ONE HAS TO DIE

ONE HAS TO DIE

BRANCHES *of* PAST *and* FUTURE
BOOK THREE

MN BENNET

Paperback ISBN: 979-8-9901493-1-1
Ebook ISBN: 979-8-9901493-0-4

Edited by Charlie Knight (CKnightWrites.com)
Cover art by Miblart (miblart.com)

www.mnbennet.com/

Dedication

To Megan for every late-night conversation, fantastic insight, and the support that helps me continue exploring all the wonderful characters in this world.

Author's Note

READERS BE ADVISED

Thank you so much for continuing to follow Dorian's journey in the third installment of the Branches of Past and Future series. I've included a list of content warnings on the following page for those interested. I absolutely love this story and as you may have noticed by now, I enjoy adding so much joy and humor to my books; however, I do add grief, sorrow, and the emotional struggle to confront that pain.

The title is not misleading. There will be a character death. I'm not going to hint in any way about who this character might be or when this event will take place, but I will add a note here saying it's okay to step away from a book at any time if you're not in the headspace for that story. Sometimes we love a story but we're not ready or able to handle certain content and that's okay. Dorian, Milo, and all the wonderful students in this series will be here for you if and when you want to return to their world.

I’ve never been the kind of person who kills off characters. Yes, some important characters have died before the start of the story (sweet Finn), a handful of minor characters, and of course, a few lovely villains. But this was a very painful and deliberate choice. And I’m just awful for it.

This book contains the following elements:

Foul language
Smoking and alcohol use
Blood and violence
Scenes of graphic sex between adults
Character deaths (on the page, graphic and violent)
Strong themes of grief and guilt
Depression, anxiety, and self-hatred (both mild and overwhelming)
Strong themes of possessive behavior
Gaslighting and manipulation
Stalking
Mental and physical assault
Bullying
Torture

I believe in HEA and HFN in all my works, something I strive to bring no matter how long winding the journey is. I hope you’ll enjoy this installment as much as I did.

REJUVENATION
PRIMAL
PSYCHIC
HEX
ENCHANTMENT
AUGMENTATION
BESTIAL
COSMIC
ALTERATION
ENTROPY
ARCANE
TELEKINESIS
SENSORY
BANISHMENT
LEVITATION

Chapter One

I awoke to the sound of nothing. Not a buzzing thought. Not a humming musing. Not a weird dream latched onto my telepathy from some random nearby mind sorting through their subconscious bullshit. Nope. The singular joy of a full night's rest woke me.

Milo had curled himself into one of the body pillows, practically hugging the life out of the plushy cushion. I smirked. This blissful slumber didn't even require his embrace. And from the cuddling stranglehold he had on the pillow, I considered myself fortunate I'd avoided his spooning for the night. The third night in a row where I slept with utter ease, thanks in great part to Milo dragging me out of the city for a second time this summer.

Admittedly, when Milo suggested a three-day weekend before the kickoff to the school year, I remained skeptical, considering our first vacation that I helped him plan involved a cruise that turned into an impromptu 'Enchanter Evergreen saves the day' mission when some deep-sea fiends attempted to disembowel the hull. He claimed to have no clairvoyant knowledge and supposedly improvised his heroic actions, but I very much doubted it—even if his wily surface thoughts supported the story every time I snooped.

Still, after a vacation turned photo op, followed by a whirlwind of events celebrating Milo's rise into the Global Rankings, I hadn't had much of a summer break. Everything after Enchanter Evergreen's induction ceremony was met with Cerberus parties, press arriving to Milo's simplest missions for Q&As after closing a case, and every other guild reaching out hoping to curry favor with Illinois's top-ranked enchanter. And I did mean every guild. From California to North Carolina, they reached out for a Global Ranked enchanter's insight.

Naturally, when he decided to whisk me away for a long weekend outside Chicago at the most expensive resort imaginable, I suspected an ulterior motive. Turned out Milo's only motive was for a quiet trip before the school year started for me.

Delicately, I traced my fingers against the muscles of Milo's back, scooting closer to him and wrapping my arms around his. Despite all my focus, all my efforts, I couldn't slip into his mind and observe whatever blissful dream had him drooling on the pillow he bear-hugged.

"Wake up," I whispered, nuzzling my face into his neck.

Milo moaned, resisting my call as his forehead crinkled. This was an expression I'd seen many times over the years, the face of a man lost in a silly dream and desperate to retain whatever oddities his subconscious concocted as an escape from reality.

"Come back to me." I kissed the back of his ear, allowing the stubble on my face to graze his skin. "Milo."

Our time at Tranquil Orbits was almost at an end, and while I might've been reluctant at first…well, the entire grueling flight all the way to the front doors of this resort, I did truly want to make the most of the few hours we had before checkout. Honestly, I wished we never had to leave, loving every part of this serene place, including every obnoxious couple's activity Milo booked from sunup to sundown of our stay, such as massages, facials, deep tissue cleanses—which I still didn't fully understand—all the way to Mani Pedis he insisted on.

Each treatment involved contact with another person and should've offered me an exhausting headache from pushing away the thoughts and memories of those working on my cosmetic…eh, beautification? I didn't know the word. Milo did. But I couldn't exactly peer into his mind and find it all thanks to the intensive sealing wards lined throughout Tranquil Orbits. Each wall had enough nullifying magic to withstand a dozen simultaneous casting assaults, so even my persistent telepathy couldn't pierce through the protective layers soaked into this intricate building.

Tugging on Milo's body pillow, I yanked it from his grip. "I'm about to get a whole lot more unfriendly if you don't wake up, mister."

"Why?" Milo rolled into me, burying his head onto my chest and laying his entire body on top of mine. "Sleep, you need to sleep."

As he pinned me beneath him with a hug, his expression furrowed into something groggy yet snarky.

"Are you thinking at me?" I raised an eyebrow. "You know I can't hear you."

"You're supposed to be the sleepy one." He huffed, bare chest pressed against my stomach, which only worked to further rouse me into a state of eager morning desires.

Attempting to coax him awake, I teased him with gentle, seductive sensations. I ran my fingers through his curly, blond locks that he hadn't once styled or gelled into his trademark spiky hairdo since we arrived at the resort. Nothing. I tugged at his waistband, hoping the sudden snap of elastic would elicit some spark of enthusiasm. Nothing. Finally, I pulled a move from Milo's playbook and brushed against him with my morning wood. Nada. Despite my best playful efforts, he was having none of it. I pouted, contemplating abandoning him in the bed for a morning stroll…all the way to the bathroom on the opposite end of this suite where I could at least enjoy my own company for some morning relief.

Suddenly, Milo shifted his weight, resting his thigh against my boner, and kept me locked in place while he finished his dream or beauty sleep or whatever. I guess as grueling as I'd found Milo's busy summer, he'd probably found it tenfold more exhausting. This really had been the first time in months since he'd stopped and done absolutely nothing work-related. I submitted, running my hand along his back with a caressing gesture, lulling him back to sleep so he would waste what little time we had before checkout.

Milo snoozed, letting out wispy snores as he lay his head on my shoulder, and the joy of the quiet faded the longer I sat here doing nothing with no thoughts to entertain me but my own. Sunlight pierced through the curtains, managing to somehow strike only one part of this bedroom—where my fucking head lay, making me squint. Biting back a grumble, I tried not to disturb Milo. Well, any more than I had already attempted and failed to do.

"Mm." Milo's lips smacked, gently kissing my collarbone. He took a deep inhale, his expression twisting into a waking minxy grin. He kissed my skin again. Little pecks made their way across my chest as he ran his hands along my torso, fingertips tickling the hairs on my stomach and creeping further down my waist. "Morning, Sunshine."

"I think that's my line." I kissed his forehead, grateful he brought me here to escape the heavy weight of a thousand minds funneling through mine but missing his thoughts after so much silence.

"What time is it?" He trailed his tongue between my pecs—if one could call my flat chest muscles pecs since they weren't nearly as filled out and firm as Milo's.

"Early still." I pushed him off, rolling him onto his back as I straddled his hips.

Milo's beautiful blue eyes shot open, bloodshot and making the blues more illuminated. Somehow, Milo's break from his clairvoyance made him more restless during this vacation. It was like he lived for the future and the infinite possibilities that came with his branch magic. Being disconnected from rifling through his inner core of magic didn't offer him relief, only impatience as he sought to be productive, like somehow the world itself might stop turning on its axis if he didn't keep chasing everyone's happy ever after.

"It's kind of sickening you can't simply enjoy a few days off." I pursed my lips, attempting and failing to appear playful. Milo's quirked expression made that obvious.

"Huh? Where'd that come from? I was the one who dragged you here, mister pouty I've got lesson plans and annoying checklists to cross off before the first day." Milo's voice turned raspy, imitating me with a poor excuse of a surly expression. "And you better make those arrangements so I—"

I leaned forward, planting a heavy, sloppy kiss. "Shut up."

I slid back, making my way down Milo's body, kissing his soft skin, then rested my knees between his legs as I slipped his boxer briefs down around his thighs.

"Yes, sir." Milo grinned.

Grabbing ahold of his cock, I slowly stroked him from a partial bulge to fully erect. Milo brushed my bangs off my face when I prepared to wrap my mouth around the t—

The room landline rang, an annoyingly repetitive chime that echoed so loudly throughout the room the actual phone buzzed atop the base, practically thrumming against the nightstand.

"Oop." Milo went to pull up his briefs until I intercepted him.

"Ignore it."

"No. That's our courtesy call."

"It's not so much a courtesy as an interruption." I licked his inner thigh, slowly working my way toward his shaft.

"You're insatiable."

"I am," I said as coyly as I could while holding Milo's rock-hard cock. "So you better help satiate me."

"If they're calling, then we're already behind schedule." He reached for the phone.

I huffed.

"Sorry," he whispered before answering the phone. "Yes? Thank you so much for the call. We'll be down shortly for checkout."

After he hung up, I licked the V cut of his lower abdomen, watching him stifle a moan of satisfaction. Next, I cupped my hands on his firm, round ass, preparing to go down on him with a grip on his cheeks. God, I loved his ass. It didn't matter how eager his expression was—he hopped out of the bed all the same.

I collapsed, sinking deep into the mattress, and sprawled out. "Can't we stay another day? Or at least another morning?"

"No, we can't stay just one more day. This place is hella expensive."

"I'll cover it." Since I hadn't paid for anything on our trip from the flight, the car, the days at the resort, or any of the added amenities, which were all apparently add-on features. I'd roll my eyes at Tranquil Orbits declaring their nullified magic was the premium experience folks came for and everything else an extra luxury, but damn if they didn't deliver on the tranquil environment.

"Dorian, I don't think you realize just how much a single day at this resort costs."

I didn't. Milo kept his thoughts quelled on the way here, and the moment we stepped inside the resort, his every musing, along with the world's thoughts, became quiet.

"Checkout can't be this early."

"It's not. But if we don't leave soon, we'll miss our flight."

I went to protest.

"And before you say it, no, we can't reschedule our flight. There's no guarantee we'd be back in time, and then you'd miss work too." He waggled a finger at me instead of the one thing I wanted him to waggle.

"It's gonna be PD trainings the first week anyway. What the fuck do I care? I'll take a sick day or comp time or salary deduct." All of which would be more than worth it for another day here with Milo.

"But it's probably important you're back at work in time, especially if you want to get the headmaster's approval for my arrangements."

"Wait. You actually got them?" I perked up. He hadn't brought it up once since I made my not-so-subtle inquiry. "I figured nothing came of it."

"All arranged on my end, so you just need to get Headmaster Dower to sign off on your very special first-day activity."

"I can't fucking wait. And you're sure Cerberus is fine using valuable *resources* for academy students?"

"Definitely."

"Good." My lips tightened into a thin smile. "I can't wait to break them on day one."

"Er. That sounds more like torture and less like the helpful lesson you pitched it as."

"Oh, it'll be helpful. It'll teach them for slacking off all summer."

"You don't know that."

"I've been at this long enough to know what my first-years do after making it through a year at Gemini."

It'd be nice to deflate their egos on day one, and because of Enchanter Evergreen's help making this arrangement with Cerberus Guild, my homeroom coven would think of this as a reward. They'd probably thank me for the suffering defeat I had in store for them. After the chaos of their first year at Gemini Academy between the warlock incursion to the Spring Showcase, all the way to a nearly fatal encounter with a demon—I wanted what was best for them the minute they walked back onto campus, which meant utilizing every resource at my disposal and molding them into the best witches possible.

"You look positively maniacal right now."

"What can I say? I'm a wicked witch some days." I grabbed Milo by his belt and yanked him toward the bed. "You know, a little morning loving might mellow out my malevolent ways."

"Ha. As much as I love a quickie, you've got seductive distraction written all over your face." Milo tousled my hair until I rolled over and away from him. "I can't have you using your wiles to distract me."

"You're insufferable." Even without clairvoyance, it was like he'd prepped a counterargument to every single suggestive suggestion I made.

"We could always enjoy a little mile-high fun on the flight back." Milo winked.

"I already said no on the way here. I'm not getting screwed in some airplane bathroom." I turned away from him, a little pouty and very disappointed about the long flight awaiting us. "It's just not sexy."

"It's first class. The plane's bathroom is bigger than yours, and we've made do with those humble accommodations on more than one occasion." Milo kissed my nape, grazing his teeth over my skin and nibbling. "And who said you'd be the one getting fucked?"

"Tease."

"Just wait until you can actually hear what I have in store for you later." Milo slapped my ass and rushed toward the closet to begin packing.

"Fucking tease," I growled, reluctantly following Milo's lead and making my way out of the perfect bedroom, down the hallway to the elevator, and through to the front desk where he checked us out.

I recoiled the second I stepped outside Tranquil Orbit's front doors, unable to quell a single mind. Waves of staff and incoming guests overwhelmed me with their obnoxious surface thoughts.

"*Is that Evergreen? Cuter in person.*"

"*Run my hands down his...*"

"*He's that witch who channeled a hundred others!*"

"*Looks like they'll let anyone with a meager audience into this resort.*"

"Single-handedly sparked a coup against Tobias Whitlock. Good showing."

"...killed a devil."

"Wasn't he just accepted into the Global Rankings?"

"Bet he'll be joining the Global Guild."

"Who's that on his arm?"

"Scowl much."

"I hate when enchanters bring their flings here."

Milo squeezed my hand, silencing the onslaught.

"It's just the post-resort chaos." Milo's grip remained firm even though his stance wobbled a bit, enduring his own collision of magic bombarding him once we crossed the threshold. "Damn. Gotta love those dampened wards, but the return of magic in the atmosphere really hits like a tidal wave, huh?"

"I wouldn't mind having those sealing wards applied to the foundation of my house." I chuckled.

"If only. The cost alone—yikes." Milo ushered me toward their front driveway, where guests shuffled in and out of cars. "Plus, there's a reason we had to sign a waiver before entering. They offer a unique experience which requires lots of permits that somewhat border on unethical or unconstitutional practices."

Of course, a place with this much money and prestige could bend the rules however they or their clientele saw fit. I took one final look at the entrance of Tranquil Orbits from the marble columns lining the walkway leading to the front doors surrounded by luminescent glass walls that offered a twinkling star night to outsiders but gave guests a perfect view of the lush estate outside.

Milo reached into his pocket and fished out a pill bottle. He took two and popped them into his mouth without water. His Adam's apple bulged with the heavy gulp.

"Dampening pill?" He raddled the bottle in my direction.

"Nope." I cracked my neck and followed Milo to the car he'd arranged to take us to the airport. "They barely work on me, anyway."

Those medications meant to silence unruly magics hardly took into account magical variations, even when designed to be branch-specific like the Psychic Blockers brand Milo had.

"You sure? Never really stops my visions either, but sort of eases me back into the routine after walking out these doors."

"No. I'd rather just grit my teeth as my telepathy kicks in full blast." I slid into the backseat.

"So no foreplay, just ram you into submission, huh?" Milo clicked his tongue. "I'll keep that in mind."

"Shut up." I interlocked my fingers with his, allowing his thoughts to quiet the world on the drive.

Admittedly, I should've considered the pills since everything became a haze of delirium on the trip home. I just hated the side effects those medications gave me, from the nausea to the migraines as my branch resisted the magic and chemicals intermingling to the fog of my own thoughts, barely capable of stringing together coherent sentences. I often found living with others in my head tiresome, but dampening magic made me feel like a puppet inside my own skin.

I'd bear through it. This was the best my life had been in a long time. No more lost days in my grief; I mourned Finn and missed him dearly, but I loved each new day with Milo more. There was no more regret. No fear of impending visions, dangerous warlocks, or deadly demons. Despite the excruciating headache settling in, all was right in the world, and I was eager to see what the new school year would bring.

Chapter Two

Doppler

"Dorian! About time you got here." Finn eyed me, alerted by the jingle of rattling chains Dorian wore too often on his pants. Something he considered trendy in his goth phase. This was the version of Dorian that Finn remembered at twenty-two, so I ensured I always presented myself in this manner.

I didn't care much for Dorian's try-hard style, from the heavier eyeliner and eyeshadow to the constant over-accessorizing of silver chains: necklaces, bracelets, and the thin chains looped on his overly tight black jeans. Fuck, I hated that man.

Still, my chest warmed at Finn's sweet smile, taking me in.

He sat up, ready to hop out of the hospital bed, until I added a little trickle of magic to leave him woozy. It was cruel to leave him locked in this illusion of a hospital room, reliving the same few days of recovery on loop for months on end. My magic couldn't erase his memories, but thankfully, Finn's retrocognition controlled all facets of the past, including his own. A subtle shift here and there, and I managed to sway his branch to repress those horrifying experiences bound in tar and trapped for over a decade as some magical battery to a power-hungry monster. It wasn't control or force, mere suggestion. A whisper in the corridors of the mind we borrowed for safety, guiding and instructing Finn's branch unbeknownst to him.

It felt manipulative, like I was stealing pieces of him. But it wasn't. I wasn't. I had every intention of divulging the whole truth to Finn, to Milo, but they needed time. Once I'd fixed everything, they'd see they needed me as much as I needed them. Finn wasn't ready for the full extent of the truth; I sensed his fragile subconscious, still scarred by the atrocities inflicted at the hands of the chimera.

And there was so much for Finn to absorb and reflect upon when the time came. He was dead. Well, he'd died, but his memories lived on in a piece of fragmented magic stolen by that chimera who sought to take Finn's branch. The only blessing in Finn's cursed fate was that the actions used to torment him had kept him alive in a sense. He could live again. He would live again. I'd ensure it.

Still, it was too much to fully unravel, from Finn's torture to his death all the way to a small piece of his being, his magic, his consciousness, ending up bound to the chimera. I scowled. That damn demon had proven harder to remove than anticipated.

"You look like you're in a mood," Finn said. "*At least you're not stuck in here all day. Feels like I've been in this hospital forever.*"

"It's been three days." I approached, sitting at his bedside. "Don't be dramatic. It'll just make your recovery longer."

Finn chuckled. Slowly, he slid his hand across the bed, reaching mine, then pausing. My heart thumped. My throat dried. Everything froze in those fractions of seconds as our skin tingled so close to contact. I felt more like Dorian in these seconds than I'd felt in years. The desire to brush my pinky against Finn's, the hesitation, the wonder, the unexplored feelings.

Yes, Finn had feelings for me. Or had feelings for who he believed me to be. But I wasn't Dorian. Not anymore. I'd broken free, expunged from the shackles of that worthless witch. Still, under the guise I'd taken, it would be cruel to indulge in Finn's affections. I didn't deserve it, not until I'd saved him. Truly freed him and found a way to resurrect this piece of his soul into physical form. Dorian lacked the knowledge or stomach for the measures I planned on taking.

With a delicate touch, Finn interlocked his fingers with mine, and all the anxiety for what came next washed away. Such a beautiful man whose gentle aura soothed one as monstrous as mine.

Finn squeezed my hand. "*So, your branch is working then?*"

"Why wouldn't it be?" I asked, delving into what sparked such a curious question from him.

"My branch has been off since I got here."

Not that I needed to pry into his thoughts. Finn remained an open book, trusting me implicitly. And why wouldn't he? I loved him. I wanted what was best for him. Always.

He traced his thumb along the knuckle of mine, his eyes staring off while his mind trailed into theories. "*I figured the hospital put up wards to block branches, but it's just me. Just my magic not working. Maybe you were right, and that gorgon did a bigger number on me than I realized...*"

"It's just a few days." I scooted closer, bringing our interlocked hands to my chest. The thump of my heart hit harder, banging so loudly I worried it'd echo in the witch's mind I'd borrowed. Finn had that effect on me. Always had. He saw me as more than a piece of Dorian's magic, some manifestation puppet of a weak witch's willpower.

"Since when do you dwell on your manifestations?" Finn asked, joy in his hazel eyes. "*Hey. I just glimpsed a memory.*"

I forced a cough, offering an excuse to pull my hand from his and clear my throat. "See. Your branch is just fine."

And that'd be a problem. I hated retreating from him, but if Finn glimpsed my memories too deeply, he'd see past the façade of shallow memories I guarded my surface with on an illusion of Dorian. He'd see how I spent months torturing that demon latched to Finn's being. He'd see how I skirted around Milo's clairvoyance, avoiding The Inevitable Future because I sought to paint a new future for us.

Most of all, he'd see the deepest memory of my manifested core—the day Dorian consciously summoned me based on research he'd done at Gemini Academy during his first year as a student. Dorian really had no comprehension of how deep his branch ran or the fullest potential it held. If he did, he'd have known manifestations were but the tip of the iceberg. Finn called me real that day while Dorian smothered me back into his subconscious because he was incapable of handling the dual vision we shared, having compared it to a kaleidoscope. Fool.

"You really should quit smoking." Finn grinned, boyish and teasing. "If not for you, how about for me? Or Milo?"

"Not happening," I said, adding the gravelly rasp of Dorian's typical disdain he held in his early twenties. "I don't like either of you nearly enough."

"But you do like us," he said with a joyful lilt.

Love. I loved them. My face heated. Finn and Milo accepted Dorian's brash hostility too willingly. Anyone else would've brushed that prick aside, which he deserved. But those two were truly the best.

True to Dorian's fashion, I kept my feelings to myself, unwilling to let Finn see too deeply. This masquerade of bodily reactions was something I took solace in despite my very hollow creation. I didn't have blood that flowed up to my face, making pale skin burn bright red. I didn't have a heart to thump so loudly it might burst from my ribcage. None of that existed in my core, but the illusion of them, the sensation, all came from the fine craftsmanship of magic sewed into the stitching of my very being.

"You play it close to the vest, but I see you, Dorian."

"I don't know what you mean."

"It's like Jasper. He acts like he doesn't care, clocking in and out, doing the day-to-day…"

"What?" I cocked my head while Finn continued comparing me to Jasper.

Fuck.

I'd allowed myself to be distracted by Finn, and now his retrocognition had bloomed in full effect. Not only had he latched onto my memories, but his magic had seeped beyond this phony hospital room and into the deepest recesses of Jasper Cononley's mind. I'd spent too much time analyzing Milo's magic to avoid his visions, too much time failing to carve out that chimera latched to Finn's being, and plotting ways to remove the obstacle of Dorian.

I had to prioritize all that I'd worked for if I wanted a happy ending for Finn, for Milo, for myself.

"Finn, you're truly the smartest man I know. You always find a way to stumble onto the mysteries of the universe without even trying." I leaned over, kissing his forehead. "But I need you to rest for now."

"Huh?" Finn's mind spun beyond the parameters of what I'd dimmed from his perception and into a blur of Jasper's mind.

Jasper. I ground my teeth. A worthless witch whose mind I'd borrowed to store Finn and myself away from Milo's magics. Jasper was a boring man with a rudimentary understanding of his root magics, no effort to improve his lot in life, and an underwhelmingly dull branch magic that offered him no potential for greatness. Couple that with a bland personality, a sloppy physique, and poor features, and Jasper really had nothing grand to bring into this world. Honestly, if he had even an inkling of our presence in the inner core of his mind, he'd relish it since this was truly the highlight of his droll existence.

I kissed Finn's closed eyes, careful with the beautiful curl in his lashes, and wiped away Jasper's memories that'd soaked into Finn's thoughts.

Soon, I'd take Finn from Jasper's hovel he called a mind. I trembled, skin tingling in anticipation. Soon, I'd set everything into motion, saving Finn from the demon latched to his consciousness like a parasite, revealing the best future for us to Milo and removing the stain on existence that was Dorian Frost.

Before I could bring any of this to an end once and for all, I had to remove the demon, kill that false devil, and finally free Finn of it. Since Finn was technically dead, the piece of his magic still alive, needed to be cleansed of demonic energy if he ever had a chance to truly live again.

But in order to exorcise that monster, I needed more power. Power that'd help purge the feral beast locked deep inside this mind. Once I obtained the magics necessary to remove the chimera, I could return to Dorian's mind with Finn at my side.

There were so many variables to consider when overtaking Dorian's mind and claiming the body and life that rightfully belonged to me, but when he saw I'd done what he couldn't. When Dorian realized his failures to their truest extent, it'd shatter his psyche. I'd show Dorian that I'd saved Finn where he'd failed. I'd show Dorian every potential future of Milo's magic that'd synchronized within me because Dorian's feeble being couldn't fathom such overwhelming force. I'd reveal the full extent of our branch magic and use it to shatter Dorian Frost's mind into nothingness.

I deserved to finally be happy, and Dorian deserved what came next.

Chapter Three

The first week of teacher trainings weren't nearly as excruciating as I expected. I remained buzzed by the arrangements Milo made, and the afterglow of Tranquil Orbits left me fuzzy, but I was unwilling to release the fleeting sensation. Whether my telepathy still needed to adjust after three days of silence or I'd actually gained more control over the growing fluctuations, my magic stayed mostly grounded here at the academy for the first day of classes. Even the extension of my branch that sought Milo above all else in the city had simmered. His image became a spotty portrait in the corner of my eyes, his voice a hollow echo, and his thoughts static pulses, each of which I could make sense of with a bit of focus. But today was about the kids, not Milo.

Enchanter Evergreen's chipper morning mind did flood my emotions with more excitement than intended, though. I shook it off, keeping my expression dower and preparing for the onslaught of student minds that'd bustle through Gemini Academy's hallways any minute.

"*Why do you look so happy?*" Chanelle strolled toward my classroom, where I stood propped against the wall, reading a tablet. "*I can see disdain in your eyes, yet no scorn, no bitter twist in your frown, no contemptuous huff to my 'oh so intrusive' thoughts bursting whatever bubble you're floating on. You look positively effervescent. Well, for you, sourpuss.*"

"*Shut up,*" I thought at Chanelle, which was a massive mistake.

She practically levitated with delight that I'd linked my thoughts to hers and immediately went to work, hammering as many surface thoughts in my direction as humanly fucking possible. I caught a dozen half-stories about her summer vacation zipping around each other like railroad tracks colliding into other stories and leading to a bombardment of images from her synced mind before I managed to quell the bulk of her surface thoughts.

Ignoring her proved challenging, but I returned to rereading my homeroom covens' profiles after their ranks had been finalized based on their first-year scores.

"Christ." I sighed, unable to quell Chanelle's thoughts. "I didn't ask."

"There's that scorn."

The ringing of the bell drowned out whatever witty addition Chanelle had as a follow-up and thankfully sent her swaying back down the hallway to wrangle her homeroom coven.

"*I can't believe summer's finally over.*" Caleb's thoughts spiked above everyone else, making him easy to pinpoint in the cluster of chaotic teens wading into the building. "*It was nice having more flexibility around my work schedule, but I didn't get anything done. Still can't figure out how to utilize that perfected root casting. Maybe it was just a fluke which is gonna set me back. Everything I researched says things get intensive during the second year, and I've got to make sure I keep up.*"

I buried his bursting thoughts, cycling over a hundred checklists. While slacking off was a go-to for most students during the summer, I shouldn't be surprised Caleb spent the duration training, working, studying, and tutoring—all while believing he hadn't invested enough time in any to consider himself successful. That wasn't the most shocking thing about Caleb, though.

He'd shot up at least a half foot since the last time I'd seen him. His academy blazer was snug around his chest and shoulders as he started filling it out. This wasn't the scrawny, frantic teen who'd walked into Gemini last year, completely unaware his life was in peril by some unforeseeable future. No. He'd started growing into himself, feeling more comfortable in his root magics, which he continued training. The weighted blocks he used hovered behind him, enchantment sigils glowing to signify his focus on all four in tandem. Confidence radiated off him in equal waves of calm, collective energy. I bet a bit of that pride came from the massive jump in his ranking.

```
Name: Caleb Huxley
Branch: N/A
Ranking: 100
```

Sure, one hundred remained far from the top, but out of six hundred second-year students, that said a lot about his place here at Gemini. Not to mention, he'd entered the Spring Showcase, barely squeaking by at one-sixty. Between his high placement at the showcase, the training progress monitored by his Cast-8-

Watch, and his stellar exam scores, it was no wonder he'd soared past so many other students.

"Good morning, Mr. Frost." Caleb smiled and tightened his hands around the straps of his book bag.

"Morning." Because there was never anything *good* about being awake this early.

"How was your—"

"***Too many fucking people.***" Kenzo's familiar rage sliced through everyone else's thoughts and Caleb's words. "***Who just stands in a hallway carrying on a conversation? Move, assholes!***"

I fought back a snarl in response to the collision of his wrath pounding against my head like a damn drum.

"Eh," Caleb muttered. "*Guess the summer didn't melt away any of Mr. Frost's attitude. Too bad.*"

Did he just use my name as a pun? I glared.

"*Shoot. Did he hear that?*" Caleb gulped. "*Did you hear that?*"

"Find your seat, Mr. Huxley."

"Yes, sir." Caleb scrambled into the classroom, not quite so confidently and reminiscent of his first-year self.

Kenzo stormed through the hallway, brushing past people thinking profanities so loudly it buried their disdain for the rude way he shoulder-bumped them out of his path. Honestly, I was grateful he didn't fling anyone into the air with his telekinesis since the idea crossed his mind more than once by the time he reached my classroom.

```
Name: Kenzo Ito
Branch: Hex (Disruption)
Ranking: 1
```

Not much had changed about Kenzo since the last time I'd seen him, from his appearance and his threatening posture all the way to angry musings over expectations he had going into his second year. Well, one thing had changed. He'd added dark crimson streaks to his jet-black hair.

Flashes of his summer exploded along his surface thoughts, carrying images of his rigorous workout routine, wisps he'd banished, and precision casting he'd done with his root magics and hex branch. My muscles held a phantom ache for the strain Kenzo put on his body in order to push past his limits. Like Caleb, he'd also spent the bulk of his summer training, determined to increase his skills beyond anyone at the academy. No. Anyone he came across.

Maybe Milo had a point. Perhaps I underestimated my students, daring to compare them to those I'd taught over the years like they sat in some one-size-fits-all mold. With more than a decade of education under my belt, I should know better than that.

"***Why the hell are you staring at me?***"

I cracked my neck, quelling the desire to punch Kenzo—knowing full well that came from his palpable fury colliding with my mind, spreading the rage he kept in check…mostly.

"Hey, hey!" Gael weaved through the hallway, carefully avoiding others so his spikes didn't accidentally jab anyone else. "I turned for half a second, and you vanished."

Kenzo clamped his jaw, recalling Gael's five-minute hellos to everyone he walked by, which clearly indicated Kenzo hadn't vanished but gotten bored of the small talk from students he didn't bother naming in his thoughts.

Gael had grown over the summer, too, now standing taller than me at 5'11 and actually probably taller than Milo at 6'2 with a broader build as well. His muscle definition caught nearly every student's attention since he wore a white tank with the Gemini Academy logo to compensate for the development of his spikes.

```
Name: Gael Martinez
Branch: Augmentation (Spikes)
Ranking: 35
```

They'd remained slender like thick hairs along his forearms and lower legs but easily doubled in the number covering his limbs. It was the massive spikes sprouting from his shoulders, curving inward, that explained the need for a tank. No tees with those two protruding bonelike appendages.

"How was your summer, Mr. Frost?" Gael's sharklike teeth beamed, and the bright orange of his aura illuminated his pale complexion and the short spikes framing his face. "Hope you did something fun for yourself. You won't believe what I did over the summer. I had so much..."

Gael's genuine compassion and delight collided with Kenzo's anger, creating a soothing vermillion in the air around them. As I composed myself from the swirling orangish reds, Gael rambled about his summer, carefully avoiding topics on how much of it he spent with Kenzo. He didn't speak aloud, but Kenzo consumed his thoughts. Granted, I couldn't understand much of the Spanish trailing along the surface of Gael's mind as he spoke in English, but Kenzo's name continued popping up between phrases I didn't grasp, and with the thought of the angry boy's name came a radiant blossom in Gael's joyful aura all over again. I blinked a few times, helping the auras in my vision to turn spotty and fade while I quelled my telepathy.

Kenzo grunted, too aggravated to insult Gael and too annoyed to listen any further, so he cut between us into the classroom. It didn't stop Gael, who continued talking. Nonstop. Christ, had he copied Enchanter Evergreen's chatty persona along with the spiky blond hairdo?

Thanks to my lack of responses and natural set-in scowl, Gael finally went inside in search of someone more conversational as others from our homeroom shuffled inside the classroom.

Katherine made her way down the hall, literally levitating from the exhilaration buzzing off her and fueling those she chatted up. Her yellow aura glowed, accentuating her light brown complexion and highlighting her short, curled hair that now framed her face.

```
Name: Katherine Harris
Branch: Enchantment (Spell Craft)
Ranking: 7
```

Despite making it into the second round of the Spring Showcase, excelling in her classes, and acing her exams, Katherine's ranking had only moved up by one. It crept into the corners of her thoughts. Every time she greeted someone, envious whispers festered at the edges of her happiness for friends. Katherine had hoped for more improvement, yet landing in the top ten didn't leave much room for growth, something I'd help her come to realize. She'd spent the entire night before memorizing the massive jumps in some of their rankings from first-year to second-year students.

Reaching the top ten and maintaining such a high ranking—not an easy feat. Katherine was a student to watch. Things would get even more competitive at Gemini now that rankings had been shared for all to see. Every second-year student would aim for the top ten since those positions all but guaranteed first-choice internships during their third year.

I needed Katherine to understand her achievements mattered. She had an understanding of subjects equal to Caleb, root precision nearly on par with Kenzo and Tara, and mastery over her branch magic in ways some industry professionals lacked when it came to enchantments. Still, moving into the second year, I'd like to see her shine a little more outside of Caleb's bubble. Easier said than done, given her mind spun on all things about him, causing her to linger at the doorway, searching for the right words after her trip abroad.

Every other thought in her mind fizzled out once she reached the doorway. She paused, adjusting her grimoire strapped to her hip and plucking at a loose thread on her skirt.

Caleb's eyes widened; a flurry of thoughts zipped so fast I couldn't grasp a single tangible word. Not that I wanted to once the whirlwind of auras between Caleb and Katherine swirled. It radiated loudly, bringing their memories to the forefront of the surface, painting the room in vibrant pinks and soft violets. Their lustful pining mixed with fragments of words whispered to each other over the summer, declarations of love, questions on boundaries, and grunting noises from awkward first times.

FUCK. No. Nope. Not allowing my telepathy insight on that one.

I cleared my throat until their thoughts became faint. Summer had made me lazy when it came to blocking unwanted thoughts, and the last thing I wanted in my head was their teenage lust.

Katherine stared like a lost doe. I glared, sending her scurrying into the classroom. Caleb shrieked internally, straightening in his desk and pressing his knees close together as if that somehow settled his raging hormones, which became a goddamn beacon of desire shimmering across the classroom.

"Fuck," I muttered to myself. Oh, how I despised horny teenagers. If my branch didn't simmer soon, this would be a long school year.

Since my telepathy evolved, I'd found myself latched to Milo's mind most days to where it'd almost become second nature. Not quite. It still took extreme focus to separate myself from wherever he currently was in the city, prioritizing the here and now. Based on the wind ruffling his hair, I'd wager flying somewhere. That cool breeze was much more inviting than the stale air in my classroom. Still, the auras of other's emotions springing out so effortlessly knocked me off guard. It didn't happen with everyone. In fact, I'd only really accounted for this occurring with my homeroom coven since my near-death experience when I latched onto their minds, desperately trying to see the events unfold as they fought off warlocks invading the academy. Something about my magic, my branch, changed that day.

Without wasting another second, I severed my telepathy, channeling telekinesis to rearrange texts in the back of the classroom. It took extra effort since I kept my body still, moving weighty books into whatever random order looked semi-logical. Casting telekinesis with the subtle flex of my muscles ached but suppressed my branch magic.

"I can help with that." Gael swaggered into the classroom, a mischievous smile on his face where he stuck out his tongue, revealing his new piercing, and flexed biceps, which he internally screamed "*my guns*" about while flashes of lazy beach days played in his mind. Along with images of volleyball and walking the Navy Pier with a dozen different girls.

"Ba-ba-bawk!" King Clucks flapped his wings, perhaps assisting in the chaos or merely advising Gael based on the young witch's thoughts.

"*I got this, Clucks.*"

Ugh. He waved a hand and sent the books flying from my hold and across the classroom.

```
Name: Gael Rios-Vega
Branch: Bestial (Familiar)
Ranking: 92
```

Pages fluttered, spines cracked, and students yelped in shock when several textbooks thudded onto desks and the floor before Tara swooped in behind him, gently shifting their trajectory and lessening their impact without the slightest strain or notice.

"Figured you'd want us all prepared to read on day one." Gael grinned, awed by his awesomeness. "You're welcome, Mr. Frosty."

"*His roots really are improving,*" Tara thought. "*Though, they'd probably be better if we actually spent time training together instead of concentrating on my fledgling permit.*"

It turned out Tara had crafted a methodic and manipulative ploy to trick Gael into working on his magics with her without realizing they were working on both their magics. Little did she realize that his slacker ways were five steps ahead of her, finding every opportunity to avoid her plans and enjoy their summer. Apparently, he'd done a good job convincing Tara those ideas were hers, too. Hmm. If professional guild work didn't pan out for Gael, he might have a place in politics. Lazy. Smooth talking. Vulgar.

Gael's slacking off should've made it easier to tear him down on day one, get him back on track with training, but my breathing hitched from how so many summer festivals, tourist attractions, day trips, and simply living life floated above the ever-present ocean in Tara's mind. These thoughts made it easier to stand above the waves stirring at the surface. She'd explored more of Chicago this summer, thanks to that goofball and his rooster, than she'd seen in all her years living here. The storm of sorrow remained, yet Gael continued serving as a reliable lifejacket of friendship.

"Badass, right?" Gael wiggled his eyebrows.

"The baddest of badasses." Tara snickered, then skirted by him to take a seat in the front of the classroom directly at a center desk. Such a subtle yet bold move for her. I nearly smiled, so proud of how far she'd come.

```
Name: Tara Whitlock
Branch: Ward (Sealing)
Branch: Cosmic (Shadows)
Branch: Arcane (Intangibility)
Branch: Primal (Icicles)
Ranking: 9
```

"I see you went ahead and resubmitted your fledgling permit over the summer." Something I didn't have to encourage or remind her about. Tara was taking charge of mastering her branches, which was a fantastic sight.

"Yeah, thought it'd be nice to figure out how this branch works," Tara said, almost smiling. "*The only thing I've figured out is it's not linked to the others, and I can't find where to draw and channel the casting from.*"

"We'll get there."

Tara sighed. “I forgot you did that.”

“Sorry. I’m usually better about it.”

She twisted her lips, making quite the judgy little expression. Especially for Tara. “*Are you, though?*”

The bell rang, and I used that opportunity to pretend I hadn’t caught her last thought while settling my homeroom coven. We didn’t have a moment to spare. Well, maybe a few, but considering I’d made some awesome arrangements thanks in part to Milo, I wanted to utilize the most of our morning before sending them limping off to their classes worn out and regretting goofing off over the summer.

“We’re entering your second year,” I said, drawing their focus. “Which means I need to get every single one of you ready for internships. If you want an internship, you’ll have to impress guilds during the second-year rankings, academic proficiency, Spring Showcase performance next semester, and a slew of other industry factors. That doesn’t give us much time to prepare.”

“Wait.” Gael raised his hand, spikes expanding. I nodded for him to ask. “I thought internships were guaranteed. It’s academy policy, right?”

“Oh, they are.” I tightened my eyes, glaring at each of them. “But do you really want the academy scraping the bottom of the barrel because none of the top-tier guilds expressed an interest in working with you?”

Gael gulped. His mind buzzed faster than normal, thoughts bouncing between Spanish and English with the same frantic concern that boomed from several others in the room. Hell, it wasn’t only my homeroom coven panicking. Nearby teachers had started bursting bubbles the minute class began, and their students worried over their rankings. Admittedly, I counted myself fortunate my homeroom coven currently sat among the top hundred—making my job easier on getting them ready—but guilds rarely showed an interest in anyone below the top fifty.

"We'll be skipping today's orientation since you already know Gemini's expectations, and I'd like to see who here has improved over the summer"—I rested my gaze on Gael and his familiar—"and who's floundered."

"*Don't know why he's looking at me.*" Gael scrunched his face. "*I spent the entire summer working my magic on the ladies.*"

"Ba-ba-bawk."

"*It's a type of magic. Hello, enchanters need to charm their clients.*"

No amount of scowling caught Gael's attention or stopped his blathering telepathic conversation with his damn rooster.

"***This is such a waste.***" Kenzo huffed, his thoughts cutting above the others. "***At least I could work on my studies during the orientation. Bet Frost's special lesson is just gonna be another basic ass training. What'd he do last year? Promised demons and delivered wisps. An academy should offer more. I could get this on my—***"

"This won't be like last year."

Kenzo's eyes widened; gray static popped around his brow, dimming his thoughts but not blocking them despite his best hex work.

"We kicked off day one by testing out your root magics, seeing how you faired against wisps while working as a team. But today, you'll be testing your abilities alongside professional guild witches."

"Wait, really?" Caleb perked up. "Actual guild witches?"

Katherine raised her hand and proceeded to ask without

waiting. "So, we're going to be working with them? Like wisp training with professionals?"

"No, it'll probably be fiends this time." Gael chomped his teeth and grinned at Tara.

She rolled her eyes, biting back laughter. "*We've done lots of fiend trainings, though. This has to be something different.*"

"It's the only way I can assess how much improvement each of you will require in order to hold your own working alongside a professional enchanter next fall." I rested my eyes on Kenzo's piercing glare. The room fell silent—bated breath galore—as everyone's thoughts buzzed at the staring contest of daggers between the two of us. "I assure all of you, though, today's lesson will make your training last year look like basic training wheels. Honestly, I don't expect much from any student outside the top ten here at Gemini. Might even be a more successful lesson if I wrangled those top players from a few other homeroom covens."

"***Finally, something worth my time.***"

Not only did it entice Kenzo, but it lit a fire under the rest of my class, each one determined to make me eat those words. I relished in their confidence, fueling my own. Once the excitement settled, I led them across campus to the auxiliary gym while the other classes went to the auditorium for Headmaster Dower's orientation.

"*Dorian's gonna kill me,*" Milo's mind reached out, which I gladly embraced to settle the onslaught of hundreds of students talking and thinking in tandem. "*This news is gonna ruin his day. Hope the kids react better.*"

My chest swelled. The fuck? What'd Milo mean? Did he just cancel on me through a subtle telepathic thought he perceived I might've eavesdropped on? Damn clairvoyants.

"*Milo.*" I reached out telepathically. Gritting my teeth, I tuned out the bombardment of student thoughts. Between their internalized theories and their vocalized chatter, I couldn't establish a solid link to Milo's mind at this distance. If Milo canceled, fell through, forgot to arrange the Cerberus Guild request I asked him to do weeks ago—which he said he'd done—then that meant I was dragging my homeroom coven to the auxiliary gym with no actual lesson.

I sighed. Kenzo would have a riot mocking me for talking up such a big game, only to end up improvising whatever bullshit I could string together.

"*Dammit, Milo. Can you hear me or not?*" He knew how important this was to me.

We stepped into the auxiliary gym, everyone casually taking in the layout. Even with news on the first-day lesson, few showed much of a wow reaction to the setup they'd seen a hundred times over, from the glass ceiling allowing sunlight to shine down on the dozen different terrains each setup to provide training in different environments, to the fitness station which Gemini had added new and improved gear to improve proficiency, all the way to the proctoring station which now included an added amenity for students to upload their Cast-8-Watch data. I wanted to test those functions since they were supposed to highlight the terrains most suited to strengthen student casting capabilities, streamlining their growth.

"*You sound super surly,*" Milo thought, finally reaching out to my psychic calls, his mind syncing to mine so close I could practically touch the words floating throughout the auxiliary gym. "*Have I been naughty? Gonna keep me for detention?*"

I frowned. "*You know I hate when you say stuff like that.*"

"*What don't you hate?*" His smile filled my vision as he flew through the sky.

"*Well, right now, I don't hate you, assuming you made the arrangements I asked for.*"

"*Of course. I always come through.*"

"*Then why were you worried I'd be pissed?*"

"*Huh? Was I?*" Milo's mind drifted into song lyrics, hiding something. "*Guess I always expect you to be grouchy about something. Maybe I thought you'd be disappointed starting your first day back without a good dicking. You've been so eager for sex, but I've been busy with cases. You know me with work. Always on call. Maybe after you're done for the day, I can give you a nice pound—*"

I scoffed, severing the link and returning my attention to the students. Whatever Milo kept to himself would have to wait. All that mattered right now was this training.

"Go get changed into your fitness gear, then head on over to terrain seven." I nodded to the far-off rock terrain. Aside from the cliff, this setup remained the most open space in the auxiliary gym, which would force my students to use their wits and magics to handle the combat I had in store for them this morning. "Last one there owes me an essay explaining why they're falling behind on the first day back."

"Wait. Seriously?" "*He can't do that, can he?*"

"You wouldn't."

"It's Mr. Frosty, he likes to see us suffer." "Cluck cluck."

"*Time to show off how much my flight's improved.*"

"***As if any of these losers are even worth racing.***"

"Try to keep up, Kenzo." "Real funny, porcupine."

Half of them scrambled toward the locker rooms while Kenzo and Tara took their time. Honestly, they both flew faster than I did, so the head start wouldn't do the others much good. Gael threw off his tie and blazer, sprinting ahead.

"Don't just leave your uniform on the ground," I shouted.

"No time." Gael flung off his shirt. "Can't be last."

Seriously? I needed a cigarette. "I'm not picking up after you, and if you think—"

"Course not." Gael squeezed past Caleb into the locker room, leaving his rooster to retrieve his discarded uniform.

"Ba-ba-bawk." The rooster carried the tie in his beak and telekinetically lifted the blazer and shirt, smoothing out the wrinkles with precise control. Damn, that bird had better skills than I did.

After changing into their fitness gear, the bulk of my students flew out of the locker room toward the rock terrain, leaving only a few who preferred using their branches to run faster than their levitation and telekinesis could carry them. Of course, Gael and King Clucks were among those racing ahead, still avoiding all things flight-related. I'd have to put an end to that this year. With so much on my mind their first year, I let Gael's aversion to flying slip through the cracks, but he'd never land a successful gig as an enchanter if he didn't master the skill. I couldn't think of one enchanter who didn't utilize their roots with expert proficiency. Whether his rooster envied the skies or Gael had a secret fear of heights, I'd resolve it this year.

"Whoa, is that…"

"No way!"

"These are…"

"They work with Enchanter Evergreen all the time."

One by one, they reached the terrain where two Cerberus guild witches awaited their arrival.

"***He brought acolytes, seriously? What a waste.***" Kenzo tsked. "***Frost underdelivers yet again. What's an acolyte gonna teach me this moron can't?***"

I frowned, resisting a smile, which was pretty easy considering the internalized rant Kenzo had about wanting a *real* lesson. "They're not here to train with you."

Katherine clutched her grimoire. "But you said—"

"These are some of the highest-ranked acolytes in the state," I interjected, "so they'll make for the best opponents to test out your readiness for this industry."

"Wait, we're casting against them?" Gael's spikes shrank.

"I want to see how each of you fair against professional guild witches. It'll let me know how much work we've got to put in to have you ready for your third year."

Gael smiled, expanding the spikes along his forearms and calves. "Hell yeah! We got this."

I liked the confidence; it'd make deflating their egos easier. Getting their asses handed to them by a guild witch would give them a taste of the stakes in this industry, which they definitely needed. Nonetheless, I was eager to see the fight each of them put up because not one student wavered when I revealed the news. In fact, their thoughts teemed with excitement, curiosity, and strategy. But there were three that rose above the others, three I silently rooted for even if they didn't stand a chance against these acolytes.

"*If I use everything I know about my branches, I can do this.*"

"***I'm gonna destroy these so-called best-in-the-state acolytes.***"

"*Time for everyone to see how much precision I've added to my roots.*"

Chapter Four

"*I can't believe it's Finesse and Mercury Rising,*" Caleb thought, studying the two pro witches here to test out my homeroom coven's casting skills. "*They're…they're Enchanter Evergreen's personal coven. Mr. Frost got pros who work side-by-side with The Inevitable Future to train with us. So cool!*"

After Ellie and Lena helped Milo put a stop to the demons plaguing Chicago earlier this year, he'd taken them on as his official acolytes, where they landed on everyone's radar, and their stage names became the talk of the city. Milo and his need for stage names, anything to offer a performance to the citizens he swore to protect. Although working with Milo often saddled these acolytes with cases he claimed bettered the future for all, when in actuality, he was probably too lazy to do the paperwork involved. I couldn't complain, considering it offered me acolytes to gauge my student's proficiency in a way I'd never had the opportunity to do before.

That said…

"*There's supposed to be three, Milo.*" I furrowed my brow, linked to his mind but staring at Lena and Ellie.

Lena straightened her shoulders, glaring back, assuming my scowl had to do with her, and gave me a clear piece of her mind with profane thoughts on how this exercise was beneath her time. Ellie, on the other hand, smiled in an attempt to break the tension. Her mind wasn't even remotely fixed on the lesson I had planned. She'd gained more weight since the last time I'd seen her, already a short and stout woman, but the stress of balancing two jobs on top of working full-time at Cerberus made for a lot of evenings catching up on missed lunches during rush hour traffic and eating her feelings of the pressure.

Geez. Now I felt like shit dragging her here.

"*Three what?*" Milo asked.

"*Acolytes. I specifically said—*"

"*Oh, yeah. On it. Don't you worry. Totally got it covered, babe.*"

"*Covered?*" My face flushed. "*And don't call me babe. I'm a grown-ass man.*"

"*Whatever you say, lover.*"

"Whoa. We're really facing off against these two?" Goosebumps traveled up Jamius' arms, sending pin prickles along his neck and steering my attention back to my students.

I blinked away the sparkles in my vision from the tether of Milo's sight. "Yes. You won't be fighting them independently, however."

"Oh, I never cast solo." Jamius grinned; his cheeks twitched, forcing a smile almost as bold as the one his copies maintained every time he created one.

```
Name: Jamius Watson
Branch: Alteration (Duplication)
Ranking: 52
```

His timid nature was still deeply rooted in his reactions, but since landing into the Spring Showcase finale, Jamius had begun to brush away the whispers of self-doubt that dwelled inside the well of his inner core. Instead, he prioritized the assurance of his copies that he'd always hoped to express independently. The massive jump in his ranking added to the boost in his ego, too. A shame I'd have to burst that bubble by knocking him down a few pegs like everyone else in my homeroom. Once the dust settled and the lesson was seared in each of their minds, I'd help rebuild that confidence again.

Each of my students stared in awe, curious and bewildered by what I had in store. My emotions bounced between the bubbling pride I had for making these arrangements, excitement to see my students in action, and uneasy nerves that wafted from a few kids, latching to my telepathy. Settling the rollercoaster of emotions took work, but I maintained a calm composure so none of them could gauge my intentions. Not even our class empath.

"Since this is their first time training with you, we thought it'd be best to see what each of you is capable of," I explained.

"Wait." Katherine raised her hand. "First time? As in there will be a follow-up combative lesson? Or…hmm… What is the lesson here? I'm not sure what I'm supposed to be learning. I already know our magic can't compete with a pro witch."

"*Your* magic, maybe." Kenzo scoffed, turning his scowl toward Katherine. "Are we actually fighting them, or is know-it-all going to insist on a lecture the entire morning?"

Whereas others shied away from Kenzo's temper, either intimidated or too annoyed to engage, Katherine refused to relent. Rarely did her upbeat demeanor shift, yet almost every single time these two interacted, they shot daggers at each other—one of these days, I worried it'd be actual daggers. The silent fury raging between their unblinking eyes was only fueled by awkward, mousy grins Gael and Caleb gave one another.

"The purpose of today is to see where your collaborative and combative skills are," I said, attempting to get the topic back on the objective. "Today, they'll be evaluating your casting limitations just like me, and we'll determine what type of regimen will be best suited for you this year. Ideally, this will ensure you're each ready for your third-year internship."

It'd also help me cut the strings loose on this group next year. And yes, a year away sounded far, but school years tended to drag one second and vanish in a blink the next. I wouldn't waste a moment. In the past, I was able to follow my homeroom coven all three years at the academy and have a hands-on approach when guiding them during their internships, helping smooth over issues, talking out difficulties, and so many other hiccups that occurred. The academy's new motto meant they'd be virtually independent next year.

So, with some suggestive nagging, I convinced Milo it'd be imperative the students got to work with actual acolytes during their second year to hopefully mitigate the drop in proficiency that'd already been reported based on last year's newly independent third-years. Who would've thought one administrator couldn't properly coordinate or conference with six hundred student interns? Shocking, truly.

I buried my own smug satisfaction over the state's approach to independence backfiring. The joy was outweighed by the cost of education those students would never get back. Their shot was spent on a new strategy, nothing more than guinea pigs meant to collect data and improve success rates in the future. I wouldn't let my homeroom coven end up lumped into a percentile.

"The first thing I need everyone to do is split up into your four-person covens. We'll be—"

"*Whoa. That light.*" "*When'd they get here?*"

"*So fast.*" "*So pretty. The glitter's nice, too.*"

"*Holy fuckity fuck. Clucks!*"

I squinted. Milo and his third acolyte flew into the auxiliary gym.

"*See. Told ya I had it covered.*"

When I asked Milo for this arrangement, I wanted all three of his acolytes for symmetry, allowing each of my student covens their own unique opponent and an opportunity for them to see different techniques, training backgrounds, and magics, all leading to the same career path.

"*And I told you I didn't want you to come.*"

"*What? You love it when I come.*"

I grimaced, partially from Milo's innuendo and partially because his acolyte left a trail of glitter on the way toward us. Sunlight reflected off each speck, casting light in every direction. Christ. He didn't need to stroll in with his branch at the ready. He was already late.

Kenzo ground his teeth almost in unison with me. "***Motherfucking disco ball looking witch.***"

He practically took the words right out of my mouth. Or head.

"*The Infinite Light,*" Caleb thought, mind trailing off to a thousand notes he'd taken on Milo's newest acolyte: Hayden Russo.

I couldn't believe Milo showed up. I'd explicitly explained multiple times, slowly, his presence would ruin the purpose of this exercise.

It took everything I had to ignore the flurry of thoughts. No point attempting to continue discussing the objective of today's lesson since none of them would actually hear the words coming out of my mouth with so many gushing over Enchanter fucking Evergreen's arrival.

"*Enchanter Evergreen! He's actually here.*"

"*He's gonna see my star shower fireworks in action!*"

"*I'm too tired to cast.*"

"*I knew I should've reviewed my grimoire last night.*"

"*I can't drop the ball. Gotta make sure my vitality is ready for anything. Combative, defensive, support.*"

"*Wait. Is Mr. Frost gonna make us fight Enchanter Evergreen, too?*"

"*With Mr. Frosty as our teacher, we're all but guaranteed an internship with The Inevitable Future. Definitely why he brought him.*"

"*Is he here to evaluate us or his acolytes?*"

"*Everyone's too emotional. I'm gonna puke.*"

"*Me pregunto si mi magia sería útil para Enchanter Evergreen.*"

"***Is it bring your boring boyfriend to work day or something?***"

"*Enchanter Evergreen would be amazing to work with—not that he's ever taken on an intern before. Then again, he has acolytes now, and that's a first for him, too. But maybe I should be aiming for easier guilds. Cerberus is likely to reject any branchless witches. Still, Enchanter Evergreen is the dream mentor. And...*"

I clicked my tongue against the roof of my mouth, drowning out the drizzle from all their thoughts. As if I'd ever recommend one of my students to intern with Milo. He was too aloof when it came to training young witches—they wouldn't learn nearly enough stuck handling all the paperwork the great Enchanter Evergreen was too busy for. Well, if his poor acolytes were any indication. Then again, I was grateful Milo pawned them off on whatever task met his fancy. Not that I'd exploit it too much, but it made for a hell of a first day and a strong year ahead.

Jennifer huffed, her body vibrating from the visible aggravation of standing beside both Gaels. "*Fucking fanboys.*"

Fiddling with the silver chained necklaces hanging around her neck, Jennifer scoped out her classmates. "*I get it—he's cool, but Christ... is everyone's emotional state really this wound up? It's not even the first time he's been to our class.*"

```
Name: Jennifer Jung
Branch: Psychic (Empathic)
Ranking: 18
```

I might've lacked empathy on the magical level, but I had enough to understand her frustration as she fought to quell everyone's eager emotions.

"*Frost's typical irritation won't cut it.*" She bit the inside of her lip, careful not to smudge the black lipstick while she subtly scanned her classmates. "*Plus, he's probably thrilled showing off his hottie boyfriend for some secondhand high. Poser ass.*"

Well, fuck you too, Jen.

She looped her branch toward Kenzo, believing for good reason he wouldn't be bursting with positivity over Milo's arrival like the others. She was half right. But exhilaration exploded off Kenzo in waves while he calculated strategies on how he'd dominate today and prove he could hold his own against any of the acolytes. Seriously, his thoughts were methodic and maniacal but too abrasive. His internalized shouting gave me such a headache, I had to latch my telepathy onto others to keep from passing out.

Equally exhausted or hit by a wave of my mental fatigue, Jennifer wobbled.

"Hey." Carter gripped her shoulder until she steadied. Well, until Jen's gaze turned sour, and her glare was strong enough to melt faces. "Sorry."

Carter released his grip and returned to the quiet anxiety festering in his mind. The trepidation that dripped from his surface thoughts didn't carry the wave of dread and blood like last year.

```
Name: Carter Howe
Branch: Rejuvenation (Vitality)
Ranking: 75
```

My dying body no longer haunted him, something I was grateful for, but the fear of mastering his branch to its fullest purpose and beyond continued worming its way into his training goals. Goals he apparently slacked off on, ignoring the entire summer. I should relish teaching him this lesson, yet all I wanted was to absolve him of the horrors he endured while tending to my injuries, my slashed throat still carrying the light scar of that event. But I couldn't remove the trauma etched into the cracks of his subconscious.

I continued fearing I'd failed Carter.

"Check your emotional baggage at the door, Preppy Dick." Jennifer leaned over, shoulder-bumping Carter. "No one's got time for that shit."

"But, of course, Emo Queen." Carter took a dramatic bow, a spark of joy striking when Jennifer made a queasy expression of revulsion.

A smile filled Carter's face. Elation swelled into certainty and then nosedived into a bit of cockiness, which Jennifer's empathy fed on. The pair stood silent, sharing in an emotional high. They'd grown closer, so much closer, they seemed to share subtle gestures, inflections, secrets even their thoughts kept guarded. Apparently, the pair regularly tossed gentle barbs back and forth—and some not-so-flattering ones, too. Though, that wasn't so different than when I roamed the academy halls at their age, telling Finn and Milo to fuck off, secretly delighting when they brushed aside my phony annoyance.

Whatever lingering guilt I held for Carter's trauma, however our emotions synced in the air, Jennifer had used her empathy to shatter those shackles linking us in this moment. It was funny because in all my years of teaching—even with telepathy—I never registered a full-scale read on the emotions that radiated off others, the way they bounced in the air, shifting the chemistry and hormones in a classroom.

As my mind pulled away from Carter's, I found myself drawn to Milo, seamlessly syncing to the joy he held above all else. He enthusiastically chatted up my homeroom coven, doing his best to recall their names—though he only had about half memorized.

Beneath that wave of professional positivity lay hidden concerns. I tilted my head, studying his thoughts but finding no real answer. It could be a fleeting feeling from when he thought his acolyte's late arrival would ruin my lesson. It could also be a case he didn't want to discuss. Something about this concern gnawed at me, though. All the same, I'd learned my lesson about interfering with Milo's work more than once.

Chapter Five

Once my homeroom had finally had their fill of talking over one another and internalized gushing for Milo's arrival, I took it as my opportunity to finally get us started.

"No holding back, these acolytes won't," I said, gesturing for them to split off into their four-person teams. "Individually, none of you could compete, but as a coven, you should, at the very least, put up a sporting match. Who knows, if you spent the summer training like you were supposed to, you might very well win."

They wouldn't—though some truly believed if they planned accordingly, they would. After all, none of my trainings last year set them up for a guaranteed failure, but that was something they needed. Handling losses and pivoting for future successes were as important as securing victories in the guild industry.

"The rules are pretty simple." I waved a hand, telekinetically reeling ropes over that I'd set aside from the fitness station and moving them into a circular shape covering a large portion of the rock terrain. Not enough to allow anyone space to hide, pause, and plan a counter, but enough for mobility and evasion without tripping over each other when casting. "This is where you'll compete. Get knocked past the designated arena, immobilized, or knocked out, then…well, you're out."

"Knocked out?" Carter gulped. "So, we're really not holding back?"

"Do we ever?" I asked, ignoring the twinge of guilt as his thoughts swirled into every protective measure he'd mastered with his branch.

Jennifer stood with her arms folded and her fingers reaching out, poking him with her sharp, stiletto-shaped black nails.

"Looks like rejuvenation's gonna be a game changer," Carter boasted, hands on his hips, shoulders squared, and a goofy grin oozing bravado…even if only for show. "I just feel bad for the other teams."

"Speaking of." I redirected the discussion. "First up will be Ben's Coven."

"No, no, no, Mr. Frosty." Gael waggled his finger back and forth, practically shaming me. "You have to properly announce us by our official coven's name."

I stared, doing my best not to express how irksome I found their coven name.

"What's the matter?" Gael asked. "You're the one who insisted we fill out the forms over the summer."

"*Kind of a dick move too, giving us paperwork over the summer,*" Yaritza thought, rolling her eyes in equal annoyance for me and the coven's name that Gael had somehow talked her, Jamius, and Tara into agreeing upon. Well, apparently, Gael hadn't so much talked Yaritza into the name as he'd agreed to never comment even remotely on her improved ranking if she signed off on the name. So, let's add extortion to Gael's growing list of terrible talents.

```
Name: Yaritza Vargas
Branch: Cosmic (Star Shower)
Ranking: 69
```

I ground my teeth. "You realize this is your official documented coven name. It's the name you'll have to introduce yourselves to industry panels with. It's the first name prospective guilds will see when looking into your file."

"Wait, what?" Jamius raised his brows. "But Gael said…"

"Chill, bro. It's our temporary official coven title." Gael batted his lashes, devious thoughts weaved in between a hundred innuendos I couldn't actually figure out what he intended on blurting. "Mr. Frosty said the paperwork had to be filled out before our second year but that we could update the profile anytime so long as we had any and all coven updates finalized by April 1st."

Seriously? Gael couldn't remember a single assignment the moment he'd stuffed it in his book bag, but he recalled one offhanded conversation I had between lessons months ago? Gael was a vexing paradox of mischief and mayhem.

The purpose behind students picking their coven names over the summer came down to collaboration, independence, and initiative. Forcing them to work together over the summer to contact each other, decide on a name, and file the forms allowed students a small taste of the industry paperwork they'd be expected to keep up on without much oversight from a nagging instructor. Did it always work? No. But I always had plenty of time to rectify those shortcomings during the school year. That said, I'd never had a group come up with such a crude, overused, and frankly tacky coven title.

I sighed. "First up, Ben Dover's Coven."

Gael beamed; students giggled; Milo's so-called professional acolytes chuckled, too. It didn't help when Enchanter Evergreen wheezed, fighting back laughter and egging on the humorous energy.

"Yes, so so funny," I said, completely deadpan. "Let's see if your coven's collaboration is half as skillful as your team's puns."

"We got this in the bag." Gael punched a fist against his palm.

"Cl-cluck!" His rooster fluttered, leaping onto Gael's shoulder.

"Right." Gael nodded. "Any rules to this battle? Branch magics allowed, or is this one of those trainings where you're afraid of what'll happen if I unleash the full fury of my mighty cock?"

I glared, ignoring the bubbling laughter Milo fought back. To be fair, he kept himself completely composed on the surface, but with our minds so intertangled, I could hear every cackling thought of amusement that crossed his mind. Gael's immature humor resonated with Milo. Ugh… Had he found a favorite student?

"All right." I waved Tara and her coven over. "Let's begin."

"Wait, wait, wait!" Milo swooped in the air, hovering behind me. "We gotta make it official."

"Huh?" I quirked a brow.

He zipped by, flying to the proctoring room at the far end of the auxiliary gym. The billboard display lit up, projecting our first coven training.

Ben Dover's Coven
VS
Finesse

"Try not to embarrass yourself too much, El." Lena folded her arms, scowling. Underneath that angry façade lay soft support rooting for Acolyte Reed—not hopeful she'd win, Lena expected that much, but that Ellie would impress my class with her skills.

"When do I ever embarrass myself?" Ellie waltzed forward, tripping over her own foot. The one saving grace she had was the swift activation in her levitation root to keep from falling face-first onto the gravel. "That was on purpose."

No. It wasn't.

She popped a hip in Lena's direction. "Keeping them on their toes."

It had the opposite effect, making Gael's absurdly named coven drop their guard. I rolled my eyes.

"Well?" I cleared my throat. "What are you all waiting for?"

"Are we starting?" Jamius asked.

"I am." Ellie raised an arm, aiming her large key used as a support item to channel her branch magic.

```
Name: Ellie Reed
Branch: Ward (Skeleton Key)
```

"Lock. Lock. Lock."

Gael shoved Tara, knocking her headfirst onto the ground while his familiar kicked Yaritza with a telekinetic burst, throwing the young witch into the air. A reckless move, but Yaritza's telekinesis and levitation roots were her best, allowing her to quickly shift her trajectory and find balance midflight.

I scrunched my face, studying Gael's locked pose. Out of everyone in his coven, he was the last one I anticipated to predict Ellie's move set, yet as a major Enchanter Evergreen fanboy, he knew all about his favorite idol and those he worked alongside. The second Gael saw Ellie lift her key, he acted. Though his thoughts swarmed with doubts. This was his chance to show off his abilities, but instead of saving his coven and rushing ahead to fight the sexy, full-figured Finesse—*ugh, this kid*—he ended up locked in place from head to toe.

"*Sorry,*" Gael thought. "*I fucked up. I should've done better...*"

His thoughts sank into despair, all the sunshine in his mind dimming to dust that he'd failed to impress—

King Clucks crowed, cutting through the sorrow. The two shared a few seconds of silence until the light in Gael's thoughts returned. Whatever words of communication they shared, I couldn't glean them. Not on the rooster's end, anyway. Gael might've had a locked jaw of shock on his face, but internally, he was all smiles thanks to his familiar's emotional support.

The rooster puffed, unable to move. Even though Ellie's lock strike hadn't hit the rooster since he used root magic to knock Yaritza out of the way, familiars shared a very close bond with their witches. Perhaps Ellie's ward magic took that into account as some ripple effect. If so, fascinating.

Jamius vibrated, the only one Gael hadn't been close enough to push out of the way; watery replications stretched far, flowing against his brown complexion and brightening the warm undertones of his skin. His body convulsed, and the elasticity of his duplications snapped back with loud pops like a flurry of rubber bands.

"Son of a bitch," he shouted.

"Careful, or I'll lock that potty mouth next." Ellie smiled.

"*She's good, managing to lock Gael in place and Jamius' magic from making copies,*" Yaritza thought, digging into her purse. "*But let's see her lock up fifty targets at once.*"

Yaritza let out an enthusiastic shout along with a frenzy of explosive rocks. She hurled them from overhead toward Ellie, who used telekinesis to whip Jamius in her direction.

"What the hell?" He spun in the air, squeezing his eyes firmly shut and recalling how many times Yaritza's star showers had smashed his clones. "Stop!"

"Wait. Hold on." Yaritza waved a hand, shifting the direction of her star shower projectiles. "*It's still not enough.*"

They whirled wider, spinning past Jamius and looping around behind Ellie.

"*Wow. I've gotten hella good.*" Yaritza released the tension in her shoulders, channeling her root magics seamlessly.

Standing to her feet, Tara subtly added a layer of her telekinesis and weaved it between Yaritza's to strengthen the redirection. Still, the strongest in her group with her roots and the most humble, allowing Yaritza to bask in the success while Tara studied Ellie's movements.

"Smooth," Ellie said, pivoting around Jamius.

While I expected a few cuts and bruises, I really didn't want one of my students to be seriously hurt. Here, I figured Lena would be the heaviest-handed in combat.

"Unlock." Ellie pointed her key at Jamius, unleashing every copy he'd attempted and failed to release once she'd locked his branch. Two dozen duplicates burst out, colliding with Yaritza's star shower.

The exertion of expelling that much branch magic simultaneously immediately rendered Jamius unconscious.

"It wasn't me. Well, not on purpose! You can't blame me for blowing up your extras this time." Yaritza flew down to help Jamius, unaware he'd passed out.

"Possessing a powerful branch is amazing"—Ellie waved her key like she was slicing through the air—"unless you lack the precision to properly redirect it."

Yaritza's entire body stiffened, every muscle locked in place, leaving her incapable of continuing.

Tara studied the invisible strike, her mind spinning back to Darla's hex branch that sent waves of counter magic every time the warlock aimed a dagger at a target. It didn't raddle Tara, instead providing her with a familiar sense of strategy. The key to winning this battle was literally removing Ellie's key from play. Not a bad idea, except Ellie held the opposite channeling issues Darla had. That hex warlock required a support tool in order to cast her branch. Ellie possessed so much magic, she used the key to keep it focused and allowed her to live up to her industry stage name: Finesse.

"*If I want to stand a chance against her, I need to use all my branches.*" Tara hovered toward Ellie, who crinkled her brow.

"*The threads are so entangled. How does she even cast?*" Ellie aimed her key at Tara, wavering.

Fascinating. Acolyte Reed didn't only possess the ability to lock or unlock matter; she actually saw the threads that connected everything down to a molecular level. I couldn't visualize how she processed this second sight as it remained veiled behind her magic, similar to how Milo's visions usually remained hidden from my telepathy. That said, the many overlapping branches in Tara's body left Acolyte Reed wide-eyed.

Her hesitation afforded Tara an opportunity to move in for an attack, unleashing a half dozen shadows in the form of whips. Their tips were laced in golden hues. Incredible. She'd finally found a way to use her three overlapping branches together in a combative form. The shadows served as a conduit connecting her intangibility arcane magic and sealing ward magic. She made the shadows themselves phase through the rocky terrain, leaving everything unscathed because the entirety of the tendril was merged with her intangibility. The only real danger in her strikes came from the shadows' tips that were coated in gold and sealed tight, holding a heavy amount of magic channeled in a singular location.

Tara had literally transformed her channeled magic into a battering ram she flung at targets.

"Lock. Lock. Lock." Ellie weaved between the shadow whips, barely evading the strikes. "*Dammit. I hit two dormant threads and her sensory root. I can't pinpoint the veins holding her active branches.*"

Dormant? Did she mean damaged threads that Tara channeled her branches through or other potentially unharnessed branches? After all, she'd only recently unlocked her fourth branch last semester. She could have more that'd yet to blossom.

Clink.

Tara landed a strike on Ellie's key, reeling me from my thoughts and focusing on the battle.

"*Yes.*" Tara soared closer. "*Gotcha. Just need to alter the flow, and I'll win this.*"

Pride burned brighter than the sun, shining down on the ocean in her mind. My heart hitched. I clamped my jaw, awaiting what would happen next.

The golden hue exploded, sprinkling flecks everywhere, and the shadow's tip wrapped around the key…then…nothing.

Acolyte Reed pivoted, flying around the shadowed whip and charging directly toward Tara.

"Still can't switch branch frequencies once they're laced together."

I understood. Tara's goal was to release her ward that sealed things and replace it with her intangibility funneling through the rest of the shadow. If she'd done that, the magic would've made Acolyte Reed's key intangible, removing the support tool from play. A brilliant strategy. But Reed had already decided the elegance of her key wouldn't work on Tara.

Reed flew in close, planting a hand on Tara's stomach. "Lock."

Tara's entire body froze; magic, muscles, even her thoughts ceased momentarily—it seemed the only measure Reed had to severe all the threads connecting Tara's branches.

"That's the match," I said. "Not that it could be called much of one. Maybe I should see if any of our incoming first years could put up a better showing."

"*Harsh,*" Milo thought.

I wanted to complement their coordinated attempt, but this was an overall failure on their part. They needed to sit with the loss, feel the sting, the brief wave of embarrassment. I could mold it later, harness their drive, and focus it to ensure these little slip-ups didn't happen once they graduated. In the field, it'd be more than a bad performance. It'd be the difference between life and death.

Chapter Six

Pulling the first group aside, I picked apart every flaw their team had down to the lack of communication—something they should've prioritized instead of one-liner jokes that weren't funny despite the headache of laughter Milo's mind gave me. After the moment alone, we returned.

"Almost two minutes. That's gotta be a record for you and your cock, Gael," Layla said, brushing her fingers through her low-hanging ponytails.

```
Name: Layla Smythe
Branch: Bestial (Therianthropy)
Ranking: 20
```

Seemed she hadn't mellowed out much over the summer. Her mean-spirited jabs were as sharp as her claws.

"Well, his part lasted about thirty seconds," Melanie added, fueling Layla's comment. "Not at all surprising."

The pair snickered. Such a headache. These two had bonded too much over their intolerance for anything not to Layla's standards. From Kenzo's brash attitude to Caleb's obsessive rambling, plus the mountain of other students who offended her sensibilities, and all the way at the peak sat Gael's horndog humor that somehow worked in his favor with too many girls at Gemini. She didn't understand it. She didn't like it. And she especially despised that he'd landed not one, not two, but three dates with her ex-girlfriend. It was bad enough Layla couldn't remove her feelings for her ex, but it was made worse by the fact Gael kept things casual as he chased every girl who—

Dammit. I didn't have the energy for teen drama. Especially not on the first day.

Despite wanting my students to develop rapport with each other, I sometimes loathed how close my homeroom covens got over the years, forming into tiny cliques. Their dependency on one another made them lax in their own pursuits, their goals, and Melanie had become a prime example of why it was important to emphasize one-on-one instruction. I no longer had the excuse of the void vision, the guilt of Finn's loss, the concern of finding my footing in a relationship with Milo, or the difficulty of balancing my evolving telepathy.

It was time I made an effort to get to know all my homeroom coven students and ensure they reached their full potential.

```
Name: Melanie Dawson
Branch: Primal (Fire)
Ranking: 50
```

She'd shown up with the same low-hanging pigtails, though her thick red curls added buoyancy, and she wore the same oversized blazer and dress shirt as Layla—despite the fact her branch didn't augment her stature requiring the loose threads. Though Gemini seemed to have a lot of students adopting the style, along with the shorter skirts completely hidden by the oversized tops. Layla could trend set outside the academy uniform policy all she wanted; I didn't care.

I did care how Melanie's individuality slowly fizzled out the more time she spent with Layla. Ironic, considering how bright her flames burned last year, literally and figuratively. Now, her interests had all become identical to Layla's, but not without added effort. They rose to the surface of her mind like balloons she had to constantly blow air into, forcing the idea while simultaneously popping actual passions that naturally inflated in her thoughts because her best friend found them absurd.

"Ba-ba-bawk!" King Clucks pecked at the air until Layla and Melanie settled.

While Layla did well to hide the initial terror the rooster's crow had caused, she considered how quickly she could fly if the bird dashed toward her.

"I didn't mean you," Melanie said. "I meant, well, you know… He says it so suggestively. His cock this, his cock that. I-I was being funny."

"We've had enough jokes for today," I said. "Can we focus?"

"*Oh, when we make a joke, suddenly, Mr. Frost wants to focus. Asshole.*" Layla crossed her arms, snarling in my direction.

I contemplated sending Layla's coven next, but in truth, the longer she and Kenzo waited, the more impatient they'd become, which would favor the acolyte I paired them against. Truthfully, those two possessed enough aggressive strategy between them they might win—not part of today's lesson—if they actually collaborated together.

"Next up will be The Coven of Inevitable Potential," I said, ignoring Milo's pride for a name that clearly paid homage to his stage name.

Caleb's strategic mind had the opposite effect of Kenzo and Layla. His patience allowed him to plan and account without getting worked up. Already, I'd glimpsed a dozen thoughts he'd abandoned on how his coven could face off against Acolyte Reed. Meanwhile, he plotted which of the two remaining acolytes his coven would be most suited against.

The monitor announced the next round.

The Coven of Inevitable Potential

VS

The Infinite Light

"*Gotta say I figured you would've paired their group against Mercury Rising,*" Milo thought. "*After all, isn't her branch all but perfect to take them down?*"

Milo knew my intentions, but he didn't know his acolytes as well as he thought. Or maybe he did and kept it to himself, so close I couldn't hear the many thoughts he had when assessing them. Too much remained wrapped in the potential outcomes of their futures while working under him.

Caleb huddled with his group, muttering directions to a plan that weaved throughout his mind. I couldn't glean how much he shared versus the overly detailed contingencies he might've kept to himself. Plans for Ellie and Lena dimmed from his surface as he prioritized everything he knew about Hayden's magic—which was far less since this acolyte had only hit the streets of Chicago since late July. Still, Caleb's mind was a labyrinth of twists and turns, accounting for every possible dead end he sought to avoid.

"Are they beginning or not?" Lena asked, hands on her hips and disinterest on her face. All the same, it didn't fool me. She wanted to see firsthand what the branchless kid who defeated Jamie Novak singlehandedly at the Spring Showcase could do. A spike of resentment sparked, but she buried the thought as quickly as it occurred.

Caleb had unleashed a perfected strike of banishment against Lena's younger brother. He'd all but defeated the devil wearing Jamie's face in front of nearly a hundred enchanters, yet he hadn't put enough force to free him then and there. No. Jamie lay dormant, possessed, for weeks longer until Enchanter Evergreen's plan came together, and the witches of Chicago rid the world of that disgusting devil.

I couldn't discern how much of Lena's rage was self-inflicted toward her own shortcomings and how much might've been buried spite for the branchless wonder who failed her brother. All the same, I had no intention of pitting them against one another to figure out where that rage landed.

"***Guess that means I'll be facing off against the Novak witch,***" Kenzo thought, his fury reminding me of when I'd tested Caleb's luck against the angry tyrant when searching for clues to the mystery behind his near death.

Yep. Best I avoid pitting Caleb against those with so much budding rage.

"All righty, your crew ready?" Hayden had a glittery smile plastered on his face and spoke with a slight Southern lilt—something not quite covered by the deep accent of his inner thoughts that were lost on the shape of clouds overhead.

"Huh?" Caleb asked. "Wait. Did we start?"

"Yes," I said.

"Nonsense." Hayden strolled to the center of the makeshift arena, a swagger in his steps. "Take your time. Looks like you've got a big plan. Hash it out. I can wait."

"*Is he screwing with us?*" Katherine thought.

"*He usually seems upbeat in the interviews with Enchanter Evergreen,*" Caleb thought, trying to recall what he knew about Hayden and his magic. "*But I've never seen him prior to a case. Just post interviews—most guild witches are all smiles, then. He could be faking to throw us off.*"

"It's just an act," Carter said.

"*It could be an act, but his emotional state is completely carefree. Serene. Not the slightest hint of winding up for combat.*" Jennifer swallowed hard, burying her nervousness. "*Even Acolyte Reed's emotions shifted with pangs of anticipation. This guy, though... It's like he doesn't even register a remote threat from us.*"

"We don't have all day." I checked my phone. Well, we easily had another hour before Headmaster Dower wrapped up her long-winded orientation. "Begin."

"Aw shucks." Hayden stretched, raising his arms high above his head. "Hope y'all put together a solid strategy. Can't wait to see what you've got in store."

"Everyone, get ready," Carter said, snapping his teammates back to attention.

They each entered the edge of the territory, careful to maintain distance from Hayden, who'd conveniently stood dead center while he let them plan.

"*He might have two branches.*" Katherine unfastened her grimoire. "*But only one of them is a threat, so once I neutralize it, we'll have the advantage.*"

```
Name: Hayden Russo
Branch: Cosmic (Teleportation)
Branch: Cosmic (Glitter)
```

Katherine flipped through the pages of her grimoire, searching for a spell to prevent teleportation. Immediately, twinkling lights shimmered between the letters of her spells, so jarring it knocked her back a step. Brushing a hand over the glitter didn't make it easier, and the shock of Hayden's glitter blocking the words frazzled her. Suddenly, Katherine couldn't recall a single spell she'd written down. They were all there. Hundreds of spells she'd rehearsed a thousand times over. She knew them by heart, yet in this anxious moment, all memories of them vanished. All she could think about was how she should've read over her grimoire before school, how she should've had more warding spells at the ready, how the match had just started, and how she'd failed to complete her job.

It left her coven mates vulnerable. Most of all, it left her vulnerable.

Hayden wiggled his fingers, and the glitter leapt from the pages of Katherine's grimoire. Shiny lights sprinkled and scattered all around her like a frenzy of bees. Katherine shrieked, dropped her grimoire, and backstepped—stopping short of falling out of bounds.

"A lot of folks look at my glitter and think it's just for arts and crafts, but they don't realize the beautiful versatility that comes with bringing a little light into the world." Hayden wiggled his fingers, controlling the shift of the glitter into a rope-like formation. "Especially if you've got razzle-dazzle and spirit fingers."

He clapped his hands together. The glitter coiled around Katherine's legs; Hayden pantomimed a gesture like yanking a rope. Suddenly, Katherine fell back.

"Out of bounds," I said, eyeing her elbows propping her up past the designated arena. "You're down to three."

"I'm so sorry, guys." Katherine retrieved her grimoire, noticing the glitter had trickled away, revealing the perfect spell to counter cosmic magic like Hayden's branches.

"When did you… How did you…" Carter focused on his telekinesis, knocking away glitter directed at Jennifer and Caleb.

"*He wasn't casting at the start of the round,*" Caleb thought, simultaneously recalibrating his scenarios to account for Katherine's loss. He hated thinking it, but he would've preferred it if Hayden had knocked Jennifer or himself out of bounds first. Katherine had the most to contribute when handling Hayden's magics, and Carter had become a perfect support witch with his branch and root magics.

"*Too bright.*" Jennifer gritted her teeth to stifle a shout. Barely any glitter surrounded her, yet the twinkling lights made it impossible to bear with her eyes open or closed.

Quite remarkable. I figured there was more to Hayden's simple glitter magic but never suspected he could shift the frequency of its casting. Of course, he could. That magic was part of the cosmic branch, which made slipping between planes of reality easier, and as a psychic, Jennifer saw the emotions of others by analyzing their radiating auras on a separate plane. Hayden struck a chord by infesting that emotional wavelength, basically neutralizing her.

"You set this up before the round started," Caleb said, drawn back to Hayden's arrival, trickling glitter throughout the auxiliary gym as he rushed in late beside Enchanter Evergreen.

"You're pretty darn clever." Hayden smiled. "I should keep an eye on you, huh?"

"That's cheating," Carter snapped; his telekinesis raged, lashing out at Hayden, who jumped back to evade.

Interesting. It would've been the perfect opportunity to teleport behind Carter, yet Hayden dragged out the round.

"Mr. Frost," Carter yelled. "He cheated. Do something!"

"It's not cheating," Hayden said. "Your instructor never set any stipulations on when or how we prepared for a potential match-up. I had to ensure my magic was ready for whichever coven I was fortunate enough to face off against."

Layla snatched Melanie's lighter, flicking the zippo open and pouring the grains of glitter out. "*Son of a bitch targeted the support tools.*"

"He's not wrong," I said. "Continue or surrender. Those are your options."

"You gotta remember"—Hayden pivoted around Carter's continued thrashing strikes—"an enemy won't play fair. They don't care about guild guidelines. They don't care that you're holding back because of the law. They don't care about you."

"***Fuck.***" Jennifer leapt forward, channeling telekinesis and levitation along with a lot of rage. "*The only thing that'll smother my empathy is my roots.*"

She flew furiously toward Hayden, reeling back a fist. Her flight waned. Ah, it made sense. She wasn't simply channeling two roots, but all four—even though sensory and banishment offered her zero assistance in this match, they helped quell her psychic branch that Hayden had hacked into.

"I got you." Carter redirected his telekinesis, assisting Jennifer's trajectory and speed.

In almost an instant, she reached Hayden, fist balled and magic ready to punch that glittering smile off his smug fucking face. I swallowed hard, burying the anger surging from Jennifer and Carter.

I blinked, and Hayden vanished, reappearing a few inches to the left. Jennifer bolted past him through the air and out of bounds before Carter could snap his telekinesis back and pull her to safety.

"Out," I announced.

Carter panicked. He'd failed two of his teammates. Every part of the plan relied on his support skills, and now he believed he didn't have anything to offer. Nothing he did stopped the waves of anxiety that rocked inside his mind.

"Relax." Caleb placed a hand on Carter's shoulder; it wasn't the same as Jennifer's empathy feeding on Carter's fear, but something about the calm, collective energy Caleb radiated helped temper the furious storm of turmoil in Carter's head. "I got a plan."

Caleb's thoughts zipped through so many scenarios I lacked the ability to navigate the labyrinth of his planning. While the pair whispered, I found myself at a dead end to one of his contingencies that was no longer relevant. Whatever he wanted to do, it didn't seem to concern Hayden.

The acolyte allowed them to plot, taking a chance to bask in the shift of clouds above. He soaked in the sunrays, blissful and excited. Glitter seeped from his pores, making his entire body glimmer.

"Got it." Carter ran ahead, headstrong and fully intent on punching Hayden. None of his blows landed, not even a rippling side effect.

"*He's not channeling telekinesis in his blows.*" Hayden evaded Carter's punches.

Carter was built for offensive combat, between his intense workout regime to ensure his body reflected who he saw himself as on the inside and his branch magic, which revitalized his wavering muscles. But since switching to a more supportive role, his coordination and heart were no longer in sync with this type of tactic. Still, he fought on because he needed Hayden to prioritize him.

There it was. Each missed blow revealed a hidden layer of the plan at the surface of Carter's mind. He acted as an angry decoy so Caleb could move in behind.

Caleb swung his fist, missing Hayden, who teleported a few inches to the left.

Without a second of hesitation, Carter threw every ounce of vitality he could Caleb's way, which allowed his teammate to spin midair, swinging a leg with all the telekinesis he could muster.

Damn. Caleb and Carter might actually win this round.

The kick nearly collided with Hayden's chest until he vanished in a blink, appearing a few inches away.

"*As expected.*" Caleb spun around again, relying heavily on Carter's added vitality and telekinetic assistance, but he continued chasing Hayden.

The blows missed, yet enough of his telekinesis rippled through the air to knock away stray glitter from forming. Hayden continued zipping out of range, a few inches left, a few inches right every single time.

"*Why's he doing this?*" Caleb struggled to keep his composure; frustration festered, almost at a distracting level, but he kept swinging. "*Shouldn't he attempt long-range teleportation? Aim for Carter. He's wide frickin open!*"

Caleb continued, waiting for Hayden to surprise them and go for Carter—which the boys planned for. Instead, Hayden dragged Caleb further away, pressing himself closer and closer to the edge of the arena.

"*Screw it.*" Caleb descended, funneling his telekinesis into his core and allowing Carter's vitality to strengthen his tired muscles. "*I'll hit him with such a wide strike it won't matter whether he weaves left or right—I'll hit every direction at once.*"

Hayden stopped moving, studying Caleb's breathing and taking slow breaths of his own. "*Calm the nerves. Remember, your body is your own support tool. Easy breaths, calm chest, slow the heartrate a tick or two.*"

Caleb unleashed everything he had, casting a wave of telekinesis so strong it nearly struck those on the sidelines until a subtle shift in Milo's wrist altered the direction and sent it toward the forest terrain, cracking branches and snapping bark off the trunks of several trees.

"*Nice save.*" I eyed him.

"*It was nothing.*" Milo winced, rotating his aching wrist. "*Okay. It was something.*"

"*That's what you get for showing off.*"

"*Right?*" He grinned. "*Gotta keep these wrists up to par for handies.*"

"Shut up," I muttered.

"*Where'd he go?*" Caleb's fear snapped me back to attention. "*Did I... Did I get him?*"

Hayden had disappeared from Caleb's line of sight.

"Look out!" Carter shouted.

But it was too late. Hayden stood behind Caleb, casting a telekinetic wave nearly equal to Caleb's a moment ago, which knocked him completely out of bounds.

"And then there was one," I said, biting back the twinge of guilt when fear consumed Carter.

"You got this," Jennifer shouted.

"Yeah," Katherine cheered. "You have enough endurance to outlast him."

"Carter, remember what I said," Caleb added, the plans of his contingency surfacing in his mind.

"I... I can't." Carter's eyes welled up. "I give up."

It wasn't what his team wanted to hear, yet they didn't show it in their expressions. Instead, they clapped, congratulating him for being the last one standing against an acolyte.

"I'm sorry." Carter lifted his arm, burying his face into his sleeve.

Jennifer grimaced; she didn't latch onto his emotional state or take away the sorrow inside Carter, but for a fraction of a second, I glimpsed the colors of auras she saw nonstop. A soothing white apparition cradled a sea of somber blue. And then it faded as the terrain took full effect again.

"You made the right call, Carter," I said. "Knowing when you can't win a battle is as important as knowing when to fight on."

"*Fuck that,*" Layla growled. "*Coddling him isn't gonna change his shitty performance.*"

"***Is that Frost's lesson today?***" Kenzo folded his arms. "***Some bullshit on perseverance?***"

"It takes a lot of courage to know when to fall back." Hayden patted Carter's back as the rest of his coven approached. "The first time I took on a case too big, I learned that lesson a little too late. Got myself injured. Got a coven mate injured. You did amazing today. Even had me on the ropes a few times. Literally, I was tiptoeing on the edge of that rope marker your teacher set."

"Question." Caleb approached Hayden, notebook in hand and ready to decipher the methods of the acolyte's process. "Why'd you use your teleportation that way?"

"What way?"

"Um, well, you had plenty of opportunities to dart across the field." Caleb's face scrunched, visibly confused. "I even, you know, planned on that. Did you guess my strategy? I'm sure a lot of people see your branch in action and account for the distance, then extrapolate the best course of action, which in turn means you have to plan for what they'd theorize, so I was just wondering—"

"Whoa, whoa, whoa." Hayden gestured for Caleb to slow his ramblings, which helped quiet him but didn't silence the onslaught of theories and tangents bouncing around the boy's head. "You're giving me way more credit than I deserve. I'm not nearly bright enough for all that."

"Then why?"

"It comes down to a birth defect." Hayden pointed to his chest. "Had some heart issues as a baby. Even though the docs did good work, it sort of caused a hiccup in the way my branch developed later."

Tara turned her attention to Hayden's conversation, intently eavesdropping on every word. She'd already watched him closely, considering how rare it was to meet someone else with more than one branch, and he also struggled to control them, yet all she noticed during the match was effortless skill.

"See, my range is based on the beat of my heart. The faster my heartrate, the shorter my range. The slower, the longer." Hayden looked up to the clouds, his eyes momentarily glossy before the shape of a dog brightened his mood. "Honestly, my average distance is about six to eight inches. On a good day, I can probably teleport a solid two feet."

"What a shitty branch," Layla said, ignoring my scowl.

"Guess it's not the best, that's for sure." Hayden brushed his hand through his shaggy brown hair. "Glitter and short-range teleportation. Not the most sparkly branches to put on an application—still, got me a gig at a great guild."

Which had far less to do with his branches and more to do with how he utilized them, how advanced his root magics were, and how he handled himself in the field. Hayden was the perfect example that this industry required well-rounded training, something I wanted ingrained in my homeroom coven's heads. Lena and Ellie also possessed styles I wanted them to learn from. Ellie's support tool was something more than a few needed to study. Lena's versatility in her branch didn't come naturally. I wanted my students to start getting creative in how they operated and accessed their magic like her.

Speaking of…

"Guess we're down to our last coven," I said. "Hopefully, The Roaring Rainbows of Flame and Lightning can put up a better showing than the rest of the class."

The Roaring Rainbows of Flame and Lightning
VS
Mercury Rising

Gael's sharklike teeth beamed with pride over the displayed name, but that was immediately tempered when he realized I'd used it in conjunction to undercut his classmates. He very much disapproved.

"***Hell yeah.***"

"All right, Kenzo." Layla stretched, her body shifting into her therianthrope form in the process. "Let's show them how this is done."

"*I can't believe they actually came up with a plan…together.*" Melanie took her place next to Layla in the arena.

"*No estoy seguro de qué da más miedo, Layla y Kenzo discutiendo o trabajando juntos.*"

Lena walked into the ring, hands on her hips and mind prioritizing paperwork she needed to finish before the day ended. Between her aloof arrogance and The Roaring Rainbows actually collaborating, I started thinking my lesson would yield a sixty-six percent success rate.

"*You'll wanna take this group seriously.*" I linked my telepathy to Lena, attempting to forewarn her how Kenzo had—

"As if a couple sixteen-year-olds are worth my time," she said aloud, snapping the link of our minds with a small flurry of exploding bubbles around her face. "Are we doing this or not?"

"Make your move." Kenzo smirked.

"I already have." Lena flicked a wrist.

```
Name: Lena Novak
Branch: Arcane (Bubble Burst)
```

Kenzo's smirk grew, and gray static pulsed from his body, lashing out at his teammates and connecting with disruption magic he'd already coated over Gael, Melanie, and Layla. Bubbles dripped from their pores like sweat; a few popped when colliding with Kenzo's hex, while the rest fell to the ground like marbles.

"You really think we wouldn't see that coming after the last match?" Layla growled.

"***Like you could've done much about it.***" Kenzo kept the thought to himself, surprisingly, and nodded for Layla to make the opening move.

They had an entire long-range, short-range barrage planned to keep Lena on the ropes until they'd pushed her over them and won the round.

Layla took a single step and coughed.

"Hayden didn't sprinkle his shitty glitter to teach you kids a lesson," Lena said, raising her arms. "He did it because he's a professional."

Gael and Melanie coughed, too.

"The first thing I do when I walk into a room is assess every single witch's casting frequency," Lena continued her explanation. "Ally or enemy, I like to know what I'm working with—or against. Your hex is good, kid. But my bubbles do more than disrupt magic; they absorb it, channel it, funnel it, and mold it into the moisture of the atmosphere to do my bidding."

Kenzo grabbed his chest, fighting back the same cough that consumed each of his coven mates.

"This match was set the second you walked into the auxiliary gym." Lena snapped her fingers.

Bubbles that Kenzo had knocked to the ground rose up and exploded. Each tiny pop disoriented him, tipped his footing, and knocked him into Layla. By the time he'd composed himself to telekinetically wave away the assault, a new cluster of microscopic bubbles erupted from his mouth.

He gasped as Lena's magic pushed him back out of bounds along with each of his teammates.

"You were breathing in my magic this entire time."

Kenzo stood frozen as the bubbles dissipated. His mind went blank. No furious thoughts, no cursing, no flashing back to where he went wrong. Just silence.

This was the first time Kenzo had completely failed at something. He'd never in his life failed to account for an opponent, an objective, an opportunity so profoundly. Of all my students, he needed this lesson more than anyone. It'd sting, but together, we'd work through this, and he'd learn failure was just another part of life. In the long run, he'd benefit.

"Holy shit." Gael strutted toward Kenzo and the others. "You guys got your asses handed to you. I mean, like thirty seconds or less delivery. Wow. And you're the top-ranked second-year witch at Gemini? Maybe they should reevaluate those scores considering—"

And just like that, Kenzo's unbridled rage exploded, having found an outlet. His fist collided with Gael's nose. Blood gushed everywhere, and Gael thudded backward.

"What the fuck!" Tara said so loudly even the rooster's crow could barely be heard.

"Don't worry." Gael chuckled with a wince. "I just gotta hold out another twenty-five seconds with his track record."

Gray lightning coursed across Kenzo's entire body.

"Shit," I muttered. "Kenzo!"

He quelled his magic, his rage, and his scowl and stuffed his hands in his pockets. "***Yeah, yeah. I'll be in the headmaster's office or whatever.***"

Tara and Yaritza rushed to Gael's side, tipping his head back and blotting his nose. Layla vocalized her disgust for Kenzo's childish reaction while silently gloating that Gael had it coming. Milo attempted to redirect the students, but they were lost in the drama of the moment.

And like that, the lesson had ended. I started to think maybe, like my students, I'd also failed today.

Chapter Seven

Doppler

Dorian trained his teens for failure. A fitting lesson for what I had planned. Still, the most grueling part came down to how I handled the fallen devil, the disease of demonic energy latched to Finn's soul, the filthy chimera whose name I'd yet to learn.

Not that I cared what it called itself, but it was further proof that nothing I did to break its spirit had an effect. Demons guarded their names like a point of pride, secret and rarely divulged. No amount of hacking, slashing, blunt, or brutal force coaxed anything other than a chuckle from that beast. Torturing the demon only offered me momentary satisfaction. It didn't loosen the tether of his being to Finn, it didn't yield answers, it didn't even make the chimera more compliant.

I stood outside the chamber of Jasper's curiosities, a barren waste of space I'd converted into a prison for the chimera. Conjuring a cigarette, I took calming puffs, replaying how I'd broach this topic with the demon.

Cleansing Finn once and for all would require skills beyond what I possessed. The only way to obtain that power was by skirting around Milo's predictions and unleashing something even he didn't see coming. Someone. And that meant I needed a host with better connections than Jasper, the associate assistant manager of the seventh-best insurance claims office for magical disruptions in Illinois.

I shuddered, having memorized the positive affirmations that hummed through the corridors of Jasper's inner core like bad mall music.

"Care to have a word?" I finally stepped inside, taking in the chimera's frail form.

Starved of magic and freedom had made his human image withered and decayed. If I cared to house him in demon form, I imagined that would be easier now that he'd dwindled so much over the months. Not enough to die. Cease to be. It was never enough to rid me of this pestilence that clung to Finn.

The chimera tugged at the chains around his wrists, futile but an effort he exerted every chance he could, testing the limits of my magic, hopeful it'd wane. It hadn't. It wouldn't. "If it isn't my favorite puppet."

I glowered. If I responded, reacted, he won. He'd goaded me into arguments more times than I cared to admit during our conversations.

"But you're not like other puppets," he continued, seeing as I hadn't interjected this time, smiling as blood and tar dripped down his chin, staining his trimmed beard. Another test of pushing the confines of his limitations, biting his own tongue, lips, anything to bleed his demonic bile and release fragmented energy. “No, siree. You’re special. No strings on you, Pinocchio.”

He took every opportunity to remind me he believed me less than. He didn’t see a manifestation as anything other than an echo to Dorian, an extension of magic, a spell gone awry. I wasn’t real to him. I wasn’t real to Dorian either. Something these two had in common, I supposed. But I was real. A fraction split from the whole, formed into my own being. He couldn’t take that truth from me. I wouldn’t let him.

“You finished monologuing?” I banished the tar droplets as they glimmered white and wisplike.

“What else am I to do? You leave me alone for days at a time, then when you do visit, you just root around my insides, jabbing me in all the wrong places.” He sighed, feigning exhaustion—something I hoped keeping him bound and awake nonstop would cause…but it didn’t. Simply added to his nauseating personality.

I stared, unwilling to engage.

“See. No civil conversation. I’m bored in here with no one’s thoughts but my own to keep me company.” He grinned. “Well, Jasper’s too, but he’s rather dull, wouldn’t you say, puppet?”

Even bound in this room, he’d found ways to whisper horrors into Jasper’s subconscious, startling the bumbling fool and giving me a bigger fucking headache. Despite all I’d done to confine the chimera, he hadn’t lost every ounce of strength. Even the few times I shattered his being entirely, a single wisp would surface again from Finn, proving nothing could truly eradicate him so long as they were linked. The one saving grace I had was that Jasper proved an easy quarry, which left the chimera unamused after causing a few nightmares and reawakening old phobias in the host we borrowed.

"Since you find Jasper to be such a bore, perhaps my news will intrigue you."

"Oh?" The chimera tilted his head, curious brown eyes studying my unchanging face. "*Unchanging? Dearest puppet, your expression is worth a thousand words.*"

Goddammit. I extended my arm, slamming enough psychic energy to crush every bone in his body.

The crack and crunch of bones, the grind of meat twisting on itself, the heat of blood boiling, all of it brought little satisfaction. Torture wasn't a strong suit of mine, despite all my efforts and willingness to break this beast. He knew it and relished the pain. A sadist and masochist wrapped into one murderous, sociopathic monster.

Once I felt the tether of his telepathy snap and break away, I stopped my assault. He hadn't lost every branch when Milo had exorcized him, possessing five I was aware of thus far. Every now and then, he'd taunt me with a branch, testing his limitations but also foolishly revealing them, which allowed me the time to properly bind them.

"Come now. I've had rougher massages than that." He grinned.

The problem was, this chimera wasn't a fool. If these were the magics he revealed, it meant there was more he kept to himself.

"I have no patience for your nonsense." I cast telekinesis, tightening the shackles that bound him, and used my telepathy to box away his casting limits inside Jasper's mind. Here, I reigned superior, so locked inside a witch's head he'd have to remain until I eradicated him permanently. "I'm going to be moving from this mind soon."

"Really, puppet? Taking me along for the ride?"

"Obviously."

"Good." His eyes remained locked on mine, then flitted ever so, eyeing the ceiling of his prison before returning their gaze back to me. "I don't suspect these shabby accommodations will hold much longer."

"Don't get any ideas. Your next accommodations won't be any nicer. And if you resist in any way, I'll make your life Hell."

"Promises, promises." He puckered his bloody lips, gaze flitting momentarily upward again.

Ignoring him, I searched the depths of Jasper's mind where a tiny whisper the chimera had uttered days back echoed in the farthest reaches.

I ground my teeth. Too much energy was spent keeping Finn at peace, Milo unaware, the chimera bound, and distancing myself from the gravitational pull of Dorian's magic drawing me back to become complete again.

Fuck. I'd missed the latest attempt to derail this host body's sanity.

Reeling telepathy outward, I studied the absent-minded Jasper. He looked sloppier than usual, sweating profusely as he rushed down the sidewalk back to the office while lost in a daze of childhood embarrassments.

For Christ's sake.

"No one cares about what you said when you were twelve years old," I screamed through every fiber of his being. "Pay attention, dumbass!"

His eyes widened, feet planted on the crosswalk, like a deer in headlights quite literally as a truck barreled down on him.

This chimera took any opportunity he could, filling Jasper's mind with old regrets, leading him off into traffic while dazed, and threatening to kill the host body we all dwelled inside.

"Bastard," I hissed.

If Jasper died in this instance, I'd have to abandon the mind or risk being bound to the corpse without release. If I left now, unprepared, could I keep Finn calm? Keep the chimera docile? Would Milo be alerted through clairvoyance of such a random and untimely death? There could be major ripple effects in Jasper's death that I hadn't accounted for. Would Dorian feel my presence surging through the atmosphere, clawing my way into a new host? A host that might just as likely be too high profile, already on Milo's radar.

A hand snatched Jasper by the shirt, saving him right as I prepared to leap out of his mind.

"You all right?" A glittery smile filled Jasper's vision, so sparkly even this dank prison glimmered.

"Yeah, I…" Jasper's heart pounded, racing faster against the back of his ear as he took in the scene of traffic around him. His briefcase lay several feet away from the crosswalk. "I'm so sorry."

"Don't apologize." The young acolyte waved a hand, retrieving the fallen briefcase and raising it high above traffic to avoid obstructing those driving. "Just try to be more careful in the future."

"I-I will." Jasper gritted his teeth, desperate to apologize again but swallowing the words because he worried he'd annoy the young man who'd rescued him.

Hayden fucking Russo. *Are you kidding me?*

Of all the luck in a city this big, filled with thousands of professional casting witches, Jasper stumbled onto one that worked for Milo. I clenched my fists, wanting nothing more than to strangle Jasper until his apologetic face turned beat red. There were countless visions I'd studied in Milo's infinite list of potential futures, but I'd never stumbled onto a single pathway that involved Hayden Russo.

With no inkling of what drew this acolyte to the city or why Milo found an interest in this witch's potential future, I needed to avoid him at all costs.

"Oh, geez." Hayden checked his Cast-Watch. "Enchanter Evergreen is gonna kill me. I'm late again."

"I'm so sorry," Jasper blurted because of course he did. "It's my fault. If I'd been paying attention, if I'd waited, or left the office on time, then…"

"Relax." Hayden patted Jasper's shoulder. "Don't beat yourself up over what could've or would've. I could've also left sooner, but if I had, I wouldn't have been here when you needed me."

"I'm sorry." A fog ate away at Jasper, making it difficult to find the right words. "Lately, it feels like my mind hasn't been my own. So easily distracted."

"Look what you've done to this poor man." The chimera rattled his chains, chuckling.

I scoffed. As if my presence caused this. I'd barely left a trail, walking on eggshells in this man's mind. This fog came from Jasper himself, his fatigue, his pathetic life, and his age catching up to him. If anything, I'd cleared the cobwebs of insecurities to better him a bit.

"Lena is going to yell at me." Hayden typed away on his phone. "She's gonna say I'm lying like yesterday."

"Are you late a lot?" Jasper asked, craving conversation, interaction. His sad sack life was going to compromise my future.

"Sometimes, just a little." Hayden smirked. "Depends on your definition of late."

"What happened yesterday?"

"Well, you see, I was flying to work—I left early and everything—when I heard a woman crying. She'd lost her grimoire. I couldn't just abandon her, but I'm not the most suited for searching for books. It took forever, but we found it. Of course, Lena didn't believe me. I tend to get distracted. There's just so much good to do in the world. Even simple things, you know?"

Jasper believed every word of the farfetched tale. It sounded like a lie. A lazy one at that.

"Oh, I've got an idea." Hayden held up his phone. "A picture's worth a thousand words of evidence. How would you like to be on my Insta? It's Bright Life Spotlights where I do a selfie and post case Q&A for those interested."

The idea tantalized Jasper. He'd never been a part of anything so glamorous. Never needed to hire the services of a professional casting witch. Sure, he'd seen guild witches pass him by every day, even had a few close calls with demonic energy. But that usually came with a crowd of citizens, and Jasper was just another nobody in the background. Here, he had an opportunity to finally be recognized, to stand out, and with such a young up-and-comer—an acolyte who worked alongside the most famous witch in Chicago.

"That sounds—"

"Fucking horrible," I shouted, delaying Jasper's delight. "You really want to take a selfie next to this glittering god? You'll be a laughingstock, you fat, ugly nothing. Worthless witch can't even cross the street correctly. Everyone will see it. See you. Know you."

Jasper shivered; every ounce of self-doubt carried high to the surface of his mind, reminding him of the truth of his life.

"Disgusting," I hissed, cementing all the anxiety.

"I…I can't. I'm already late." Jasper brushed by the young acolyte.

"Of course." Hayden retrieved a card from his pocket. "We can always chat when it's convenient."

"Leave me alone." Jasper swatted the card away. "No one asked for your help."

I smirked. Hayden unlocked too many variables to fates I'd never seen, which could, in turn, lead me down a path toward Milo's clairvoyance. Thankfully, I'd kept Jasper off Enchanter Evergreen's path. Most likely. Long enough to move hosts, set fortune and the future in my favor.

"You're wicked, Pinocchio."

"Shut up."

"Took what little shrivel of self-worth this witch had and shredded it." The chimera tsked, shaking his head back and forth.

"Please, it's no worse than what the actual voice inside his head reminds him of on a daily basis." I'd merely said it a little louder.

"I like you, puppet. You're vindictive and callow. It's a fun combination."

I glared. How I hated this abomination. "Are you going to behave or not?"

"Gladly. Make your moves. It'll put me one step closer to finally uniting with Dorian. Oh, how we'll laugh about the puppet who dreamt he was real."

He didn't believe this was a possibility. He knew it. It was cemented in the foundation of his thoughts, true as truth could be. That was the most frightening thing about the chimera. Almost all the crevices of his mind remained open for me to explore, and in the deep recesses sat futures he declared impending and unstoppable. Not sure if it was bravado, arrogance, or a warning.

I'd undo his very being soon enough. He'd never know what possessing a perfect host body felt like because Dorian would be dead. Gone. Shattered into a million fragmented, intangible thoughts. And I had no intention of sharing my body with this demon.

Chapter Eight

The rest of the day went more or less according to plan. It was hard to fuck up first-day expectations. By the time I got home, I was ready to pass out. Too many lazy summer days washed away how exhausting running around a classroom all day working with students got. Eventually, the routine would return.

Charlie's meows for affection kept me alert as I stepped into my house. He sat on the end table beside the door, stretching as far as he could to rub his head against my hip while keeping his paws pressed to the very edge of the table's top. I picked him up, cuddling him close to my chest. Charlie purred, completely content while I filled the food bowls, ensuring his whiny sister Carlie wouldn't starve to death. She strutted into the kitchen, lapping down big bites of dry food.

"Wow, you must be hungry."

For a second, I almost confused the frustration flooding my mind for hers. Carlie loathed dry food. It was merely sustenance to tide her over until the wet arrived. This wasn't her emotional reaction. Sure, my telepathy had evolved, but not enough to glean my cat's thoughts, thankfully.

Charlie made biscuits, tugging at the fabric of my shirt and keeping me fully planted in the kitchen of my home while my mind synced to Milo's. I couldn't see him or hear him, only feel the stress going through him as he worked a case. Setting Charlie on the floor, I ignored his meows of utter betrayal and reached out to Milo, listening more intently.

This frustration didn't come from work. Something had him in knots, similar to how he'd felt this morning before my lesson. Had the results left him upset? Did he see some unknown future I'd fucked up? Was it unrelated?

I could ponder all day and night, or I could do the adult thing and ask.

"*Milo—*" I clamped my jaw.

There was an ache in the back of my head, almost like my magic was tugging on my hair, pulling me in strange directions to muffled thoughts so soft they were like whispers. There was no hint of sadness, not that I detected. Still, this individual's inner voice spoke in a hush, like they didn't want to be heard. Bizarre, hauntingly synchronized to my frequency, but somehow wrong.

I shook it off, focusing on Milo's mind. The last thing I needed was for my telepathy to randomly pick up on people's minds outside my range. Balancing my connection to Milo was enough work, keeping up with my students and the staff at Gemini on a daily basis was enough, enduring my noisy neighbors' thoughts was enough. I didn't need more growth in my branch magic.

My telepathy faltered, and I remained in my own mind yet again, so I decided to use this freeing break to be productive. While I worked on tweaking lessons around the notes I'd taken for my homeroom coven, I sorted through my curriculum scaffolding content for the new first-year students in my general history course. This batch struggled a lot with the introduction diagnostic I gave. The test at the end of the week would determine just how much I needed to backtrack my lessons in order to cover material they'd missed before attending Gemini Academy.

Milo's thoughts trickled into the back of my head as I worked. Not surface thoughts but a feeling of dread, one reminiscent of the trepidation that rose in his mind before he arrived during my lesson.

"*You okay?*"

Nothing. Scratchy static and chords of stress. The melody played above his words, above the link I attempted. His thoughts were scattered, and as such, his image remained fuzzy in the corner of my eye. So close I could practically touch him, but in actuality, he was halfway across the city meeting with witches. Kraken Guild, I think?

I blinked away his image and continued working. Retrieving my phone, I shot him a text. Before the growth in my telepathy, we were pros at playing texting tag.

Me: How's work?

Nothing.

Me: Today was interesting to say the least.

Not even read.

Me: Still swinging by tonight?

The floating bubbles of his reply went on forever. I stared at their rhythmic dance the same way Charlie became entranced by the strum of my fingers when playing. Must be writing quite the essay. Or a crude joke with lots of twists and turns.

Milo: Yeah. See ya soon.

Wow. See you soon? He didn't even offer up a single sexy emoji for me to overthink the intention. No flirty banter. No flurry follow-up with a dozen tangents. Just yeah…

Me: You okay?

Milo: Busy.

I swallowed hard, letting the trepidation clinging to Milo's mind sit in my chest, weighing heavy on my lungs. Feeling stressed for absolutely no reason of my own was somewhat comforting in a terrible, standard routine kind of way. I just hated how this stress came from Milo. He'd been a bubble of pure joy for months that I'd forgotten his thoughts could even gravitate toward sadness. And sure, I might've occasionally delighted in bursting that bubble over the summer, but I didn't like feeling actual stress wafting off him in waves. Tidal waves that distracted even my most basic thought processes.

Tossing my laptop on the other side of the couch, I decided work would be there in the morning.

Charlie stared at the abandoned laptop, then at me.

"I could watch TV?" But the only show I wanted to watch was one Milo insisted we binge together. Not that we ever finished more than two episodes at a time when work came crashing into our evenings. "Chores? I should actually clean."

Charlie cocked his head, ears twitching.

"Yeah, fuck that." I stood and lit a smoke to calm my nerves. Each inhale smothered the emotional tether linking to Milo and the little pang of hunger in my stomach. "That's it!"

I had a plan for distraction and productivity. Milo would be hungry after work. And he'd stocked my fridge with tons of stuff—his insistent way of reminding me the best meals came from dishes cooked for oneself. Sounded like a load of garbage to me. The best meals came from trained professionals and the satisfaction of knowing I didn't have to do the dishes afterward. But I'd make something for Milo when he swung by.

"How hard can it be?" I grabbed a little of this and a little of that from the fridge. Milo always just threw things together, and I'd seen him cobble up delicious meals out of the most random ingredients.

Charlie stared at me, judgment in the way his tail swatted.

"I've got this. Learned through osmosis."

He swaggered away, likely annoyed he'd get zero affection as I ran around the kitchen preparing an awesome dish. Milo was hungry, stressed, tired. The least I could do was offer him something when he got home.

I started chopping veggies and tossing seasoning on the meat. While I hadn't decided exactly what I'd make just yet, all of Milo's meals began with prepping the supplies. This was actually pretty easy.

I had literally no idea what I was doing. One second, I was searching my memories for the many meals Milo had strung together while making casual chitchat, and the next, I was stirring three pans of food. When did I add a third pot to the stove?

"Not good, not good, not good." The kitchen was smokey, and the meat had burned in the singular minute I turned to focus on the sauce. "It's like grilled, though."

I turned to Carlie, who sat on a countertop, eyeing the human food.

"Wanna try?" I sawed a knife back and forth until I managed to carve off a small piece for her.

Carlie turned up her nose to the dish I'd charred. She never turned down human food.

"Well, fuck."

My front door swung open, and Milo swaggered inside, takeout in hand and a flirty smile on his face. "*Thank God I planned ahead because neither of us needs food poisoning from this somehow overcooked and undercooked meal.*"

He then searched his mind for a synonym for the word meal that also meant inedible because, apparently, I couldn't fucking cook.

"If you knew I was going to screw this up, you could've texted me. Saved me the effort."

"Thought today was about learning from failures?" Milo laughed.

"Ha," I croaked.

"Besides, for every dish you ruin, you're one step closer to a future where I get breakfast in bed. I'm talking waffles, poached eggs, crispy bacon, and a *thick* sausage." He winked.

Milo maintained a carefree smile and even had positive surface thoughts, which might've manipulated me into believing everything was okay in the past, but I'd felt the stress weighing on him. I'd plucked at the strings, carrying it close to my heart. There was no way I could ignore it, ignore him.

"Why were you so concerned?"

"Huh?" Milo had a perplexed expression, feigning ignorance of my question as the same dread that'd followed him all day continued swirling beneath his surface thoughts.

Granted, he did well to hide it, but our minds were too close to hide these feelings.

"I thought maybe you were worried about your acolyte not showing up, and somehow that'd ruin my lesson. But you both showed, and everything moved forward as planned. Then I figured you dropping in was what worried you—because, you know, I explicitly told you not to—but that isn't it."

"You didn't want me there?" Milo twisted his lips, resisting his trademark minxy grin. "Completely forgot about that."

"Liar." I pouted. "Did you predict Kenzo's outcome? I assure you, that's not the worst thing that kid's done. Hell, it's not even in the top ten worst outcomes I've had during a lesson."

"That says a lot about your teaching method, Mr. Frost."

"Oh, fuck off." I paused as Milo sent me salacious images of things he could fuck. Burying my arousal, I continued. "Look, I recognized the spike of insecurity in your thoughts when you got to the academy. Same spike that hit when you walked through my door. Same spike you're currently repressing so I don't notice. Just tell me what's wrong."

Milo strummed his fingers against the counter, eyeing the takeout while wondering if he stuffed his mouth with food, it'd take his mind off whatever bothered him.

"Tell me what's wrong." I rested my hand over his, settling the shaky motion. "Or… Is this something you can't tell me? For reasons? Work? Future? Both?"

"No, it's not privileged." Milo sighed. "I just really wanted to save this conversation for after dinner. Not sure you'll have much of an appetite once I tell you. Actually, I'd prefer holding off on this conversation for as long as possible. Bury it. Ignore it. I just wanted you to have a good first day. Well, first week would've been nicer. First month, even better. But that's not the case. It's gonna be affecting your students soon, and the last thing I want is for you caught off guard so—"

"What's this got to do with my kids?"

Milo grimaced. It looked as unnatural on him as a smile did on me. "That's the thing. I don't exactly know."

My heart pounded. "A vision? Void vision?"

Could something like that be happening again? Had I merely delayed the inevitable? Was my homeroom coven cursed? I struggled to take a deep breath.

"Not a vision, void or otherwise. In fact, this is sort of outside my magical purview."

"What?" My chest tightened. Milo's thoughts rattled against my own swelling fears and concerns. Had I taken on the full force of dread he carried with him all day? It was awful. I couldn't focus or think or move.

"Theodore Whitlock's trial is being announced soon," Milo said.

My stomach sank, nearly dropping me to the floor. "The warlock incursion on Gemini Academy."

"Each of the warlocks involved will be having their day in court soon, and as you know, trials are highly classified. Especially one that'll be dragging Whitlock Industries through the mud."

Courthouses, law firms, the companies they outsourced—Hell, even those employed were cloaked in powerful warding magics. The kind of stuff that made the Tranquil Orbits gimmick look cheap.

"I have no idea how things will turn out, but I suspect there will be lots of feelings, reactions your students have."

"Am I going to be approached?"

Milo shrugged. "No idea. That's sort of been what's weighed on me today."

Normally, Enchanter Evergreen didn't allow himself to become too attached to a case that required legal action. Once he'd passed it onto law enforcement, he released the hold it had on him. He knew how to compartmentalize what he could and couldn't control, something I never learned and doubted I ever would. With trials, the state and the nation did their best to keep up with magic and technology, preventing either from interfering. I had no clue one way or the other how effective their methods were. All I knew was Milo had glimpsed nothing of this and couldn't give me the answers I craved. How would this turn out? Would my students be okay? Would I?

"I only found out thanks to a friend who passed along the info. It'll be hitting the news cycle soon, and they thought I'd want a heads-up. And thought you deserved a heads-up, too. I'm not sure how hard it'll hit your kids, if they'll be called on, or what's going to happen. The whole mess is unknown. I hate it."

Milo glanced at the faint scar lining my neck, a reminder of what happened when he struggled against a current of unknown futures, a reminder that the best one he'd predicted nearly killed me. Anything beyond a perfect outcome haunted Milo, even when he repressed it with a smile.

"I don't see it that way." I slid my hands up Milo's arms; the goosebumps hit me almost as hard as they did him. "Every time I see this scar, every time I'm reminded of that day, I remember it was when I finally let go of my grief. It had swallowed me whole for years, all-consuming and immobilizing. Every time I see this scar, I am reminded how I finally allowed myself to be loved by someone far too perfect for me, yet blessed that he sees something worthy in me."

Milo's eyes teared up. His mouth went dry.

"*Have I left you speechless?*" I linked our minds.

He rolled his eyes up, letting the emotional state fade before shooting me a minxy grin. "You are worthy, Dorian."

Milo moved closer, wrapping his arms around me and holding me in a tight hug, then his hands went a bit further, cupping my butt and squeezing. "And honestly, with an ass like that, how could I not love you?"

"You're insufferable. Can you take nothing seriously?"

"I think you've got a serious, stern face enough for the two of us."

"Hell, record shows I had enough for the three of us. How I ever ended up in bed with two annoying goofballs is beyond me."

"It's that good dick."

I shoved him away, hand pressed to his smiling face. "We were having a moment, and you made it crass."

Milo zipped his lips, and we stood silently, a few inches apart but thoughts colliding, intertwined on every sexual experience we'd explored with one another. His beautiful mind and body silenced the world, and the burden of stress weighing on him vanished and became almost instantly replaced by a boner.

“I suppose it can’t be helped.” I kissed him, but he turned his head, only allowing my lips to hit his cheek.

“Wouldn’t wanna be too crass.”

“You’re the worst.” I yanked him by the back of his head, turning it toward me and kissing him again.

Leading with my tongue, I kept him quiet, which only worked to silence his snarky comments aloud, not the ones playfully being thought at me. His kisses were sweet at first. I savored the smack of lips, the wispy breaths, and the assertive way he rubbed his arms over my body.

Milo paused, glossy-eyed and running his fingers along the scar of my neck. He softly kissed it. Little, sweet pecks across my neck. But there was nothing sweet running through his mind. Oh, no. A primal urge swelled triumphantly above everything else in the world. It swept away the stress of his day. Perhaps the emotions had merged as he found a new outlet, one where he intended to fuck away his anxiety.

I’d gladly allow him to pour that frustration into me, empty himself of all the worries he carried.

“I want you,” I whispered, tickling his ear with a hot breath.

He caressed me with his hands, pushing up against my body while holding back. “I want you, too.”

“No.” I pushed away. “I want you to use me.”

Milo stared wide-eyed until my words synced with his desires, igniting an urgency to drag me out of the kitchen and into the bedroom without a second of hesitation. He kissed me each step, leading us into the bedroom and guiding my backward steps when my footing fumbled.

"On your knees." Milo pushed me back; his commanding tone made every submissive fiber of my being tremble.

Craving his dominance, I dropped to my knees obediently and immediately unfastened his belt. Milo ran his fingers through my hair gently but then gripped a full head of hair, shoving his cock into my mouth. Gagging, I stretched my jaw, bracing for the throb against my throat. My body warmed; my dick hardened with each thrust of his hips. His pace didn't yield for a moment, giving me no chance to prepare. I loved it. His aura radiated throughout the rooms; scarlet and deep purples filled my vision as his cock filled my mouth.

Tenderly, Milo wiped a tear from my eye, then traced his thumb down my jawline and wrapped his whole hand under my chin while his other hand held my hair. He fully controlled my head, face fucking me. I went to unzip my pants.

"No," he hissed, the tone intoxicating.

Enthralled, I obeyed his desire that beckoned with primal thoughts. I gripped his butt with my hands, steadying his fast thrusts as my throat finally adjusted to the full length of his shaft.

My erection pressed hard against my tight jeans, throbbing for release and stiffening with each grunt Milo made. He took slow breaths, holding my head all the way down. Finally, the pressure lessened. Not on my throat, which I loved, but on my body. Somehow, Milo had begun to undress me. Opening my eyes, I saw the threads of my clothing unstitching, leaving me bare and on my knees as Milo continued using my mouth.

"Ugg mmm," I struggled to tell him to stop. Not his eager pounding of my throat but the tearing apart of my clothing. I gagged with garbled words instead.

"*Think it, don't speak it.*" He stroked my face.

Right.

"*That's my favorite fucking shirt.*" I bobbed my head, continuing because Milo's satisfaction made me quiver, and I couldn't allow this exhilaration to fade, not even for a second. It was too enticing.

"I'll buy you a new one, a hundred new ones." Milo groaned. "Fuck."

He pulled his dick out of my mouth and rubbed the tip against my lips, covering them in precum and spit.

"On the bed," he commanded, undressing himself.

I crawled onto the mattress, assuming a position on all fours, back arched and vibrating with excitement as he lubed me up.

"This is what you want, right?" He wrapped a hand around my neck, pulling me back and into a deeper arch as he pressed the tip of his dick against my hole. "You want me to fuck you?"

I nodded.

"Say it." Milo smacked his cock against my ass. "Tell me what you want."

"I want you. I want to feel you. I want to—"

In a swift motion, he entered me. I muffled a gasp, and he paused, allowing me to adjust to him inside me.

"Relax." Milo rubbed my back, easing my tensed muscles.

Kissing my nape, I knew the moment had passed as a surge of desire blossomed. He shoved my head forward, burying my face into the pillow as he pounded me out. I whimpered, panting and begging with inaudible grunts of satisfaction. His pleasure heightened, and the slap of his skin against mine made me quake, begging for more. Harder. Faster. Anything he wanted, I would gladly give him.

"Wait." He stopped.

I turned, glimpsing his slacks telekinetically floating into his grip. He rifled through his pockets, retrieving his wallet and pulling out a small plastic square-shaped something. Was he grabbing a condom? We were well past that stage in our relationship.

"Got something I really wanted to try out with you." He ripped it open with his teeth. "Do you trust me?"

"Implicitly."

"Good." He slapped something onto my back.

He rubbed it, pressing his palm between my shoulder blades as my skin tingled from the sensation. It sent a jolt through me, cascading in the strangest way. My telepathy soared. Milo licked the space between my shoulder blades, and with that sensation, the entire world vanished.

Everything disappeared, and I stood inside the confines of my inner mind, taking in the sights of elegant décor, an exquisite banister, and the marble flooring where my legs wobbled.

"Fuck," I howled, unsure how I stood here as Milo continued railing me outside.

He hadn't missed a single stroke, making my knees weak and ready to buckle.

"You okay?" His whispered question came from behind, but his words stirred all around.

I convulsed, biting my lip and holding in a moan as he grabbed my cock. Just as I was about to fall forward, Milo materialized in front of me. In my mind.

"How?" I fell into his embrace, clutching his shoulders in my mind while outside, he continued screwing me from behind. "What's happening?"

"It's an enchantment," he whispered. "I've always wanted to delve into your head the way you do mine."

"While fucking?"

"Practically the perfect time." Milo held me, brushing his hand through my hair but yanking it out there. "It's not as powerful as your magic, obvs. Requires trust, willingness, and a bit of your psychic branch melding with mine. Still, pretty sexy, right?"

"It's kind of awkward." I winced, and Milo's thrusts eased.

"What about this?" He raised his brows, and the chandelier above twinkled and dimmed, then flickered as the ballroom of my inner core grew dark.

"What are you doing?"

"Helping add a few of my favorite memories, hoping you'll indulge and add a few of yours, too."

"Relax," Finn's voice called out.

I spun around, searching for his steady breaths, finding a memory playing out before us a few feet away. My legs wrapped over Finn's shoulders, his lips inches from my own, and Milo pressed to Finn's back, guiding the motion of all our bodies.

"What is this?"

"Thought it'd be nice experiencing moments that brought us together, indulging in a few youthful kinks, while trying out some new ones."

This was something I'd experienced on my own many times before, locked in Milo's memories during sex. But he'd never seen firsthand what it was like watching a memory play out so crisply while in the midst of screwing. I tasted Finn's skin on my lips the same way I did the comforter I'd bit down on outside my mind. I felt the gentle guidance of Milo's hands on Finn's hips as they slapped against my skin.

If Milo had tried something like this a year ago, I would've bolted—gone silent and disappeared off the fucking map for months—but somehow, now, I found myself entranced by the recollection, the vivid overlap of then and now and what could be in the future.

"It's hot, right?" Milo wrapped his arms around me. The tight embrace settled the quiver, but my breathing hitched. "We're in your brain, watching some of our best bang sessions while I'm literally fucking your brains out."

My body warmed, convulsed, and I squeezed Milo's forearms.

"I'm gonna, I'm gonna…" I sighed, shaky and satisfied and flooded with so much serotonin I was surprised my inner core hadn't erupted.

"Easy, Dorian." Milo stroked my hair. "Catch your breath, enjoy the show. I've got a long night planned for you."

I chuckled. "What have I gotten myself into?"

This was more than a single memory of Finn; soon, others blossomed in my inner core, playing all around us. Flashes of sex between the three of us but also first kisses, awkward date nights, declarations of love, quiet gestures of understanding, soft moments of affection, conversations both serious and silly, and so much more. It overwhelmed me in the best way possible. Every single event the three of us had together from mine and Milo's perspective, meaningful or trivial, became seared in my mind.

Floating in Milo's embrace, I held him as memories unfolded all around us, relishing every second we spent reliving these moments together while he literally railed me deeper into the mattress outside my mind.

Chapter Nine

Milo was gone by the time I woke up and staggered into the bathroom to get ready for work. Damn. I couldn't walk straight this morning. Today was going to be a long one between replaying the lust of last night and attempting to figure out a segue from my intended lesson to the bombshell I had to drop on my students. Ugh. How exactly would I connect failure and growth to the upcoming news of the trial? I could simply not tell them. Wait for the news to announce it. Wait for the prosecution team to reach out to them. I gulped. Christ, would they be expected to testify?

I rushed to get dressed and ready, eager for the wind to whip some sense through me on the flight to the academy.

The flight hadn't offered much insight, so I guess I'd just wing it.

"*Love that pun.*"

"*Huh?*" I spun around my classroom. "*Milo?*"

"*You're the one who linked to me.*"

"*Not on purpose.*" I quelled my telepathy. "*Talk later.*"

"*Kisses...*"

I severed the link connecting us before Milo could send a flurry of dirty images my way. My damn branch really just did its own thing some days.

"Good morning, Mr. Frost." Gael was the first to arrive, sharklike teeth beaming even if his usual aura was less luminescent.

Maybe that came from dimming my branch, or maybe it came from his experience yesterday. A few other students trailed in this morning, each carrying thoughts on their combat against an acolyte. Some surface thoughts fixated on how sore they were, others preparing for whatever written follow-up I might require of them, a few proud of the role they played, and one in particular fueled by anger so fiery it almost hid the embarrassment that buzzed at his core.

Kenzo stormed past Katherine, cutting in front of her and into the classroom where he sat in his usual seat, front and center, despite yesterday.

"*Ass.*" Katherine rolled her eyes. "How is he not suspended?"

That was an easy enough answer I wouldn't be providing. Headmaster Dower, in her infinite wisdom, handled the situation amicably. According to the write-up, she'd conferenced with the students and resolved all conflicts. I scoffed. Anything to keep from adding a suspension to the academy's end-of-year report. Those numbers never looked good. Guess that meant I'd have to actually conference with Kenzo and Gael sooner or later.

"Gael told his moms it happened during training," Tara explained to Katherine, curt and aggravated. With Kenzo. With me.

With Gael. Even with King Clucks, who apparently supported the choice of lying to Gael's moms.

"It's not a lie." Gael winced when he grinned. The swollen bruising around his face was hardly covered by the bandage over his nose.

"Ba-ba-bawk!"

Seemed the only thing that came close to embarrassing him during the ordeal was the idea of his overprotective mom barreling into the headmaster's office demanding an explanation. He'd already devised a plan to tell his mother what had happened when his mom wasn't around.

Christ. I was a shitty instructor, allowing him to skirt the truth and hide the incident by pointing out to his parents how they'd signed the waivers to attend Gemini, which naturally came with a few bumps and bruises. Taking a deep breath, I added contacting Gael's moms to my mental to-do list; I would explain the situation and hope they limited the full extent of chewing me out to my planning period.

When the bell rang, I invited everyone into an open conversation, leaning against my desk. "How's everyone doing today?"

"Sore," Jamius said, filling the silence in the classroom.

"The lock has left my muscles tired, too," Tara added.

"Oh no." Jamius stretched, finding his desk unbearably stiff. "It's my magic. I overdid it yesterday, so I'm all tapped out on duplicates."

"And?" Yaritza scrunched her face, visibly confused. "How does no copies make you sore? You don't make them massage you or anything, do you?"

"What? No!" Jamius' cheeks puffed. "I just sort of put off a few things around the house, and without them…it was a long night."

I stifled a chuckle at the flashes of chores swirling in Jamius' mind. Apparently, he'd 'put off' more than a few things, and his parents decided with his branch completely drained, it'd be a valuable lesson on procrastination.

Yaritza and Jamius went back and forth for a bit, leading the conversation from awkward silence to random rambling.

"Question." Gael jumped into the conversation. "If you make a copy of yourself and that copy gives you a handy, is it gay or a really awesome form of masturbation?"

What. The. Fuck.

"Because if I had your branch, I'd make a copy of myself and have him on his knees—"

"Stop!" I glared, waiting for the snickers in the classroom to simmer.

"What?" Gael tilted his head, a mischievous grin on his face. "It's a valid question on magic. Maybe even on the ethics of magic, which—"

"You can save for another class with another teacher," I interjected.

Despite being vulgar as ever, Gael's comment had eased the tension in the air, finally calming the nerves of yesterday, so I steered the discussion back on course.

"I want to talk to all of you about failure. Losing is a difficult lesson to learn," I said, wincing at the especially sharp chord of anger coming from Kenzo.

"*Between pissy pants and the fuck boy, I can't catch a break on hormones.*" Jennifer huffed, glaring at a particularly boastful Gael who wore the bandage over his broken nose like a little badge of bruised honor.

"Some of you may already have an understanding of falling short of an achievement, but since attending Gemini, I've seen all of you demonstrate success after success, from the first semester where each of you persevered in the most frightening of situations." I took a breath, easing the tension, sending pin prickles up the back of my neck, raising the hairs. Whether this was my nerves or the students', broaching the topic of the warlock incursion wasn't going to be an easy one. "Even during the Spring Showcase, you all defied expectations. Each of you rose to the challenge, ranking among the top students, and you all passed the first round."

Pride blossomed around the room, many recalling their role in the tournament.

"And while there was only one winner, none of you failed during that event."

"Not that the top title does any good." Gael snickered.

Kenzo's embarrassment collided with his rage, and a swirl of mixed emotions burst from the thoughts of everyone in the room.

"Enough," I snapped.

Gael grinned. "Just saying…"

"No. You're taunting. You're picking a fight for no reason other than to get a laugh." I paused, letting that sink in. "Is that who you are, Gael? A jokester, sure. But one who pokes fun at someone else's expense? Pouring salt in the wound just to stoke the fire."

Gael got quiet; the entire class stared, silent even in their thoughts, except for Kenzo, who made it clear he didn't need my meddling.

"That metaphor might've gotten away from me." I cleared my throat, waiting for the awkward silence to pass.

"No, it made sense." Gael and his familiar sighed. "You're not incompetent, Kenzo. You're irritatingly good at everything. And you're an asshat, so it was just nice seeing you fuck up for a change."

"None of you fucked up," I said, watching a few eyes widen at my word choice. "The acolytes I picked were specifically pitted against your covens because your magics were vulnerable to them. Your fighting styles weren't suited. Your tactical approach wasn't ready. I wanted you to lose."

"*¿Apoyándonos para que fracasemos? No genial.*" Gael frowned and gave me a thumbs down, which was quite possibly the meanest thing I'd ever expected from him.

That disapproval stung, but I shrugged it off and continued. "Understanding failure, sitting with it, and moving forward is the only way to be successful in this industry."

"*I've got the failure part covered,*" Jamius thought. "*Was really hoping to learn the success part for a change.*"

Ugh. That tugged at me.

"You know I was part of the industry, right?" I asked. A few nodded. "In fact, every teacher at Gemini has been affiliated with one guild or another. They all have their own reasons for leaving, walking away, but do you know why I did?"

Silence met with curious thoughts, but none were bold enough to ask.

"I failed a mission. Not one. Several. I wasn't the best enchanter; I was part of the best team of young enchanters. Even so, I didn't have the constitution for the guild industry. I didn't learn from my mistakes. Eventually, I was put on a mission I was nowhere near ready for and lost someone. Someone very close to me. It wasn't only Fi… A lot of people died that day. I didn't learn from that failure. Instead, I dwelled on it until I couldn't function as a guild witch any longer. I couldn't do much of anything. Not even teach. Still learning that one."

It took everything I had to keep my composure. My skin buzzed, and my telepathy lashed about, searching through the sea of the city for Milo, my eternal life jacket. But I remained here, taking uneasy breaths until I settled the tremble that came from speaking about my greatest failure. I couldn't say Finn's name in front of my students. Perhaps I still carried too much pain for his loss, even if I ignored the grief that'd hollowed me out for more than a decade already.

"I'm not saying this lesson will teach you the big values of what it means to fail with grace and learn to do better, but I am saying the more you resist being imperfect and accepting that you have room to grow and improve, the more this industry is going to eat you alive."

"***Some of us don't need a lesson on failure. We already know it.***" Kenzo turned his head to the window, staring at the brewing storm clouds. "*Some of us also understand the sting of death too, Frost.*"

I ignored the other buzzing minds in the room, focusing on Kenzo's mellow words, something that rarely pierced through his sharp surface thoughts. His mind shied away from surfacing memories of his parents, but their deaths, the loss that ate away at him, the broken friendship with Caleb, and the vow he made to be the strongest enchanter the world has ever known blossomed in thoughts.

Allowing Kenzo to sit with his past, a past he usually kept buried, I continued my discussion with the class. "I do want to let you all know we'll be working closely with these acolytes throughout the semester. Expect many more pro lessons this year."

"So, are we going to have to fight against them every time?" Katherine asked.

"***I won't underestimate Novak next time.***" He clenched his fists, and static popped across the room, so light it hardly registered, but the subtle sizzle sliced thoughts, making minds muffled momentarily.

"*Like getting our asses handed...*"

"*How much failure...*"

"*...a lot...for the...*"

"*¿Qué más...decir?*"

"*...maybe...*"

Impressive. Kenzo had already taken note of Lena's technique of maintaining her branch in constant flux, adapting his disruption for the same method.

"Not exactly. There won't be more sparring. Not until your midterm finals, where I'll be evaluating what you learned from this failure, how you showed growth over the course of the semester, and finally determining your overall grade based on whether your coven can win in a rematch."

Before their curiosity and concern swarmed me, I pushed on because I had bigger news to share. Information they deserved here and now. While I didn't look forward to the bombardment of thoughts or emotional reactions, I had to tell them what Milo had revealed.

"There's one more thing I need to tell you." I cleared my throat.

"Oh, man. Mr. Frosty, you've already dropped one bomb for the day. Let's save whatever evil class lesson you've got up your sleeve for another day."

How I wished to follow Gael's advice.

"I've been informed the warlock incursion on Gemini Academy, on our homeroom, will be moving forward with a trial."

Everyone's eyes widened at the news, thoughts streaming while some actively worked to simmer their internalized questions, waiting for me to continue. "It's not released yet, but I imagine it will be soon. Some of you may be approached."

"*Some of us already have.*" Tara averted her gaze from her classmates. A tidal wave of guilt crashed onto her, sweeping away all the work she'd done to improve herself last year. Of course she'd be approached early on since her brother was the ringleader of so much devastation.

"The academy will have an official stance; your counselor will be there for anyone who needs to talk. But I want you all to know that if you need anything, I am here for you. Here to talk, to listen, to offer support in any way possible. What happened that day was unlike anything you should've experienced in the halls of Gemini Academy. Each of you carried yourselves exceptionally during that ordeal, afterward, and into this new school year. I want to ensure that you continue carrying yourselves this successfully well into your careers, whatever they may be."

Kenzo raised his hand, thoughts stirring so quietly I wondered if the events of the warlock incursion weighed on him more than I realized. On that day, he blamed himself both times I'd nearly died at Theodore Whitlock's hands. He also harbored so much hatred for the man who slaughtered his parents during their time at Phoenix Guild. It was something that rarely surfaced beyond the depths of his rage, but I worried about how he handled those emotions, those regrets.

"Yes." I gestured to him to ask his question.

"Are we gonna actually do something productive in homeroom or just sit here talking about our feelings all class?"

"*Ass.*" Katherine strummed her fingers against the cover of her grimoire.

She wasn't the only one who found the question grating. Some saw the sharpness in Kenzo's tone as taunting, as if he would mock them for dwelling on the events. But in truth, all Kenzo fixated on was what he could control. There was something meticulous about his thought process when it came to coping with things out of his control—he'd prioritize what he could change, compartmentalize what he couldn't, and make himself ready for a future where he could.

His determination was admirable, even if he was an ass.

Chapter Ten

I found myself in the staff lounge, of all places. Something about Peterson and Thompson's inane rabble kept me grounded during my planning period. The silence of my classroom allowed every worried thought that swept across Gemini Academy from my homeroom coven to hit harder. I couldn't handle my own feelings about the situation—how the hell was I going to handle theirs, too?

"Well, well, well. If it isn't Mr. Frost." Chanelle stepped inside, beelining for the copier near the table I sat at. "How're your classes treating you?"

"Horrible."

"For you or them?"

"Yes." I sipped my coffee.

"Wait. Which?"

"Huh?"

"You're the most frustrating person in the world, you know that?" Chanelle looked back over her shoulder, judging the layout on the table for four that I'd claimed all for myself with everything covered in papers. "Why are you even in here?"

"For the refreshing atmospheric change, obviously."

Chanelle rolled her eyes, rushing through prompts on the copier as she printed off stacks of colorful packets. Some cheery questionnaire intended to spark conversation in her classes. Ugh. "*I'm excited about dinner this weekend. I've been trying to land a reservation at Dollop of Desire since it opened. Gotta love knowing an enchanter with connections.*"

I quirked a brow. Why think it instead of saying it?

"Oops." Chanelle's thoughts quickly pivoted away from a text exchange she'd had with Milo about this weekend. "Never mind."

I sighed. Milo. He must've arranged some outing with Chanelle he'd planned to spring on me at the last minute.

"Oh, that." I ground my teeth to fight off a frown. "Can't wait."

"*Liar.*" Chanelle smirked, rushing out of the staff lounge without so much as a witty one-liner.

I sipped my coffee as the lounge emptied out, allowing the tension that brought me in here to fizzle. It seemed I no longer needed the bustle of others to alleviate my wandering mind so I could enjoy what remained of my planning with a bit of peace.

The bell rang. Shit.

"Shit, shit, shit." I scrambled to pack my laptop and papers into my satchel, exiting the lounge and squeezing between the crowd of students that'd flooded the hallway.

I shoulder-bumped a student. Turning to apologize, I froze. Jamie Novak looked up at me, eyes glazed and mind an empty cavern of sorrow.

```
Name: Jamie Novak
Branch: Arcane (Whirlpool)
Ranking: 32
```

His academy uniform hung on him; he'd withered away, barely reminiscent of the teen jock from last school year. His face was flushed, and wispy stubble did little to distract from his pale exhaustion. Messy blond hair helped hide his sunken eyes, filled with deep bags from sleepless nights spent reliving the lifetime of horrors inflicted on him by the chimera.

I grimaced at his vacant expression, the lack of purpose floating in from his thoughts, the way his ranking had plummeted, much like his desire for life. Despite ranking third in the showcase and already sitting among the top ten first-year students, he'd lost a lot of points since he didn't take any of his final exams. Sure, Gemini was *kind* enough to exempt his grades given the extenuating circumstances, but they couldn't be bothered to account for that on his student ranking. That'd be too considerate. The system was inflexible to case-by-case scenarios, and no one with the authority to do anything about it cared enough to change it.

I swallowed hard, consumed by guilt. His. Mine.

"Sorry," he said. "I wasn't paying attention."

"No, it was me."

"No. It was my fault." He stepped around. "*Everything is my fault.*"

Jamie's inner core was a wasteland of empty spaces and black holes, devoid of pathways like they'd broken off and vanished entirely. His dreams had died. His passions had been crushed. His memories were crumpled and destroyed. Even with the chimera exorcised, the toll of carrying a demon inside him, living for months on end as a devil, had broken him.

He'd been on my roster but never showed up the first day, so I assumed he would be dropped from Gemini's attendance soon, figuring the boy would need or want more time to recover. It turned out Jamie didn't want anything, but he needed so much more than Gemini or I could offer him.

Jamie walked by a large group of students circled around Layla and Amani, who eyed his rumpled appearance and snickered. The group took up so much space in the hallway, I couldn't find a path between or around them. I furrowed my brow, understanding why Kenzo often considered flinging those who stood idle aside with a bit of telekinesis.

I squeezed by Amani, who barely noticed as she continued chatting with Layla.

```
Name: Amani Williams
Branch: Psychic (Glamour)
Ranking: 6
```

She stood taller than everyone around her, both in stature and her self-appointed throne. Confidence and belief oozed from her pores. Cascading sunlight hit her face, brightening the undertones of her dark brown complexion, and it seemed she found the spotlight no matter where she was in life, even a seemingly innocuous hallway.

Amani had already proved quite an exemplary student last year, excelling in her academics and magics, but after partnering with Kenzo during the showcase and landing in the finale, her success skyrocketed. As Jamie's rank and reputation spiraled, she became the top student in Chanelle's homeroom coven.

"...dragging our class down any way he can." Amani took one

last look at Jamie, who cut the corner, then ran her fingers through her braided hair that was split into two low-hanging pigtails similar to Layla's style.

"I can't stand him." Layla's face twisted into a snarl. "He's always been a dick. Now he's just a limp dick."

"I don't know," Vik said. "Sort of feel bad for him."

Most of what I knew about Vik came from observations Layla had on her cousin. A lot of Smythes attended Gemini. Now and for many years before. The latest generation hadn't taken their place at the top of the academy, the closest being Layla herself, who prided her ranking and reputation, along with the fact that she was the only Smythe to make it into the Spring Showcase last year.

```
Name: Vik Smythe
Branch: Arcane (Copycat)
Ranking: 158
```

Even though they'd improved their ranking by the end, Vik still hadn't found their footing here at Gemini. They'd been part of Jamie's four-person coven, and due to the yearlong stress that came from teaming with a Novak, Vik struggled to keep up with their magic. It didn't help that their cousin flourished at the academy, finding her place immediately. They were much taller than Layla—much taller than most of the students at the academy, with broad shoulders and a slender build, while Layla remained petite and shorter than the rest. Doubt swelled inside Vik, yet they pushed it down, not wanting to look out of place among their friends.

"Being possessed by a demon must've sucked," Melanie said.

"Yeah." Vik fidgeted. "I just feel bad. I never even noticed. What's that say about me?"

Layla scoffed. “No one knew because he’s an asshole. Don’t let what happened to him and those puppy-dog eyes fool you. How was anyone supposed to tell the difference between Jamie and a demon?”

“I don’t know. I should’ve been tipped off,” Amani said, a twinkle in her deep brown eyes. “He was actually nicer once he got possessed.”

The group laughed, a roaring delight encouraged by the glint in Layla’s eyes landing on everyone. Even Vik joined in quietly.

I walked past them, glaring. Amani and Layla rolled their eyes, unfazed. Melanie clammed up, grinning and sincerely believing I hadn’t heard a thing. In her defense, she considered my frown a constant and unchanging expression.

“*Eavesdrop much, bag of dicks.*” Layla popped her hip, continuing her cutting comments with Amani as the pair entertained their obnoxious audience.

Vik was the only one who expressed guilt from my glare. They stopped laughing, but it didn’t deter the others.

I cut through the crowd of students, returning to my classroom and fighting to keep my mind focused on the lesson I’d prepared. The introduction to my History of Magic was one I’d delivered a hundred times over the years, yet so much pulled at my thoughts. No matter what changed, the one constant in my life seemed to be the guilt I carried for things I couldn’t control.

The upcoming trial.

The horrors caused by the dead devil.

The fractured minds of teens.

As I went over a mini-lesson on what to expect from History of Casting Laws, I hung onto my encounter with Jamie, who sat in the class completely isolated from everyone else. Last year, he'd taken a seat in the front and center. Now, he practically glued himself to the wall in the back corner, where almost no one lingered.

The closest person to Jamie was Tia, who still remained a solid three desks away. I grimaced. Even Chanelle's homeroom students avoided their classmate. Though, based on Tia's surface thoughts, she didn't acknowledge Jamie or carry mean-spirited jabs but instead fixated on her interpreter.

```
Name: Tatiana Owens
Branch: Enchantment (Invocation)
Ranking: 162
```

Similar to Caleb, Tia wrote down everything in class, not wanting to miss a single word of knowledge. Pride filled her chest, painting a purple aura over her light brown skin. This year, the only thing on her mind was proving to Mrs. Whitehurst she'd be one to watch as she trained to improve her ranking.

"*I'm not letting Gemini push me aside this year.*" Tia fiddled with the pendant around her neck. "*I belong here. They're gonna see that. They can't keep me out of the showcase on a technicality this time.*"

Each word sparked a burst of belief, swinging the door of Tia's mind wide open and practically spilling the memories of her inner core out into the classroom.

My vision flitted from the students in the room to the office Chanelle got once she took on the role of academy liaison last spring. Tia sat in a chair opposite her teacher, ignoring her parents and absorbing the words lipped by Mrs. Whitehurst.

"We've fixed the error, but Gemini won't retroactively adjust the points you may've potentially earned the first few weeks."

And there it was, the reason Tia wore a pendant instead of the standard Cast-8-Watch the other students wore. While the academy ordered tech specifically designed for every student's branch magic, they hadn't specified it to Tia's needs. Yes, it registered invocation, but admin didn't account for her disability, for the necessary accommodations. The watch never picked up half of the training time she'd accomplished, only documenting when Tia channeled magic.

According to her watch, she never once practiced her versed invocation. But invocation wasn't a spoken magic. It was a language-based branch. Just as Katherine had to write her spells, Harrison had to concoct spelled recipes, and Tia signed her spells. The watch had designs for recording vocal patterns but not recording her signs. The oversight took weeks for Chanelle to fix, demanding the academy provide a new, appropriate model, but by then—by the time this memory of Tia sitting in Mrs. Whitehurst's office, watching the apologetic words spill from her lips—the Spring Showcase was practically underway.

Tia knew then she wouldn't place. Her ranking sucked. Her chances were impossible. She had to start from scratch because of…

Vibrant purple washed away the memory, forcing me to close my eyes. Tia refused to let it dictate her success this year. That was what she repeated to herself every time the memory surfaced. The problem was, it remained at the peak of her mind, unrelenting.

I was drawn back to how I snapped at Chanelle last year over Tara's waiver rejection, how it affected her chances in the competition, how I didn't even realize the uphill headache Chanelle fought for her own student. And a student with a documented need for accommodations the academy willfully disregarded when making their Cast-8-Watch requisitions.

I pushed Tia's thoughts away, hating when people relived their past so vividly, but understanding why this memory cemented itself to the surface of her mind, why it clung to her every thought, why it made her question her abilities time and time again.

I coughed, buying myself a bit of time for my fumbling words as I quelled my telepathy so I could continue my lesson.

Tia cocked her head, then signed. "*She's seriously gonna bring up my vaping again? Fucking hell.*"

Apparently, Tia's interpreter had taken it upon herself to add a little lesson of her own, signing how my cough stemmed from a nasty habit that'd kill me. Fucking hell was right.

Clearing my throat, I ignored the glances in the classroom and Mrs. Fleck, having finally composed myself.

I briefly highlighted what we'd cover this semester. In order to be successful in the guild industry, it was important for students to not only understand the rules and regulations enchanters had to abide by in today's society but also understand the evolution of the legal system when magic returned to our world more than two hundred years ago.

That last bit clung to Tara's mind, who jotted notes. She wanted less information on the legal system—something that already haunted her given her brother's upcoming trial—and more insight into why magic returned, why it'd been lost, how both events occurred, and what the world was like the first time magic entered it.

"*Had it always been here?*" She tapped her pen in the margins of her notes, creating a dotted smiley face. "*Did people just forget how to cast? Was there an entire generation of duds like me, incapable of mastering their magic?"*

These were questions with answers still highly debated by scholars with far greater understanding of the history of magic than me. Some theorized that too much demonic energy devoured the magic of our world, others believed a spell had dampened it for a period, and a few entertained the idea that divine intervention stripped our world of magic as a punishment. No one had the answer. Not even Finn.

He used to delve deep into the history of the earth, searching for answers to all the forgotten questions of time, but he couldn't glimpse the era where magic ceased. His branch required a connection to magic for his retrocognition to relive the events, and for the centuries without magic, there was nothing for him to latch onto.

I swallowed hard. Finn. It seemed my mind wandered to him every day, sometimes a cherished memory, sometimes a silly word, and sometimes a fleeting fantasy of how I would've changed things if I had another chance. I didn't, though. Finn was dead. And I couldn't dwell on his loss, not during class, not when I had Milo, not after over a decade of grief.

Allowing his beautiful smile to fade from my memory, I telekinetically distributed packets to my students. "I'd like you all to fill out this packet so I can get a sense of what you all remember from last year's class."

Gael grumbled while King Clucks bawked with such authority it startled several students.

"You're more than welcome to work with each other"—I glared at the now grinning Gael—"but I expect this to be completed by the end of the block."

Without hesitation, he yanked Tara's desk toward him with a

telekinetic pull and partnered with his quiet bestie who had all the answers. The only people who scored higher on the history final than Tara last year were Caleb and Kenzo, who each had perfect scores. Something that irritated Kenzo.

Normally, I didn't allow group work during diagnostics, finding blank responses as helpful as those answered. After all, if students didn't know or understand questions, it gave me insight into areas I'd need to revisit this year and how much of last year's curriculum I'd need to include to bridge those gaps of knowledge. But I took notes on my tablet, eavesdropping on surface thoughts where students floundered, relying on someone else in the group to provide the correct answer.

As everyone worked, I found myself wandering toward Jamie, who remained isolated. His desk sat close to the wall, his thoughts dim, and his body crouched over his desk, inviting no one to approach. I'd hoped that, maybe a little, this would offer him an opportunity to work with someone else in the class.

"*He looks just like Teddy.*" Tara's bright blue eyes lingered on Jamie while an image of her bloody brother Theodore ascended to the surface of her ocean of thoughts.

I recalled this memory, one that stabbed at her heart regularly. She was so young, and she'd found him locked in the basement of their home, bound and on the verge of death. Their father planned to strip Theodore of his magic, and Tara helped release him. All she wanted was to go back and undo that choice and prevent the horrors of his release from ever happening, change her role in unleashing him upon the world.

"*Not Teddy.*" Tara turned her desk slightly. "*Me. Jamie looks as lost as me.*"

"Just you two?" I asked, standing close to their desks.

King Clucks flapped his wings, and Gael made a judgy

expression. "Clearly three, Mr. Frosty."

"Well, if you wanted to work with any others," I hinted, not-so-subtly, as my head tilted toward Jamie, "it might help finish this very thorough packet before the end of class."

Gael flipped through the pages, skimming the question numbers. "We got it covered."

His flippant disregard reeled Tara back to her senses. "Yep. Between King Clucks and me, we'll get this answered quickly."

"Hey," Gael whined.

Tara smiled, allowing the sense of empathy that tugged at her heart to pitter-patter away. While she didn't possess a psychic branch, Tara could feel the devastation radiating from Jamie. She'd never felt the horrid touch of a demon in her mind, rooting through her body or carving up her insides, but she knew what it was to be bound on a path set forth by powerful and demanding parents. She knew the pain of everyone's eyes falling on her, believing they had her figured out because of everything they'd read or heard. She knew what it was to carry such sorrow.

All the same, Gael refused to allow Tara to waste a second feeling bad for someone who spent his life being an utter jerk to her. I couldn't fault him for that. The horrors Jamie endured didn't excuse his bullying tactics. They didn't undo the cruel things he said or did for years on end. Still, I felt for the kid. That chimera picked Jamie Novak so it could stalk me. Hunt me. It knew how shallow I could be, ignoring the pain of those who irritated me. Ignoring Jamie's pain because, frankly, I didn't care what happened to the kid last year so long as he left my students the hell alone.

Gael might be a jokester nine out of ten times, but he was a loyal friend, protective, and I needed to respect that Tara's empathy couldn't and wouldn't be the life raft Jamie needed.

I ended up stuck at the academy, enduring the most exhausting staff meeting of my life. Seriously, I might actually die here listening to Peterson ask for clarification on every single bulleted item on the agenda and Thompson ask just one more unnecessary question that didn't relate to the topics at hand.

"I'm going to murder them." I sighed, seeking Chanelle's snarky commentary, yet her mind was lost in administrative duties.

I quirked a brow. No, not administrative, but something field trip-related.

"Dear god, what are you planning?"

"I got the green light from the headmaster, so I'm composing an email to send over to Guild Master Campbell, explaining why Cerberus would benefit from opening their doors to our students."

"Guilds don't do visits."

"They also don't send acolytes to work with students one-on-one, but you managed to pull that one out of your ass." Chanelle grinned. "*Well, you might've done something with your ass to pull that one off.*"

"*Don't be crass.*" I linked our thoughts, sending a hefty psychic pulse her way.

"Dick." Chanelle cracked her neck, then continued rewording her drafted email. "I just think this is a good opportunity for the students."

"Half of them have already walked the halls of guilds." I rolled my eyes. That was the biggest push in the academy pipeline of education—alumni sending their children to continue following the family career path and landing in the guilds through the strongest magic of all: nepotism.

"Sure, but what about the students who haven't? Don't they deserve to land the experience? Or do you really think it benefits them to wait until their third year before ever stepping foot into a guild? Seeing the inner workings? Gaining a sense of the atmosphere? Learning—"

"You made your point." I waved a dismissive hand, not requiring another rhetorical question to cement how correct Chanelle was.

Peering over her shoulder, I skimmed the email. A pretty solid proposal with valid points on how it'd benefit both the guild and the academy. I paused at the date, chest tightening.

October 27th

"Is that really when you're planning the field trip?" I immediately went to work scouring Chanelle's surface thoughts, seeking a hidden fluctuating thought that didn't exist.

"Yeah, seemed good since it's right after the quarter." She shrugged. "Shouldn't interfere with any units."

I might've leaned a bit closer than usual, searching for a reason behind why she picked the date. Nothing. Well, nothing aside from the fact Headmaster Dower approved the date, insisting it not interfere with summative assessments most teachers assigned as a wrap-up to the end of the quarter. "And that's the only reason?"

"Yes, creeper." Chanelle's thoughts immediately shifted from the field trip to concern she had something on her face.

I backed up and slouched in my seat. That date was the day of Theodore Whitlock's trial hearing, the first day he'd leave The

Metropolitan Detainment Center and make his official plea, and from there, everything would whirlwind into a court case that might drag me and my students into the chaotic spotlight. I didn't want to think about it. Given how Chanelle or the headmaster didn't make the connection, I guess no one else wanted to either.

Chapter Eleven

Doppler

After Jasper's royal fuck up, I had little choice but to seize the reins of his mind. A rather easy task once he'd fallen asleep, but not something I could maintain over the course of long periods. However, I wouldn't need to guide his body after today, simply until I crossed paths with the witch who'd help align me with the future I sought to bring to fruition.

Even as the sun set, the summer heat clung to the air, making each inhale of humidity exhausting as I trudged downtown. Whether it came from Jasper's lack of endurance or the resistance his body put up from my suggestive guidance, I found the feel of his sweaty skin disgusting. The more control I exerted, the more I synced to the sensations of his body. Each step was laborious and grueling. Unable to continue, I propped up against the cool glass of an ice cream shop, unconcerned by the annoyance the owners or patrons carried for my fat, sweaty back filling their view.

"What're you doing?" Gael asked, voice shouting down the block.

I tensed, releasing my grasp on Jasper's mind. Did Gael recognize my magical frequency? He wasn't a psychic, but as a witch linked to a beast, he held a practical understanding of the particulars in the branch's fingerprint. How'd he register Dorian's unique casting signature so quickly? What was he doing here?

Jasper's sleepy body slumped over, nearly falling face-first onto the pavement until I snapped to attention, stopping him. Turning my gaze, I searched for the loudmouth obsessed with his dick and joking about cock all day. Peering through Jasper's groggy eyes, where his heavy eyelids fought to stay open at my bequest, my nerves settled.

As I should've expected, that clown wasn't speaking to me. No. I wasn't even on his radar as he chased some girl in a skirt who skipped overhead through levitation.

"Come on," Gael pleaded. "Why do you gotta tease me?"

The girl spun around, her expression ditzy, her pose flirty, but her thoughts calculating. I recalled this one running circles around the simple-minded Gael last year, and Dorian's observations of her had shown she'd improved after the Spring Showcase.

```
Name: Tiffany Sparks
Branch: Bestial (Familiar)
Ranking: 60
```

It wasn't easy peering in on Dorian's thoughts from afar, but he had no reason to suspect my presence, and unlike Milo, he wasn't constantly searching for threats in the darkness of the unknown. It helped to check in from time to time, keeping tabs on the witch with enough magic to destroy a devil yet no will to control such a magnitude of power.

I silently observed Gael and Tiffany, taking deep breaths that didn't assuage the ache of this body's muscles or the annoyance Gael's presence brought. How I wished Jasper were a smoker. But he never cared for the vice, yet I had a phantom craving for the calm a cigarette offered. Another offense brought on by Dorian Frost since he picked up the habit during his teenage years. Prick.

Gael followed close to Tiffany, who hovered a few feet above the pavement in front of the ice cream shop. While Jasper had no skill with his magics or a branch notable of mention, his real talent came from vanishing in a crowd. The man could disappear without a single soul noticing, which made him perfect for my previous needs. As his bland presence went unnoticed by Gael, I caught my wheezing breaths while faced with Dorian's worst student.

"You could always join me." Tiffany extended her hand.

Gael scrunched his face, searching for his familiar who'd stayed behind at their previous destination to finish some card game. A minor fortuitous turn of events since I found that rooster exasperating.

Gael's core tightened, slowly allowing him to ascend off the ground, and I watched with wide eyes. His legs dangled, no trembling or uncertainty. More of a swimmer's grace as he moved through the air, sunlight shining against his bronze skin once he moved from the shadows of the concrete. He floated close to Tiffany, more graceful than her, with a well-trained stance to distribute his weight. So much for lacking skill in his root magic. It seemed the only hesitation he held for levitation came from his foul bird.

Tiffany's expression softened. She waved him over, pulling him with her telekinesis and ready to kiss him while they drifted through the air.

"No." Gael descended. "King Clucks will be here any minute, and if he lost to that damn jackrabbit again, he's already gonna be pissed off enough."

"But you didn't mind chancing your familiar's wrath at the carnival last week." Tiffany crossed her arms, glaring down at Gael. "With Jackie."

"What?" Gael grimaced. "The Ferris wheel broke down. She was the real hero there, making sure we didn't spend all night waiting for repairs. I was a total damsel in her arms."

"Uh-huh. So I heard."

"We went as friends. We are just friends," Gael clarified, using the term 'friend' quite loosely, too, considering what flitted through his surface thoughts on all the things that corresponded between them before and after the carnival. "She's hung up on her ex. You know we're only hanging 'cause it pisses off Layla."

"And what about all the other friends you made over the summer?" Tiffany pouted.

"Don't tell me you're worried?" Gael posed, hands on his hips.

"Not worried, never worried. Just curious how many girls you spent the summer with. How many guys, too." Tiffany widened her eyes, studying Gael's expression shift from a sheepish grimace to a flirty grin where he stuck out his tongue, flashing his piercing. "Heard you played with the lacrosse captain's stick."

"Funny." Gael's bronze cheeks flushed a bit. "I didn't join his team if that's what you're fishing for, but we did go for a few rides. He's got a nice car."

"Uh-huh."

"What can I say? Those Aries Academy guys are quite compelling." He snickered. "Always figured myself more of an automatic guy—turns out driving stick is pretty fun, too. Guess I'm comfy riding in anything, really."

Tiffany rolled her eyes at the car metaphor, and I joined her since Gael's boasting had a nauseating effect.

"Hey," he said loudly, steering the conversation away from his curious exploits. "You didn't see me say anything about all those Aries Academy boys you were going to parties with. You seemed quite popular, Tiff."

The two played a mental game of tug-of-war, each debating how much of their hand to reveal on the amount of stalking they'd done of the other's social accounts, how much they actually enjoyed the other, how much they wanted to take their hanging out to the next level. It was tragic and dull and not remotely useful information. Gael was a ball of smutty thoughts and pining emotions for Tiffany. Tiffany went from being calculating and crafty to starving for Gael's attention. Pathetic.

"Come on, Tiff. You know you're the only girl who makes my c—"

Tiffany descended, slapping a hand over Gael's mouth. "If you make a dick joke, I'll knee you in the nuts."

"Fine." He grinned. "Seriously, though. King Clucks is quite picky, but he loves hanging out with you and Duchess."

"She's become rather fond of King Clucks, too." Tiffany twirled a finger through one of her long blonde locks, flaunting and flirting to draw Gael's gaze, which followed the strand she played with. "She normally despises other familiars."

"See. Our chemistry's synced on a magical level."

Gael offered nothing to a brighter future. He was a jester with half-decent casting, and even that came from his better half. The most frustrating part about this child was how he emulated himself off the worst parts of Milo. Yes, Enchanter Evergreen knew how to cut loose and have a good time, but he wasn't all jokes. He was a professional, something Gael never grasped, and I doubted he ever would.

One of the few commendable things about Dorian was how he tolerated Gael's thoughts. Everything inside this kid's head was dirty jokes, porn, and terrible one-liners that seemed to work more often than not. When I finally took hold of Dorian's body, my body, I'd have to continue the charade of education for a time. Long enough to cement my future with Milo and Finn. But if I had to endure the students in Dorian's class, I'd have to set some of them on a better path. Gael's antics wouldn't be allowed anymore.

Dorian believed himself to be strict, but he wasn't. At his core, he allowed children too much freedom of expression so they'd find their potential. He believed too much in his students and wasted years on their trivial futures.

Gael could keep his silly thoughts for today; he could waste his days flirting with girls and playing his games.

"Ba-ba-bawk!" The rooster flapped his wings, feet clicking on the pavement as he stormed toward us.

"Whoa, King Clucks, look at you!" Gael pointed to the stuffed bag floating behind the rooster. "Looks like you cleaned house."

"Duchess of Damnation must be a good luck charm." Tiffany turned her head, searching for her familiar.

"I'd say. Hey, where is—"

The rooster squinted at me and crowed, a loud, repetitive croak as he clicked his claws on the concrete. Suddenly, a beaver hovered toward me, grumbling and grunting, chewing on a stick. I straightened.

"Chill, King Clucks." Gael smiled at me. "*He's not that creepy.*"

"Sorry about that." Tiffany grabbed her beaver. "Duchess is temperamental sometimes. She's very friendly, though."

The two young witches wondered why their familiars reacted so strongly, each concerned about the limitations of their waivers, and fledgling permits wouldn't excuse an outburst if their pets cast magic on someone. That raised the hairs on my arms. Those beasts sensed something foul in my scent, in Jasper's scent. I needn't linger and draw awareness to a man I'd soon abandon to his simple life.

"Uh-huh." I slouched, growing exhausted from these two and wanting to escape the walking cesspool of Jasper's body.

I continued making my way to my destination, ignoring Gael complimenting the prize purse his rooster had won.

Trailing along the next few blocks, I arrived at the busiest street in downtown Chicago and stood outside Gwendolyn's Guns & Gals. This place would definitely land me on Milo's radar if the mere contemplation of seeking out Cassidy Gardner hadn't already.

Not that my brilliant clairvoyant would know what to do with images of Jasper's future mulling around in his mind. Or would he see me? See Dorian? That idea might perplex him more. All in all, there was no evading Milo's magics forever.

Even knowing all I did about his visions, how they worked, the systems by which he organized and prioritized futures, I couldn't account for everything that went through his mind. He played the flirt, the goofball, the smiling friend to everyone he met, but above all else, Enchanter Evergreen was a brilliant tactician. So, instead of skirting his visions, where I'd lack insight into the predictions he plotted, I decided to lean into things, controlling the narrative.

Cassidy remained the most well-connected criminal in a sea of filth that lined the shadows of Chicago. Why Milo bothered contemplating her future stumped me more so than it did Dorian himself. Supposed we had that much in common.

Still, she had the connections I sought, the illegal enchantments I required, and the perfect host body for the next phase in my plan.

Chapter Twelve

My students proved more resilient than expected. No. That wasn't true. They'd always shown strength when faced with information meant to derail their hopes. As the week passed, news about the warlock incursion was announced. The city flooded with intel; damn near every citizen had an opinion, and Gemini had an official stance—something encouraging for those brave individuals involved and the perseverance we as an academy would exhibit moving forward.

While I found the whole thing unsavory, I didn't despise Headmaster Dower's approach as much as anticipated. She'd spoken with me before sending out an email to every student, staff member, and family connected to Gemini Academy. She'd talked to my class before going on the morning announcements. It was peculiar feeling her genuine concern, her honest acknowledgment of the situation. Dower had never been my favorite, but all things considered, I didn't hate how she handled this awful hand we'd been dealt.

I still didn't know how any of this would turn out, how involved my students would be, how involved I would be. As I got dressed for the evening, I put it out of my mind, along with Milo's very judgmental thoughts. It was nice to ignore the things I couldn't control while playfully mocking the things I could.

"*Why don't you wear that suit I got you?*"

Changing into a long-sleeved casual black shirt, I hummed, pretending I hadn't heard his thoughts. He wasn't the only one who could use a melody to dodge telepathy. It might've been petty, but I didn't want to go to a fancy dinner. I didn't want to go on a double date. I didn't want to spend my Friday evening in a highly publicized location on the arm of the delightful Enchanter Evergreen.

"This place is a little fancier than ripped jeans." Milo pursed his lips, fighting off a frown with a twitch in his nose like he was allergic to my bad wardrobe.

"How am I supposed to know? You said we were just getting a bite."

Milo squinted, taking a long silent pause even in his thoughts. "I know you know."

"Know what?"

"About Dollop of Desire." Milo snatched the ripped jeans from my hands and grabbed a pair of dress slacks. "Sorry. I wanted to surprise you with a nice night out."

"Admitting your faults is the first step." I chuckled, changing into the something Milo had approved. "Chanelle tell you she spilled the beans?"

"It was half and half you'd find out from her or the students who work there." Milo rocked his head from side to side.

"Enchanter Evergreen making a reservation at a trendy restaurant tends to get attention."

"Should I be expecting a photo op?" Since going public, I'd landed in more than my fair share of pictures alongside Milo between guild events, Cerberus celebrations, and his inauguration into the Global Rankings.

I sighed. It was part of the territory that came with loving Milo. As much as I loathed sharing him with the world and hated seeing my image displayed publicly to be scrutinized, I couldn't imagine going back to a life where I boxed my heart away, beating just enough to survive the day. I loved how it beat with Milo in my life, the excitement, the happiness, the contentment, even the annoying events.

"No photos." Milo slid his hands under my shirt. "Part of the appeal to such an elegant evening."

"I suppose this is a nice way to kick off dinner."

"Oh?" Milo smirked, pulling the shirt over my head. "I'm just trying to get you out of this and into something nicer."

I stood in front of him with the shirt fabric tugged against my upper back, sleeves draped over my arms, while my chest and stomach were exposed. Standing in my saggy slacks that I hadn't buttoned yet, I pressed my hands on Milo's shoulders, sending some suggestive imagery between our linked minds.

"We're gonna be late."

"And?" I grazed my teeth against his neck, gently nipping. "It's been a long week."

"Mmmm." His mind synced to mine; the tender bite of my teeth registered like the sensation struck my skin. "Suppose we have a little time before heading out. And you do look awfully tense."

"I'm not that tense," I said, knowing he was referring to the news he'd shared about the trial, but nothing had come of it. Not yet. And if something did, I'd be ready. Ready for myself and for my students.

Pushing me off, Milo kissed me, soft and sensual. Each smack of our lips came with whispered thoughts and tantalizing desires. Who needed a restaurant that specialized in desire when my boyfriend knew exactly which thoughts elicited the most eager arousal? My skin tingled, warm and enticed.

Leading with his tongue, Milo kept my mind and mouth so distracted I hadn't even felt the subtle shift in my body. The carpet tickled the heels of my feet as Milo lifted me off the floor just enough to telekinetically position me against the wall. I shuddered from the cool surface against my back and bare ass, pants and boxers around my ankles. When had he slipped them off? Maybe the quake came from anticipation.

Milo dropped to his knees, kissing my lower abdomen. His warm hands rubbed my thighs. It definitely came from anticipation. Licking my shaft, Milo teased me. I ran my fingers through his hair, unable to form words, thoughts, a link—only a carnal urge. Without a single word between us, Milo sucked my cock.

I gripped a handful of his blond hair, thrusting my hips in a steady motion with my hand and shoving him further down inch by hardening inch. I lost track of time, lost track of everything except the pleasure his tight throat brought. Every time we were together, it unlocked new sensations, new radiant emotions as fresh as the very first time, continuing to explore every facet of the other.

Milo grabbed my ass, heightening my pace, and looking up at me as he choked. His glossy blue eyes were stunning. Intoxicating.

I continued. Faster. More assertive. Each pump into his warm throat made me throb. Thinking purely on instinct, on what I wanted in the moment, on what Milo wanted, I levitated just a bit, just enough to alter my position. Wrapping both of my hands around Milo's head, I tilted him back further, hovering above as I buried my cock all the way down his throat, which constricted and only further enticed me.

My breathing tightened, and I slowed down. "*You okay?*"

There was a good chance this struggle to breathe came from the link of my telepathy, and Milo might very well be gagging a little too much for his liking.

Ignoring my question, Milo grabbed my legs and pulled them over his shoulders. With a hand at the small of my back, I obeyed his prompting and squeezed my legs. Here I was, floating in the air, straddling my boyfriend and face fucking him.

The more I continued, the tighter my muscles tensed, everything on the precipice of buckling. My toes curled, levitation waning. My body warmed, and I erupted.

I panted, body twitching, hips bucking with a spasmed pleasure as I came down Milo's throat. He gurgled and gulped. Running my fingers through his damp hair, I held my soft cock in his mouth, taking slow, satisfied breaths before collecting myself and standing on my own two feet.

"Did you seriously just give me a blowjob so I wouldn't complain about this evening?" A fantastic blowjob at that.

"Damn straight." Milo slapped my butt. "Now, get your ass in that suit."

I was buzzing the entire drive to the restaurant, practically floating by the time we arrived at Dollop of Desire. Milo might not have

been a mind reader, but he knew exactly what to do when getting me off. It was so much more than the sheer satisfaction of his mouth around my cock. Residual primal energy radiated between us, washing over me so much so that I barely absorbed the elegant entryway or path leading us to a table large enough to seat ten.

"Told you we didn't need to rush," I said. "Could've made sure you had a little fun before rushing here."

Milo tilted his head closer as we walked, his sweat and cologne wafting together and sending my senses right back to the bedroom. "I had plenty of fun, trust me."

We took our seats in the boxed-off quarters, much like all the tables in Dollop of Desire, where guests had a private experience when indulging in a taste of passion unlike anything Chicago had to offer.

I gagged on the rehearsed motto circulating through the minds of every employee, forced to maintain an enthusiastic demeanor inside and out.

"I swear, Chanelle's worse than that acolyte of yours when it comes to punctuality."

"It was one lesson. Hayden's usually better about that stuff."

"Not according to your other two acolytes."

Milo grinned, boyish and cute and irritatingly aloof. "Well, some of the best futures work on a later schedule."

Our server stepped into our room, speech prepared and already brimming with nods about his magic in case the enchanters dining were looking for an intern next year.

"Mr. Frost." Harrison clammed up; every thought he had trickled away as he scrambled to point out the history of the dining experience.

```
Name: Harrison Heywood
Branch: Enchantment (Potion Craft)
Ranking: 25
```

One of Chanelle's homeroom students, a small, wiry kid with a fantastic magic similar to Katherine's spell craft but a keen interest in explosive potions much like Yaritza's star shower. He fared well when teamed up with Kenzo during the Spring Showcase. Although, much like most of Chanelle's homeroom, he got knocked out of the finale in a blink by Kenzo, too.

"*I was hoping it'd be a business dinner. Usually, when they drop the enchanter title, it's work-related.*" Harrison's cheeks trembled, forcing his smile. "*I don't wanna wait on Mr. Frost. He's probably gonna make me take his meal back and redo it a hundred times over.*"

Oh, fuck off. As if I'd ever. Harrison's thoughts cycled through every assignment I'd made him redo. I scowled. Maybe he wouldn't have to go back over his work so much if he didn't rush through tests, half-assing his explanations all the time.

Annoyed, I tuned him out while he explained the craftsmanship behind our table. The metallic surface was similar to the Teppanyaki grills at a Japanese restaurant where they cooked their meals with a side of entertainment. But Dollop of Desire didn't cook in front of their guests. I quelled my telepathy, pushing away the enchanted experience coming from every nearby patron. Sigils were etched onto the table, capable of absorbing the effects of any meal heightened beyond what one's pallet could handle.

Before Harrison could continue, the host brought the rest of our party. I forced a smile on Milo's behalf, bracing myself for a fucking double date. Milo and Chanelle were exhausting enough on their own.

"Mrs. Whitehurst?" Harrison straightened up, a squeak in his voice. "*Seriously? I can't catch a break tonight.*"

You and me both, kid.

Chanelle sauntered to our table, wearing a strapless red dress that accentuated her deep brown complexion. She'd already taken out the braids she'd had the first week back to school, sporting a short, spiky pixie cut that highlighted her high cheekbones and helped frame her face, along with the gold earrings among other jewels she'd adorned this evening.

Her husband trailed behind. If she had a train to her shortly cut dress, he'd be carrying it on her behalf. Truly. In his mind, she was a queen, a goddess of beauty and love and lust and charm, all things that captivated him every day. It was fascinating—and nauseating—seeing the passion burn so brightly between them even after ten years of marriage. Not so much as a subtle sign of boredom or loss from either of their surface thoughts.

"This is Kyle." Chanelle beamed, introducing her husband to Milo.

"Nice to meet you." Milo shook his hand, and Kyle let out a low grunt in response. "You ever been here before?"

Kyle tilted his head and shrugged.

"A few times for work," Chanelle answered, patting her husband's chest. "I've never been so lucky, though."

I'd met Kyle a handful of times over the years at staff outings Chanelle had dragged me to, where Kyle had gladly attended despite having a limited understanding of the teacher lingo. Well, teacher bitch sessions. Looking back, I couldn't recall once where he'd actually spoken. Sure, I'd heard his thoughts often; even now, he was reciting some statistics to some game or event or work—between the numbers and my tired telepathy, I couldn't be certain. Still, he was a quiet, lanky man, towering over his wife and silently observing us all.

Harrison took orders for our drinks and left us to mull over the menu for a bit.

"It's always so awkward seeing my students out in the wild," Chanelle whispered to Kyle.

He nodded.

"More so for him." I sipped my water. "Pretty sure 'cringy' crossed his mind about a hundred times in the minute since you've arrived."

"Liar."

Not a lie. She'd hinted about the Heywood restaurant on more than one occasion, and Harrison had dodged every single not-so-subtle inquiry about the waitlist.

"Milo, dear, thank you again for setting up that meeting with Guild Master Campbell."

"Anytime." Milo smirked. "The more meetings she's in, the less time she has to hound me about paperwork."

Unlike his previous guild master, Campbell didn't like Enchanter Evergreen shirking his duties onto acolytes, despite his many protests that it'd help prepare them for life as an enchanter. He was just too lazy to sign all those documents.

"What are you meeting with Campbell about?" I asked.

"Arranging for more acolytes coming to Gemini. Though, I'm not gonna teach my kiddos how to fail with grace during the first lesson."

"You can save that lesson for when they land subpar internships their third year."

"Oooo, someone's feeling feisty tonight." Chanelle grinned, perusing the menu. "Can't wait to see what a few cocktails brings out."

I gleaned Milo's mind while everyone read over the dishes. Turns out, Milo had pitched the idea I suggested to Campbell, who immediately leapt at the PR opportunity. That and the tax exemptions Cerberus would get by providing free labor to an educational institute. A double win since acolytes were paid in experience and professional recommendations, not cash.

"*So, you took my idea?*" I linked to Milo's mind.

"*Did you want credit?*" He squinted at the menu, avoiding reaching for his readers. "*I'll gladly let Campbell know right now.*"

"*Absolutely not.*" I scoffed. "*Guessing you didn't see an outcome with me being pleased about my involvement being revealed?*"

"*Don't need to be clairvoyant to know you'd be unhappy with all those eyes.*"

He was right. I definitely wanted the academy and guilds who worked with us to implement more of my suggestions, but the idea of actually sitting through curriculum meetings and stroking egos while filling out a detailed analysis on all the reasons it'd benefit our program made me want to hurl. Milo could gladly take the credit. Plus, when the state inevitably altered an already perfectly functional model and made its tweaks, I could blame Milo instead of myself.

Milo scrunched his brow. "*Why do you look so happy? There's a twinkle in your eyes.*"

"Divine Diet." I pointed to the menu. "Sounds delicious."

"Uh-huh."

After we all ordered, Kyle and I took the socializing back seat while Chanelle and Milo bantered about… I honestly stopped paying attention. Something funny. They both cackled enough, that was for sure.

Harrison came back with a round of appetizers. Given his parents provided the best enchanted food in the city, I sort of expected the dish to look more appetizing. It was gray and mushy, sitting inside a seashell.

"Don't make that face, Dorian." Chanelle grabbed a shell and slurped up the goop in a big gulp. "It's a taste of deep-sea diving with just a hint of a lazy beach day."

"So, they're like oysters?"

Kyle nodded, then slurped up his own right about the same time as Milo.

I followed suit, then quickly wiped my mouth with a napkin and spit out the sludge along with the sensation of sand between my toes, sun on my face, and wind blowing through my hair. Guess my slug shell had an extra serving of lazy beach day.

This was going to be a long meal. I didn't even want to come here. Why the hell would I want to experience another outing on top of this?

"Here, try my drink." Milo eyed the crumpled napkin on my lap.

"I'm good."

"Trust me," he pleaded. "You'll love it."

I wouldn't. Nothing about these magical meals was to my liking, but I took a sip anyway.

Euphoria washed away all the stress like I'd stepped through my front door, dropped my satchel, and escaped into my house after a grueling day.

"It's called A Quiet Night In," Milo said. "Thought you might enjoy it."

"It's pretty nice," I said. "But I could enjoy an actual quiet night without spending fifteen bucks to drink the experience."

"As if Charlie or Carlie would ever offer you a quiet night."

"Touché."

It turned into a pretty fun evening, with me sipping A Quiet Night In while Kyle lost himself in some skydiving salsa, mountain climbing poppers, and anything else on the menu that sent his adrenaline surging along with his acid reflux. Chanelle and Milo favored bites that allowed them to experience events neither had time for with work. Concerts long since passed, tourist attractions at the peak of the season, championship games flooded with cheering audiences, and so much more, it made me queasy every time I considered taking a bite.

I brushed my fingertips against the etched sigils to mellow out the experiences my food sought to offer, content simply indulging in Milo's happiness.

"*What the hell is going on with Cassidy?*" Milo turned his head. His eyes fluttered, lashes flitting as his thoughts vanished, tangled between shifting futures. "*Why's her future so grim?*"

I twisted my lips, trying my best not to frown, while Milo joked with Chanelle about some random nonsense. But I found it frustrating how Milo was scouring his mind, searching through visions tucked away behind the deepest workings of his inner core, during our double date. And for Cassidy, of all people. She peddled dangerous products illegally, compromising citizens to make a profit. Whatever dangers lurked in her future were of her own making. Honestly, Milo needed to stop helping people who caused their own problems. It'd allow him a few moments of peace.

"*Something's stalking her…but not? It's like they're right on the cusp of her potential pathways, hiding or…*" Milo bellowed, loud and obnoxious, giving Chanelle's joke far too much credit, so much so even she quirked an eyebrow, questioning. "Sorry. It's just that it reminds me of the time…"

There he went, saving face and remaining fully engaged in the conversation while his thoughts weaved behind future events that even my telepathy couldn't sense. How he did it was beyond me.

"Okay, you gotta try the Singing Tayters." Milo handed me a plate of crispy tater tots, each with a grilled imprint of one of his favorite songbird entertainers.

"You all right?"

"Always." Milo smiled, big and goofy and unwilling to spoil our night out.

He'd share later—or not, if the future's best interest dictated he keep things to himself. I was okay with that. Milo's eyes bounced between me and the plate, smile growing increasingly irritating.

I frowned, fighting a smile because, for once, despite everything, I wasn't obsessing over the worst. Milo's mind often drifted toward terrible fates, exhausting cases, and potentially dangerous futures, and yet that need to search for more answers, that side of me, faded. The part always gnawing to chase and solve and fix what I couldn't control. That piece had slowly fizzled away, so subtle, so slowly, I didn't recognize its absence until now.

Mostly, I wanted to make sure Milo had fun tonight, pushing every other thought away with ease in a way I'd never been able to do before. Maybe this was what unconditional love felt like. Maybe this was what emotional growth meant. And maybe none of it mattered because life had finally gravitated toward simple joys.

Reluctantly, I grabbed a Singing Tayter and popped the fried potato in my mouth, savoring the salty crunch before a concert enveloped my mind.

Chapter Thirteen

Doppler

My newest host prepared for work while I skimmed memories of Enchanter Evergreen's latest exploits. It didn't take much, whispering my will into the mind of this witch. Witch. More like a warlock given the criminal activity, yet the term warlock was only ever applied to witches who were convicted of their wrongdoing. Ignoring the semantics of law and the actions of this deviant, I prioritized learning what Milo was doing, which cases he'd solved, and where his fate fell. Strangling the subconscious of my current host and changing desires subliminally allowed me to control this witch from afar without actually having to exert command.

Deep in the depths of this mind, the hairs on my neck rose. A fabricated sensation, sure, but one that grounded my nerves into something tangible. Did Milo sense my movements? Did he feel the acute shifts of my frequency, the familiarity of synchronization I offered? I smiled, studying Milo while evading his ever-present clairvoyance. Not entirely, that much I could be certain of.

Dragging Jasper throughout the city by the reins to Cassidy's club had already left me drained. Moving Finn without suspicion took a degree of delicate maneuvering even my best infiltration skills struggled with. Most of all, that goddamn chimera put up more resistance than anticipated. Loud clanks came from the deep pits of darkness in this new witch's inner core. So much for willingly accompanying me during the transfer.

I chuckled, skimming posts about Milo locked here in the subconscious memories. In fairness, the demon probably didn't appreciate his new housing accommodations, and I savored the joy it brought me, knowing nothing the chimera whispered or attempted would faze the current mind we stayed inside. There were already so many twisted fantasies dwelling in this witch, sinister and sadistic, that the chimera's haunting words wouldn't rattle him like they had Jasper.

Carl Kevins @MagicWandInMyPants
Okay, but can I get sandwiched between these boys?!?! 🥵 I got serious warlock problems, I swear! 🔥🔥🔥 Send in the pros. STAT!

A reposted selfie of a shirtless Milo and Hayden standing beside members of the Chicago Fire Department after wrapping up a case against some fire-casting warlock that'd scorched their dress shirts. I smirked. Milo wouldn't have struggled against this low-ranked wannabe criminal, but he knew how to set up thirst traps for his audience while also promoting a young acolyte. Seemed the public clambered for more on the mini-Milo, Hayden. I didn't like that. It presented potentials I couldn't predict.

Sarah Sunders @EvergreensGirl
My baby looking real cute. Can't wait to see what's next for #TheInevitableFuture! 😘 @CerberusGuild must be loving this.

She'd tagged @GlobalGuildCompany in the picture of Enchanter Evergreen meeting with representatives from the Global Ranking. These types of posts helped steer my next steps.

As the top-ranked enchanter in the city, the state, it was easy following news on Milo. There were entire Instagram pages set up for Enchanter Evergreen sightings. There were dozens of Twitter fan pages posting The Inevitable Future's solved cases. News alerts, articles, videos, and so much more funneled online every day.

A layman would see the glorious work of a dedicated enchanter; I saw the paths of futures Milo followed. While I no longer had access to the newest visions passing through his mind each day, I did study the tens of thousands I had glimpsed nearly a year ago when all Dorian observed was a single void vision. Knowing which cases Milo took on, which events he handled, delegated, or ignored—all of it helped me dodge him until my final arrangements had been made.

"Hey!" the chimera shouted, followed by a loud bang. "Puppet! Puppet, can you hear me?"

I waved a hand, sending the images studied by the host back into the subconscious. "What?"

"You can hear me." He strummed his fingers, a rhythmic pattern against the metallic box I'd encased him in.

Floating through the darkness, I approached the only sliver of light reflecting off the silver box I'd conjured.

"It's such a tight squeeze in here." Even tucked inside a box half the length of a casket, I could feel the smile on his face. His jovial tone, the light snicker between his words, and the damn strumming of some melody. "You've put me in a box with so many locks. It's like you don't trust me. Why even ask me to behave? I told you I have no intention of compromising your little plan, puppet. I'm thrilled by the initiative you're taking. It's bold and brazen. Foolish and foolhardy, too."

I ground my teeth, almost tempted to hurl him into the deepest depths of this mind, but if I couldn't hear him, track him, he'd win. With even a second of privacy, that demon could dole out too much trouble. Let him mock me from his prison; that box will be his coffin soon enough.

"How ever will you join me in here? Don't you want to torture me? Find ways to break my link to your beloved? Sorry. Dorian's beloved."

"Is this what you intend on doing? Pestering me with pointless barbs." I folded my arms. "I expected better from a former devil."

"Patience, puppet. It's all about patience." He hummed. "Something you clearly lack. When you strolled into Cassidy Gardner's place, I expected you to grab her. Lock us inside the mind of the witch running Chicago's undercity. But you didn't. Why?"

"Because I have no use for her."

"Or were you worried her magic would sniff you out?" The glee in his voice was grating. "Afraid a real witch might be able to fend you off? Is that why you avoided her lieutenants as well?

"Shut up."

"I just want to know why you went someplace where you could've grabbed a witch with enough magic to end Dorian Frost, yet you left housing us inside the body of some second-rate patron who actually goes to the most notorious arms dealers in the city to see the dancing witches."

There it was. The chimera didn't understand my intentions, couldn't glean it from my guarded thoughts, and more than anything, he wanted to protect his perfect host body—Dorian Frost. He didn't understand how a simple witch with no real power in his magics or his connections held such a vital role in my plans.

Besides, I didn't need a proper host to end Dorian. I could do that on my own. What I required was a warlock with the magic to unravel the chimera from Finn.

"Pay attention, demon. If you listen closely, you might catch on."

Ronald Kowalski drove through the first checkpoint into the parking lot of his job, already sick and tired of what awaited him. He hadn't even clocked in, and he was ready to go home. Couldn't blame the guy. The Metropolitan Detainment Center housed some of the deadliest witches and warlocks in Chicago accused of criminal activity. Heavy emphasis on accused.

While each of them awaited their day in court, they sat inside a heavily enchanted facility filled with thousands of sigils meant to ward off intrusion, prevent casting from those wearing dampeners, and allow for the best detection of any magics at play.

I quelled my branch, holding my breath and hoping the release of my telepathy didn't rouse Finn's awareness or allow the chimera an opportunity to break loose from his confinement.

Ronald crossed through the second checkpoint, scanned his badge, and walked through the long white corridor. Not a single sigil glowed. It seemed my presence remained hidden.

As Ronald continued going through various layers of detection and crossing through each new entry point, I smiled, having chosen the perfect host to tuck away my consciousness. Ronald had a way of evading the alerts, allowing my magic to bypass the systems. Unbeknownst to him, of course. After all, Ronald didn't only attend Gwendolyn's Gals & Guns for the girls; he found a way to supplement his income by occasionally delivering packages to those inside the MDC. His deliveries consisted of gifts for magic or luxuries conjured by magic and easily concealed by those inside their tiny cells. A lucrative business for Ronald. Not that he made much profit since he ran up a tab every night, showing the lovely ladies what a big spender he was. I doubted anyone was impressed, but Ronald believed this gig would take him to better places.

It would. It'd take him on a necessary path that'd offer me the best future I deserved. When I joined Milo, reunited us with Finn, and lived my best life, perhaps as a thank you to Ronald Kowalski, I'd steer his fate off The Inevitable Future's radar. He was but a blip, nonessential, and unlikely to cause much harm anyway.

In order to break Dorian's mind and take possession of the body that was rightfully mine, I needed the one man who came the closest to killing Dorian, not once but twice. Inside the MDC, Theodore Whitlock awaited his day in court. With his magic, I would soon have everything I deserved, and Finn would be released from the shackles of the chimera.

I twisted my thoughts toward Ronald's desires, piquing his interest in seeking out Theodore, patrolling his cellblock.

"Puppet," the damn chimera called from the depths of the

subconscious, locked in his box but resisting the restraints I'd placed. "Were you thinking of me? My ears were ringing."

Liar. Guarding my thoughts, I remained more vigilant, not to let the chimera glimpse my intentions. He didn't know Theodore Whitlock like I did. He didn't know how that warlock would snuff him out instantaneously. I merely needed to time my strike.

Drifting toward the shadows of this mind, I pulsed magic against the metallic box, shrinking its size, tightening its constraints, and doing all I could to leash this demon's connection to magic. My eyes were heavy and tired. So tired of balancing everything so meticulously.

"Hey, Kowalski," a scratchy hiss of a voice drew Ronald's attention, snapping free of the suggestion I'd whispered.

Dammit.

Already aggravated by another early shift that'd last twelve hours, Ronald eyed the twitchy, bug-eyed warlock, who he knew would only further piss him off. Something about this scrawny man seemed familiar. I scrunched my face, looking deeper through Kowalski's blurred vision. Too much late-night drinking, among other vices, left the guard's sight sensitive to the bright lights. It didn't help that my energy waned, and I couldn't filter the shiny haze clouding Ronald's sight.

"What do ya want, Pete?"

Pete hunched, folded his arms over his chest, and averted eye contact while distancing himself from inmates traipsing by. Not enough. Ronald knew they'd been hassling Pete, pushing the boundaries to see how far they could test him since his return to the MDC. Despite the booze drowning most of Ronald's memories, the details he had on Peter Graham rose to the surface, and I was finally able to recall where I knew this scrawny inmate.

Christ, without his branch, this warlock was nothing. And he was a warlock. He might be in the MDC awaiting trial for now, but he'd been through the Chicago prison pipeline long ago. A powerful, deranged warlock who razed West Chicago during his heyday with his deadly branch that spread through the air like a toxic plague and fed off any magic nearby until, of course, Enchanter Evergreen put a stop to him well over a decade ago.

Name: Peter Graham
Branch:Entropy (Cellular Absorption)

That was a name I hadn't seen in a long time, one Dorian barely held in his own memories—just some random warlock who made the news before disappearing from the public eye. But I took caution to memorize every threat Enchanter Evergreen dispatched, every warlock he encountered, every life he brightened because, unlike Dorian, I cared about Milo beyond measure. Hell, I even cared more for his grating students, understanding the intricate facets of their being better than my lesser half.

Dorian professed to care about his students, doing everything to better them, but he knew so little about their lives. Except for the ones he favored because Dorian was transparent and petulant. I knew Peter Graham as the warlock who nearly slaughtered half of the enchanters of Basilisk Guild. The same guild that the Martinez family ran. Gael's family.

Dorian never made the connection. Why would he? He didn't watch Milo closely a decade ago, too lost in his grief to function. But I watched Milo, studied him and the lives he gently guided. In my observations, I always wondered what he saw in the futures he nudged. Did he layer every life he bettered in such a way intentionally, or was it serendipity that led to fates he saved crossing paths at later dates?

If Peter was in the MDC, that could only mean he'd served his sentence and yet again found his way back inside the lovely institution of corrections. It was a shame since magic like his could've likely flourished in the guild industry. Then again, he didn't have the temperament to handle the disgust most people held for the entropy branch, vilifying it for its poisonous, venomous nature. I didn't care for the man or pity his blight behind bars. Neither did Ronald, who made it abundantly clear the warlock had nothing to offer him, so in turn, he wouldn't offer any of the goods he procured for inmates.

"You got a few weeks left in here, Pete," Ronald said firmly, intent on squashing the subject before Peter continued pestering him. "Keep your head down and try not to fuck up your parole next time. Doubt they'll send you back here if you screw up again."

"It'd just be more bearable if—"

Ronald shoved Peter back, reminding him of his place. I half expected Peter to lash out, say something threatening, but there was no fury in his thoughts, no vengeance, merely survival. Truly fascinating to see a warlock so profoundly powerful humbled by the silver trinket bound to his right wrist. Something so delicate, engraved with the same symbols lining the walls of this jail, and yet the dampener cuffs synced specifically to each inmate's casting and frequency.

Ronald continued his shift, making his rounds, peddling his products, blowing his own fucking ego on loop. It was nauseating, but I used the time to study this institute, recover my strength, and read up on Milo's cases so I could navigate my way around his clairvoyance. Still, with all the changes I'd made, the ripple effects,

I couldn't be certain any singular breath wouldn't have a butterfly effect on Milo's magic, shifting the winds of futures.

Walking up to a cell, Ronald slammed his baton against the bars. Inside sat two men, one face down with his head on a pillow while the other hunched over him, jabbing him in the back with a melted pen he kept heating with an enchanted matchstick.

"This isn't fucking art class," Ronald snapped. "What'd I tell you about this, Cromwell?"

"More discretion and always have your cut ready," Vincent said.

I chuckled. Seemed his time behind bars hadn't left the warlock easily humbled. However, I doubted anyone would find the muscular, heavily tattooed man who tried to murder a bunch of students nearly as intimidating if they realized he'd been taken down by some branchless kid who was practically destined to die that day.

```
Name: Vincent Cromwell
Branch: Enchantment (Brand)
```

Still, quite impressive that he'd flourished so well in holding. Ronald had a business arrangement with Vincent, who'd become everyone's favorite tattoo artist. His brands might've lacked magic behind bars, but a lot of inmates liked his tattooing talents. Too bad they didn't realize the hidden brands he tucked inside the ink of their exquisite pieces. Crafty. Too crafty for someone as dimwitted and greedy as Ronald to realize. He got so many different ingredients, yet never bothered checking what the right alchemic combination created.

It seemed Theodore already had machinations of his own, keeping his fellow warlock friends well-placed in the MDC. That simply wouldn't do. Carefully, I surveyed Vincent's limited knowledge about the worst Whitlock and his agenda, all while ensuring the chimera didn't suspect my intentions or investigations.

"Take this shit somewhere else," Ronald said, standing at the open doorway of the cell.

"We're almost done, boss." Vincent kept working with a smile almost as cheerful as the woman he etched onto the back of his most recent client.

"He's not threatened by you," I whispered, having no patience to follow his long rounds any further and wishing to find the warlock that drew me to the MDC.

Ronald fumed. Damn. It did not take much to light the short fuse on this guy. He was half a second away from unloading pent-up rage onto Vincent and the other inmate before I steered his anger.

"You think that's gonna work?" I dug my voice deep into his thoughts, hacking away at the insecurities that fueled his fury. "You wanna send a message? You need to send a message. You don't deal with punk ass grunts."

Ronald clenched his jaw, grinding his teeth so much it almost dulled the constant pain in his molars. Almost. And that pissed him off even more.

Perfect. I cracked my neck, straining as I cemented my sensations with the already aching body I borrowed. I'd nearly regained my full strength, but I didn't want to push the boundaries yet. I wanted to wait until I'd guided him where I wanted.

"You should take this up with Theo—"

"Teach him a fucking lesson," the chimera roared, banging against his box. "Beat him. Break him. Show this little warlock who's boss!"

"What? No!" I turned my attention to the depths of darkness below, glaring at the shiny metallic box which shook and shimmered.

Ronald approached Vincent and went to snatch the warlock by the collar of his uniform. Vincent jumped back, instinctively guarding himself with his hands. A defensive maneuver when retreating but one we'd all regret since his makeshift tattoo kit jabbed Ronald in the arm.

The tiniest prick and droplets of blood pooled on Ronald's arm, swirling with black ink. Fuck. Ronald stared at the blood and ink representing the fury and hatred this man carried with him each day. Holding back the tsunami of rage in Ronald took nearly all my strength.

"Attack him." The chimera cackled at my efforts, relishing the futile chaos he'd provoked. "Show him who's in charge."

"No!" I shouted. "Stop."

I pulled at the fibers of violence that seeped into Ronald's conscious and subconscious mind, the same strings the chimera tugged upon to provoke such easy control over the correctional officer. Once I'd torn the rage from the demon's grasp, I manipulated the anger, conjuring more blades than my eyes could count, and impaled the chimera again and again. He might claim pain did nothing to faze him, but obviously, I'd made his accommodations too comfortable.

The chimera spent so much time riling Jasper's mind with forgotten fears, I'd forgotten there were so many other buttons in the human psyche one could push if they sought to elicit a reaction. Of course, that monster would incite Ronald's worst qualities.

"When you hinder my objectives, you don't anger me, demon," I hissed. "You only add to the satisfaction I'll gain when I finally purge you from this plane of existence."

"Right back at ya, puppet." The chimera wheezed through the agony.

Ronald wiped his arm. The black ink had disappeared, but the blood pooled yet again.

Fuck. Fuck. Goddammit! Can nothing go right for me?

Releasing my own anger so it wouldn't sync to Ronald's, I took a deep breath.

"Take this up with Vincent's boss. Show him who's really in charge. Not Vincent. Not some chump. He's not someone worth your wrath." I fed into his ego, cradling this man-child's need for respect, for authority, for dominance. Oh, how it left a sour note of putrid sludge in my throat. "You need to confront the one who thinks he's running things, the one who caused such an action to occur. Do you think Vincent would've ever dared if the warlock he follows didn't believe himself above you? Remind him you are the authority here. You."

Ronald bolted down the block, abandoning a bewildered and frightened Vincent, ready to confront the warlock I sought. Unbridled rage painted Ronald's already blurred vision in shades of red and hot white. I squinted, ensuring I didn't act too soon or too late. I didn't need C.O. Kowalski actually doling out his authority. I simply didn't have the patience to follow his long rounds any further.

There he was in all his glory, perched atop a table, legs planted on the bench, and haunting blue eyes that sent a shiver so strongly through Ronald it cut deep to his core, making even me tremble.

```
Name: Theodore Whitlock
Branch:Arcane (Demonic Resonance)
```

This was the man who nearly slayed Dorian. Me, by extension.

I unleashed my magic, sending waves of agony through the nerves of Ronald's mind. In an instant—a searing, brutal instant—he passed out, leaving me to control his body. Slipping into his body, I fought the urge to wriggle as the weight of his muscles, his fat, his exhaustion pulled at my being.

There were a lot of correctional officers who worked for the MDC. Some had easier minds to mold, some knew how to skirt the security check-ins, and some had better branch magics for when the time came to approach Theodore Whitlock. But I chose Ronald because the notion of hijacking his waking mind didn't bother me. It wasn't the same as puppeteering the sleeping, sluggish Jasper. No, no, no. Snatching control over a host while consciously awake had long-term effects. It shattered memories, broke desires, changed personalities.

I wouldn't wish that upon the many C.O.s here doing their best to enforce structure in this lawless place. It was something Milo and Finn would disapprove of, but the sanity of this corrupt man, the warlocks he detained, didn't concern me. If I broke his psyche beyond repair, it'd be worth it knowing I saved Finn and reunited the three of us again. They'd understand. It was a small price to pay to carve out the happiness I deserved.

I positioned myself at a warded pillar, silently observing Theodore from a distance and ignoring the curious thoughts of onlookers who wondered why C.O. Kowalski remained idle. Apparently, he was a man who often over-asserted himself when displaying his authority behind these bars, whether by pedaling his products or stomping on the throats of anyone brazen enough to talk out of turn. Burying every unwanted insight I continued gaining on Ronald Kowalski, I focused on my true target.

Theodore had the same observant eyes as his sister Tara. There was a quiet understanding that came from generations of knowledge bestowed upon the Whitlock family. They sat atop a throne of wealth and power; it made sense they kept it by remaining aware of the peasants clamoring to reach their heights.

He saw everyone in this cellblock as nothing more than pawns to a game of chess he waged against his father, a battle he believed he hadn't lost. Fascinating and disturbing.

I squeezed my chest, Ronald's chest, fighting back the psychotic pleasure wafting in the air. It carried a drumbeat, something so potent it gave me palpitations when listening too closely to Theodore's eerie thoughts.

Whereas Tara's ocean swept all those who dared enter into the undertow, her brother had an inviting inner core, yet I dared not enter the open gates of his depraved fantasies. Darkness lurked at the edges of the illuminated space, ready to pounce and consume the weak-willed. A trick a lesser telepath would fall for, one I was certain other state officials had fallen for, too.

Theodore shared a striking resemblance to his sister. The same blond hair and blue eyes. But his eyes held a hollowness more like his father's than the sorrow dwelling in Tara's. The same model-like features and a tall, slender build had painted him as soft in here, though it seemed that was no longer the case. Theodore sat in the center of the rec room of his cellblock without a single inmate encroaching on his space. Distance was offered out of respect or fear—perhaps both.

Definitely both.

Delicately, I tiptoed at the edges of Theodore's mind. His deepest desires lay bare. His biggest fears exposed. His secret hopes revealed. All ploys because this warlock knew how to turn his thoughts into venom, decaying anything that sought to create a connection.

What I needed, what I required, was the piece of his mind he didn't use as bait. I strained, focusing on not only Theodore but the many minds around. Piecing together the scraps of knowledge they possessed mixed with the snippets he kept buried.

My prodding caused a spike of hatred so sharp the thoughts practically sliced through the air, painting grainy images of Theodore's first days behind bars. Bruises. Blood. Stabbings. Carnage. Death. So much pain radiated off Theodore, the fight for his survival mixed with the pleasure he gained from subduing those intent on snuffing him out.

It seemed Tobias Whitlock liked loose ends even less than I did, but in his arrogance, he sent the wrong men to remove the threat Theodore presented, allowing his son to rebrand his image almost immediately here in the MDC.

Theodore didn't have friends in the Metropolitan Detainment Center; he didn't have enemies either. Those bold enough to oppose the slim, rich boy with bound magic, like everyone else, had fatalities in one place or another. The medley of minds around conveyed as much.

All that remained in the MDC were sheep who followed the Whitlocks' suggestions and wolves who knew to stick to the outskirts of the forest, for a demon acted as the shepherd of this cellblock. That was what they saw him as—a demon in human flesh, a monster who controlled monsters. Even without his magic, he ignored his pain, he held no empathy, he offered only death and brutality.

But I knew a real demon. Theodore was dangerous, yet controlling him was something achievable. Unlike that chimera.

Theodore's lips curled into a twisted smile as his thoughts stretched out like a gnarled tree, looming over me and everyone in this cellblock. It was maddening, glimpsing his exposed mind. "*There's a psychic in the air.*"

Theodore's open mind encouraged the energy I trickled outward into his thoughts. Even with his magic dampened and no indication of telepathy rummaging through his thoughts, Theodore felt the gentlest tug. I plucked at his thoughts, delicate, but they were not strings. They were webs, and he was a spider who'd laid a trap for anyone daring enough to leap into his mind.

"*I've missed the rough thrust of a telepath in my skull.*" Theodore cocked his head, searching. "*Who are you?*"

He studied the guards first, crossing off each one, including Ronald, because surely there had to be someone new in the rotation. Next, his eyes flitted to inmates in the cellblock, each with magic as bound as his, but curious if someone had landed a little trinket to bypass the wards and cast a bit freely.

"*No, no, no. I know every branch here, so where have you been hiding?*" Theodore closed his eyes, creating a silhouette of his image, rising high in his mind and climbing to the edges of those decayed tree limbs he considered lively thoughts. "*Where oh where are you, my friend? Come say hello. I won't bite. Unless you like that sort of thing.*"

I had no desire to address Theodore, to tip my hand, to end up wrapped inside this psychopath's mind. It was layers upon layers of hatred, arrogance, conviction, remorseless lust for carnage, and a thousand other culminating factors that would make controlling him that much harder.

"*Come out, come out, wherever you are.*" Theodore strummed his fingers against the table he sat at, feigning boredom while his thoughts raced in every direction, sniffing at the magic in the air, desperate to find and latch himself to my telepathy.

Every sinister whisper of his mind made my skin itch. The hairs on my neck rose, and goosebumps trailed my arms like I could almost feel him reaching out for my magic.

For the time being, I needed to remain on guard against Theodore's thoughts, carefully analyze them without being bound to his being. He controlled demonic energy. Based on the research I'd gleaned from the doctor who worked with Theodore, she'd implanted brands that housed fiends into the minds of branchless witches. I could also use his magic to control the chimera and remove it with ease. It'd be difficult, damn near impossible, but I needed his branch to properly contain and eradicate the demon tethered to Finn.

"Is that your plan, puppet?" The chimera chuckled from the depths of the subconscious, wriggling against the blades I'd impaled him with.

I ground my teeth. I needed to remain vigilant and on guard against the chimera, too. Soon, I'd rid myself of him, and so long as I kept my attention focused, I'd keep him imprisoned where he could do no harm.

"You think you can jump into his mind?" The chimera strummed his fingers against his prison walls, with a startling similarity to the rhythmic beat of Theodore's.

Blocking my thoughts, I tightened the shackles containing the chimera and whatever foolish attempt he contemplated about casting magic.

I knew I couldn't jump into Theodore's mind at this moment. There were too many factors. The MDC dampeners made Theodore's branch useless to me right now. Theodore's chaotic mind proved another complication. I needed to observe everything about him, learn ways to manipulate and control his very being. Then, only then, I could take hold of Theodore. But I'd have to wait for the right opportunity.

Chapter Fourteen

Milo's bear hug woke me before the morning sun. Work hadn't been hitting him with heavy cases, and he'd spent nearly every night of September at my place. His arms tightly squeezed me, keeping me pinned with my back pressed to his chest, my butt against his crotch. And to really keep me from moving, he had one leg wrapped over both of mine. It was comforting; here, I eased out of my slumbering dream state, awakening only to Milo's mind. My eyes were heavy, groggy, ready to drift back to sleep in the warm embrace, maybe even scoot against him and rouse some frisky morning thoughts.

I was too tired, though, too comfortable, so I dozed off momentarily. An actual moment, too. I closed my eyes for a blink when Carlie's paw started patting my head. She rubbed her face against mine, purring and offering the most affection in the world.

Shit.

My eyes sprang open. If she was acting this sweet, that meant I'd dozed off way past her feeding schedule and my alarm.

"Just a few more minutes." Milo strengthened his hug, trying to cuddle me into submission. "You won't be late. Clairvoyant guarantee."

With a bit of telekinesis, I loosened his grip and slid off the bed. "Not taking that chance. I've got the auxiliary gym reserved for the day, and I can't afford to lose any time."

Milo huffed, snatching my pillow and hugging it in my stead.

"This is really all your fault, you know."

A month had gone by, and it'd proven difficult to find time with Milo's acolytes, my students' schedules, and booking the auxiliary gym. Milo kept his acolytes busier than I realized. It also didn't help that he'd pitched my proposal to Guild Master Campbell, which she springboarded across the academy. Thanks to my noble idea, every damn teacher with a second-year homeroom wanted to pencil in time to have their students train with pro-witches, so that meant fighting even harder than usual to schedule the auxiliary gym.

"The next time you steal one of my ideas, try not to fuck me in the process."

"But I love fucking you."

I glowered.

"It's for the betterment of the city, of everyone." Milo smiled, giddy at the idea of what he saw.

Potentially saw. Something glorious wrapped in some vision where my telepathy only glimpsed fragments of his thoughts on how this simple streamlined idea carried a ripple effect that might truly change the foundation of how academies and guilds interacted. Of course, it was just Cerberus offering up all their acolytes to work alongside the students at Gemini, but that'd change soon enough. After all, if Cerberus offered up acolytes for good PR, it wouldn't be long before other guilds followed suit. Soon, pros would be helping facilitate training at every academy in the state, maybe even making their way down to a few non-academy facilities from private, charter, and public schools. If that happened, if industry professionals actually took the time to help kids harness their magic, it could very well change an entire generation of casting.

Carlie weaved between my legs, nearly tripping me on the way to the bathroom. "Fine. I'll feed you first, fat cat."

I didn't waste a second getting my students to the auxiliary gym, even with Milo's thoughts syncing to mine in the distance. He worked on cases, planned for meetings, kept the press guessing what was next for the globally ranked enchanter, and a thousand other things, but nothing in his mind rang with urgency. Nothing called to me like it had months ago when my telepathy first expanded, seeking him out in the sea of minds across the city. It was genuinely nice not to constantly fret about some horror lurking around the corner, so I looped my telepathy onto the minds of my students, which helped keep me grounded in the here and now.

Since I'd reserved it for the full day, even after the acolytes left to work on cases, my homeroom could continue training. Hopefully, this would help them apply what they'd picked up from these ongoing lessons. And I could pull aside the few who were already shirking off on their coursework.

I rolled my eyes at Gael and Melanie, each completely aloof about their studies. They were lucky to have such a knack for decent, half-assed work turned in at the absolute latest possible deadline. Seriously, even champions of procrastination would admire their slacker ways.

"Speaking of slackers," I mumbled. "Just a friendly reminder, make sure to bring in your permission slips if you want to attend the upcoming field trip."

"Thanks for the reminder." Gael fished a crumpled, overly folded, half-ripped permission slip out of his back pocket. "Totally not the last one to turn in my form this time."

He grinned, handing me his paper.

"If this is another forged signature from that rooster of yours again, I'll make sure you never see the inside of a guild—field trip related or not."

"Bawk!"

I flinched. Fucking familiar.

"It's definitely one hundred percent parent signatures." He pointed to a jam smudge, then redirected to the signatures that'd been smudged after spending god only knows how many days in his back pocket. "They both signed and everything. See?"

"Fine."

Inside the auxiliary gym, I divided my students up and sent them right off to work with an acolyte. Having the extra helping hand was perfect, and it allowed me to focus on the different components each kid needed to work on during the visits. While they went to work, I pulled up notes I kept for tracking their progress as they trained.

I made my way to Acolyte Novak's group first since she'd taken it upon herself to work with the largest group.

```
Name: Lena Novak
Branch: Arcane (Bubble Burst)
```

Kenzo joined Lena's group, where she planned a lesson on maintaining branch fluctuations in a constant ebb and flow. It was her specialty, making her already powerful branch nearly invincible in combat. Kenzo still had quite the chip on his shoulder after being shown up by Lena. Every week, the acolytes came to work with my students, whether for one period or an extended afternoon homeroom, and Kenzo continued training to counter her branch, convinced he wouldn't be outdone a second time.

```
Name: Kenzo Ito
Branch: Hex (Disruption)
Ranking: 1
```

It didn't even matter if I assigned him to work with Acolyte Novak that day or not; he made it a priority to hone in and search for her hidden magics. Static popped in the air, nullifying Lena's magic. She seemed to enjoy Kenzo's efforts, taking a certain delight in how he searched for her frequency tucked across the auxiliary gym. Every time he cast a hex, she sent out hundreds more microscopic bubbles, which he went to work snuffing out, aiming for a hundred percent proficiency.

"We're going to be working on consistent casting flow," Lena explained, not missing a beat between her own fluctuating branch magic as she gestured for Kenzo, Layla, Katherine, Carter, and Melanie to line up. "You five are the most suited based on your casting frequencies and the particulars of your branches.

Enhancing your endurance for longevity regimes will go a long way in improving your stamina."

"I practice maintaining my branch every day," Layla said, texting Amani—I could tell from the way she pursed her lips and the cutting surface thoughts she had only one friend who would truly understand. "I know full well the limits of my therianthrope form. You might need to revisit Mr. Frost's notes on me."

Hmph. Seemed Layla didn't reserve her snotty comments for just my lectures.

```
Name: Layla Smythe
Branch: Bestial (Therianthropy)
Ranking: 20
```

"Maintaining your branch in full effect leaves you depleted after about fifteen minutes, correct?" I asked.

She shrugged, more focused on her texting conversation.

I waved a hand, shaking Layla's grip on her phone until she understood there'd be none of that right now, and stuffed it in her jacket pocket. "You won't be expected to improve the duration of your fully formed therianthrope shift. That's not what Acolyte Novak's lesson is on."

"Exactly," Lena interjected, ready to lead her lesson and wanting no assistance from me on the matter.

Sure, Enchanter Evergreen forced her to work on this like a case, wasting her 'very valuable' time. But if she was going to do this, she planned on doing it the best, which meant independently and with the highest success rate between herself, Ellie, and Hayden. Geez—she was as bad as Kenzo when it came to being a perfectionist.

"Therianthropes can learn to do minor shifts, augmenting only the animalistic features they require for a situation," Lena explained. "Finding ways to isolate which components you change and when they will improve your proficiency with shifting and allow for longstanding endurance is important."

This clicked for Layla, finally engaging her in the lesson. Often, she'd transform just her hands into their clawed form. It helped sharpen the direction of her telekinesis or intimidate men she didn't know, asking her how she was doing, what she was doing, and where she was heading, among other prattle she didn't tolerate.

"I get it." Fine hairs covered Layla's hands as her nails transformed into thick, black claws. "There. Mastered. Am I done with this little lesson?"

"Not bad, but not very useful either." Lena crossed her arms. "A therianthrope's tracking skills are some of their most beneficial attributes to the guild industry. Yes, the brute force of a therianthrope is an added benefit, but it doesn't do any good if the witch fizzles out halfway through a case."

Layla fought a snarl.

"Focus on partial shifts," Lena said. "Such as just your eyes, your ears, the olfactory system of your nose—any of these can heighten your senses tremendously without overexerting yourself."

Layla attempted to redirect her casting by shifting just the parts of her body that heightened her senses while Lena maintained an unamused expression. But I caught how her mind was briefly distracted, sending her bubbles throughout the auxiliary gym and avoiding Kenzo's pursuit. He was tenacious, as always, which kept Lena hard at work, even if she pretended Kenzo's casting barely fazed her.

"While Layla ponders over the lesson, let's get you started." Lena eyed Carter up and down.

```
Name: Carter Howe
Branch: Rejuvenation (Vitality)
Ranking: 75
```

Her eyes rested on the honorary Cerberus emblem pinned to his blazer. Some of my homeroom students still prided themselves on the successes they had the first semester of their first year, wearing those emblems on their uniforms daily—namely, Caleb and the Gaels. I was more impressed by the trans flag pinned next to Carter's emblem. He hadn't hidden his identity last year, willingly sharing with those he trusted, but now he seemed quite comfortable taking pride in himself, so much so that thoughts of joining the Gemini LGBTQ+ Club flitted across his surface thoughts. A showman like Carter would definitely bring a spark of life to the organization.

Lena got Carter situated on a training course to distribute his vitality to different muscles in his body. Admittedly, the continuous flow she'd picked would help strengthen the parts of his body that he drew telekinesis and levitation from.

"*Nice observation, Acolyte Novak.*"

She scowled, partly from my intrusion and partly because it seemed a default expression for her. "As for you two, it's time we made you less reliant on your support tools."

Katherine did her best to remain calm and composed. "What about Kenzo?"

Melanie, on the other hand, couldn't hide how nervous Lena's scowl made her. "I think, based on my branch, Acolyte Reed would be better."

```
Name: Melanie Dawson
Branch: Primal (Fire)
Ranking: 50
```

"No," I interjected. "She's not doing any review on support items."

A nice mini-lesson Acolyte Reed offered during a previous visit. Honestly, I still preferred dividing Melanie's training from Layla since she tended to goof off in favor of impressing her friend, but Lena didn't seem to tolerate talking or distractions when here, so I figured keeping Melanie in this group couldn't hurt.

"Precisely," Lena said, annoyed by Melanie's request and my continued interruptions. "I want you two focusing on ways to channel your frequency into your support tools without making contact."

Katherine clutched her grimoire tightly. "That's not how my branch works."

```
Name: Katherine Harris
Branch: Enchantment (Spell Craft)
Ranking: 7
```

"I know exactly how Spell Craft works." Lena telekinetically yanked Katherine's grimoire and Melanie's zippo lighter away.

It was a useful lesson. Root magics like sensory and banishment allowed all witches to cast their energy outward. Any witch, no matter their branch, could funnel their magic anywhere with the correct training and understanding for their frequency.

After she got them started, Lena made her way toward Kenzo.

Each stood tall with crossed arms, unmoving—taking shallow breaths and resisting the need to blink like that somehow played a role in their casting. It didn't. Not a single word passed between them, and even their thoughts were difficult to hear with the echoes of static brought on by Kenzo's disruption circulating throughout the gym.

"*You know, Kenzo, you've gained an incredible understanding for feeling Acolyte Novak's casting in the air, coordinating your disruption.*" I linked to Kenzo's mind, ignoring the blatant profanity at the sheer audacity I believed he required a compliment from me. "*But it's important to remember that your branch, while versatile, may not be suited to fend off her arcane magic. It's not a lack of effort on your part—you know that.*"

"***Say your peace without the fucking pat on my head so I can focus. I'm not a damn child. I don't need the buffer speech.***" Kenzo ground his teeth, practically snarling from the shift in Acolyte Novak's bubbles and how he was forced to endure conversation with me. "***You're rambling worse than branchless right now.***"

"*Just remember you have more at your disposal than your hex.*"

Lena's branch wouldn't be bested despite Kenzo's precision. Her bubble burst carried its own mixture of hex magic, nullifying and striking back at Kenzo's disruption. Arcane branches were difficult to compete against, no matter how commendable and capable the other branch user might be. It was a valuable lesson Kenzo had no intention of listening to as he harnessed his spark of disruption further.

I left them alone, content Lena had this lesson more than under control. Obviously, I welcomed the assistance of other instructional guidance, but I didn't want to simply unload my homeroom students onto others, like some cheap tactic to abandon them or my duties to improve their skills—though I'd noticed other teachers indulging in the break that came with having access to acolyte's visiting to offer professional lessons.

I bet Milo didn't account for folks leveraging the system to shirk their duties in his potentially positive futures. I sighed. Actually, he probably already accounted for that. Damn clairvoyants.

Making my way toward Acolyte Reed in the forest terrain, I found their lesson already underway.

```
Name: Ellie Reed
Branch: Ward (Skeleton Key)
```

Jennifer hovered in a seated position, legs crisscrossed and hands on her knees.

Ellie pressed a hand against Jennifer's back, straightening her position. "You're still allowing too much channeled magic to flow toward your branch. Deep breath and redistribute."

Jennifer opened her eyes, glaring so foul Ellie nearly yelped. Unlike Lena, who had a drill sergeant approach, Ellie very much represented a butterfly of creative expression who sought to flutter about offering positivity and acceptance to everyone. Ugh—she would've been one of *those* teachers.

Kindness was good and well, but students often took advantage of weak-willed consideration, always seeing how far they could push the boundaries. In this case, Jennifer ignored the parts of Ellie's instructions that she didn't want to attempt.

```
Name: Jennifer Jung
Branch: Psychic (Empathic)
Ranking: 18
```

"*This would be easier without Tara and Gael.*" Jennifer furrowed her brow, fighting against the two polar opposite emotions yanking at her branch magic. Between Tara's ocean of sorrow and Gael's inferno sun of joy, she really had her work cut out for her when it came to Acolyte Reed's dampening exercise.

"Why aren't you using your sensory and banishment in conjunction with your other roots?" I asked. "It'd help with the lesson."

Jennifer turned her glare toward me, to which I returned with my own.

"*Eep,*" Ellie thought, fighting the external shout and allowing it to ring through my head.

So irritating.

Feeling a bit snarky, I sent those emotions Jen's way, knowing sass was her least favorite thing to latch onto her empathy. "Perhaps I can release some wisps, offer you a target for this training. Unless, of course, you're content with—"

"Targets would be wonderful." Jennifer ground her teeth. "*I can picture Frost's shiny fucking forehead when I strike those damn wisps.*"

Ouch. How big did she envision my forehead in her mind? It was like a billboard. I shook my head, allowing my shaggy bangs to cover my face.

"Miss Reed?" Gael raised a trembling hand.

"Yes."

"Is it okay if I go to the bathroom?" He grimaced.

```
Name: Gael Martinez
Branch: Augmentation (Spikes)
Ranking: 35
```

Ellie deferred to me, unsure she had any authority to say yes or no on bathroom policies.

Gael didn't need the restroom, but he desperately needed a break. He'd prioritized the objective of Reed's lesson, but the shift in his channeling shrank his spikes, making his skin tingle. It was an ache he often gave into, yet he wanted to learn how to ignore it. He wanted to be an enchanter, one who fought through the pain and saved the day.

"Go ahead, Gael." I didn't have a bathroom policy. Even when students just wanted a breather to goof off in the halls of Gemini, I usually allowed it. Life was exhausting enough, and classes were tiresome when confined to eight consecutive hours of productivity.

"Thanks." Gael shuffled past Tara and rushed out of the auxiliary gym before releasing his repressed channeled casting. The sensation of relief struck, sending an effervescent sigh through the air.

He needed this lesson on repressing branch flow since the constant flux of his branch affected his overall root performance, but I didn't want any training to break Gael or the positivity he brought to our homeroom.

"Nice work, Tara." Acolyte Reed studied Tara, who continued meditating while channeling as much casting into her roots as possible.

```
Name: Tara Whitlock
Branch: Ward (Sealing)
Branch: Cosmic (Shadows)
Branch: Arcane (Intangibility)
Branch: Primal (Icicles)
Ranking: 9
```

"*How's this much magic still sitting in her branch receptors?*" Ellie thought. "*She might have an endless supply like Hayden.*"

I frowned. Great. Another hurdle tossed toward Tara's already difficult branch overlap and newly developed fourth branch. The Infinite Light wasn't just some catchphrase for Hayden's glitter magic but a reference to his rare magical trait known as infinite draw, where a witch's channeling never waned. The receptors had no limitation on casting capability. Well, no limitation on his branches or roots. A witch's body always had a breaking point.

Having no answers for Tara, I allowed her to continue her training with Reed and approached Jamius, who channeled his casting into his roots alongside three copies.

```
Name: Jamius Watson
Branch: Alteration (Duplication)
Ranking: 52
```

Unlike the others in Reed's lesson, Jamius didn't struggle with a constant flux of magic drawn by his branch, but he did struggle with properly distributing that magic. Every time he created a duplication, he created them with full access to his roots, which in turn ate away at his access to his magic. Each copy chiseled away at his proficiency. Thanks to Reed's branch, she saw the actual threads he pulled from when manifesting them and assisted in locking them during this exercise, giving him a feel for his root casting receptors. Of course, he'd eventually have to master this skill independently.

"I was brought into this world to fly," a copy cried. "Why can't I fly?"

"You can levitate." Jamius shrugged. "That's basically flying."

"Oh? Is that so?" the copy floated toward Jamius. "So, I guess that dirty fanfic you're writing is basically a novel, wouldn't you—"

Jamius clapped his hands, and his copy exploded into a puddle of water.

"He was a traitor and got what he deserved," a second copy said.

"Concurred." A third copy nodded, hand on his chin as he attempted his most sophisticated expression. "A thought has occurred to me. We were both brought into this world with only sensory at our disposal, yet there is nothing to sense in the nearby atmosphere."

"Ah, yes." The second copy mimicked the third's behavior. "That thought was also thought by me."

These two were clearly some of Jamius' more annoying duplicates.

"What do you think it means?" the second asked.

"It means we were created without purpose," the third answered. "The world is a lie, life is pointless, we are simply cogs in the machine."

"Can you guys chill for like a minute?" Jamius sighed.

"A minute? You mean a whole thirtieth of our lives?" the third copy let out an exacerbated gasp. "It might be a mere sliver to you, but I intend on living my life to the fullest."

"But you have no purpose," the second chimed in.

And the third copy started crying.

"I'm gonna give you a minute with yourselves." I backstepped.

Jamius sulked. "*This is why I don't limit my roots when creating them. They get so damn whiny.*"

Interesting and tragic how Jamius' duplicates carried such an existential crisis in their short-lived existence.

Flying through the thicket of trees, I exited the forest terrain and made my way toward the rock terrain where Acolyte Russo had allowed his group to take a break. Though I hadn't caught Hayden's lesson, it didn't look like he bothered with any of the objectives I laid out.

Gael grinned, internally boasting how impressive his roots had gotten despite flat-out refusing to train the one root magic I wanted him to focus on today: his levitation. The rooster crowed, probably bragging too in some fucking bird language only Gael comprehended.

```
Name: Gael Rios-Vega
Branch: Bestial (Familiar)
Ranking: 92
```

While those two stuck to the ground, Yaritza played on her phone during the break. Based on the scorch marks lining the boulders in the terrain, it was clear she'd prioritized her branch training even though Acolyte Russo's group was specifically designed to focus on root casting.

```
Name: Yaritza Vargas
Branch: Cosmic (Star Shower)
Ranking: 69
```

Yes, Yaritza's levitation and telekinesis were solid, mainly in conjunction with her branch, but her sensory and banishment were mediocre at best.

Ignoring the nonsense of their surface thoughts, I allowed them to enjoy their little break while I had a word with Hayden, who was already locked in a deep conversation with Caleb. It seemed even Caleb slacked on his root training, favoring the only thing he liked more than casting lessons—studying. With a smile on his face and notebook in hand, Caleb had pulled Hayden into a discussion that already overwhelmed the young acolyte.

A hundred different questions floated around Caleb's head, linking to the handful he'd already asked and the notes he'd jotted based on Hayden's answers. Each answer seemed to only add more follow-up questions which, based on Caleb's history of curiosity, would turn into an endless discussion.

```
Name: Caleb Huxley
Branch: N/A
Ranking: 100
```

"Shouldn't you all be focusing on root training?"

"Definitely." Hayden smiled, big and goofy, with a bit of glitter shimmering around his face. "But these three were doing such a fantastic job, I thought they deserved a little break before round two."

This fucking acolyte and his holly jolly bullshit cheer. It was extra annoying, given how fucking genuine it was. Seriously, how could someone be this positive and uplifting all the time? My head hurt just glimpsing his sparkling surface thoughts.

The whole point of Russo working on roots was because he might've actually been able to help Yaritza finetune hers, Gael *attempt* levitation, and Caleb master his perfected banishment, all of which I'd floundered at helping them achieve.

"The scheduled break isn't for another hour; they're more than capable of enduring until then."

"Agreed, but you should've seen how hard they all pushed themselves."

"It was nothing." Caleb continued writing, questions percolating the more they simmered in his mind. "Honestly, I wish I could keep up with your casting rollovers. The way you switch between your roots so quickly. Not to mention your branches, which you didn't even use…"

"My roots are actually better than my branch casting."

"Because of your medical limitations?"

"Um, yes and no? I don't know." Hayden shrugged. "It probably has more to do with the fact they didn't develop until I was sixteen."

```
Name: Hayden Russo
Branch: Cosmic (Teleportation)
Branch: Cosmic (Glitter)
```

"Really?" Caleb's eyes widened.

I prepared to interject and end this Q&A until Caleb's hope blossomed, superseding the countless questions he had. Even as he worked to finetune his roots, Caleb secretly yearned to develop a branch of his own. It was something I'd never seen surface in his thoughts, but the desire was there, fresh and bright and hopeful. Caleb wanted to be great and knew if he had unique magic, it'd guarantee his success.

"Docs explained my branches laid dormant for so long in order to compensate for the stress on my weak heart." Hayden's grin was inviting, making Caleb return with a happy half-smile. "I relied on my roots to carry me through while I was an academy student. Although, I did have a little fun showing off my branches when my third year rolled around."

Caleb wondered how that must've felt, surprising everyone with two branches, showcasing amazing root proficiency, and finishing top in his class.

"Yeah? Bet they were shocked."

"At first." Hayden's grin turned into a forced pouty face. "Only problem was when they finally did emerge, they weren't very strong—well, I mean, you've seen them in action."

"Oh." Caleb scrunched his face, his expression quizzical, ready to ask a dozen questions about clarification.

"I think the point Acolyte Russo is making is that while his branches are unique and strong-*ish*, it was his root proficiency that landed him a solid internship and an offer at a guild."

"Yeah, that sounds about right." Hayden smiled.

"So, how did…"

I sighed, almost resigned to let this play through since Caleb's curiosities wouldn't yield until he got his fanboying out of the way. Since joining Enchanter Evergreen's team, Caleb had researched everything he could on Hayden Russo, Ellie Reed, and Lena Novak. Hayden had been the most forthcoming thus far, Ellie's responses left Caleb more confused, and Lena intimidated him almost as much as Kenzo.

"Enough questions." I glared at the both of them. "Back to training."

Chapter Fifteen

The days of the week bled together in this blissful normalcy, and somehow, it was already mid-October. Occasionally, my telepathy would seek out Milo's mind above all else, but without the urgency of danger lurking in the air—the future—I found it easier to unravel my magic when it wound around Enchanter Evergreen's cases. Maybe I was gaining more control. Maybe I was just learning to be less controlling.

My mind wandered after a lecture on the foundations of guild life and the economic impact it had on America. Nearly every student in my first-year History of Witchcraft course had fogged over surface thoughts, absentmindedly reading over the assignment I'd distributed. I couldn't blame their faltering attention spans or my own for this activity. The lesson was as dull as they came but a necessary evil for the state standards students would be required to exhibit proficiency on by the end of the year. Not every learning opportunity came with fun engagement. Sometimes, it required boring, repetitive study tasks.

As the class's focus waned, my telepathy drifted throughout the academy, and I allowed it. Following the bustle of excitement kept me awake as I strolled around the classroom, keeping attentive if someone required help.

Magic exploded from the auxiliary gym, wave after wave of channeled energy that skirted against my overactive psychic branch. The casting frequencies wrapped around active thoughts and strong emotions.

I followed the sensations, buzzing from the palpable adrenaline in the air.

The excitement nearly pushed me away, but I latched my telepathy to Chanelle, whose mind buzzed with an aggravation reminiscent of mine. Much like me, she'd reserved the facility for the entire day, hoping to make the most of her time with Cerberus acolytes. And like me, she sweet-talked Milo into offering up his acolytes to assist in the training.

If it were anyone other than Chanelle, I'd be annoyed. Okay. I was annoyed since that meant I had to work around the fact Milo's acolytes were double booked. But I understood the importance.

Chanelle studied Amani, who snapped her fingers and telekinetically redirected several projectiles thrown by her classmates, which sent them hurling back with a barrage of copies hiding the originals.

```
Name: Amani Williams
Branch: Psychic (Glamour)
Ranking: 6
```

Not only were her glamours difficult to identify, but her root proficiency was on par with some of the best in my homeroom. While I wasn't certain what the objective of this training exercise was, it was clear from the grimacing Acolyte Reed on the sidelines that this wasn't what she'd intended for the students. It wasn't what Chanelle had planned for either, equally vexed and impressed how Amani had taken the reins of the lesson, making herself the de facto instructor, and turned it into an opportunity to finetune her coven mates' techniques.

A huge tidal wave of water crashed beside the opposing students. Between the powerful current of water and the redirected projectiles hiding among a sea of glamoured duplicates, it forced the competing students to retreat deeper into the forest terrain, where their mobility and flight were further hindered.

```
Name: Derrick Lowe
Branch: Primal (Water)
Ranking: 82
```

"You got this, Tiff!" Derrick shouted, shifting his arms and moving a singular wave above the others.

Tiffany straddled a large branch like a broomstick. Ugh—so grateful that trend died out well over a century ago. And like the stage names Milo tried to make trendy, no amount of retro styling could breathe life into riding brooms for flight again. I recoiled at the thought. Her familiar rode a smaller branch, gnawing on it while using her tail to pivot their direction.

```
Name: Tiffany Sparks
Branch: Bestial (Familiar)
Ranking: 60
```

She cackled, twirling round and round on the stick, propelled faster by her familiar's casting. The mayhem in her laughter frightened those she chased, driving them directly into the crosshairs of the final member of their coven.

```
Name: Harrison Heywood
Branch: Enchantment (Potion Craft)
Ranking: 25
```

He chucked two vials. The first exploded, releasing green goop, which clung to all the students like a thick slime. The second erupted, shifting into a mist almost instantaneously that solidified the goop into a hard lime-green concrete.

Each member of Amani's coven was perfectly in tune with each other's magic, strengths, weaknesses, and personality, unlike the five peers they sparred against. It wasn't what Chanelle wanted, but there was a calm that helped settle her thoughts as she observed their seamless collaboration, believing she'd done at least one thing right.

I quirked a brow, nearly drawn back to my classroom, but I latched onto the anxiety in Chanelle's heartbeat, staying close to the stirring dread as she counted off how too many students had wandered from their assigned tasks to partake in Acolyte Reed's lesson—well, Amani's lesson—leaving all but three of her homeroom students to work elsewhere.

Chanelle eyed Jamie working with his sister, Acolyte Novak, and immediately levitated in the opposite direction to see why another student had distanced herself from everyone and chose to work alone. Well, not entirely alone. Tia practiced signs with her interpreter. Chanelle tried interpreting the meaning of Tia's signs but struggled to remember the motions as Tia's hands moved in rapid succession.

```
Name: Tatiana Owens
Branch: Enchantment (Invocation)
Ranking: 162
```

Skimming Tia's thoughts gave me added insight. Apparently, she worked with her interpreter on alternative phrases to find ways of reducing the chanting necessary when creating an invocation. Smart. Similar to Katherine and Harrison's enchantment branch, Tia's invocation allowed her to create a spell for any purpose so long as she channeled the magic correctly and created the right verse in her spell. It was a language-based magic, requiring every sign to be cast correctly with enough channeled magic to summon her spell. Too little and the spell would fizzle out; too much and the invocation would explode.

"How are you today?" Chanelle signed.

Her eyes followed Tia's hands, catching every third sign. Smiling, she tried not to show how utterly confused she was. Admittedly, she'd done better picking up ASL than I had with Spanish to benefit Gael. Okay—I'd made zero effort because Gael spoke fluent English, and I often relied on the emotions my branch caught when his thoughts drifted into words or phrases I didn't understand.

"I'm fine," the interpreter said. "Working on simplifying my invocations with phrases that'll carry through. The problem is they tend to create weaker spells, but that's probably because of my channeling output. It's hard balancing what to put into my branch while directing my root casting elsewhere."

Tia had learned at a young age not to rely on her hands for root magic, unlike most witches who used the easy gestures of directing their telekinesis or banishment. While levitation and sensory were easier for her, the other two floundered when signing for her enchantment branch.

"Still can't maintain them together?" Chanelle asked while signing. "Finding ways to make my branch more versatile was difficult until I learned how to conjure my whip. Something my husband actually taught me about my casting. Keeping your roots in play as you train your branch is commendable, but I find when trying something new with my branch, I wait until I've perfected it before reintroducing my roots to that training. Does that make sense?"

"*She does what with her whip?*" Tia's eyes widened.

The interpreter quickly worked to correct Chanelle's signs, blushing a bit at whatever provocative mishap Chanelle had signed when mentioning her whip.

As Chanelle continued working with Tia, I found myself slowly drifting away. My focus returned to my class, assisting the few first-year students who struggled to find the answers to the content covered in the assignment. I'd nearly severed my telepathy when a spike of guilt struck, pulling me back to Chanelle's mind.

She struggled when watching Jamie and Acolyte Novak interact, wanting to help redirect the lesson that Lena had completely disregarded. Chanelle's stomach churned, adding to the discomfort and blame eating away at her. A similar chord of guilt plucked at my insides.

"You can do better than that." Lena kept her arms folded across her chest, guarding her heart from spilling out as she lectured Jamie. "You're barely casting. Stop and properly channel your branch."

Bubbles popped around the outer swirls of three of Jamie's whirlpools, disrupting their flow and breaking the water into puddles on the ground.

```
Name: Jamie Novak
Branch: Arcane (Whirlpool)
Ranking: 32
```

He furrowed his brow, expression twisting into the same spiteful and sour face I'd seen too many times last year. Hateful, harmful words festered along his surface thoughts. I winced at the cutting comments he planned to hurl toward his sister, venom oozing from the cracks of his mind.

"It's my fault." Vik grimaced, having experienced Jamie's wrath firsthand and desperate to avoid it. They weaved their arms round and round, summoning three shadow cats that each worked to manipulate the broken droplets of water and regather them into a single vortex of transportation. These cat silhouettes batted the air playfully, totally aloof in comparison to the strenuous efforts Vik displayed when directing their behavior. It seemed even magical kitties didn't listen to directions.

```
Name: Vik Smythe
Branch: Arcane (Copycat)
Ranking: 158
```

Jamie eyed his coven mate, eyes softening. It pinched at my heart and Chanelle's, who observed the pair as silently as me.

"You're doing fine." All the rage inside Jamie washed away, replaced by guilt and regret and horror that he provoked such fear simply by existing. Taunting Vik used to be a sporting event for him; watching a member of the Smythe family squirm so easily made him question how they ever became such renowned enchanters in the first place.

"You're both shit at this point." Lena eyed Vik. "You've got built-in radar for frequencies. Your branch allows you to manipulate and alter your frequency to mimic another witch's magic."

"It's more complicated than…" They swallowed hard, as frightened of Lena's scowl as they were of Jamie's.

Vik reminded me less of their cousin, Layla, and more like Caleb—both were equally nervous when it came to confrontation. The difference being that Caleb didn't allow himself to believe the comments that said his branchless status made him worthless, whereas Vik became consumed by every word directed their way. Instructors, family, peers, even friends who pointed out how great their branch was sent a constant reminder that the only flaw with their magic was them. Vik Smythe's deepest casting struggle came from being gifted with a powerful branch and believing they were unworthy of it. Cursed, in fact, since every other Smythe inherited a bestial branch, and they were just a subpar copycat.

"Watch how I conjure the portals," Jamie said, feigning a weak smile. It was a difficult effort, something so unnatural for him that he thought his face might crack and fall to pieces. "And ignore Lena. She's all bark because she's a…"

Jamie's smile faltered just as it almost slipped into something snide, just as he was about to cut Lena down and call her a bitch, just as he reminisced Lena's many failures, shortcomings their father brought up at the few holiday dinners Lena attended. Jamie despised this hatred latched to his very being, believing he'd never shed the desire to pick people apart, pick them apart the same way the chimera had picked Jamie apart for months.

It didn't just torture him physically. It broke his spirit with as many words as it had bruises and breaks.

Jamie hadn't recovered since the possession. Not emotionally. Not even sure he had physically. Skirting away from Chanelle, I hovered toward Jamie. Floating as a ghost of psychic energy, I attempted to delve deep into his mind, search for those broken pieces, find something salvageable. Normally, I preferred a manifestation for these tasks, but I wanted to help, to do something…anything.

Guess I hadn't untethered from Chanelle's mind entirely since that same sensation, same yearning, screamed from her inner core, silencing the entire academy if I listened to her regrets loud enough.

I stepped toward Jamie's open, vacant mind and immediately jolted from the agony that seethed inside him. Every pain was as fresh as when first inflicted. A hundred haunting past memories he wished had been lost to the ether with the thousands of others and a million moments with the chimera so overwhelming it hurled my mind back to my classroom.

Clenching a fist, I fought the tremble in my hands. A searing pain burned the muscles of my wrists—exactly where Jamie's branch threads were located. His body was riddled with pains and aches, from his strained muscles to his foggy mind, all the way to the phantom pains that continued haunting him.

Chanelle's guilt drew me back to the auxiliary gym. She watched Jamie from afar, allowing his sister to work with his coven, unsure how to assist herself. I'd never known Chanelle to doubt herself so much, to lack a new strategy of engagement, or to have the resolve to work with a student. Jamie was a challenge last year, and now she believed her own shortcomings brought on what happened to him.

"*Lena's probably the worst pairing for that coven.*" I linked my telepathy to Chanelle, unable to silently stalk her.

"*Dorian?*" She bit the inside of her cheek, resisting the agitation that bubbled in her thoughts.

"*I know you're struggling with Jamie...*" With his whole coven, really.

Chanelle swallowed the words she wanted to say about how she'd failed Vik, too. Most of all, how she'd utterly failed that entire coven. Chanelle's guilt expanded, filling my mind as if it were my own. This whole coven struggled in every single way, and that failure belonged to Chanelle. She'd taken on too much last year, believing after so many years of balancing a hundred projects, she could carve out an added position just for herself. The liaison position was a stepping stone, sure, but she deluded herself into thinking it wouldn't take away from her passion in the classroom.

"It hasn't," I said, eyeing my students who hadn't noticed my out loud mutterings and continued working—and goofing off—on the assignment I'd given. Burying Chanelle's doubts that surfaced so loudly, I tried to find a comforting word. "*You haven't failed this coven.*"

"*Yes, I have.*" Chanelle studied Jamie, her gaze fixated on him and frightened she might break if she looked at the other members of his coven, who she believed she'd failed even more.

The bell rang, pulling my mind back to the classroom where every student stared, awaiting me to dismiss them. This was a good batch of first years in my Introduction to History, and most had aching surface thoughts of their teachers in the past using telekinesis to hold a student who attempted to zip out of the classroom when the bell rang. Guess some teachers really took the philosophy that 'they dismissed their classes, not the bell' as if I could be bothered to give a fuck about a kid trying to savor the few minutes of freedom they got between eight consecutive classes.

I waved a hand, dismissing the class, and sat in my desk chair. Thankfully, my planning block was starting, so I channeled my magic back toward Chanelle.

Stepping inside her mind, I ignored the bubblegum pink interior of an inner core stylized almost as extravagantly as her closet. Well, I assumed, given her extensive wardrobe. "Knock, knock."

"What the f—"

I pulled Chanelle deep into her thoughts before she finished speaking.

"Figured a little face-to-face might be helpful."

"You could've walked to the auxiliary gym instead of…whatever the hell this is."

"Like I'm walking all the way across campus. You realize I'm already sacrificing my smoke break for this chat." I frowned, fighting back a smile.

Chanelle studied the single circular screen representing her optic reception. A nicety added by me so she wouldn't wonder what was happening outside her head since she'd never had the pleasure of standing inside the inner core of her own mind. Not that her students noticed her absence.

"So, what are you thinking?"

"I'm thinking I need to regroup the kids, but I waited too long, and the other covens are so comfortable with each other, I'm…I'm afraid I'll…" Chanelle fought the thoughts and the frown on her face.

"You're afraid you'll fuck it up more."

"Exactly." An easy smile lit up her expression, even if it was a self-deprecating grin.

"Lena's attention is split. She's not helping all your kids because she's prioritizing Jamie."

"At least they have a connection, something I can't make."

"She doesn't though," I said. "Lena has as much guilt and regret—if not a hundred times more—as you do. She's not helping Jamie. She's letting half the coven assigned to her flounder while projecting her frustrations onto Vik. It's not good for them, serving as a proxy to this little family…bullshit."

"It's not good for any of them, I know. I tried putting Jamie in a one-on-one with Acolyte Novak, but they just yelled at each other the entire time."

"What about Ellie?"

"She's a pushover." Chanelle tsked. "Jamie did absolutely nothing during her lesson. Though it was good for his coven."

True. I'd seen how Amani had taken charge of their group lesson and turned Acolyte Reed into a glorified cheerleader.

"Okay. How about Hayden?"

"He's even worse. Notice he didn't show up to today's training?"

Acolyte Russo was frustratingly tardy.

"I don't wanna give up on Jamie, but I'm out of solutions. Not that I had any to begin with."

"Have you considered maybe he shouldn't be here?" I twinged, doubting the words as they escaped my lips. Did I ask because of

Jamie's best interest or because seeing him every day made Chanelle question her role as an educator? No. I asked because seeing him was a haunting reminder of my own failures.

"I have. I know he has as well, but Novak's don't quit," Chanelle explained. "I had that very uncomfortable conversation with Jamie's mother over the summer."

The confrontation—not conversation surfaced in Chanelle's memories. A scowling woman stood between us. She looked just like her daughter Lena, only older and meaner, with the same wicked glint Jamie's gaze cast last year.

"What the hell?" Chanelle trembled at the surfacing recollection, her whole body outside her shaky mind, in fact.

I waved a hand, repressing the representation of her memory. Since I usually only dived into Milo's mind these days, I forgot other folks didn't understand how to navigate the insides of their own heads.

"Christ, that woman." Chanelle took an uneasy breath as the image of Guild Master Novak faded away. "She's spiteful as hell, too. When I so much as made the suggestion that Jamie take a leave of absence, she tried to remove me from my liaison position."

The coordinator role, where she served as a delegate between Gemini Academy and the guilds of Chicago.

"Not that it would matter if she managed. Clearly, I can't handle the responsibility on top of everything else."

"That's not true."

"It is. I failed Jamie. I am still failing him. Failing every student in my homeroom coven—you should see some of their rankings this year. What the actual fuck am I even doing here? I had a devil in my class last year, and I was so busy I wrote it off as a spoiled brat living up to his douchebag entitlement."

Every uncertainty Chanelle kept tucked beneath meticulous belief in herself, her goals, her hopes for everyone bubbled inside her inner core. A necrotic rot eating away at her.

Guilt swelled, festering in her mind like an infection. Even with the chimera dead and gone, that monster had a hold on those of us left alive. A silhouette appeared, taking the form of Jamie's possessed body, a haunting apparition that flashed fresh in Chanelle's mind because she believed what had happened to Jamie fell on her. But it didn't. This guilt was mine, a torch of regret she shouldn't be burdened with carrying.

"You know that devil was there because of me, right?"

"That's what it said." Chanelle averted her gaze from the recollection of Jamie smirking, snide and menacing, before I wiped it away with a wave of my hand. "I wondered, but I didn't want to pry. You, Milo, or Jamie himself."

Given the massive amount of agony Jamie Novak endured while possessed, I highly doubted he had any semblance of understanding what had happened that day.

Telling Chanelle the truth about the devil, the chimera, wouldn't change what happened to Jamie. It wouldn't remove the guilt buried deep in her chest, rotting away at the smile she almost never let falter. But I owed her a piece of my history, the truth that led to her and her wayward student caught in the chaos of my life.

"I should probably start at the beginning when I lost one of the two men who's ever held my heart."

Chanelle stood captive and curious, and I finally shared a piece of myself with someone I considered a true friend.

Chapter Sixteen

Divulging everything I kept to myself was like releasing this unknown weight off my chest. I could breathe again. It helped that Chanelle found the news absurdly fascinating, more intrigued by my sordid history than the parts where I'd inadvertently brought on the worst possible outcomes.

Her curiosity buzzed around my head the rest of the day at the academy, allowing her a beautiful distraction from the gnawing guilt that'd settled in her chest. I nearly smiled once or twice. Nearly. An obvious side effect of latching my telepathy too closely to Chanelle's thoughts.

Still, I sort of enjoyed how light I felt on the flight home. The only other person who knew this much about me was Milo himself. It was strange trusting someone with my shortcomings, my failures, my past, but I found solace in the fact it brought relief to Chanelle's weary mind, allowing her nauseating cheerful personality to shine like a bright beacon at Gemini again. She'd undoubtedly do something to make me regret divulging so much, probably decide to overshare more of her life, which I already had too much insight into, thanks to my branch.

Once I'd gotten home, I fed the cats and gave Charlie all the cuddles he could handle as I lay on the couch unwinding after a long day. It was oddly comforting to have the biggest challenges in my life feel almost bearable. Everything had this aimless opportunity. Nothing, even the worst of the semester, held this dire urgency of impending doom. Yes, there was an upcoming trial because of the warlock incursion last school year, but I'd taken a page from Milo's playbook. I couldn't change or control it, so I pushed it out of my head because it was out of my hands. It helped that most of my homeroom didn't dwell on the events, the potential outcomes.

"Maybe I should be more paranoid?" I hugged Charlie tighter than he preferred, kissing the orange fluff of his face. "Nah. Think I'll just coast on these easy currents."

Speaking of calm waters, Milo's mind synced to mine as he flew across the city, closer to my home. The ebb and flow of his thoughts would've settled any lingering doubts, except I didn't have any. For the first time in a long time, I was genuinely happy.

My phone buzzed. Ugh. Chanelle.

"This is why you don't talk to people, Charlie." I waved my phone in his face, showing him the invitation to some revolting staff outing. "Pass."

Charlie bapped my phone, further encouraging me to leave the message on read. Hopefully, Chanelle would realize our conversation didn't mean our dynamic had to change. Meh. I'd just ignore her until she got the hint.

Chanelle: Get your ass over here! You can't sit at home all night.
Fine. Guess we'll have this very important impromptu staff meeting without you.
Folks are buddying up for the field trip. I was gonna put our homerooms together but
Thompson makes a pretty good argument. Maybe I'll ride with her kiddos.
Guess that'll leave you with your fav. Peterson.

Me: You're the literal worst.

Chanelle: Come convince me to pair off with you.

I shuddered at the idea of chaperoning with Peterson, but I knew Chanelle too well to believe the idle threat. No way would she endure Thompson just so she could have a laugh at my suffering.

Me: Have fun with Thompson. She's got a mental list of all the academy changes she'd like implemented. Bet she'd love having you all to herself.

Chanelle: 

Me: Sexy cowboys? Now I am jealous.

Chanelle: Asshat!

I spent the rest of the evening playing with Charlie, tossing his favorite toys around the house with the guidance of telekinesis. He loved the hunt almost as much as he loved delivering his bounty and cuddling up for praise on the masterful kill. Carlie, on the other hand—quite literally since I used telekinesis to tease her—wanted nothing to do with playtime. However, she wanted treats, so I provided them.

Milo had been kind enough to buy her an exercise wheel she never used, but we found hovering a treat just out of reach encouraged her to run a few laps. It was a delicate process. The treat couldn't be too far out of reach, or she'd quit, too close, and she'd snap it up. If she ran too long, she'd cry and quit. If she got rewarded too soon, she'd learn to manipulate her way into treats for less effort. That really only worked on Milo, though. He spoiled my tabbies far too much.

As I unwound, I stretched my telepathy far and wide. I hadn't by any means mastered this long-ranged technique, but I'd found better control over casting it toward Milo. Like a large net, my telepathy spread across the city of Chicago, scooping up dozens of passerby thoughts before finally syncing to Milo's mind. The shift from outstretched psychic energy to precision focusing was almost instantaneous, where the net of thoughts vanished as my telepathy threaded to Milo like a needle.

Every time I linked to Milo, there was such a serene buzz that followed. Even when his thoughts were outside the positivity, he maintained for public appeal. Thankfully, this wasn't one of those times. I floated alongside him during the bustle of meetings, the excitement of prepping for upcoming interviews, the dreaded filing of paperwork for cases. It made my evening routine effortless, listening to the podcast of thoughts from the man I loved with all my heart.

While he worked, I graded student assignments and rearranged mini-lessons based on which classes needed to revisit older content, and I even prepared an activity for the field trip. Chanelle pitched it as a learning opportunity, and Milo suggested the kids deserved to walk the halls of a guild. If I was being real with myself, Chanelle and Milo actually saw it as a fun day off for the kids. I could keep it fun. Scavenger hunts were fun. This would be ideal, so my students didn't just fawn over their favorite enchanters.

I'd managed to get through a week's worth of to-dos by the time I checked the clock. Quarter to ten, and Milo still hummed as he worked.

"*Are you seriously spending the entire night at the office?*" I thought as I did my nighttime ritual.

"*That a problem?*" Milo had a minxy grin, figuring my link offered him an invitation to come over.

He had a standing invitation, no matter how annoyed I acted when he showed up unannounced.

"*Only if you barge in at two in the morning, waking me up.*" I hopped into bed. "*Why don't you just make one of your acolytes fill those out?*"

Milo sighed. "*Can't. I've got them working an actual case.*"

"*Sucks to be you.*" I rolled onto my side, shifting my tone and my mood, making sure the right emotion spiked across the city. "*You know what else sucks?*"

"*Oh?*" Milo tilted his head, running a hand up his thigh. A sensual act that sent a wave of his arousal through the link holding our thoughts together. "*Do tell.*"

"Not me at two in the morning."

"Evil!"

I severed the link of magic, making the snap of the tether as loud as possible so Milo would notice. It didn't take long for my phone to vibrate. He might be spending the night at the office, but at least he knew what he was missing. I could feel his excitement, anticipation, and desire all wash over me as I dozed off to the buzz of missed messages that undoubtedly got dirtier with each unanswered reply.

Milo's embrace roused me from sleep, not enough to fully wake, but enough to shiver as his chilled body huddled close to me. The night air clung to Milo, making me clutch my blanket tighter as his cold arms wrapped tighter around my stomach and stole my body heat. He must've flown quickly—even for him—as his ragged breaths took a bit to ease and sync with mine. I wanted to roll over, to say something, maybe even tease him a bit, but it was late. I was exhausted, more so when Milo's groggy mind invaded mine, sending his sleep-deprived thoughts through my head.

Just as I was about to pass out again, wrapped in Milo's bearhug, I heard him sigh. Not aloud. No, his wispy exhales tickled my ear as he nuzzled against the nape of my neck.

This sigh came from within, where he continued working somewhere deep inside the inner core of his mind.

Seriously? Resisting my heavy eyelids, I forced open my eyes, squinting at the bright light of my phone. One in the morning and twelve missed texts from Milo.

I huffed. Now I'd never get back to sleep. Whenever Milo pulled all-nighters, I found it impossible to simply ignore him. My mind craved his peace.

"What are you doing?" I strolled right into his mind, walking past the endlessly high wall of screens. Each one contained a grainy static picture of a vision I couldn't make out. "Hello?"

He called this space his Fateful Viewing of Infinite Possibilities—something he'd never hear me utter out loud. I refused to give him the satisfaction over the absurd name.

Pushing deeper, I reached the second layer of visions where the luminescent board of fates interlocking along infinite pathways dwelled in a circular white room. His Dispatch Board of Destiny. I half expected not to see him, to have to push through to the filing room where he sorted visions like paperwork—funny that his mind created an office space for him, considering how much he actually despised paperwork.

Still, he wasn't there. He stood silently studying a pink pathway. More of a magenta, I supposed. The spectrum of colors was so grand the wall looked like a rainbow yarn conspiracy board.

"Well?" I reiterated my question since I knew Milo heard it. My words echoed loudly through all the chambers of his mind.

"Sorry. Distracted." Milo kept his eyes locked on the strand he studied. "Theodore Whitlock is having his first court appearance soon."

I froze, drawn back to the warlock incursion, my students fighting for their lives, the void vision unfolding and fizzling out, Finn's goodbye, the taste of death in my mouth… I ran my hand along the scar on my neck.

No matter how much I buried the events of that day, the horrors, the slightest mention sent it all flooding back into my mind. "Have

I mentioned how much I despise the fact Gemini assigned our field trip the same day as that?"

"That was my doing." Milo had an apologetic smile, and his eyes had this annoyingly sweet puppy dog effect. "I pushed for it. Really prefer you and your students somewhere safe while Theodore's outside the walls of the MDC."

I huffed. Funny since I didn't think I'd feel truly safe until Theodore Whitlock and his warlocks were behind the heavy wards of a maximum-security prison. A trial would drag on for months, much like setting the date of this sham of a trial intended to prove guilt for something everyone knew he'd done.

"Do you suspect something?" I struggled to ask, frightened of what answer I'd receive. "Did you see something?"

"No. And I wouldn't." Milo continued studying the magenta string. "The MDC is so well-warded that all the inhabitants are challenging to read. Though, given I haven't seen a single fate in the city crossing paths with him or his warlock allies in the future, that should be enough to assuage this feeling."

"Then why doesn't it?"

"My clairvoyance is being blocked or avoided. Hard to say."

"And you suspect he's doing it?"

"Not at all. Maybe. No. I don't know. It's too fuzzy to tell."

The last time someone blocked Milo's clairvoyance, preventing him from reading potential possibilities—making every outcome too fuzzy to interpret—it came from a woman affiliated with Theodore's warlock faction. Darla. She possessed a hex branch known as counter.

Memories of her sparkling blade as it emerged from tiny pocket portals flashed in my mind. The nicks and slashes across my body. It wasn't her branch alone that blocked Milo's magic, though. It required the brands from Vincent, who placed an enchantment of Darla's hex onto all those aligned with them in the months Theodore Whitlock spent conspiring to overthrow his father and destroy the guild industry he considered tainted and corrupt.

"Whoa." Milo cocked his head, smirking. A carefree expression hiding his concern. "You're thinking aloud. Or is it because you're in my head?"

"Both."

"It's not Darla Monroe." He plucked an olive-green string. "Her paths are blurred but there, meaning her hex isn't at play. She's very much detained. And based on the charges the state has for her actions prior to joining the warlock incursion, I'm surprised they didn't toss her right into a maximum-security prison. Guess everyone's entitled to their day in court."

"Is this the work of other warlocks making a move with the upcoming trial?" I asked hesitantly. "A few months ago, during your investigation with the demons, you stumbled onto a faction of warlocks—would be warlocks, whatever—who idolized Theodore Whitlock's revolt against the guild system."

He'd faced them when seeking intel from Cassidy Gardner outside her club. It seemed so inconsequential, but they'd used enchantments to block his psychic branch. Not strong or durable like Darla's counter hex, but enough to evade Milo's clairvoyance all the same.

"Unlikely. Since getting the guilds back to collaborating, I've been passing intel to Kraken so they could get the glory of squashing rogue warlocks."

"Could there be other factions who…who are… I don't know." I lingered on what I wanted to ask.

"I don't think so. I'm not even sure how or why it'd involve the warlock incursion. Just grasping at straws because of the timing with the trial, and I can't seem to make a connection elsewhere."

Fuck. This was what I got for doubting the world was conspiring against me for a full fucking minute. Containing my aggravation and concern and anxiety, which'd looped to Milo's encroaching dread, I took a deep breath and sent the most calming energy his way as I possibly could.

"Relax." Milo stepped close, rubbing his hands up and down my arms.

"What's happening?" I asked, remaining pensive, not paranoid.

"There's someone skirting my magic."

"Someone or something?" I swallowed hard. "Something demonic?"

My heart hammered in my chest so intensely it nearly pulled me from Milo's mind. He steadied me here in his inner core.

Very few things avoided Milo's visions, but resisting branch magics came easily to demons. They were deadly and dangerous and nearly destroyed Chicago when one sought to make me his new host body. His perfect host. I was a fool to believe with the devil dead, the threat of new demons surfacing in the city was over. Was it a small, random threat? With demons, no such thing existed. Was it one that'd survived the slaughter when the guild witches united against the chimera and his forces? I had believed Milo had ended every single threat that day.

He believed he had ended them all, too. How I so wanted to believe the horrors of our past were gone. How I wanted to believe new threats like this trial with Theodore Whitlock meant nothing. How I wanted to believe my students wouldn't cling to their grief, how students like Jamie wouldn't be locked in hellish trauma, how friends like Chanelle wouldn't lose themselves to the same guilt that consumed me for so long. I wanted to ignore the bad, fake it until I made it, and live the happily ever after Milo promised.

"Not demonic. Not really their MO."

"Then what is it? Not demonic. Not a hex at play."

"I really don't know. I thought it was a really bad void vision at first, the type that didn't even come with a grainy image, just a nagging feeling. Something in the corner of my eye, but when I turn to look, it's gone." Milo shrugged. "It's like someone is walking around the edges of my visions, almost as if they know them."

"How?" I couldn't even see Milo's visions.

"No idea." Milo pointed to the magenta string.

"The obsessive side of me wants you to work, to remain vigilant on any potential threats, but another part of me knows there will always be something lurking in this world." While standing close to Milo in his inner core, my body outside turned over, and I buried my sleeping head in the crook of his shoulder. "Another part of me wonders if this is actually intentional. Is a danger really out there dodging The Inevitable Future's clairvoyance, or is it just a coincidence? Are you afraid that maybe things have gone too well? Too calmly? Are you searching for any possibility of someone or something interfering with those happy futures you work so hard to create?"

Letting go of Finn, accepting Milo, and looking to the future I still had all helped strip away the pricklier sides of who I was, the paranoid side, the part that constantly worried if I wasn't looking over my shoulder for danger at all times than it'd swoop in and harm those I cared most about in life.

"I can't see everything and everyone, but I've had my branch wound throughout Chicago for close to a decade. Nothing accidentally or coincidently avoids my magic. Not the brightest successes, the foulest hearts, or the seemingly mundane. I observe it all, ensure paths converge to the best possible outcome." Milo's serious expression crumbled away, transforming into a sweet smile. "Get some rest, Dorian. Your field trips coming up, right? You gotta be presentable when you bring the kiddos to Cerberus."

"You know I'm not going to be able to sleep with you working all night, running yourself into the ground."

"I'm fine. Really. Still catching my beauty rest, don't you worry." Outside his mind, Milo's sleeping body hugged me tighter. Whether on instinct or instruction, he wanted to reassure me, like cuddling would wash away my anxiety. Admittedly, it helped some.

"If you don't sleep, I don't sleep." I crossed my arms, firmly making my stance inside Milo's mind. "So, if you have a theory, let's hear it. Sometimes, the best way to work out a problem is to share it."

"That one of your teaching approaches?"

"As a matter of fact." I frowned, fighting back a smile because if I smiled every time Milo made me happy, the muscles of my face would break from being overjoyed. "All right. You suspect the upcoming trial. That's not grasping. You have a reason to feel it. You always do."

"I've always suspected Theodore might cause trouble, even after being detained. But like I said, Kraken Guild has helped pick up the slack there. They've been instrumental in keeping tabs on the MDC."

"But?"

"I don't know where to even begin."

"How about where this feeling first started?"

"I first noticed it on Cassidy's pathway. A blip then gone."

His mind had drifted onto Cassidy weeks ago during our double date. Had he been carrying this fear for that long? Had I been so wrapped up in my own happiness that I overlooked it?

"Looking back, there are others where it's happened." Milo pointed to a blue string, a red one, and a violet one far off on the opposite end of the board. "Yet no one is connected anywhere, and nothing has happened. Nothing I'm aware of. I'm having trouble pinpointing what's going to happen, what the goal is, but this level of caution suggests something truly nefarious."

Ignoring my own paranoia, I listened intently, hoping any little bit helped Milo piece together the scattered thoughts entwined with futures he couldn't make sense of.

Chapter Seventeen

Doppler

Milo's magic searched for me, hunting me, seeking out the mystery being that dwelled at the edges of his visions. The touch of his psychic branch elicited a quiver deep within the confines of this current host body, so much so even Ronald's sour scowl softened when he arrived at work.

I lingered close to the door housing Finn and pressed my hands firmly against the metallic surface as I cast waves of slumber to allow him to rest through the horrors I'd soon unveil. Every fiber of my being wanted to step inside and explain it all to Finn, seek his guidance that came with a history of knowledge on magical warfare. But he wasn't ready yet. Hiding my presence from Milo's clairvoyance ached. All I wanted was to reach out and wrap myself in the touch of his magical embrace. Not yet. Soon. Soon, I'd have the men who belonged to me.

"With me," I muttered, pressing my ear to the door where Finn slept. "You belong *with* me."

Taking my leave, I rose to the highest heights of C.O. Kowalski's mind, who sluggishly made his way into the cellblock where Theodore stayed. The thoughts of my host were fogged over, crumbling to dust every time I took hold of his active mind. It couldn't be helped.

Everything had finally culminated in this moment. I'd studied Theodore's mind enough to force my hold over him—at least long enough to control his branch and eradicate the chimera—and not a moment too soon.

"Whitlock, you're coming with me."

"Finally." He shivered, clicking his teeth with juvenile anticipation.

Leaning into C.O. Kowalski's gruff attitude, I instructed him to reel it back, then led him to the Prisoner Holding Area.

Once inside the small, warded chamber, two other guards awaited. One stood at a switchboard, reading the standard guidelines about exiting the MDC, asking questions based on protocol while double checking the sigils were aligned to contain Theodore's casting frequency. The other performed a full-body search on Theodore. After ensuring he held no threat when leaving for the courthouse, the guard waited for Theodore to redress. Then he placed a set of cuffs around his ankles and wrists, using a long chain to shackle and limit his mobility.

"Kowalski." The other C.O. indicated my role. A small, vital opportunity.

Reaching for the keys I carried, I did as I was commanded and prepared to unlock the dampening cuff that bound Theodore Whitlock's casting efforts. The sigils lining the silver bracelet were specially crafted to bind his branch but were still too strong for my own magic to supersede, which meant breaking into his thoughts would be a futile effort unless I timed this exactly right.

I had one minute while his mind lay free, and his magic remained unbound.

Dampening cuffs were strongest when designed with a home base location, a spot where their energy could easily be rejuvenated. The cuffs worn in the MDC were imbued by the enchantments lining the walls of every cellblock—this detainment chamber included. He'd be issued a separate set during his transport and a final pair when bound in the courthouse.

A minute might seem relatively short, but for dangerous warlocks, some only required mere seconds to wreak havoc. The sigils lining the walls all focused on Theodore Whitlock's channeling frequency, ready to inform of any casting discrepancies so the guards could strike him down. They wouldn't detect my movements, my frequency, so long as I remained cautious.

The biggest issue here came down to containing Theodore once I leapt into his body, which was why I spent weeks observing him, learning his history, his strengths, his fears, and his failures, all while avoiding his detection. He had an exceptional understanding of psychic energy, so once inside his head, I'd hurl every ounce of doubt this psychopath buried and lock him within the confines of his own mind.

Would it be enough to strike him down before the guards placed the next set of dampening cuffs on his wrists and synced it with the sigils of his transport vehicle?

I unlocked Theodore's dampener cuff, revealing his bare wrist where ink had indented his skin. The timer began. The next cuff couldn't be placed until the residue vanished. It was basically a semi-permanent tattoo that sort of reminded me of the sticker lick-on tattoos Dorian's students used to wear. Well, back when they were trendy in what seemed like a lifetime ago. I hadn't thought about that first batch of students in forever.

"Happy to see me gone, Kowalski?"

"Huh?" I furrowed my brow, replacing the smile that'd inadvertently taken hold.

Theodore cocked his head, thoughts twisting into snide comments he didn't want to press his luck by uttering aloud. Even he knew not to gamble with his chances of stepping outside the MDC. One false move, and he'd be remanded to isolation.

Now came the difficult part; I had to unleash my current host and overtake Theodore's mind. It'd take all my magic, but I'd bombard him with so much psychic energy he'd never recover, not even after I abandoned his body. Ronald would be too weary to react, but I'd need to deal with the two guards swiftly so they didn't interfere. I trembled as I stepped to the edge of this mind, about to leap into the ether of the world without Finn.

I'd only be abandoning Finn for a few minutes, but I couldn't risk dragging him and the chimera into Theodore's mind. Once I had full control of his branch, I'd command the chimera to release Finn, remove the threads that bound their connection, and unravel its demonic energy from the piece of Finn's consciousness that still held life.

I'd pull Finn out, exorcise and banish the demon, and then leave this forsaken hellhole with Finn at my side.

"Quite the plan, puppet." The chimera's voice echoed from the box where I kept him contained.

I lingered at the edges of Ronald's mind, double-checking the confinement of his prison. Every blade remained in place, and the box itself was reinforced with enough magic to contain him until I'd unraveled his connection. It'd hold. It'd hold long enough to see this through.

Leaving all my fear behind in this host body, I leapt out, lunging for Theodore's mind.

"Quite the plan indeed." Theodore turned his attention toward the empty air where my psychic energy floated.

Did he see me? Impossible.

"Anything's possible if you put your mind to it." Theodore opened his mouth wide. A white light flickered from within his throat, illuminating the bulge of his Adam's apple, and a tiny ball floated out of his mouth.

A wisp.

How'd he acquire demonic energy? When?

"That'd be my doing." The chimera clawed at his box, making Ronald twitch.

As the chimera wriggled loose from the blades embedded through him and fought to break from his box, I leapt back into Ronald's mind and barreled toward the chimera, unconcerned that such an invasive burst of psychic energy would rattle Ronald's entire being. I had to stop the chimera in his tracks while the other guards contained Theodore. Forcing Ronald's beleaguered body into obedience, I shouted through him. "Stop his casting!"

The wisp sprang ahead into the mouth of the guard by the switchboard.

"Detain him," I repeated before sinking into the darkness of the subconscious.

Instead of listening, the second guard went to aid the gasping officer. He wheezed, each breath making his face turn red as his throat swelled like a frog.

"That sonic branch isn't doing you much good, is it?" Theodore snickered. "It's a perfect feeding frenzy for my little friend, though."

The guard's face turned a deep purple before his head erupted, blood and tar glimmering as the last fragments of the wisp transcended into a fiendish form the size of a rat with enough limbs to make a centipede blush.

"Free me," Theodore ordered.

The tiny fiend leapt from the falling body and gnawed on the shackles holding him in place.

"Who am I to defy such a command?" The chimera cackled, his body rumbling with such force it cracked and tore at Ronald's insides.

Every ounce of demonic energy expanded tenfold, sending sludge circulating through Ronald's veins and feeding on the magic to further magnify the chimera's indomitable ferocity.

Ooze burst from every orifice of Ronald, tearing him apart from the inside, flooding the entirety of his mind. Everything I did to contain the demon failed. His thoughts weren't his own, fading into something primal and fiend-like. Most of his demonic energy spilled out into the holding cell. Tar bubbled and popped into white wisps, which quickly went to work, eating away at the enchantment sigils lining the walls.

With a wave of his hand, Theodore slammed all three guards against the wall. His telekinesis didn't waver for a second, unyielding and immobilizing me as I unraveled my mind from the broken, dying receptors of Ronald Kowalski's body.

I had to grab Finn. Drag him out, take the chimera as far from Theodore as possible. Reaching the door where I kept him safely tucked away, I found tar blocking my path. Banishment cleared it away. I rushed inside the empty hospital room.

Empty.

My body trembled.

"Finn?" I shouted as the illusion I painted for him evaporated, eaten away by tar funneling into this tiny sanctuary.

"*I shall miss you, puppet.*" The chimera's thoughts surfaced above the frenzy of the fiend that'd leapt from Ronald. Was Finn with him?

I fought my way through the demonic energy, banishing it in waves as black tendrils lunged forward, gripping me, eating my psychic magic, dragging me deeper into the depths of this hollowed-out mind.

"*I'll send Dorian your love. You were right. Breaking Dorian is the best way to take hold of his mind; however, Finn's survival, facing the guilt of failing him yet again when you planned to burst into his thoughts unfettered by my being—that wasn't the way to break Dorian Frost. Oh, no. I have much better plans for my perfect host.*"

How? How'd he do this?

I sank deep into the subconscious of the dying Ronald, bound to the body as I fended off demonic energy still circulating through this form, devouring all the magic and leaving nothing but rot and waste in its trail.

A few wispy fragments of thoughts lingered by the broken scraps of the box I'd conjured, lying free and exposed. They fed on the magic of the prison I made. Deep in the darkness of Ronald's mind, the chimera didn't whisper horrors but suggestions.

"*You're not the only telepath, puppet. While you studied Theodore, I conspired. A soft suggestion here, a manipulation there.*"

When?

And the moment revealed itself: the nick on Ronald's arm from Vincent's tattoo kit. A jab that pooled with blood and ink. Only it wasn't ink. The black blob was a tiny inkling of fiendish tar that'd transformed into a meager wisp and fluttered away. I was so fixated on containing the chimera and reeling back Ronald's wrath, I'd missed it entirely. But not now.

I could see his guarded thoughts so crisply.

I was a fool. He'd fluttered away in the form of a wisp, found Theodore before me, fed the psychotic warlock his energy, filled with whispers of my intentions.

"Dorian, Dorian, what's happening?" Finn's voice called out frantically. Startled by the shock of being ripped from the safety only I could give him.

I clawed my way to the surface, tearing through mountains of demonic energy standing in my path, doing everything I could to escape this corpse.

Two wisps fluttered around Theodore as demonic energy continued gnawing at my magic. It severed any connection I had to Finn's thoughts, any hold I held over the chimera, any chance I had of achieving the happily ever after I so desperately craved.

With the fiend of the chimera at Theodore's side and access to his magics, he'd be too formidable.

I failed. I failed Finn.

My knees buckled at the edge of this void of a mind, finding escape impossible. Pointless. I let the darkness of death and demonic energy swallow my very being.

Chapter Eighteen

Chaos. Pure and foul. The crunch of death that littered the ground only added to my growing headache. I huffed. Maybe I was being a bit dramatic as I eyed students stomping about, crushing the withered leaves that started to fall, but getting them organized for this field trip was a disaster. They completely broke apart from their groups and reformed into a huge blob one might mistakenly call a crowd. Whichever administrator had the bright idea of sending all the second-years down to the buses at the same time instead of calling homerooms one by one could go fuck themself. Hard.

Rounding students up was worse than herding cats. At least with Charlie and Carlie, I knew what to expect. Not my homeroom students. Oh no, they delighted in surprising me with new trends. The Gaels were usually my go-tos when it came to leading the class single-file anywhere we went on campus, but Kenzo was having none of that—so he tore Gael away, and they wandered toward the back of the line, which quickly deteriorated once Gael Rios-Vega spotted Tiffany and abandoned our class.

Caleb had many talents, but leading the class line wasn't one of them. He absentmindedly bumped into a few students from another class while reading from one of his textbooks. Katherine, Melanie, and Layla had wandered off to a large group of girls who all couldn't be bothered to muster even a modicum of enthusiasm. Not sure if they were all actually so above a boring office field trip or if a few dominant minds hadn't led the charge to enjoying anything educational automatically resulted in losing cool credit or whatever the fuck bounced around Layla's head as she cemented herself in the center of the group with Chanelle's top-hitter Amani.

I made my way to the bus with the only three students who bothered following my directions: Carter, Jennifer, and Jamius. Everyone else slowly drifted through the sea of second-year students using this time to talk to friends outside of class, plan ways to switch which bus they were assigned, or simply waste time—successfully, I might add—since it ensured we'd be back late, and they wouldn't have to attend an afternoon class.

Cerberus had sent the acolytes to help organize the students even though most stood idle as teachers wrangled students. And I mean every acolyte at their guild, even the ones assigned to enchanters who'd refused to hand over their charges for the purpose of instruction. Well, not everyone. Per usual, Acolyte Russo was late. He'd probably get to campus by the time we arrived at Cerberus. Then again, the chaos would certainly delay our departure. Acolyte Novak and Reed each positioned themselves by our bus. At least Reed greeted the students when they hopped on; Novak simply scowled, clearly aggravated she'd been put on babysitting duty.

Seeing the acolytes ignited my concerns for Milo. Since our conversation, he'd spent nearly all his time working, looking for a threat I wasn't entirely sure existed. Wishful thinking on my part. Today of all days, I desperately wanted Enchanter Evergreen to be wrong. I hoped Theodore pled guilty and saved everyone the horror of reliving his actions through a lengthy trial. I hoped whatever person stalked Milo's clairvoyance proved to be a figment of an overworked guild witch who simply needed another vacation.

Me: How's the stakeout going?

I contemplated sending a stick emoji or grilled meat, but neither properly conveyed the pun, but after a week of him working, planning contingencies, avoiding me, I wanted to send more than just a question.

"*This is going to take for-fucking-ever.*" Chanelle sighed, making her way to the bus we were sharing. "We're supposed to leave in ten minutes. Does no one read my emails?"

"Pretty sure it's that none of the kids actually listened when we told them which bus to get on." I stuffed my phone into my pocket. No sense waiting for a message that wouldn't arrive.

"Listen up, everyone," Chanelle shouted in some futile effort to draw attention. It didn't work. Not with six hundred students roaming all over the parking lot.

I could abandon her, sneak off for a cigarette because I had more than enough time for a smoke given the sluggish rate the students moved at, yet I had this annoying nagging chord that struck. Was this empathy? For Chanelle's plans gone awry? Ugh. I shuddered. It was fucking awful.

"*Listen up.*" I linked my telepath to about thirty kids. "*Right now, we're trying to file onto the buses. The longer you take to get on the bus, the longer I'm going to have to stay inside your head, pestering you to follow the directions. Do you want me in your head? Pretty sure about half of you are a moment away from thinking about that really embarrassing time you did something you definitely don't want your history teacher—who has a long memory—to know about.*"

After a handful of frightened gulps, a half dozen eyerolls, and hearing the word cringe muttered more times than I could count, as well as one very loud "fuck you," I abandoned their minds and sent the same message to a second group of students.

Rinse and repeat my meanest telepathic voice, and in a matter of five minutes, I'd wrangled every student onto their assigned bus.

"That's what I'm talking about." Chanelle raised her hand to high-five me, convinced she'd pulled this off with her teacher voice. "You know, you could've helped."

I simply frowned at her and got onto the bus.

The bus filled up with mine and Chanelle's students. My head hurt from linking to everyone's mind, even in batches, so I let Chanelle take attendance.

"Whoa, you got a tattoo?" Jamius asked, eyeing Gael, who stood in the seat beside his as he scrolled through his phone.

"Yep. King Clucks knows a guy." Gael grinned. "Best. Birthday. Present. Ever."

"Please tell me this wasn't some basement parlor." I groaned, having the misfortune of sitting within earshot.

"Of course not." Gael beamed. "Only the best right here."

"You're sixteen. Who's gonna give you a tattoo?" I glowered, resigned not to search for an answer as Gael's thoughts twisted into the absurd.

“What’d you get?” Carter asked.

“Where’s it at?” Jamius followed up.

“Kind of hard to show in my uniform, but I’ve got pics.”

I turned away as Jamius, Carter, Harrison, and a handful of other students all moved in closer, hanging over their seats, to see the tattoo. A decision they’d undoubtedly regret based on the minxy surface thoughts weaving around Gael’s head.

“Dude!” Jamius shouted. “The hell?”

“Why?” Harrison fought the intense urge to throw a potion in his eyes, but that wouldn’t wash away the memory forever seared in his thoughts.

“It’s just a picture of your ass.” Carter laughed. “What’s wrong with you?”

“No, my tattoo’s right there. See.”

“I’m not looking,” Jamius said.

“It’s a snowflake,” Gael clarified.

“And why do you have a snowflake on your butt?” Carter asked.

“So anyone lucky enough to see me in all my glory knows this ass is one of a kind.”

Too many students started laughing, almost as loud as the rooster’s clucks of validation, which further heightened Gael’s need for attention. This was going to be a long day.

“Man, Enchanter Evergreen’s not even gonna be here!” Gael Martinez pouted; the light of his phone reflected against the spikes on his face as they swelled from his deepened frown.

“What’re you talking about?” Gael flung himself across the aisle, legs planted on his seat as his arms braced his position on the back of another seat while his body stretched across the bus like the worst fucking cat so he could snoop at Gael’s phone.

"Enchant Track says he's all the way on the West Side."

The West Side, more specifically outside the Metropolitan Detainment Center, where he awaited Theodore Whitlock's departure to the courthouse.

"That app's always wrong." Gael gestured, almost falling as he released one hand, but he caught himself just before plummeting face-first onto the aisle of the bus. "Besides, he could make that flight in five minutes flat."

"I think he's working a case, which means no Evergreen." Gael sighed; utter disappointment followed his heavy exhale. "*¿Qué sentido tiene ir si Evergreen no está allí?*"

"Sucks, but at least there'll still be some cool enchanters there, including Guild Master Campbell." Gael grinded while keeping himself braced on the seats, thoughts twisting into the completely perverse as his imagination of Campbell ran wild.

I flicked my hand, telekinetically gripping Gael, who panicked when he suddenly floated above the seats, limbs flailing. His rooster clucked furiously, half-convinced Gael dared levitate in his presence—which was a reminder I still needed to find a solution for that issue—but Gael's protests made it clear this wasn't his doing.

"There are safety precautions in place for a reason, Gael." I shifted my hand, sending him plopping back into his seat. "The next time you think about climbing over seats, don't!"

The jostle of the bus made me queasy, and gripping the leather of the seat didn't ease the ride. It didn't take long for my telepathy to wander, seeking a reprieve from the bustle of the bus, seeking answers on Enchanter Evergreen's case.

I eagerly followed the thread, wanting to know Milo was doing well since our conversation.

I blinked. Fire and blood flooded my vision, a filter of carnage painting a frame of death over all the students on the bus. Tensing, I tried to settle my frantic nerves as they synced to Milo's muscles. His body was stiff and unmoving. I couldn't hear his thoughts. I couldn't hear any thoughts as the tether that bound us over such a distance snagged and tightened.

Gasping for breath, I quelled my telepathy.

Where was Milo? What was happening to him?

"Are you okay, Mr. Frost?" Jamie Novak had this pained sincerity in his eyes as he was the only student not lost in conversation or music or staring at their phone.

I looked at his concerned expression, watching the filter of blood and flame shift into a splotchy, tarlike image.

"I'm fine." I turned away, delving deeper into the hollow thoughts around me, snapping this horrible link so I could see more.

I hovered above the empty mind that'd reeled my magic close, terrified of what had befallen Milo. Taking a shaky breath, I exhaled with relief once the face I hovered above revealed itself. This wasn't Milo. It wasn't anyone I knew.

My telepathy ached, testing the limitations of this bizarre bond to some random person in a small white room. Demonic energy poured out of his nose, mouth, ears, and eyes and oozed down his chest, where I saw the glimmer of a name tag before tar ate away at it.

Ronald Kowalski.

Who the hell was that? And why was my telepathy latched to his mind?

Clenching my teeth, I resisted leaving. I couldn't abandon this witch, this place, until I understood why my telepathy had gone haywire and attached itself to some unknown mind in such a horrid state. It wasn't easy; it was like the push of magnets from the same pole fighting against making contact. I'd never experienced such a force when linking to a mind. It actively tried to push my telepathy away. It was like someone or something identified my specific frequency and didn't want me here. Wherever here was.

Searching my surroundings, I saw several broken sigils lining the walls. Warding magic was meant to prevent casting. Perhaps that was where the pounding pulse against my telepathy stemmed. They were damaged but still functional in the most chaotic sense. I couldn't gain my bearings, searching for the source that had invited my magic from across the city.

This outstretched link, pulled far beyond its limits, had become a familiar sensation since I'd learned about the development in my branch when syncing to Milo's mind, yet this bond offered no comfort from the tumultuous world.

"*Well, well, well.*" The eerie hum of the most hateful mind I'd ever experienced rang through my head. "*I knew there was something familiar about your telepathy. I never forget a psychic's touch.*"

I spun around this blood and tar-splattered room, my vision fluttering in every direction and making it difficult to navigate, to ground myself, to comprehend the carnage. Carnage. That was what this was. Three slaughtered bodies lay strewn on the floor, including the one my telepathy connected to—somehow, impossibly. A swarm of tiny fiends crawled along the walls; they devoured the magic dripping from the sigils, they lapped at the blood spilling onto the floor, and they tore apart the hinges of the bolted doors on either side. Finally, my mind settled, the swirling round and round ceased, and my sight rippled around the most terrifying warlock I'd ever encountered.

Theodore Whitlock.

I hovered behind him, watching the destruction he commanded while simultaneously finding myself buried inside a corpse beneath the fiend that'd burst from the chest and now gnawed on broken bones protruding outward.

My chest tightened like I was drowning in the tar funneling out of the guard. Every attempt to figure out what was going on, see more inside this room, and escape this bizarre, rippled effect on my sight was met with splotchy black spots.

Sludge obscured my vision, yet my line of sight bounced back and forth like staring at Theodore between a set of mirrors infinitely reflecting their image off each other. It was like my telepathy had collided in on itself while collapsing all at once.

What the fuck was happening? I hadn't experienced anything like this since summoning a manifestation, the two of us staring back at one another, but this wasn't that. It couldn't be since I no longer had the ability to create extensions of my branch in such a way.

Theodore stood tall with a proud smile on his face as he turned around, facing my psychic presence. "*Do you remember the sweet embrace of my mind, Dorian Frost?*"

He reached out, touching the empty air, searching for my magic that'd sought him above all else. Milo was right. Theodore had horrible plans; his surface thoughts were painted with murder and mayhem and such unbearable hatred it almost broke my mind, staring into the abyss of his being.

"Dorian." The touch frightened me as if he would grab my telepathy in the air before him and steal me, drag me to where he was, kill me. "Dorian."

Chanelle shook me. "Dorian. Christ. You listening?"

I blinked away the image of Theodore, finding my magic completely quelled as I returned to the bus, which had stopped. All the students had filed off, and only Chanelle remained.

"I-I need to make a call." I fished my phone out of my pocket. "I'll be inside soon."

"You okay?" Chanelle quirked a brow.

"Yeah, just a headache."

"Take your time." She strutted down the aisle to exit the bus, turning with a second-guessing look before shifting back true to form. "But don't hide out here the whole time. No slacking or pawning your tour group off to someone else."

Chanelle played it cool, yet I already glimpsed her piecing together rearrangements for who to send my group with. She'd split everyone up into small groups with either a teacher or acolyte chaperone so we could tour the facility in sections without six hundred kids piling on top of each other in one room at a time. Not that sending six hundred students off in different directions helped much.

My call went straight to voicemail.

There was one way I could contact Milo to ensure he knew what Theodore had done, but the idea of accidentally linking to Theodore and tasting death in my mouth again sent an unnerving tremble through my body. I steadied the terror, the horror. It didn't make sense why my telepathy latched to Theodore in the first place. Maybe it had to do with how much concern I really carried about the warlock, the trial, everything I ignored, and repressed trauma bubbling to the surface demanding answers.

I swallowed every ounce of trepidation and cast a wide net of telepathy across the city, ignoring the sea of minds. Once I'd spotted Milo's frequency, the calm in the storm, I tightened my branch and synced to him.

He walked out of the MDC unscathed, unconcerned, and unhappy. Not what I expected to find, but the aggravation he carried outweighed the horrors I'd seen minutes earlier. Milo—correction, Enchanter Evergreen—eyed the team of enchanters he'd assembled outside the MDC. They stood posted in the back of the building, surrounding the armored van meant to transport Theodore to the courthouse.

Casting his sensory, Milo searched for nearby demonic energy. "Did you all handle the fiends summoned?"

"For the most part. A few skittered away, but I'll get my acolytes to patrol the area later," an enchanter said with a sour tone, completely unfazed by the events that had unfolded and coping an attitude with Enchanter Evergreen. "You know, after that field trip you and Campbell dragged them away for."

"Find the demonic energy and remove it now." The curtness in Milo's voice held a sharp edge.

"It's just a few fiends."

"I don't care. I don't want a damn thing Theodore Whitlock conjured stepping foot in the city." Milo balled a fist but released the building rage by casting another wave of sensory in the surrounding area, ready and willing to finish the job.

Rolling his eyes, the enchanter flew off with another person to scour the neighborhood for tiny fiends that he didn't believe would pose any more threat than a handful of wisps.

"*Are you okay?*" I called out, unable to observe Milo in silence a second longer.

"*Figured you'd be attaching yourself to my thoughts today.*" A natural, carefree smirk crept from the corners of Milo's cheeks. "*Guess you're more obsessed than you tried to play it off.*"

"*I know—*"

"*Theodore tried something, which I suspected. Campbell tried to get us in the MDC as escorts, but the warden made assurances his team could handle it.*" Milo's expression and mind went blank, suppressing the bodies he walked in on, but I filled in the pieces from my own encounter. "*There were injuries, to say the least.*"

"*You don't have to sugarcoat it. I saw what he did.*"

"*And here I thought I was keeping the gory details under wraps.*"

I didn't know how to tell him my mind had linked to Theodore Whitlock. Well, not his exactly. I couldn't make much sense of it right now.

"*Theodore didn't think this through.*" Milo's thoughts pulled me from my own. "*The fiends he summoned weren't enough to face one enchanter, let alone the team I had. The only real shocking part of today was that he surrendered without putting up a fight.*"

That didn't sit well with Milo, believing the arrogance of a warlock who challenged a city surely wouldn't give up because the odds were stacked against him. Yet, Milo took solace in the fact Theodore's actions had now left him boxed in isolation behind a hundred different layers of warding sigils without a chance of leaving for his court hearing. Whatever moment of hesitation struck Theodore Whitlock when confronted by enchanters outside the MDC had ended this threat before it ever truly became one.

"*Relax, Dorian. Enjoy the field trip,*" Milo thought. "*Theodore's been detained.*"

Nothing involving Theodore Whitlock would ever allow me to relax.

Chapter Nineteen

Doppler

Is this death?

I floated in a black abyss, hollowed out of every fabricated sensation that I'd clung to in my short, miserable existence with only a few fleeting thoughts to keep me company.

Dead. I expected it to come with a collision back into Dorian's subconscious. I predicted if I ever met such an unfortunate outcome, I'd at least have the satisfaction of rattling that weakling's mind to the very core, breaking it beyond repair as he tasted the memories of ten thousand visions I held, insight on the true extent of his branch, and the truth that his manifestation was twice the man he'd ever hope to be.

"It's that hubris that brought you here, puppet." The snark mixed with false sincerity fueled my rage.

Fuck. I wasn't dead. The fiend had devoured me and brought me into the clutches of the chimera's new body.

"Wrong," he whispered from the shadows. Slow, slithering darkness that wriggled across each other with the faintest distinctions in their black shades. Some faded, some sheen. "The fiend didn't devour you. Merely ate away some of your magic. Couldn't have you putting up a fight in our temporary home."

"Why didn't you just kill me?"

"You already answered your question." The chimera chuckled. "Can't chance you tipping Dorian off that I'm still here. You offered me the most fortuitous of second chances, and I intend to see this opportunity through the right way."

"What are you planning?"

"Currently?" A clawed hand plunged through the darkness and snatched me up.

I gasped, choking on tar filling my lungs as I came up for air on the surface of more darkness. Not the same pitch-black horrors below, but a dimly lit inner core. Dank, rotten, and filled with despair. This wasn't the demon's inner core but some tragic, depressing mind.

"Like you're one to talk. You don't even have an inner core." The judgment in the demon's gaze as he wore the same mortal face I'd kept him confined to for months unnerved me. No, annoyed me. Bastard traipsed about, masquerading himself in the same human flesh he so desperately wanted to make a reality. "More a reality for me than you, puppet."

"Get out of my fucking thoughts!"

"Make them less transparent, and I wouldn't read them with such ease."

I had guarded against his telepathy, against all his magics, yet he still played me. Now, I sat in the mind of someone completely stripped of my strength and bound to the bidding of the very demon I'd tried to purge from Finn.

Finn. I clenched my teeth. How I so desperately wanted to ask what became of him, but I knew the answer. The chimera had buried him somewhere in this pit of darkness, this sea of tar.

Instead, I kept my mouth shut and studied the mind we were inside. This wasn't Theodore's mind. It had a haunting hate but not worn with pride. No, the envious sort of hate bottled and pushed to the outskirts of a mind trying not to be consumed, yet the rot of it had done years of damage. That much I could tell with a single glance. The demonic energy circulating inside this mind would only add more horrors once it'd fully seeped through.

The chimera stepped toward a viewing room of his making, allowing us to peer through the eyes of whatever host body he'd picked.

"Not a host body."

I scoffed. I hated having him in my head, sniffing out every passing thought.

"Consider yourself lucky someone finds you and your shallow thoughts remotely interesting."

We hovered to the height of the surface, standing at the peak of Peter Graham's thoughts as he anxiously awaited the guards to check him over. One by one, they cast sensory on every inmate filed in line. They searched every crevice of every cell, with an extra methodical touch on those affiliated with Theodore Whitlock.

I expected to find a bloodbath among the cellblocks, a riot, chaos, and death, but everything had been contained.

"As it should be," the chimera said. "The best victories in waged wars come after allowing a foe to win a battle."

"Why jump into Peter Graham?" He had Theodore. He had the exit of the MDC at his fingertips. He had access to my mind and magic. Surely, all of that would've allowed him an opportunity to escape, to seek out Dorian, and do the unspeakable—gain the perfect host he sought for centuries of scouring this world.

"That's your problem. Impatient and arrogant. I knew, even from my limited vantage, there wasn't a single future in which Theodore Whitlock walked out of the MDC unscathed. I explained if he attempted to break free, something you observed him already plotting, then he'd fail. His plan would fail because Enchanter Evergreen had already predicted it, planned for it, and had put checkmate in motion before the Whitlock moved his first pawn. So, he's waiting. He helped me, and soon, I'll help him. Unlike you, he heeds the warnings of his betters, so with my suggestion, he painted a beautiful commotion."

Tar bubbled and popped, revealing images of fiends causing a frenzy, Theodore boasting against authority, a tiny wisp slipping between the guards back into the trenches of the cellblocks, and finally, Theodore surrendering himself without resistance.

"I believe the magicians of old called it a sleight of hand."

"Why not flee?"

"And risk being banished with the onslaught of fiends summoned? I think not. Best to maintain a low profile."

I studied the guards approaching a fidgety Peter, each easy prey for a strong telepath. Not that I possessed the magic to untangle myself from the chimera in my current state. I felt him settled inside the fabric of my being, pulse beating as he absorbed my essence like a slow rot.

"Why not jump into a guard?"

I awaited their sensory to sniff out our presence looming at the surface of Peter's mind.

A quick search and nothing. They moved on.

"We are but a wisp of demonic energy, barely noticed and requiring the truest of talent."

Peter watched the guards scrutinize and search those possessing tattoos gifted from Vincent, links that made them allies of Theodore Whitlock. For the first time since arriving at the MDC, Peter Graham was grateful he didn't have friends.

"I got the idea of housing us in Peter from you. Your comprehension of his branch was thorough, and I can make use of it," the chimera said. "While you were busy studying Theodore, I was befriending him, searching through the knowledge of our previous host, and feeding your ego with false attempts of escape, mishaps, or arrogance on my part. Mortals—even fake reflections of them such as yourself—are quite simple-minded and easily misled."

He smiled, his mind unveiling all his wicked machinations.

Peter had a powerful branch, but most importantly, he had no friends and posed no threat to staff or inmates. A soft suggestion to Theodore, and suddenly, Peter found himself off everyone's radar for the next few weeks. Weeks. The chimera didn't want Peter's branch but his access outside of the MDC. He wanted a host that'd walk out the door unsuspecting.

"Now, you're getting it. Enchanter Evergreen will undoubtedly have himself and others patrolling the guards, the facility, watching and waiting for the other shoe to drop."

"And when it doesn't, the interest will shift to more pressing cases, and you'll stroll out of here then fully possess Peter Graham's body."

"Precisely. Soon, we'll leave, I will be restored, Dorian will be broken, and you can rejoin your body as I claim my perfect host."

I sank back into the pit of tar at my feet, unable and unwilling to resist. Nothing I did now mattered, not against a demon who'd woven his energy around the crumbling matter of my magic and held all the power.

"This is a true game of patience. Pay attention, and you might learn something, puppet."

Chapter Twenty

I hid on the bus during the field trip, letting my magic settle. What a bizarre turn of events. Theodore's sadistic nature and his impulsive attempt to escape weren't unexpected, but the way my telepathy latched onto the dying body of that guard… I ran my fingers across the faint scar on my neck. Part of me believed with my telepathy evolving, that streak of empathy tethering to the thoughts I heard and revealing the emotional colors, perhaps I found myself attached to that witch because just last year, that could've and should've been me.

I could've been covered in blood and tar. I could've lain at the feet of Theodore Whitlock. I could've been dead without a second chance.

Fuck. I didn't want to dwell. Speaking of should've and could've, my telepathy began to bloom again, and the bustling thoughts of students traipsing throughout Cerberus Guild reminded me I had teacherly duties to prioritize.

Stepping off the bus, I lingered in the empty parking lot.

"Fuck it." I reached for a smoke and took a deep, blissful inhale. I was already late. What difference would one cigarette make? Aside from calming my nerves and affording me a few more minutes alone.

Each puff eased the tension in the back of my head until the sudden foul taste of cotton candy sat on my tongue. I fought back the urge to hurl, to choke on the filth of smoke.

I scowled. There was a child out here, one also indulging in a smoke break and ruining mine with their disgust of a habit they attempted to test out.

Levitating between the buses, I kept quiet as I searched for whoever had wandered away from the field trip for a little sugary nicotine fix.

Jamie's cheeks were puffed like a squirrel, saving all the smoke he'd inhaled for hibernation.

"Seriously?" I glared at him and Tia, who kept her eyes trained on my mouth. "Shouldn't you two be inside?"

Tia tucked her vape into her sleeve pocket while Jamie remained completely silent, cheeks twitching and lips twisting with disgust. He was desperate to exhale but actually believed me too dim to notice what I could clearly see.

With a telekinetic pulse, I snatched Tia's vape. "That's against academy policy. No tobacco products."

Tia signed something about academy policies contributing to an authoritative police state of bullshit, along with a few more profanities. That much I caught from her surface thoughts.

"Go inside."

Tia held out her hand, expecting her vape returned.

"No."

She pointed to my cigarette. "*Hypocrite.*"

I took a deep drag and slowly mouthed as I exhaled, "And?"

Tia frowned with deep, furious lines on her forehead, then went back into the guild while Jamie turned away, coughing and gasping and hating the flavor of cotton candy more than he thought humanly possible.

"Why are you vaping?" I asked. "You don't even like this."

"How would you know?"

"Because right now, your intense urge to vomit is palpable."

"Fine. Guess it's just nice having someone to hang out with." Jamie shrugged. "Plus, Tia doesn't talk or expect me to talk. Kind of perfect."

"She's actually pretty conversational," I said, gleaning her distant stream of curse words for me that held the same artistry as Kenzo's hurled profanities. "You just don't know how to communicate with her."

"Great. Another thing to feel like shit about."

I huffed while Jamie sulked.

"I don't want you to feel like shit." I frowned. "But I am curious how you feel."

"I'm fine."

"You realize I'm a telepath, right?"

"*Shitty one, as I see it.*" Jamie's thoughts went back to every scream for help he hurled in the pitch-black darkness of his mind, the hoarseness in his voice, the breaking bones, the blood and tar and horrors of hundreds of suffering souls beside him day in and day out. "Sorry."

"Don't be." I took a drag. "I have to ask: why are you here?"

"Because I don't wanna be inside."

"No. Why are you at Gemini?"

"Because Novak's don't quit," he said with a hollowness. "Novak's see their duties through to the end, best of the best, no matter the cost."

"I'm not an expert, but I've worked with fractured minds before."

"Saying I'm damaged?" Jamie scoffed, halfheartedly wanting to feed into his ego, the person he used to be, the one who'd have a snide and cunning comment to retort on the spot. He didn't have any, though. He didn't have much of anything anymore.

"I'm saying maybe you should consider counseling, talk with a psychic specialist." I finished the last drag of my cigarette, inhaling until the filter collapsed between my fingers. "I can see the gaps, the breaks. This isn't the type of damage someone walks off until they feel better. It requires mending, years of it."

"Novak's don't need support. We provide it." Jamie gave me a thin, forced smile, the same he had when his parents reminded him of that mantra after he left the hospital.

"Everyone needs support, Jamie."

"Not everyone deserves it, though."

That struck a chord. A thousand different chords of the pain circulating through Jamie's every waking moment, his sleepless nights, the lack of support he had at home, friendless days, and goals diminished.

"Can I ask you another question?"

"*Just did.*" Jamie sighed, burying the snark like he did so many emotions he believed himself unworthy of expressing, and nodded.

"Why do you want to join the guild industry? Correction. It seems that avenue isn't much of a choice, so much as an expectation, but what motivates you? What used to motivate you when training your casting capabilities?"

Jamie shrugged. "Stupid stuff. Doesn't matter anymore."

"As someone with an honorary doctorate in dumbassery, I assure you, it can't be that bad."

Whether my crude language, deadpan tone, or just a few walls around Jamie finally breaking down, my comment led to the briefest of chuckles before he answered. "It used to be wanting to be the best. My motivation. Well, no. That's not entirely true. It was to be better than others, remind them of their place, and prove mine."

"And now?"

"Doesn't matter. Nothing matters."

"I can see a lot of the carnage in your head, a lot of the fractured memories, the living nightmares, but most of all—I see a young man trying to swim through that abyss. Sometimes having an attainable goal, some motivation, can help when nothing else does."

"What do you think my goal should be?"

"Why not help people?"

"That's generic as fuck."

"Lots of different ways to help. Big things, small things. Dire and trivial and the infinite spectrum between."

"Ugh, you stole that from Mrs. Whitehurst. She's always saying corny things like that." Jamie leaned against one of the buses, staring up at the empty sky, wondering what it'd be like to float up there and just stay. "Help people, huh?"

"I find it to be a wonderful distraction from my own struggles."

"Seems pretty dumb, but most things are. Guess it couldn't hurt."

I remained outside with him, silent and unhelpful, but here so he wouldn't be truly alone. It was a reminder that I didn't have time to worry about Theodore Whitlock or the horrors of the past, dark mysteries lurking in the future. That was Enchanter Evergreen's world to focus on, and he had. He'd adverted whatever wicked intentions that warlock plotted. I belonged here, doing what I could, which meant helping my students. All of them. Every single kid at Gemini Academy mattered and needed my attention in one way or another. I didn't know how yet, but I'd help Jamie, too.

Once I got home, I basically drank until Milo arrived. After the day we'd both had, I figured he'd show up, and honestly, with everything that'd nearly happened, I wanted a strong drink.

I winced from the burn of vodka. Damn, my thirties didn't appreciate the heavy-handed pour mixed with a light touch of acidic orange juice.

"Honey, I'm home." Milo strolled inside, aloof and carefree, even if his thoughts held horrors at the edges where he hoped I wouldn't look.

"This isn't your home." I grabbed the bottle of white wine I'd picked up, knowing he hated liquor and my cheap reds. "I'm not even sure you have a home, considering how much time you spend here."

"Oh, it's a disaster." Milo undid his tie, tossing it in his usual spot, and strutted into the kitchen. "Thank you."

"Figured after your day."

Milo uncorked the bottle and poured it nearly to the brim. "I expected worse, honestly."

"How many fatalities were there?"

"Three. Then nothing. He got loose somewhere between the change of his dampener cuffs and just…"

"I saw."

"Sorry." Milo took a sip of his wine, savoring the tartness on his tongue before swallowing. "I tried to keep the worst of the images out of my head."

"It wasn't you. It was Theodore. Or the guard's dying thoughts. I ended up in that room, watching him the same way I watch you."

"That's newww." Milo dragged out the word like it'd somehow cover the apprehension in his voice or concern in his thoughts.

"It's probably your fault." I took a swig of my drink. "I was so concerned, a bit obsessed—I know I said I was done with that, baby steps or whatever—but I wanted to know how you were handling the whole Theodore Whitlock escort to the courthouse, so I reached out telepathically since I've totally mastered long-range telepathy."

"I mean, not as much as your skillful self-deprecation, but the telepathy is growing."

"Ha." I took another sip. Okay, gulp. Or heavy-handed swallow, which left only a sip in my glass. "I guess when I got there, I felt the pain of one of the guards, his death, and it swept me inside. Then chaos ensued because of demonic energy, broken warding that rattled my magic, and the threats of a narcissistic psychopath."

"He knew you were there?" Milo quirked an eyebrow.

"Yeah. Not surprising. He fucked up my telepathy the last time we crossed paths." I poured another drink. "He's got a rotten mind. One of the worst I've ever touched."

"That's for sure."

Milo and I stood in silence, his thoughts mere whispers as he trailed the vast layers of visions deep within the confines of his inner core. I didn't want to talk or cast, so I let him work and sort futures based on the events of today. The chaos. The horrors endured, and the many others adverted.

I unwound for the evening, reading through essays while Milo pretended to watch television even though his mind was lost in visions. Admittedly, it was a nice evening, all things considered. Quaint and quiet. Eventually, my eyes grew heavy, and the awful fucking handwriting on the paper rough-drafts all started to blur together. I went to bed, hoping Milo would settle soon and get some well-deserved sleep.

When he finally joined me in bed, he had to carefully slip in between me and Charlie, who squeaked and cried before being plopped next to my stomach, where he nestled into a tight ball and dozed right back to sleep. Carlie, on the other hand, remained on the floor, her eyes reflective in the darkness of the bedroom and watching, waiting for us to go to bed so she could join. She very much did not want to appear as if she needed or desired affection—merely food—but she found her way into the bed every single night.

"Anything you wanna talk about?" I pulled his arm under mine, close to my chest, with his hand against my heart. I liked keeping Milo's hand close to my heart, reminding him even when I couldn't say it, he owned every beat, every joy, every ounce of happiness in the future.

"Just sleep." He scooted closer, cuddling against me.

"Okay. But if you do wanna talk… I'm here."

"Just sorting work stuff, other stuff."

"The events of today?"

"Theodore's actions were bizarre, to say the least."

I did my best to remain calm and still as Milo spoke. The last thing I wanted was for my body to give away my anxiety. I also didn't want to dwell on the warlock incursion, the long-lasting ramifications, or the potential fallout their mere existence brought.

"I've seen a thousand different hellish futures fueled by Theodore, conflicts and combat between him and Whitlock Industries, a bloody battlefield across Chicago and all of Illinois—the world, in some grand stacked events—but I never saw today."

I shuddered. The idea there was ever potential for global destruction, no matter how minute, was horrifying. And such a possibility existed in Theodore Whitlock's future.

Milo kissed my shoulder, his lips pressed against my skin until my nerves settled. "It was never a real possibility. The number of factors that have to play out just precisely like juggling a stack of falling dominos."

"Despite your weird as fuck analogy, it's still a possibility, though, right?"

"Meh. We're more likely to bow down to King Clucks, Peckfender of the Unhatched Dozen. Would you like to hear about his possible international fame?"

"Never," I said, gruff and sour.

"That shadow skirting my visions also vanished. Starting to think maybe I blew it out of proportion. Maybe I was just dealing with a bad clairvoyant moment, trying to see a potential future that wouldn't manifest," Milo said, steering the conversation away from humor, which he rarely did, so I knew this weighed on him. "I just really didn't expect Theodore to surrender, to be so easily contained, to spark a flame and then squash it before burning down everything in his path."

I did my best to listen to Milo's continued comparisons of destruction as he contemplated how events unfolded, wondering what he missed, why he missed it, if there was something he should've or could've seen.

"You can't prevent everything." I pulled his hand close, kissing his knuckles. "You told me that."

"Doesn't mean I won't keep trying."

"Even if you run yourself into the ground?"

Milo squeezed me tight, pulling me closer and making Charlie release one of his pouty purrs at the movement during bedtime. "Thankfully, I have you to keep me from burning out. You keep me afloat when the world weighs down on my shoulders."

"I sort of feel the opposite."

"Ouch." Milo snickered.

"No. I feel like I'm always floating toward thoughts, away from feelings, to and from the regrets I'll always carry, and a thousand burdens I put on myself every day." I rolled over, subsequently infuriating Charlie, who trotted to the end of the bed and huffed, but I needed to look Milo in the eyes, see him, and let him truly see me. "You keep me grounded. You keep me safely here in the world of the living, looking toward the future."

Milo's playful grin twisted into something stoic and charming. Gently, he kissed me and hugged me tightly. "I love you, Dorian."

"I love you, too, Milo."

After collecting papers and wrapping up a brief discussion on today's objective, I gave my students the last five minutes to relax. No point dragging out conversation when boredom bubbled across the classroom.

Gael tsked at Tara, who sat several desks away during the lesson after I rearranged them, finding it the only way to keep him on task. Tara glanced at me, so I gestured whatever permission she believed I needed to grant before she moved back over to Gael. He was a minute from disrupting everyone by telekinetically dragging her desk across the classroom anyway, and I didn't need him scuffing up my floors again.

"You still haven't RSVP'd."

"Is that really necessary for a house party?"

"*The* house party," Gael clarified loudly, so everyone in the room who wasn't invited would be well aware of the big bash they were missing out on—not that it seemed he'd left much of anyone in the room off his list. "It's gonna be the party of the century, in fact."

"You say that about every party."

"That's because I'm nice." Gael pressed a hand to his chest, feigning sweetness. "But this is *my* party, so it's actually gonna be the party of the century." He eyed Jamie. "And I just feel sorry for anyone who isn't invited."

There it was.

Tara thumped Gael's knuckles, very much shooting him a look that conveyed her thoughts crystal clear. He knew them without a word or my telepathic insight.

"*He doesn't have to keep pushing Jamie.*" Tara's look didn't relent. "*The past is the past, and honestly... Just feels like kicking someone when they're down.*"

Tara still resented Jamie. Not for the Spring Showcase or the taunting in class. No. Unfortunately, she had years of memories to pull from when it came to Jamie's cruel antics. But she didn't want to. Not now. Not ever, really. Tara hadn't quite compartmentalized everything as well as I pretended to compartmentalize things, but she did her best to push all the negativity out of her thoughts. And she had a lot more than I endured at her age or ever. Jamie. Her brother's recent attack. Her father's lectures about the family legacy. Her branch overlap. Her expectations to take a bigger Whitlock spotlight to hide Theodore's continued spiral of destruction. A sea of sorrow that continued raging every time she came so close to quelling it.

"Why don't you just give my invitation to someone else?"

"But I need you there." Gael batted his eyes.

"Please, you'll be fawning over Tiffany, and I'll be plastered to a wall avoiding, well, everyone."

Gael squinted. "She RSVP'd *maybe*."

"She'll probably still show."

"Oh, she'll definitely show. She can't get enough of this cock." Gael grinned. "Plus, she loves King Clucks, too."

The rooster crowed exactly as the bell rang and not a minute too soon.

Everyone rushed out of the classroom except for Jamie. He didn't hang around to talk, though. It was just his way of further isolating himself from his peers, waiting for the hallways to thin out. I dwelled on how I had no answers for Jamie. No support to offer. No suggestions for Chanelle.

I went outside, shivering at the cold front that'd swept in right at the start of November, and rushed to my car to have a smoke. I contemplated hiding out here during my whole planning, but I had tasks to finish arranging my review lesson for my homeroom coven. As I made my way back inside, I found myself lingering outside of Chanelle's classroom, uninterested in returning to mine.

It was tempting to return to my cold car and spend the rest of my planning smoking. Instead, my feet moved on their own, and I walked right into Chanelle's empty classroom. "How's it going?"

"Fine. Working on liaison emails instead of catching up on a pile of ungraded essays."

"I wanted to ask you a question."

"So I guess the small talk part of our day is already at an end." Chanelle grinned.

My frown only added to her smiling face.

"What's up?"

"I've got the auxiliary gym booked Friday. I see you've got it this Wednesday."

"Nope." Chanelle's smile disappeared.

"You don't?" I was almost certain I saw her name scheduled.

"No, I won't switch days."

"I wasn't asking that…" I scrunched my face. "Wait. Why wouldn't you switch days with me? You don't do anything on Fridays."

"Exactly, and neither do the students."

"Mine do."

"That's because you're an asshole to them."

And my frown set into a natural, burning scowl. "Anyway, I wanted to ask if you'd be willing to send Jamie to join our homeroom during our practice."

Chanelle paused, fingers hovering above the keys of her computer.

"I mentioned the Wednesday thing because I didn't know if you'd think two days in a week would be too much training, but I'm planning more of a casual jig-sawing activity to review techniques with my homeroom. They'll be split into groups, alternating tasks. I thought the change might be helpful. Maybe. Probably not."

"Yeah, I could send him to your afternoon homeroom."

"Cool."

"Wanna take any others off my hands?" Chanelle's smile returned. "I'd love a peaceful Friday afternoon."

"Nope." I turned on my heel and walked back to my classroom.

"Slacker," she shouted before returning to her emails. "*Thank you.*"

Chapter Twenty-One

I'd brought my students to the auxiliary gym and then split them into groups that I hoped would bring out their best efforts during this afternoon's training. Nothing fancy. No acolytes. No new content. No pop quiz on casting. Mostly a review of what we'd covered throughout the semester.

They already had their fledgling permits; most had a solid grasp over their casting. They still had time before the second-year Spring Showcase. Courses had gotten more rigorous, but any kid with me as a teacher had already faced the worst of academic expectations their first year, so most of my students—even the slackers—breezed through their coursework.

The fall semester really was a lull period for second-year witches, and I wanted them to enjoy that since applications and interview practices would kick in next semester. Everything would fly by, and before I knew it, they'd be third-years and saying their farewells as the academy threw them into internships.

Having sent the other students off to different stations I'd arranged, I turned to the group at the station I'd assigned myself.

The first group of students I'd decided to work with on rotations was Caleb, Jamius, and Gael.

"Ba-ba-bawk!" And King Clucks, naturally.

Caleb already started eyeing the other setups, especially the rock terrain where I specified branch training would take place.

"You'll be doing a second round of root training there," I explained.

"Figured as much." Caleb nodded.

"First round of root training will be here."

Gael rolled his eyes, already aware of my intentions and doing his best to shrug off any lesson I might devise where he'd have to levitate. For someone so aloof, he certainly grasped things a lot faster than he let on.

"In fact, even when your group rotates stations, I'd prefer you three to focus on root casting."

"Not like I have much say in that." Caleb half-smiled, running a hand through his freshly buzz-cut hair.

"Your specific focus today is strictly banishment."

"On it." Caleb scrunched his face, staring off at the forest terrain where I'd set up wisp training. "So, should I go join their group or go to the proctoring office to grab some enchantments?"

Since hitting their second year, I rarely relied on the enchantments signifying demonic energy. It was important they got a real feel for fighting and banishing wisps and fiends at every opportunity they had.

"Neither. I want you to finetune your perfected banishment." Since working with the acolytes, each had noted an expectation to see Caleb's perfected root in action, yet all he'd done was showcase strong proficiency in all four. That in itself was great, something any witch branch or not should take pride in, but Caleb had more to offer, and I planned on helping him prove that.

"I-I-I have no idea how to access that."

"Exactly. So, instead of guessing games, I'm going to be helping you and others by studying the subconscious thought waves during channeling. It helps assess where the difficulty comes from."

Caleb frowned.

"This won't be a day one success, but we'll get there. For the time being, you need a live magical target to banish, so look at your new training partner." I gestured to Jamius, who'd already pulled out his phone to level up some guild character in an interactive mobile game that required his full attention. "Put it away and start creating duplicates."

Jamius sighed. "You just said I was doing a root training exercise."

"You are. You'll be focusing on maintaining and switching between your four roots while summoning no less than three duplicates at a time. Each one will be expected to have access to one root themselves, but no more."

"Ugh, why do you hate me?"

I glowered at Jamius until he straightened up and went to work on summoning specifically crafted copies of himself. His work had gotten better, but I needed him to have more fluid control when changing the specifications and access to magic his duplicates had. Giving them identical strength to his own left him too winded for long-term casting.

Once Jamius and Caleb got settled, I turned all my attention onto Gael, who grinned, already prepped with evasive ways to avoid the one root he knew I wanted him to train in.

"All right, Gael." I huffed. "We're going to focus on your levitation and only your levitation." I might've sent a persistent buzzing sound to the back of his head, distracting his train of thought so he wouldn't interrupt me. Underhanded, but a necessity with Gael. "You and King Clucks need to start showing proficiency in each of your roots before moving on to bestial takeovers."

Part of Gael's argument came from an interest in enhancing his bestial connection. But he already knew how to channel the rooster's natural strengths into his body. And while a rooster's kick might not seem like much, adding that ferocity and redistributing it into the human form gave Gael a physical edge. He wanted to hone those skills, but I wouldn't budge until he started levitating.

A dark shadow entered the auxiliary gym, carrying with it waves of pain that threatened to drag me into it the same way Tara's ocean of sorrow did when my telepathy got too close. I quelled my branch some and saw Jamie had finally arrived.

"Mrs. Whitehurst sent me." He had his hands stuffed in his pockets. "Said I needed to rework my fundamentals."

"Not exactly." I grimaced, fighting a frown but unable to smile as a show of encouragement. Gael had already soured my mood, and the chasm of depression radiating off Jamie didn't help matters. "I was hoping you could actually help one of my students."

It wasn't the best pitch, but it sounded smoother than Chanelle's 'go practice without the rest of your class with Mr. Frost for the afternoon' comment that fluttered around Jamie's surface thoughts. I doubt she worded it that way, but people really did remember things the way they wanted.

"Perfect." Gael scoffed, eyeing Jamie up and down before turning his gaze back to me. "How am I supposed to keep up with your lecturing when just anyone can walk into the auxiliary gym stealing your attention?"

I'd hoped to have Gael started before Jamie arrived, maybe even get a quick check in on the other students, too. Who was I kidding? Gael would take the bulk of my time in today's lesson, so I might as well get Jamie started.

"Please tell me he's not who needs the assistance."

Gael's familiar crowed, flapping his wings and pecking the air in Jamie's direction.

"Yep." Gael nodded. "*Total tool.*"

"Hold on one second." I gestured to Jamie, tuning out Gael—as best as anyone could—then flew over toward the rock terrain where I'd set up a station for branch training.

Kenzo and Gael seemed like an impossible pair to split, so I sent them off partnered with Katherine, figuring Gael would make a solid buffer. Kenzo continued pushing his disruption out in waves, breaking apart every single spike Gael hurled from his body. It allowed Kenzo to finetune his precision shots while Gael tested the limits on the recovery time it took new spikes to sprout from his skin.

As expected, Katherine had pulled away from Kenzo and Gael to focus on channeling from her grimoire without making contact with the pages. She didn't like the strain it put on her mind and body, but what she liked even less was the idea of limiting herself when she knew she had what it took to achieve this level of mastery.

"Katherine, do you mind joining me at the other station?"

"Thought you specifically assigned our groups to maximize our afternoon?" Katherine asked, edge in her voice and still annoyed

I'd split her up from her coven mates—mainly the one she couldn't stop thinking about kissing.

I rolled my eyes. Christ. They'd been dating for nearly a year. How long were they going to sit in the clingy honeymoon pining phase? Besides, the split had more to do with balancing a few others. Like Kenzo and Gael, Layla and Melanie were also difficult to pry apart, but I needed to see Melanie blossom a bit outside her bestie's radius if she wanted to be successful. And like every student here, she wanted a guild career. That wouldn't happen if she kept serving at Layla's altar.

Katherine strapped her grimoire to her hip. "So, where are you sending me?"

I pointed to my station, where Jamie waited. Katherine practically squealed, not even registering Jamie had walked into the auxiliary gym because she only had eyes for Caleb.

Oh, fuck me.

"Soooo, root training?" Katherine fastened the strap on her grimoire, locking it. "Guess I won't need this."

We flew back together, and I waited until we landed to steer her attention toward Jamie. "Jamie, we've discussed how you'd like to find more ways to help others as a goal toward your training, so I thought working with Katherine would be the perfect exercise in that effort."

"Wait…" Katherine furrowed her brow. "You took me away from branch training to what?"

"This will be branch training," I explained. "I was thinking you two could create a hybrid spell. You like those, and it'll help with your enchantment branch."

Katherine's hybrid spells came from combining her magic with someone else's and storing it in a page of her grimoire. Apparently, it was a lot easier than recreating a specific type of magic.

"Suuuure." Katherine pulled out her grimoire, flipping to an empty page. "Suppose I'm also used to you changing the expected lesson midway. It's a very Frosty move to make."

"Did you just use my name as a verb?" I quirked a brow, catching a distant snicker from Gael and his rooster. Of course, they set the term in motion.

While Katherine set up her book, etching sigils in the corners of the page and chanting a verse that'd help sync their casting, I stepped toward Jamie. He had a befuddled expression that almost hid the sadness in his eyes.

"It's a great practice for you," I said.

"Not sure how this helps me help people. I mean, Katherine, sure. But what's giving her access to my magic in some co-op spell really achieve in the grand scheme of things?"

"For starters, it's a hybrid spell." Katherine continued setting up. "Secondly, I might end up using this borrowed magic to save a life one day."

"Yeah, sure you will."

"It's also a great way to practice matching unfamiliar frequencies," I said. "Something you can continue working on with your coven later. Especially when working with Vik. Their magic might be able to mimic yours, but if you can match their frequency when casting, it'd make it easier on the both of you."

Jamie almost smiled, then approached Katherine and sat on his knees in front of her grimoire. I took it as a win.

Caleb had wandered further from Jamius' copies, inching toward Katherine. Distrustful of Jamie despite what the young witch had endured. It seemed everyone struggled to cut Jamie slack, focusing less on their guilt for what happened and more on the rotten person he was the very first semester.

"Shouldn't you be demonstrating a perfected banishment by now?" I scowled.

"Y-y-you said this isn't gonna happen in one day. I'll need way more time—"

"It won't happen at all if you just stand around gawking. Back to work, Caleb."

"Yes, sir."

Now that I'd gotten most of them on task, I scanned the auxiliary gym to ensure no one else's minds floundered. We'd be rotating stations soon, so I needed to take this opportunity to get my most reluctant student on task.

With a wave of my hand, I lifted Gael off the ground and telekinetically floated him toward me. King Clucks clucked furiously, flapping his wings and shooting me a menacing glare.

"Whoa, whoa, whoa!" Gael flailed his arms and kicked his legs so dramatically it drew Katherine and Jamie's attention from their hybrid spell. "This is a massive abuse of authority. It's unconstitutional!"

"We're not playing games anymore." I released my grip, dropping him directly in front of me. "You're going to levitate, or you're going to tell me why you won't levitate."

"I can't."

"More like you won't."

Gael's mind twisted to thoughts about Tara's overlap.

"Don't you dare." I glared. "It's one thing to think it, but don't even try to make that a reason you can't fly."

"I wasn't gonna." He sighed. "*Felt dirty just thinking about it.*"

King Clucks puffed his chest at me.

"You need to chill too, bird, or I'll send you flying next."

"Ba-ba-ba-bawk." King Clucks dug his clawed foot into the

ground, and I swore for half a second, I could feel his thoughts as he envisioned my head beneath his talons.

"Fine. It's totally embarrassing, but I sort of hit my head once. Not a super big deal or anything, but King Clucks sometimes, just a little bit, gets worked up about it, and he's not a fan."

"I've seen him peck you repeatedly, and you're telling me the rooster won't let you fly because he's worried you'll get injured?" I mean, that much I knew, but I always figured it came down to spiteful envy since chickens couldn't exactly fly. Then again, as a familiar, King Clucks did have access to the levitation root, too.

"Yeah, but he's just playing around when he does that." Gael grimaced. "Maybe it was a bigger deal."

Gael brushed his fingers through his faux hawk, moving the hairs until he reached a spot where he pointed. I couldn't see anything through his thick black hair, but he jabbed his finger a few times to indicate the spot.

"Took a big fall and got a souvenir, too," Gael said, explaining the incident.

The memory rose to the surface of his mind, fully formed and painting the auxiliary gym with the sunset park trail where he fell. Gael described the ordeal in the most lighthearted way, underplaying the severity because he rarely took anything seriously. Even a fatality.

Gael fell and busted his head open at seven. He was badly injured, and no one was there. Blood was everywhere.

"This was way back when King Clucks was still Prince Cheeps-A-Lot," Gael said. "Thank god they allow familiars to refile their names because the silly things you come up with as kids—cringe."

His rooster clucked with approval.

"Yeah, because King Clucks, Peckfender of the Unhatched Dozen, is far less cringey."

"Exactly!" Gael snickered, completely missing my snark. "But you using cringe is just sad, Mr. Frosty."

I huffed.

"Anyway, I hadn't had much luck with my roots until King Clucks found me."

They'd tried to make a day of it, exploring. Every day, in fact. Him and his little chick finding new places to wander and secret spots to perform their magic. Not an uncommon occurrence for young witches who were years away from their formal training but desperate for access to the magic they weren't legally licensed to practice.

Blood splattered again, and the collision of Gael's head against the ground looped over and over. Each time just as brutal, painful, terrifying.

King Clucks, the tiny chick, chirped and cheeped and cried out for someone, anyone, but no one followed him back into the woods.

"See. He gets all worked up over nothing." Gael pointed to his familiar as he recounted the story.

Gael played it off, cool and casual and carefree even as fear swirled along the edges of his memory. The contrasting colors added by the trauma made for a darker palette, turning the park forest into a nightmare world where the trees had menacing faces, and the sunset had a bloody vibrance matching the head injury Gael sustained.

That was when I realized that this palpable fear, this trauma, came from King Clucks' thoughts. Witches with familiars synced minds for communication, but I rarely connected to the animal.

Still, the terror seeped so deeply into Gael's memory, the two streams of thought overlapped. Despite that fear preventing Gael from levitating, this was a true testament to the bond he shared with King Clucks.

"What happened in the end?" I asked, uncertain how to approach a solution and curious how Gael found help.

"Sexy Enchanter Campbell found me." Gael waggled his eyebrows. "That's right. Met her before she was a bigshot guild master."

That part of the memory was painted in pink hues, lust perhaps, but most likely tied into the pink mist of Campbell's branch that could harm or heal depending on her temperament. Her mist replaced the blood loss, mended the internal damage, and sealed the gash on his head.

I did the mental math real quick. Based on Gael's age, this would've been when Campbell and Milo were an item, what felt like a lifetime ago, and shortly after his rise to fame from the events during the Night of the Fiend Massacre. I wondered if he had a role in this incident. It was unlikely Campbell had just happened to have been strolling through a park late in the evening and stumbled onto an injured child at exactly the same time he required her magical assistance, but if a clairvoyant boyfriend pointed out a path she should take, then perhaps…

I rolled my eyes. Like Milo would tell me anyway.

"That's the gist of it." Gael folded his hands behind his head, flexing his arms in the process. "Unless you know a way to get the mother hen to chill out, I don't see levitating in my future."

"Cl-clu-cluck." King Clucks pecked at the air, clearly offended by Gael's comment. Ugh. I couldn't believe I understood the bird. Not his thoughts, not outside that tangible memory, but I'd grown accustomed to the fluctuations in his noises that I knew what each tone meant. Dammit.

And as much as I hated admitting it, Gael was right. He wouldn't be levitating. Not until I worked on a solution to help King Clucks cope with the trauma associated with his witch partner coming into harm's way.

"Well?" Gael waited.

I was stumped. "I'm gonna think on this."

"I might have a solution." Jamie stood up, dusting off his slacks. "If you wanted to hear it."

Gael sighed, loud and dramatic. "This outta be good."

"It's not like a real solution, but matching frequencies with Katherine reminded me how my sister used to do that when I'd cast. My telekinesis and levitation were pretty rough, so she'd sort of loop hers around mine as an added layer." He shrugged. "Of course, she had to stay close when doing that. It was like a reverse piggyback ride."

The image sprang from the hollow pit of his fractured mind. A small boy in a fancy suit for an event flying with his slightly older sister in a sparkling dress. Lena hovered above him, looping telekinesis around him as a young Jamie giggled, leading their direction with the pivot of his arms and legs.

"It'd be super easy for you two—since you're already so familiar with, er, your, ah, familiar's magical frequency." Jamie scrunched his face. "I just mean, maybe he'd be less concerned about you levitating if he had semi-control. Well, full control. King Clucks looks like a full control type of guy."

"Hmmmmm." Gael strummed his fingertips across his chin, a façade of deep thought when he and I both knew the only thing on his mind right now was inappropriate recollections of Guild Master Campbell.

"BAWK!"

"It would seem King Clucks approves of your idea," Gael said. "We'll try it out. Maybe."

"Now might be a good time." I frowned.

"Fine, fine. We'll get to work." Gael strutted off, thoughts wrapped into a one-sided conversation with his familiar. Well, as usual, I could only hear his side of the discussion.

"That was a great idea, Jamie." I turned and tried to soften my dour expression.

"Helping people is a great motivator, right?" Jamie almost smiled, not from our talk, not from the suggestion he offered Gael, but rather the surfacing memory of joy spent with his sister.

It hovered above the darkness of his mind, illuminating the shadows and cracks of his inner core, and for the first time since I'd seen his mind freed of the chimera, it appeared some of the damage had slowly mended itself.

He had a long journey ahead of him, one I hoped to offer assistance on in any small way.

Gael watched us, already searching for a way to avoid his new learning objective. But the way his mind shifted to contemplation and conversations with Tara, and the curiosity in his thoughts bubbled, I didn't believe this was the worst of his slacker ways.

Between his impulse and perhaps a bit of kindheartedness, I finally cracked that smile I'd been holding back when the idea in his head turned into words. "You know, Jamie, I'm having a party. Not a big thing. Well, sort of. Everyone's basically going. It'd be weird not inviting you, so like, if you wanted to show up or whatever. Probably wouldn't be the worst thing."

"That sounds like fun."

"Yeah, it's gonna be real chill."

Given the time left, I went to check on the other groups and let Gael and Jamie have their awkward exchange, relieved Jamie had found a bit of joy buried in his memories and maybe a little in his future.

Chapter Twenty-Two

Doppler

Dark and dank death clung to every fiber of my being, dwelling in the mind of Peter Graham. Since Theodore's attempt to escape, everyone inside the MDC, from guards to inmates, stood on edge. Festering paranoia and brewing anger ate away at my telepathy, adding a gnawing agony to this numbing darkness conjured by the chimera's demonic energy.

He allowed me enough magic to witness his plan and gauge his intentions but not enough to break the shackles of slimy tar bound to my wrists wherever I roamed in Peter's mind. I contemplated calling out to the warlock, warning him of the horrors that'd burrowed deep into his consciousness, yet it seemed a futile effort.

The damn demon likely anticipated such an attempt—toying with me as revenge for how I'd imprisoned him. Even if there was a single oversight to this vile tactician, what could Peter Graham really do about the situation? He lacked magic with the dampener cuffs, so banishment was out of the question. The only thing on his mind currently was avoiding the ire of guards and those on his cellblock long enough to make it to his release.

Parole was the only thing on his mind. Every waking thought revolved around the ticking clock of when he'd finally escape the MDC. He wouldn't risk alerting anyone of the potential demon inside him if I whispered such revelations because he feared serving his full sentence far more than he feared a monster in his head.

"That's because Peter still believes beneath the shackles of his confinement, past the beratement of mortal peers, and beyond the years of lost influence, that he is truly still a monster worthy of fear himself." The chimera manifested behind me, hands pressed firmly against my shoulders as he pushed me deeper into the muck of tar that rotted this mind. "Witness what will unfold because of your hubris, puppet. You believed yourself something grand. Now you can watch someone who actually is perfection incarnation."

I scoffed. "And you call me arrogant."

The chimera waltzed by me, practically floating on the gelatinous flooring where I lay stuck up to my waist. We spun round and round, skirting toward the edge of Peter's mind, where my magic gained a view to observe the world outside of Peter Graham's head.

He shuffled ahead of two guards escorting him to the same white chamber I'd planned on possessing Theodore, the same room where everything went to Hell. He stood surrounded by six guards, twice the initial protocol. One guard unshackled Peter's wrists and ankles while another removed the dampener cuff. The minute

Peter's magic was released, a euphoric buzz hit him. Even without channeling, the raw release of his branch made his thoughts hazy. The sludge polluting his head became clouded over by the instinctual need to reverse the effects of an ill-gotten demon lurking in the shadows of his mind.

```
Name: Peter Graham
Branch:Entropy (Cellular Absorption)
```

"Calm yourself," the chimera whispered to the warlock. "Remember what you heard; remember they're looking for any reason to shoot you down where you stand."

The toxic smog that flourished in Peter's inner core dimmed as he quelled his magic, watching the guards at the ready while one prepared a new dampener cuff. A thinner and not nearly as potent one.

Once the new cuff had taken effect, Peter was ushered out of the white chamber to an empty room where a patrolman stood behind a glass window. He slid an envelope of Peter's belongings atop a clipboard, which Peter immediately signed to accept. Afterward, he slid his dampener cuff through a small slot beside the window that beeped.

"This holds a three-hour charge," the patrolman said, securing it to Peter's wrist after the allotted transition passed. "You'll be expected to meet with your parole officer to be refitted with your permanent cuff. Any and all property of the Metropolitan Detainment Center must be secured and returned in the condition received. Failure to comply will result in a fine equal to or greater than the price of replacing lost, damaged, or stolen property. Sign here."

Peter signed the waiver—one he'd signed two times already after violating his parole and finding himself going through the same speech at the MDC release station. It sent goosebumps over Peter's arms, pin prickles against the back of his neck, and a fierce desire to leave this place and never return.

Not that he would. He knew the future that awaited him if he screwed up again. He knew he needed to go directly to his parole officer, get properly fitted, secure new living quarters, find a job to pay the absurd fees surrounding his early release, and pray to god that he'd finally get rid of the dampener cuffs for good this time so he could taste his branch again without fear of retribution for illegal casting.

Peter's thoughts twisted to the long-winded protocols and expectations he'd be expected to meet once he left the MDC. Each word ate away at the already tight space inside his surface thoughts where we dwelled.

Ignoring Peter, ignoring the chimera, ignoring the protocol of bureaucratic release I no longer cared to glean, ignoring all the unchangeable things in this world I couldn't alter, I channeled my telepathy. Sending subtle waves of magic, I kept the ripples contained and did my best not to disturb the black blanket of tar weaved throughout this mind.

All I wanted to know, all I've wanted to know since I awoke in this hellhole, was where Finn had gone. Was he okay? Was he buried beneath the demonic energy? Had this foul monster encased him in horrors yet again because of my fucking stupidity? I ground my teeth until the self-loathing passed. I wasn't Dorian. Guilt and blaming myself wouldn't change a damn thing, so I wouldn't allow myself to sink into a pit of despair. Not when Finn was here somewhere. Not when I needed to find him. Help him. Save him.

"How would you do any of that?" The chimera appeared before me in a blink. "You really don't grasp the fact that nothing in here goes unnoticed or untended by me."

"Why offer the slack then? Why give me access to my branch?"

"Why not?" He chuckled. "What can you do with it? You can't overpower me. You can't escape. You can't even whisper to other minds without alerting me, and we both know I'm far better at swaying sad, pathetic mortals than you."

I could reach out this very second and alert Dorian, tell him the chimera still lived. Give him all the details so he could pass the intel to Milo, and then this damn demon would perish for good.

"But you won't." The smugness in the chimera's voice grated my nerves. "You won't do anything because you're still hopeful about your plan. Your future. Not that a silly little thing like you ever had one."

Dammit. I was hopeful. Hopeful, desperate, and pathetic. The emotional sensation synced to the same hope Peter held as he stepped outside the MDC and took his first free breath. My chest swelled, taking in the joy Peter held for the deep, crisp breath that hurt his lungs in the best way. Freedom. But not truly free. There was so much ahead of him, and he knew better than to screw it up this time. However, he had no idea the Hell that awaited him. Neither did I, but I wanted to see it unfold, understand and comprehend the plot the chimera intended to set in motion—as if any insight would help me thwart such things.

"But watching all this, seeing everything unfold, what is the truth of what you want?" The chimera stared down at me, truly placing himself on a pedestal above me, cementing or flaunting his superiority. He smirked, continuing to prove he not only heard my every internal thought but that he found every idea in my head laughable.

"What I want, what I truly want, is to see you dead," I said through clenched teeth. "Kill you myself."

"No." There was a sweet cadence in his voice. "No, no, no."

I turned my head. Engaging with this monster would get me nowhere.

"I suppose I should practice my benevolence." The chimera knelt, ensuring his eyes were level with mine. "Gestures of kindness are a complexity I don't fully grasp but would like to learn before claiming Dorian's body. Sharing it would be easiest if he were willing."

"You won't take it. Even if Dorian doesn't realize the full extent of his branch, Milo will—"

"Will do nothing. You taught me so much. Even in all my years of walking this world, I arrogantly relied on my demonic presence to obscure magics and detection. Too lazy to properly evaluate a foe. But you, puppet, showed me all the chinks in Enchanter Evergreen's branch. So long as I follow the roadmap of your successes, I can easily avoid him." He smiled, dark and wicked and filled with malice. "That is, until I take Dorian's body and use it to snuff out The Inevitable Future. Imagine the poetry."

"I will end you before I let you harm Milo." That wasn't an idle threat. I didn't care if he'd weaved my being to him, tethered my magic to his demonic energy. I would never allow Milo to pay the price of my mistake. I wasn't Dorian. I wasn't that selfish.

"Would you sacrifice one love for another?"

With a twist of his hand, the tar nearby swirled, unraveling sludgy layers until a human mold appeared. The body remained completely still, frozen—not by force but through years of careful, deliberate practice. Even the thoughts held a soft loll to them, careful not to disturb or distract from his betters.

My eyes welled with tears. Finn.

It was fucking devastating to see him in such a state, returned to the imprisonment I swore I'd free him from. The cage of nightmares I locked away so he could remember what happiness felt like. The life I wanted to give him once again, unbound from the burden of a devil.

"What have you done?"

"Given him back every single memory you denied him," the chimera said. "Returned to him years of training. You see, I'm used to having more souls bound to my being than your simple, hollow head could ever fathom."

The tar around Finn's face washed away, revealing his somber hazel eyes. Vacant. But his thoughts buzzed with compliant terror.

"He knows not to act out. He remembers what happens to those who misbehave." The chimera strutted toward Finn, placing a hand on his face and daring to rub Finn's chin. "You won't do anything, puppet, because you still have hope that things will be better. That you'll get the happy ending you've deluded yourself into believing you're entitled to. But spend some time in Finn's thoughts. Learn that no one truly deserves anything they get. Not the good, not the bad. The universe is a vast beast of infinite chaos. You're cogs while I'm the conductor."

"I will break you. I will free Finn. I will free myself. I will have the future—" Tar swelled and boiled, funneling into my throat.

Every hollow fiber of my being seared with white-hot pain. Every fabricated receptor ignited with agony brought on by the demonic energy. He drowned me in darkness, keeping me fully aware and silent while he plotted ahead, preparing to unleash his horrors onto the world yet again.

"All thanks to you, puppet." The chimera's cackle reverberated throughout this inner core.

Time always moved differently in minds. Having spent so many years of my existence delving into other people's memories at Dorian's behest, I could live five lifetimes in a single memory. I could spend five seconds in a lifetime of memories. Sometimes, that passage of time translated to the real world, but mostly, it didn't. Time was a fabrication my magic ignored when performing the duties of a diligent manifestation.

Now, it served as pure Hell incarnate. In the few hours since Peter Graham's release, I'd died a million tiny deaths as the chimera stripped away my will, my being, my desire to persevere. Illusions of the mind strong enough to warp my perception of reality into the chimera's image where he sent every horror that I'd inflicted on him over the course of months back at me a hundred-fold. Brutal and unyielding.

After what seemed an eternity, I floated through the tar to the peak of Peter's mind.

"Continue following this path. You're almost there," the chimera whispered the words so precisely each syllable hit like the key to a piano playing a perfect musical piece.

Against his better judgment, Peter obeyed the whispers. All his gnawing insecurity about missing his first check-in with his parole officer washed away as he took a scenic route through the city. Deep in the South Side, Peter followed a trail of wisps.

Aimless and random as they appeared, Peter understood the pattern, the purpose, and though he didn't know why, he had to reach the end. He had to know where these desires came from, this haunting need for answers.

"What are you doing?" My throat burned with each word; tar dripped down my chin.

"Watch and see true mastery unfold before you." The demon's smugness remained completely intact.

Peter turned the corner and entered an alleyway illuminated by a handful of wisps. At the end of the alley, crouched against a wall, was a fiend. Its body contorted to appear small in stature, but as Peter arrived, it unraveled and revealed itself to be a brutish beast on the verge of ascending into true demon form. So close to the cusp of self-actualization.

"What the fuck?" Peter and I said in unison.

I couldn't tell if this was his fear or mine. It was one thing for the chimera to skirt the mind of a warlock, casting influence, but if he jumped into the fiend, then he'd regain nearly all his power.

"Not nearly. It'll take decades to regather so many lost branches, but the few I have, I sent with this lovely fiend." The chimera shushed Peter, deceiving him into complicitly remaining.

Peter swallowed hard. The lump in his throat hurt my own—sending another wave of pain from all the boiling rot that'd infested my body.

The fiend cast magics I'd failed to remove or contain from the chimera.

It drew more wisps into the area. Ten turned into a hundred, and a hundred burst into a thousand. Soon, every single wisp in the neighborhood was drawn to the casting. A flurry of glowing white lights surrounded us.

"Fun fact, puppet. Theodore's branch doesn't control demonic energy. It's more like he issues commands that must be upheld." The chimera pulled me closer to him, standing on the edge of Peter's mind a single step from spilling out into the world. "He gave the fiend made from my energy one simple order: lay low and await perfection to find you."

"Impossible. They bound Theodore's magic. You showed me that."

"Even with Theodore's magic dampened, binding him from further casting, the command will still run its course so long as the order isn't too complicated. This base beast merely needed to wait for my arrival, slowly absorbing and drawing nearby wisps."

The chimera dragged me with him as we plummeted out of Peter Graham's body. I gasped as Peter choked on the tar and wispy energy pouring from his mouth, spilling from every orifice.

We splattered onto the ground, breaking every bone of my fabricated body once again. Did this action itself break me into pieces, or was that some cruel illusion cast by the chimera who now reigned supreme in my mind?

Tar exploded into a puddle of goop; droplets of my fractured thoughts lay bare on the street. Most of my being clung to the wispy light. I radiated so much luminescence, so much brightness, I hoped it'd shatter my sight for what came next. I didn't need telepathy to know what would soon unveil itself.

"Come to me, beast. Bring me the power I lent you! Return us to the greatness and majesty of godhood!"

The fiend slinked forward, boundless limbs reaching closer as it crawled beneath the light of bright white wisps attaching themselves to the tar. Peter trembled.

Left awestruck and terrified, Peter contemplated his actions. A few seconds of hesitation. His hand gripped the dampener cuff that held his magic in check, that signaled his location, that determined the rest of his future. One misstep. One fuck up. Everything would end for him. He'd find himself thrown back into prison. Not the Metropolitan Detainment Center, but the maximum-security facility he'd barely survived. No one would believe him if he cast.

Every fiber in his being told him to run, but the chimera's musical melody continued in Peter's thoughts, compelling him to remain still for just a minute. A minute. A few more seconds. A little longer, and everything would be okay again.

Peter obeyed as the chimera collided with the field and transcended into true demon form once again. All the energy, random wisps and broken pieces of magic like myself, were dragged into the transforming tar that took form into a monstrosity of a true chimera.

I kept my sights locked on Peter; his eyes were wide with shock and fear as the shadow of a towering chimera darkened the alley. In an instant, Peter's entire body shattered, bloody and bruised and broken beyond repair.

Had this happened to Jamie Novak when the demon possessed him? I knew that kid endured pain, bound and possessed, but watching the chimera shatter Peter's entire being as he wriggled his demonic energy into a mortal coil was truly devastating. Every cell of Peter's body broke apart, making room for the demon, then reformed, not so much as a scratch as tar stitched every limb, muscle, and bone back together.

The agony the chimera greeted me with when gaining control paled in comparison to the insurmountable destruction of Peter losing his body to a demon.

"Not a demon, puppet." The chimera stood behind me in his preferred human guise, adjusting a sleeve while redesigning every crevice of Peter's inner core. Before, we dwelled like a cancerous rot at the peak of Peter's mind, but now that carnage seeped through every pore of his body. Every cell radiated demonic energy. "I am once again a fully-fledged devil."

He cackled, unhinged and bursting with power as he shattered the dampener cuff that released his new host body's magic. "I often prefer the arcane. They're far more durable when containing all my glory, yet this particular branch is unique and appealing. It won't last forever, but this host should last until I gain the perfection owed to me."

I pushed off the shadow flooring, unwilling to submit before the chimera. I might be bound to him, locked in here by his magics, but I wouldn't give him the satisfaction of kneeling. "What happens next?"

"Now, we break Dorian." The chimera smirked, painting images of my plot, my ploy, my desperate attempt to claim a future where I could find happiness.

There would be no unraveling the demonic energy from Finn now, not with Theodore Whitlock locked in the deepest pit of the MDC.

There would be no banishing the chimera with Finn and me bound to his fate.

There would be no overwhelming Dorian with his failures, proving I'd accomplished what he never could, never attempted, and claiming the life I deserved.

This devil revealed every misstep I'd taken, every instance he'd acted, whether subtly or brazen, in an effort to supersede his confinement and bring his freedom to fruition.

"It was a fascinating plot, breaking Dorian's willpower to live, to resist. I will be using that strategy since it's unlikely he'll willingly submit to me. Much like your pale attempt of defiance, Dorian could prove troublesome. But unlike you, I'll take a more direct approach." The demon's cocky tone and smug smile were grating. "You believed you could shame Dorian with his past, break him with grief that he's already proven to best—albeit it took him long enough."

"And what's your plan?"

"I'm going to take away the thing Dorian values most. I'm going to remove his hopes for the future, starting by killing those precious students he holds so dearly."

I swallowed hard. I hated Dorian. Hated everything he took for granted. Hated how much time he dedicated to those students over his happiness, happiness that he should've showered Milo with during all those lost years of grief. But I couldn't allow the chimera to slaughter his students. My students, too. I cared about them. More than Dorian.

I had to find a way to stop the devil, free myself, and free Finn before he destroyed Dorian's world. My world.

Chapter Twenty-Three

Doppler

Power radiated off the chimera in waves, subtle at first, adapting to his new body, his new host, home, Hell incarnate, but as he grew in strength, the transcendence of a devil became almost unbearable to handle.

My telepathy, my magic, my being collided with his presence everywhere I turned, locked in this darkness until it buried me deep within a pit of unsurmountable agony. I lay here, immobilized and uncertain if I'd ever have the will to take action. Haunting the subconscious of Dorian's mind as an empty manifestation never felt like this. There was a satisfaction in the air; I could taste the pleasure the chimera took in drowning my being beneath the waves of his demonic energy.

"You get used to it."

My eyes snapped open, and I wiped away sludge from my face, searching the varying layers of darkness, the slithering shadows, all so I could locate Finn. His beautiful voice had called out, so soft, gentle, offering a reprieve from this horror.

"If you don't fight the pain, bear it, he'll lose interest," Finn explained, his voice somber and reminding me of every horrible memory I'd tucked away from him while we hid in our own little world, our own little happiness that I'd carved out. Even if it was all a lie. A lie I wanted to make reality.

I still could. I could fix things somehow. "Finn…"

"Here." His hand found me in the pit, pulling me closer, swimming through tar until his silhouette became bright and clear.

A fabrication of my mind desiring to see him whole and happy.

"It'd be wise not to want things here. He'll use that against you."

"My thoughts are less guarded than I predicted." Especially if Finn could read them.

"Everything is exposed in the shadows," he said. "Be grateful it's just us. I've had the misfortune of hearing thousands of others all at once, desperate, angry, frightened, hopeful, lost, relieved, forgotten, and every other sensation you can fathom, all weighing down on the bits of sanity you have left."

"Where is he right now?"

"Working. He often works. If you're quiet and careful, you can hear him." Finn glanced up. "Right now, he's sending a message."

Try as I might, I couldn't grasp what Finn saw. Even attempting to listen in on his thoughts with my telepathy, they were so faint and soft, like he'd spent lifetimes mastering the art of whispering his every passing musing.

"Here." Finn brushed the back of his hand against my cheek, the sweetest and most soothing sensation I'd ever experienced.

I never wanted it to end. I could die now, lost in joy, completely content and forgetting all my failures in my miserable life.

Memories of the chimera blossomed in my mind, exploding so quickly I barely registered the flashes. This was Finn's retrocognition in action, photo stills of what the chimera had done.

Theodore's sadistic smile. A wisp of energy. The carnage of Theodore's near escape. The delight in his eyes as he surrendered. The chimera slinking into Peter's mind as guards banished fiends and others escaped. Peter's possession. True possession. Blood. Tar. Magic. The city of Chicago flew by in a haze as the chimera—no, the devil—searched for something. He stabbed his hand. Blood. So much blood. Then, letters etched onto parchment while he whispered words in Latin. The letter burned in blue flames of primal casting, and the ashes fluttered in the air with purpose, thoughts of Theodore as the sprinkled note vanished in the sky.

"What was that?" I asked as the darkness returned.

"Not sure. I'm never sure with the devil," Finn said. "But I know he's pushing something sinister in motion."

"I'm so sorry," I cried. "I'm sorry I failed you. I'm so sorry I—"

"Took my memories? Let me live a lie? Compromised everyone for what?"

"For you."

"You should realize from the Hell you washed away from my mind, there's nothing left to save in me. The devil carved it all away long ago."

"That's not true," I shouted. "That's why I kept those memories. I needed you to see you had a future. *We* have a future."

"The only future we have is in the devil's grasp."

"I'll fix this."

Finn half-smiled, stifling laughter even in his thoughts as fear the chimera would scold him surfaced in his mind. "For someone who professes not to be Dorian, you're very Dorian-like. Guess that's in your nature, right?"

I frowned. Of all the comments, all the accusations, that cut the deepest.

"He always wants to fix everything, too, even if it ends up making things worse. Funny, for someone who acts like he doesn't care."

"I care, though. I can be honest and raw with my feelings, something he never learned."

"You'll want to be a bit softer with your thoughts here," Finn warned.

A warning that came too late as tar latched onto my pores like the suction cups on a tentacle, coiling around every fiber of my being and snatching me away from Finn, from the fragment of joy I held in this dark pit, and dragged up into the surface of Peter's mind. Correction, Peter's former mind. This inner core belonged to the chimera now, a devil incarnate once again because of my failures. What remnants of Peter remained were shattered, hollowed-out memories barely enough to stitch together one solid recollection.

I squirmed and fought against the tar that oozed over my flesh, sending the façade of scalding suffocation. No amount of reminding myself it didn't truly exist made these sensations any less painful.

"I find minds are so much more accommodating to my needs when under duress." The chimera's hand dug through the sludge. He gripped my face, squeezing my jaw and cheeks to the point I thought my bones would break. They endured as tar funneled its way down my throat, drowning me in rot and filth. "You should be so lucky to feel me inside you, puppet."

My eyes rolled back as he cast, his haunting magic tearing me apart and rooting through every thought I held. This was a psychic branch. Not his telepathy. Another he held, searching for something.

"Scrying," he elaborated.

A psychic magic that allowed the witch to locate or message others from great distances. It latched to my every waking memory.

"It's honestly the best way to locate anyone or anything," the chimera said, a wicked lilt of joy in his voice. "Only one thing better, in fact. And that's the guy calling about your extended car warranty. Seriously, best locators in the world."

I bit down on the chimera's hand, which continued squeezing my jaw, but naturally, it had no impact on him.

"Come on? Not even a little laugh? A chuckle? I'm being sweet and funny. You like that, don't you?" The smile in his eyes vanished as his expression soured, venomous disdain for me palpable. "Fine. Be that way."

He snapped his fingers, and the tar coating my hollow insides stabbed me from every direction, tearing at the magics holding my mind and memories intact. I screamed, resisting the pulse as the chimera siphoned information on each of the students in Dorian's homeroom coven.

"Always works a bit best when I have an image in my head, or in this case, yours." Tar splashed around the shadows, obeying the wave of the chimera's hands.

It funneled and formed into silhouettes taking shape around the muck at our feet. What bits of light remained in Peter's mind reflected off the etched lumps, creating tar portraits of Dorian's twelve students. My students. The chimera yanked memories and moments I held of each, events Dorian had me search for, musing thoughts Dorian never registered, and so much more I carried.

The chimera pointed a finger at the images he'd created for each student, shrinking them into tiny, sleek marble-like totems. Even though their silhouettes had faded, even though all I stared at were twelve round black blobs, I distinctly recognized which totem represented which student.

"That's the scrying in effect." The chimera smirked.

He channeled magic, more of his psychic scrying meant to pinpoint their locations. Within an instant, a wave of sludge bent and cracked and conjured a map of the city. Tossing the marble totems, we watched them roll throughout the city, whirling down long roads, taking sharp turns, colliding with each other, and making their way to a destination.

I didn't know where we were, but I worried whichever student was deemed the closest would be the first the chimera slaughtered. The day had passed, so none of them would be at the academy—not that I suspected the damn devil so arrogant he'd attempt an assault so brazen.

"Perhaps after I have a perfect host, I can show young Theodore how one sets a school of witches ablaze." The chimera tapped my head, mocking the insight he kept as he rooted through my thoughts.

I barred my teeth, practically growling.

"Lookie here." The chimera's eyes drifted to the marble totems, smacking into each other one by one, colliding and clumping together in one fixed location.

What were they all doing at Gael's home?

"Familiar with the place?" the chimera asked. "This is quite fortuitous. I'd intended on murdering them in small batches, splitter Dorian's sanity in slivers, while evading Enchanter Evergreen, but perhaps I should simply slaughter them in one big go and watch it completely shatter my host's hopes."

I pushed myself off the ground, preparing to challenge him, to do something because I couldn't allow him to harm any of those students.

"Relax, I'll retrieve you once we reach our destination. You can help me pick which witch to slaughter first." The chimera chuckled. "In the meantime, enjoy your reprieve with your dead lover, correction, Dorian's dead lover. But you should find some semblance of happiness in this life before I snuff out your existence entirely."

I seethed, biting back my words and holding my thoughts behind a thousand profanities to keep them guarded and scattered from his attention. If he suspected what I planned, what I contemplated, he'd stop me the same way I'd stopped him many times before.

With a snap of his fingers, I sank deep into the pit of tar, clawing and scrambling to drag myself back up, but the familiarity of Finn's soft thoughts lulled me into complicacy.

I sank deeper, finding myself drawn back to him while he studied the shifting shadows in the darkness. I swam toward him, goal in mind, plan unfolding softly between the loud, false thoughts I radiated with fake rage. "While he acts, I can counter his split attention. I can take control. I'll use the magics he's cultivated against him, and we'll bury him in the demonic energy of his own making, lock him in a cage, and then—"

"You're not the first to believe such things, to believe they can defy a devil, overpower his dominion in this dwelling." Finn's fingers moved like playing musical keys, the same way the chimera would, like the act had been ingrained in Finn's mind from lifetimes bound to the devil. "If he's allowed to live, you won't be the last to have such foolish notions."

"We can't kill him." I wasn't sure either of us had enough magic for a banishment of that level, but our psychic branches together could contain him.

"He's going to kill those children. Not in some distant future. Tonight. He'll slaughter everyone in his path, he'll steal their magics, devour a piece of their soul, bind their being to him like he has with us."

"I need more time."

"You don't. You know there's a way to stop this now."

The last thing I wanted was to surrender myself, forfeit the last few months of laborious efforts, or bring about Finn's death. His true death. But I couldn't allow the chimera to kill these children. I couldn't allow him to possess Dorian. I couldn't allow Milo to suffer because of my failures.

I had our location. I had insight into all his casting capabilities. I had his plan of action. Most of all, I had the ability to grab ahold of the tether linking me to Dorian. I could tug on it, snap his attention toward this horror, warn him, alert Milo, prevent any of this from unfolding.

All I had to do was act. Why couldn't I act? There was no chance of seeing Finn, saving Finn. There was no chance of surviving this myself; the chimera made it abundantly clear he'd sooner see me dead than bring me with him once he claimed Dorian's body. Not that I'd want to live in such hellish conditions.

Why was it so hard to make a choice, to follow through? I couldn't take action, not on a plan that'd see me dead because I'd never truly lived. I didn't want to die before finally experiencing life.

"I cannot live a life where so much carnage falls upon others so I can avoid a death I've already endured more times than I care to recollect. You may not wish to end your existence, but I will not bear witness to tonight. I can't continue watching the devil destroy lives to extend his own, torture countless witches to taste their magics." Finn sank into the abyss of darkness, sinking beyond my grasp.

I was a coward. Weak. Pathetic. Worse than Dorian, who I despised.

"Finn, wait." I dug my hands deep into the tar, searching for his presence and finding only haunting horrors attached to each drop of ooze.

I jumped back, struggling to compose myself. Finn would rather endure his own private Hell of torment than fight for a life rightfully his. It was devastating. This was why I hid his memories from him, knowing it was too much of a burden for him to carry all at once.

But he was right. We couldn't allow the chimera to harm these children. I couldn't allow any of them to die.

Chapter Twenty-Four

Doppler

"Come along, puppet." The chimera snatched me from the depths of darkness once again.

His telepathy echoed inside the inner core of what had once been Peter Graham's mind, yet every memory belonging to the man had been scraped out and replaced with acidic tar. A scalding rot that ate away at the body almost as quickly as it had eaten Peter's mind.

Using my magic, I skimmed the images floating around the devil's thoughts. We stood outside a house party, hidden in the backyard behind a shed and trees and shadows, concealed by some glamour casting the chimera utilized—one of the branches he kept veiled from me during our months together, an unwanted reminder of my utter incompetence. Steam seeped through his host body's pores while the chimera cast telepathy that scanned the dwellings inside.

Even with Peter's entropy branch mending damage, his body wasn't durable enough to contain a devil for an extended amount of time, especially not with the chimera casting multiple branches in tandem. I could exploit that; I just needed to push him harder, too hard.

"*There's well over a hundred witches inside.*" The chimera chuckled, his presence seemingly coming from every direction. "*Baby witches, but I'm wiser than to simply shrug off their training.*"

His mind slithered around the empty pocket of the backyard, skirting a hidden trail of a lush garden walkway and the off-limits caution tape Gael had placed. The curious musings of guests in the backyard indicated that much—his moms would kill him if their garden was ruined. They'd kill him if they learned he'd thrown a party flooded with people, too.

"*Lucky for him, we'll save him the hassle and kill him first.*" The chimera's grating words echoed in his mind while he continued searching further, proving his telepathy was masterful, precise, potent, and capable of the complexities that came with maintaining duality so few telepaths could master. Dorian and myself included. We only endured the sensation while working together, though he never saw it that way. He saw me as a manifestation without identity, a tool, a piece of magic.

"About time you showed up," Gael said, loudly greeting Carter and Jennifer at the front door as the chimera's sleuthing thoughts slinked around the side of the house and toward the entrance.

There were a few cars on the street, carefully scattered, which, given the attendance, was a kudos to Gael's forethought. He must've warned his guests of the potential of being busted by neighbors, meaning more carpooled, took the L, or flew here with the intention of maintaining a low enough profile to not get a noise complaint. The sigils lining the walls of his house had Katherine's touch, most likely something to buffer and muffle noise. Everything was so well thought out, I'd be proud, except it meant there surely was no chance of authorities showing.

"*What could a few police do that a hundred enchanters were barely capable of?*" the devil boasted.

But as strong as he was, as impossible as the odds were, he wasn't as powerful as when Milo first defeated him. I quelled all thoughts, focusing on the party alongside the curious chimera so I didn't tip my hand.

We hovered inside alongside Carter and Jennifer as Gael gave them a quick rundown.

"Alrighty, so we're pretty stocked." Gael pointed to a beaver levitating in the kitchen as she telekinetically distributed beers, mixed drinks, waters, and pretty much everything one could imagine. "Duchess is running the bar scene, but she's got her dam up and ready to collect those keys."

"We didn't drive," Jennifer said.

"And fledgling permits." Gael mouthed some silly commercial about friends not letting friends drink and fly, then slammed his hands together to indicate the heavy-handed warning every young witch saw on looped advertisements. "Splat!"

"I'm not drinking." Carter smiled.

"Fantastic, another designated bud." Gael grinned, pointing a thumb over his shoulder. "You can join Caleb at the goodie-two-shoes table, where we'll all celebrate your valiant efforts to keep us safe."

Jennifer rolled her eyes, spotting Caleb on a couch reading a book while sitting beside his girlfriend, Katherine, who cast her spell craft on a round of Jell-O shots with Tia and Harrison, the three using their unique enchantment branches to alter the colors, add a hint of mist, and heighten the booze while sweetening the flavor.

I'd attended enough academy parties—correction, observed Dorian attend—with Milo and Finn to recognize the same magic party tricks had survived the test of time for a new generation of teenagers.

The high-pitched scream Katherine let out as she downed a shot and giggled bubbles annoyed Jennifer to no end. She grumbled, resigned to "enjoy" herself at another party Carter declared would be fun. Even though everything about this party felt more grueling than death itself.

"*If she only knew,*" the chimera hissed, sending a quiver down my spine.

Jennifer stared at the empty air where the chimera and I hovered. The crinkle in her face as our emotional energy wafted toward her empathy made her bite back the urge to gag.

"Point me to the beer," Jennifer said, hoping a drink would make the night bearable.

Gael slung an arm over Carter's shoulder, pulling him into a tight side-hug by the boy's neck and preventing him from following after Jennifer.

"You gotta tell me," Gael whispered, sultry and delighted. "Have you finally made a move?"

Carter's eyes practically popped out of his head, they bulged so big. "Huh?"

"On gothic Barbie." Gael waggled his eyebrows.

"Uh, um, well…" Carter blushed. "We're just friends."

"Friends who shoot each other I-wanna-bang-you glances."

Carter's entire face turned bright red, and Gael couldn't determine if he'd gripped his pal with too much of a chokehold or had struck a nerve. Either way, Gael didn't relent. He liked Carter, and he found Jennifer more bearable when with her preppy prince since she didn't tell him to "go fuck himself" half as much when she was lost in Carter's pining. If there was one thing Gael understood more than any of his peers, it was hormones, who had the hots for who, and when he could play Cupid for a friend or Casanova for himself.

Gael finally released Carter, slapping his back in the process. "Make a move."

Carter straightened his jacket as he joined Jennifer.

The chimera kept close to the party host, Gael, who did a quick lap from the kitchen where Duchess remained, using her wide beaver tail to smack anyone overindulging on booze, to the dining room where King Clucks had set up a card game in an attempt to fleece drunk teens, all the way to the den where Gael had rearranged the furniture to accommodate a dance floor. One no one used since Layla and Amani stood propped on the wall, eyeing anyone so gauche as to enjoy themselves in such a juvenile manner.

"*Buzz kills!*" Gael thought so loudly it cut through the music playing. He planned to swing back around and liven up this scene, but first, he wanted to find the only guest in attendance that mattered. His heart thumped faster, rhythmic and matching the bass, as he searched for Tiffany.

Gael strolled from one crowded room to another, further revealing the state of inebriated teens that'd make for easy targets if the devil dared to spring into action and slaughter everyone inside.

"*Oh, I dare.*" His mocking voice weighed heavy on my chest, making my heart lurch. A false sensation sparked by guilt over my inaction, my inability to make the ultimate sacrifice Finn hoped I would.

Gael quirked a brow at Jamie and Tara, who stood against a wall, avoiding the party scene. Each had their first drink in hand, though neither sipped. Tara was antsy, mind locked in her ocean of sorrow as she contemplated breaking the ice and speaking to Jamie. His vacant stare at the party was as empty and hollow as his mind that'd been broken by the chimera.

"***Not enough,*** *it seems.*" Contempt seethed from the chimera as he kept his rage in check. Despite his efforts, it bubbled and boiled the rot of his inner core, revealing the disgust he dwelled on for the weakness of Jamie's body. A body incapable of manifesting the full glory of the chimera's cultivated magics, his unmatched strength. He blamed his failures against Enchanter Evergreen on Jamie, the flaw of an imperfect host body.

Tara turned to talk, to speak, to utter words, but her face grew hot, and her thoughts swirled more chaotically than they did from her usual somber touch. "I have to pee."

She stormed off, embarrassed and completely confused about why or what she hoped to gain by burying the past with Jamie. It ate away at her the same way the darkness in Jamie's mind ate away at his future hopes.

"*Ugh, painful.*" Gael downed his drink, quickly considering ways to help offer a solution. None of his ideas seemed good, yet I'd learned that every impulsive action from Gael had a tendency of working out for the best.

"Guess who." Delicate hands covered Gael's eyes and brought a smile to his face.

He spun around to take in Tiffany, captivated by her little black dress. "Here I thought you'd never show."

"Duchess said the party had a decent turnout, so I decided to give it a shot." Tiffany timed the comment perfectly by downing a fiery shot with so much cinnamon that it left an aftertaste that weighed on her thoughts heavily enough to make my tastebuds yak.

"Sent your familiar to scope out the scene." Gael squinted, imitating his own feathery familiar, and then his very serious expression fell back into his trademark grin. "Love it."

"Gonna show me around or what?" Tiffany eyed the staircase, the crowd, and then Gael's goofy face. "Was hoping for a private tour to the real hotspots at the so-called party of the century."

Gael practically levitated as his heart surged.

"*I doubt his tour will continue now that he's found a witch he'd like to explore,*" the chimera whispered with a bitter note toward the hormones wafting between Gael and Tiffany. "*Not that it matters. Despite the numbers, their current state will make them easy to eviscerate.*"

His mind slowly reeled back into himself. Layer after layer of the telepathic cord he'd weaved throughout the party while safely evaluating the scene returned to his host body that stood stiff and lifeless, hidden in the backyard.

I needed to act. Needed to do something before he unveiled the full extent of his magics and slaughtered everyone here.

"Figured I'd find you here," Gael's voice stirred in the ears of the chimera's body; the stiff muscles flexed of their own accord, filled with venom toward the young witch.

His sharklike teeth shimmered against the light of Kenzo's electrical hex that danced atop the petals of flowers in the garden. The sparkling string lights adorned throughout the backyard highlighted Gael's revealing spikes in his matching pink tank and baggy joggers. A total opposite to Kenzo's black tank and slim-fitting joggers, which were soaked in sweat from an intense workout.

"You know the garden is off limits. Gael will flip if he catches you."

"As if I care." Kenzo curled his fingers into a fist, watching his disruption magic strangle the life out of a flower that curdled inward as the vibrant pinks of its petals blackened.

The chimera wiggled his fingers, amplifying his glamour as Kenzo's disruption nearly revealed his hidden body a mere five feet away. Peter towered over the boys, a beast in the shadows cloaked by magic and ready to devour them in an instant.

"Why'd you have to kill the flower?" Gael frowned.

"Practicing." Kenzo's disruption had expanded, distorting and breaking apart all the magical energy in the air to the point it could snap and crack organic material nearby.

"*That could be a useful branch to add to my collection.*" The chimera turned back, facing me in the shadows of his inner core, thoughts reminiscing how the darkness once shimmered when he'd stored several thousand branches together.

He mused over the idea as his body, Peter's body, flexed and stretched, extending the circulation of his entropy branch and absorbing the trickled casting that made the muscles of the body swell.

"*Then again, I'd rather not bring in the consciousness of Dorian's students. It's best to strip away their lives, leaving him in shambles.*" He smirked, unaware of the synapsis firing off as his host body took in the young witches standing before us.

"You know, you don't have to push yourself so hard," Gael said, attempting to grab Kenzo's hand.

Kenzo pulled his hand away, coiling gray static around his fingers. "You've known since day one that I refuse to compromise my future, my success, my training."

His words were meant to sting, to push back, to give Gael an out that Kenzo secretly hoped Gael wouldn't take. All the same, holding his rank at number one and entering his second year had left him feeling stagnant, mainly because Kenzo still didn't have a solution to besting Acolyte Novak's magic. Failure and weakness loomed along his surface, yet his disruption cracked the words away before they echoed aloud, almost as if he feared someone would hear them, know them, feel the same concern that ate away at him. Most of all, he hated the idea Mr. Frost had a point about compatibility, a lack thereof, but he refused to believe there wasn't a solution to any problem he faced, knowing he could master any threat.

"*That'll make him easy pickings.*" The chimera prepared to take full control of his body.

"I give you my all. Every time I want to take a break, I push forward and train, study, put my big social butterfly wings away." Gael playfully leaned, almost nudging Kenzo but careful not to, given the protruding spikes on his shoulders. "All I ask is you give me something every now and then."

The smile on Gael's face, his sharklike teeth, the joy in his eyes strummed in the fragmented memories of the chimera's host body. Peter was dead and gone, devoured by the chimera's insatiable lust for carnage, yet a glimmer of his broken psyche remained intact.

The body tensed, furious and fueled with hate toward Gael. It seemed even a shattered mind could formulate orders, willpower, desire when faced with something the person wanted. Peter had always wanted vengeance against Basilisk Guild, the Martinez family, and Enchanter Evergreen. When looking at Gael, the kid became a beacon of Peter's rage. Rage that overwhelmed and overpowered the chimera's control.

"*What's going on here?*" The chimera searched the fragments, unable to stitch anything together and grasp Peter's hatred.

I kept quiet. There might be a way to exploit this, seize control, but I needed to figure out how.

Kenzo huffed. "I'm here, right?"

"But you're training, being pouty and bratty."

"I'm not a brat." Kenzo glared.

"I like brats." Gael giggled. "The dolls mostly. I had a few—"

"You could literally be here with anyone else, everyone else."

"I don't wanna be here with anyone else. I like you. I like the way you challenge me. I like the way you push me harder. I like how strict your regiments are, even if they're super fucking annoying. I like talking with you. I like listening to you teach—well, lecture." Gael's effervescent happiness shattered the chimera's hold almost entirely on his host body, severing the devil's control. "I like that underneath that tough exterior is a slightly less mean interior, and then the gooey center just past that is like a squishy sweet, but also grumpy, guy."

Kenzo scowled; everything about this moment, this cute conversation, reminded me of the hundreds Dorian had had with Finn and Milo, reminded me how he never took full advantage and lost the best potential future of all, and how these two wouldn't have any future at all if I didn't act soon.

With the devil distracted, settling the rattling nerves of his body, I channeled my telepathy in search of the tether that linked me to Dorian. I'd shake him awake, give him every missing moment, and warn him to send all the guild enchanters he could muster to my location.

"You know, speaking of brats, I can be a bit of one when I don't get my way." Gael extended his spiky hand. "And do you know what I want right now?"

Kenzo groaned. "Attention?"

"To show off my boyfriend, even if he won't let me call him a boyfriend."

"Labels are limiting." Kenzo stared at Gael's hand, longing to hold it, to take solace in the simplicity of happiness, yet the harrowing shades of black and white from his inner core bellowed that he didn't have time for simple joys. "And I don't do PDA, affection, looking cute in front of others for the sake of, what…flaunting our romance?"

Gael pouted. The type of expression that seemed to always make Kenzo crumble into pieces no matter how hard he resisted.

Without a word, without a thought of hesitation, Kenzo grabbed Gael by the collar of his tank and pulled him in close for a kiss. Passion blossomed so brightly their auras nearly turned the night sky into a sunset. The world faded away in this moment and Kenzo knew pure happiness.

"So, where'd we land on the hand holding?" Gael grinned.

"*I'll hold your hand.*" The chimera shuddered, lumbering forward and revealing his presence even though the body continued resisting him.

The terror in Gael's wide eyes stole my focus, but I needed to act fast—reach Dorian before I lost my conviction, before every student here was killed.

Taking in Peter Graham's appearance, Kenzo quickly formed a plan. Gears of calculated thoughts already whirled far louder than those of confusion at the sudden arrival of someone lurking in the shadows with a threatening expression and magic radiating out of their pores.

"***Get Gael out of here.***"

"***Who the hell is this dude?***"

"***What type of magic is this?***"

"***Gael's face—he's terrified.***"

"***His muscles are growing like an alteration branch...***"

"***But that reveal...clearly a glamour or teleportation or...***"

"***I need to fall back for maneuverability.***"

"***Multi-branched? Rare.***"

"***Too many dumbasses outside.***"

"***Drunken stupors that'll get them hurt if I cast carelessly.***"

"***Think, dammit!***"

Kenzo's frantic thoughts searched for answers, forming correct answers in fractions of seconds to things that'd take professional enchanters minutes to unravel. But the gears of Kenzo's mind at work paled in comparison to the blossoming memory from Gael's mind as he locked eyes with Peter Graham, the warlock who nearly killed him and his family a lifetime ago.

"Aaaah," the chimera said through his uncompliant host's body, his voice echoing in layers. "Vengeance truly is at the core of all actions."

The chimera fell back into the shadows of his inner core, swimming in the fragments of memories he couldn't piece together. Sparks of lightning sizzled and popped inside his head, fueling the fury further and turning those sour recollections into a haunting shade of crimson.

"*If this broken body seeks retribution, so be it. We can kill the little spiked witch. I'll turn his boned appendages into a crown.*"

I blocked out the chimera's unhinged cackling; it boomed through every angry cell of his body, feeding more demonic energy to enhance the already tremendously overpowered entropy branch.

I needed to reach Dorian now!

Chapter Twenty-Five

Doppler

Gael's immediate terror engulfed everything around us, swallowing my telepathy and the chimera's into a memory so strong it wiped away the current layout, propelling us into a fiery building where rubble and blood and destruction reigned.

Rarely did fear strike the young witch, but when it did, it carried a torrent of power more threatening than the currents of Tara's somber ocean, which had nearly drowned me once upon a time. Every fiber of my being burned and stung from the stabbing sensation of colliding with this terror, like being impaled by the spikes lining Gael's body.

"*What is this?*" The chimera's psychic image in the memory hovered in a translucent state—attempting and failing to concentrate on the world outside where his body thrashed about, running loose in an effort to slaughter everyone in the backyard. "*I'll need to kill this boy quickly. His fear is running amuck.*"

Why not quell his telepathy entirely? If he severed the connection, he'd have no trouble escaping. Did he require it to keep track of me? Did he believe it'd help control his rebellious host body? Whatever the reasoning, I needed to pull at the threads of his focus, leave him vulnerable… But first, I had to contain Gael's nightmare memory manifesting before my eyes.

His parents were covered in blood, there was debris everywhere, and the mall was in utter chaos. What should've been a sweet family outing was ruined by Peter Graham, who sought vengeance after the enchanters at Basilisk Guild arrested his crew, shut down his business, and forced him on the run. But Peter Graham didn't run from fights. His branch made him a god, and it was time to show the guild witches just how invulnerable his cellular regeneration made him.

The young and frightened Gael didn't know any of these details—this was information I'd gleaned after studying every facet of Milo—all Gael knew in this moment was his family was in danger. He was in danger.

Every bruise. Every broken bone. Every blood mark smeared upon the ground. All of it flashed before Gael's eyes, consuming him so loudly that it outweighed the bloodshed happening at the party. I couldn't discern if the screams I heard came from Gael's memories then or the students now.

Kenzo's infuriated roar of agony bellowed, shattering pieces of the memory. It held intact, the edges fractured, but soon Kenzo's voice entwined with the same screams Gael's mother released as Peter Graham stomped on her chest. The shouting and crying and screaming carried terror in every direction here in the memory, merging with the reality out there, creating such a disharmonious melody it nearly choked me.

I couldn't breathe, the same as Gael's mother, who struggled to control the water that sprayed from overhead sprinklers despite her powerful primal branch. Her casting remained nullified and drained by Peter's ominous presence.

Gael's father gritted his teeth as he forced himself to his feet through sheer force and his collection of five spiked tails. Five. Gael wondered where the others had gone and cried when he saw his dad's bloody, broken arms dangling useless to him, but he couldn't simply surrender. Not when his family's lives were at stake.

With Gael barely hitting four years old, it already made much of this unformed memory spotty despite the stranglehold effect it had, but he sobbed so hard the entire time that everything had a splotchy filter. If he couldn't contain his fear, I wouldn't be able to reach out to Dorian. I wouldn't be able to stop this from happening. I wouldn't be able to save him like he'd been saved…

I shook my head. "That's it."

I rushed through the chaos of people screaming and pushed past the crowd that swarmed around Gael, abandoning him with his injured parents alone with only a warlock that'd kill him. He knew he would die. He didn't know what death was yet, but in that moment, he understood the word so crisply as it spilled from Peter's lips.

"I'm gonna kill every single witch in your guild, your family, your city." Peter's muscles swelled, growing bigger with every breath Gael took.

He cried. His spikes had never hurt before, bothersome sure, but now they shrank and ached and ate away at the skin they sprouted from. He didn't understand. His body burned, and he wanted it to stop.

Peter's branch fed on all the channeled casting around him; Gael's constant flux of casting offered a buffet of sorts, helping enhance Peter's physical form as he ate away at Gael's branch along with every other ounce of magic in the air.

"Snap out of it." I grabbed Gael's tiny shoulders, almost feeling the prick of his spiked nubs against my palms. This was nothing but a haunting nightmare, but it carried true weight. So much so that it'd devour my telepathy if I didn't stop him. "Think past this, Gael."

Lost in the memory of the four-year-old boy who cried so hard, Gael barely registered what I said.

"Think about what came next. Don't hang onto these awful memories." I locked eyes with the small boy, hoping to see past the child in this memory and find the young man who was shrouded in fear. "What happened next? What is the shining beacon that you hold onto?"

Gael sobbed as more horrors unfolded. The memory didn't continue; it rewound to the second Peter arrived and assaulted his parents, destroying everything in sight, attacking anyone and everyone nearby. Again and again, the memory looped only on the nightmare because, outside his mind, Gael relived that nightmare as the last person he ever expected to cross paths with again came back to finish him off.

That was what Gael believed with all-consuming conviction; it locked him in this Hell.

"I can see that torch you carry, Gael." I shook him. "I can see it trying to shine this very moment."

"I-I-I…don't know."

"Show me!" I shouted, sending all my telepathy deeper into his mind, tearing the hope he had and dragging it to the surface.

Dorian never liked forcing others to face their emotions for good or bad or anywhere in between, but I didn't have time to let him sort it out independently. He didn't have time. No one did.

A blur of a man soared through the mall, slamming a fist into Peter Graham's face so hard, it created a crack of thunder. That was what Gael believed, unfamiliar with the sound of breaking bones. All he saw was a young enchanter whip in from out of nowhere to save everyone. Gael studied his hero, taking in the spikey blond hair, the stylish suit, and the unyielding smile when in the face of danger. But I saw bruised knuckles, strained muscles, and the fire in Milo's passionate blue eyes that refused to relent. I tore away the floorboards of his inner core and pushed the memory forward, past the outstanding battle that left Gael mesmerized and toward the happy conclusion that filled Gael with hope and positivity for every single day that came after.

The blurred memory swirled round and round until we'd abandoned the debris of the mall and stood in a parking lot surrounded by first responders of every kind.

Gael smiled, watching a young unknown enchanter with spiky blond hair talk to reporters. Milo hadn't saved the city at this point, hadn't become the hero of the events from the Night of the Fiend Massacre that led to swarms of citizens idolizing him. But on this day, Milo had inadvertently found his number one fan: Gael Martinez. At four years old, Gael knew The Inevitable Future was someone truly special, even before stardom had found Milo.

"I'd like to sit here with you, relive every wonderful second of Enchanter Evergreen kicking some much-deserved ass," I said. "But right now, I need you to relax and snap out of this nightmare."

Gael took a deep breath, the kind of breath that should've calmed him, yet he gasped. The soothing memory fell to pieces, and I returned to the backyard, where I found Gael half-conscious as his branch became further and further depleted.

A filthy yellow smog clouded the backyard, swirling in the atmosphere and eating away at all the magical energy from nearby witches, sending that energy snapping through the trail of smoke back to Peter Graham's body where he absorbed the power.

Gael choked, eyes watering. Each of his nerve endings fired off tingling surges, the muscles in his body went numb, and Gael struggled to take a deep enough inhale for his body's diminishing circulation. "*No quiero morir.*"

"No!" I reeled back my fear, my anger, because I had to act now.

"*Thanks for calming him, puppet.*" The chimera stood behind me in his inner core while Peter's body thrashed about chaotically. "*Thought I'd have to snap that witch's neck to get my telepathy to settle. An increasingly difficult task with the other one putting up such resistance.*"

He didn't mean Peter, his erratic host body, but Kenzo, who wheezed, covered in blood and gray static.

Chains rattled and clinked, quickly coiling around me from head to toe. They tightened, dragging me waist-deep into tar as I watched the events unfold, incapable of helping in any way.

"*Can't have you doing something we'll both regret.*" The chimera surfaced from the pits of his inner core, holding the fragmented memories of Peter Graham in a bunched ball of lightning. "*Imperfect bodies can be so temperamental.*"

I needed to think. To act. Find a way out of these psychic chains holding me.

"*We both know you don't really want to reach out to Dorian. You want to hope. Hope you'll find a way to save yourself, save Finn, save Milo.*" The chimera waltzed past me, patting my head. "*These children's lives are inconsequential. Behave yourself, and I will reward your obedience, puppet.*"

I struggled against the tightening shackles, channeling the rage in the atmosphere. Kenzo's rage, a constant flux of fury that refused to yield no matter the odds, and I wouldn't yield either.

Even though Kenzo was seconds away from buckling over from the pain of such fierce blows, he continued casting his disruption. It wouldn't stop Peter's entropy branch from feeding on the magic in the air, but Kenzo knew that. He continued casting in hopes it'd steer Peter's siphoning away from Gael and the others lying injured or rendered unconscious in the backyard.

Over a dozen students lay strewn across the yard, bloody and wounded, much like the scene of Gael's worst fears. Amidst the carnage stood Kenzo, on the verge of collapsing but standing strong as a buffer between Gael and Peter Graham.

It didn't matter though. Kenzo knew that. The subtle smog in the air was unlike anything Kenzo had experienced before. He still couldn't place the branch, but he understood the range stole away casting no matter the distance. The limitations seemed endless. Everything he cast only added to the warlock's strength, to the devil's strength—but the young witch couldn't see the true threat veiled behind the façade of a vengeful warlock.

"***There's gotta be a way to stop him. There's always a way.***" Kenzo didn't care if he lost, if this was his ultimate failure—even though every cell of his body vibrated with fright, a feeling he couldn't quite place since he hadn't felt it, truly felt it since the day he awaited news on his parents after the attack on

Phoenix Guild. A day where so much fear and hope mixed together. Suddenly, he understood why his parents gave up their lives against odds they could never fathom. All in desperation to buy a few more seconds of salvation.

"*I don't want to die…*" Kenzo swallowed the trepidation and ground his chattering teeth. "***But I won't surrender.***"

Kenzo wanted to buy those ticking seconds now. He wanted those struggling to their feet to stand and run from the danger. He wanted to redirect enough siphoning magic toward his disruption hex so Gael could breathe. He wouldn't fail, falter, or fall until the boy he loved took a breath, a free breath, and escaped.

Icicles sprang from every direction, propelling from thin air toward the chimera's body and doing nothing but further enhancing Peter Graham's muscles, which fed upon the primal magic at play.

Not that it mattered. They were a decoy, a distraction, a perfectly timed act of heroism.

Tara phased through the grass, hovering in front of Kenzo. The shock in his eyes, the relief in his exhale—both tore at him as shadows manifested across the backyard. Springing from every direction, they latched onto person after person, hurling them against the house, where they immediately phased through the solid matter before the panels of the home became imbued with a golden hue meant to ward from entry.

I sighed, mesmerized by how much Tara Whitlock had grown into her branches since the last time I'd seen her. Sure, I kept tabs, the same as I did with all of Dorian's students, but peering at the edges of her ocean, it seemed so tame compared to the last time it engulfed my being. She'd tempered her emotions, prioritized her hope for others and goals for herself, and focused on how to cast her four branches in sync.

"About time you showed," Kenzo snapped, incapable of showing the gratitude dancing on his surface thoughts, the wave of relief that hit, but he was ready to divulge a plan he'd formulated since her arrival. "We need to—"

"Like you, Kenzo"—Tara waved a hand, summoning a single shadow—"I work best alone."

It snatched Kenzo and Gael up, throwing them at the house with the others.

Before they crossed the threshold where Tara's warding magic blocked all thought, I glimpsed Kenzo's swift mental reactions.

He had enough time to cast, to disrupt Tara's shadow, the intangibility she shrouded him in, the ward put in place to activate the moment he went through the wall. With the right push of levitation and telekinesis, he believed he could pivot, counter, and strike Peter. He could help in this fight.

Every second that ticked by, his mind processed all the possible maneuvers he could perform, ways to continue fighting, but he hesitated. For just a second, a second too long, he froze, and for the first time in his life, he let the fear of failing, of dying, outweigh his need, his desire, to prove he was the best.

Kenzo's regret boomed before crumbling to silence as all that remained in the backyard was Tara. The chilling breeze made Tara's teeth chatter until she clenched her jaw and glared at us, at Peter Graham's calmed body, at the chimera possessing him, at me. Wind whirled around us almost as chaotically as the brewing storm in Tara's mind.

Her telekinesis was fast acting and compensating for her dimming branches in the presence of Peter's magic that fed upon her casting.

"I don't know who you are, why you're here, or what you

want." Tara moved her arms in a fluid motion, weaving her branches together into a powerful sphere meant to contain her foe. "You won't hurt anyone I care about."

With Gael gone, Peter's fractured mind ceased its untamed stirring, offering full control to the methodic chimera. He studied the three branches circling him, encasing us in shadows, the subtle hue of gold shimmering to lock the sphere, and the tiny pocket of intangibility that whirled waves of telekinesis inside to knock back any attempt at escape.

"*Oh, I like her.*" The chimera ran his rough hands against the sheen shadows, absorbing the magic.

Peter's entropy branch held one limitation—one that Enchanter Evergreen had exploited long ago. When Peter absorbed magic faster than he could expel it, it made his body swell with more muscular growth than his skeletal system could bear. A burden that not only slowed the warlock down but broke him internally as his body compensated by stitching together fractures caused by the continuous inflation of mass.

The devil didn't suffer the same limitations. His demonic energy feasted on the insides of Peter's body faster than the magic could repair the liquified organs, thus making Tara's continuous casting a perfect ebb and flow.

"*I shouldn't carry the consciousness of a student in my mind; it'll be so much more haunting for Dorian to be alone with no hope of companionship or salvation when I hurl him into a pit of despair, yet this one has so much power.*" The chimera shattered the golden shadows, feeding on the broken pieces scattered at his feet like glass. "*The branches inside her seem infinite and untapped. I could restore so much of my lost collection simply by snapping up her soul, her threads of magics.*"

He rushed Tara, slamming her into the house and cracking the ward she'd put in place. Instead of resisting his grip, attempting to flee, Tara reinstilled the barrier. She poured what seemed an endless amount of branch magic until the house itself became a shimmering golden shadow of translucent energy, completely warped from reality along with all those inside. Shielded. Shrouded. Protected.

"Then again, my new friend Theodore would be dismayed if I slaughtered his sister." The chimera grinned. "Hmm. Decisions, decisions."

"You know my brother?" Tara gasped. "*Is that why he's here? Have I brought this down on everyone? Again?*"

"Truthfully, I don't care a fig for the future that reckless warlock envisions, but slaughtering you would put a major thorn in his plots."

Tara trembled when the chimera wrapped his hands around her throat. His grip tightened, and all the control she held over her branches faltered. The words he'd spoken echoed in her thoughts as the ocean raged and her branches thrashed about chaotically, ineffectively against Peter's branch.

She was going to die. Tara Whitlock was about to die, and there wasn't a goddamn thing I could do to stop this.

"*Reach out to Dorian,*" Finn whispered so softly, so gently, it brought comfort while I lay bound by chains and tar. "*You can still cast. This illusion is one conjured by the mind. Telepaths don't fall for tricks of the mind; they make them.*"

The chimera cocked his head, Peter's head, almost as if he'd heard Finn's suggestion, but I knew that Finn practiced great care in tiptoeing around the devil who'd held him captive for far too long.

If I contacted Dorian, Tara would live. But Finn would die. I would die.

Tara's face reddened, her eyes glossed over, and her breathing became wispy and haggard. I trembled as she futilely clawed and slapped Peter's arms. "*I don't want... I don't want to die.*"

Her grip weakened.

Her eyes turned vacant.

Her magic simmered.

"Get the fuck off of her." A tidal wave of water exploded between Tara and the chimera, throwing the devil back as water whirled around.

Jamie stood in front of Tara, rubbing her back as she choked on air, gasping and retching from the sudden shock of release.

"He's draining magic." Tara coughed. "Not sure how…"

"I see." Jamie studied the chimera, who he didn't recognize, guised in Peter's mortal coil. The chimera resisted the teleportation effect of Jamie's branch, slowly feeding off the molecules of water that Jamie continuously summoned in hopes of hurling the threat far away. "Maybe he just needs a little push."

Jamie cast a telekinetic punch, which proved even less effective than the arcane magic at play. In fact, the chimera lapped at the telekinesis, relishing how he possessed a branch that could finally feed upon root magic—the one weakness demonic energy held.

"Guess we gotta do this the hard way." Jamie smirked, the kind of expression that washed away the hollowness in his haunted mind and reminded him that he liked to hit hard and dirty. "Try not to judge me too much for enjoying this, Whitlock."

"Huh?"

"The guy's got a very punchable face, and I've got a lot of pent-up frustration."

Jamie flew toward us, shoving the chimera deeper into the whirlpool, hitting him with a powerful tackle meant to knock us all the way through.

"Wait, J—" Tara shouted, then snapped into complete silence as the waves of water carried the chimera through a cosmic plane, hushed like the vacuum of outer space, through instant teleportation of Jamie's branch.

We reemerged, surrounded by water, currents splashing against us and making it difficult to find solid footing. Not simply for the chimera but for Jamie himself, who'd been dragged through the portal.

He backed away, summoning the water of the beach to obey his command, which swirled into a whirlpool ready to transport Jamie far away until yellow smog burrowed between the synchronized droplets and ate away the part of the whirlpool that created the teleportation effect. The chimera fed on every ounce of magic he could, preventing an escape.

"Jamie Novak," he said through gritted teeth. "Ever the thorn in my side."

"I wanted to drop you in and leave you for the pros." Jamie sloshed through the water, backstepping from the overgrown warlock plodding through the current. "Guess you're not gonna go quietly, are ya?"

Jamie continued summoning his magic, whirling it round and round until the waves of water consumed us entirely. Every molecule vibrated with the intent to teleport us elsewhere, but Peter's branch drained it before Jamie could throw us through a portal.

"You've got a stall on your branch. It's fuzzy, but I read it. The lull is delayed against the duality of my arcane branch." Jamie had a cocky grin, confidently controlling the whirlpool which engulfed us. "*It's haunting, the way this branch works like a demon, but it's not.*" Jamie settled the quake in his muscles, shaking off horrors of things that couldn't be true, but they were true. "*It's not demonic. I knew that the moment my telekinesis ended up nullified. Demons can't suppress root magic. This guy's just got an OP branch. But so do I. I'm a goddamn Novak, and it's time to remind people what that means.*"

The chimera gurgled, flailing about and kicking against the water which contained us. His smog circulated the water, lapping up the magic but not quick enough to drain Jamie's control over the flow of movement.

"You might think you're unstoppable, you might be able to drain my teleportation factors, but I've got enough energy to channel this surplus of water to keep on trying," Jamie boasted, spinning more currents of water, unleashing his wrath into chaotically precise waves. "So, you don't want me flying you off to the front steps of a guild, that's fine. I'll just keep you locked in this water until you pass out. After all, everyone's gotta breathe."

"*That so, Jamie?*" the chimera thought, tired of the frustration an arcane branch caused. If Peter Graham's entropy magic wouldn't remove the problem, the chimera intended on using one of his other magics.

Jamie trembled; his eyes widened with terror.

"*Mortals breathe.*" The chimera linked his mind to Jamie, not a gentle click of a connection either, but more like he dropped an anvil dead center in Jamie's mind. "*Demons require nothing from this world but a host to house our glory as we ascend to true devils. You remember that, don't you, Jamie?*"

He grabbed his ears, filled with confusion; broken memories of months in bondage surfaced, stitching together in ways so much of his past remained incapable of since the chimera shattered his mind.

"*Do you remember how long I held your breath?*" The chimera floated in the torrents of water, relishing the steadying ebb and flow as Jamie's focus floundered. "*Six days. Not a record, but fun. It would've killed you. Remember how you begged me to kill you?*"

"This isn't real. You're not real." Jamie sloshed through the water currents, attempting to reach the nearby shore.

"*So many fun times we had, so many techniques of torment and torture I revealed. We could've had a lifetime of lessons and lectures, but you failed me, Jamie. You fumbled and crumbled when I needed your help to secure my perfect host, a host I would've carried you into, a host who would've wanted you to have a peaceful ever after. Being the gracious god that I am, I would've obliged. Then you failed me so horribly.*"

Jamie cried, scrambling to fly out of the water, but his levitation failed, feasted upon by the chimera's newest branch magic.

"*Why'd you fail me, Jamie?*"

"This isn't real. You're dead. You're gone. This is…this is…"

The chimera snatched Jamie by the throat and shoved him under the water. "This is your end, Jamie Novak."

No!

I had to stop this, had to do something.

The shackles shattered as Jamie choked on water, fighting and resisting the pull of the abyss. That which surrounded him and that which loomed in his thoughts every single day.

"Dorian!" I screamed, pulling the tether that entwined us and sending every ounce of psychic energy I could muster, hoping it'd be enough. "You can stop this, Dorian! You can save him! You have to!"

Chapter Twenty-Six

"I think it's fate, you know?" Finn held up the sopping wet kitten with sappy thoughts and a pleading expression at the ready. Him and the kitten. They each gave me sad eyes, demanding I agree to adopt the furball.

"It's not fate," I protested—because of course I did—folding my arms to buffer any attempt of making me cuddle the kitten. "I can hear the concerned owner a few blocks over. Let's return the little fella and go home."

Finn huffed, pouty and disappointed. "Fine. Defy fate."

"Life's a random construct of chaos, Finn. Nothing happens for a reason. It's all bullshit."

How I wanted to roll my eyes at my past self and his morose outlook on life, the universe, fate, but I settled into the memory, hoping to indulge in some much-missed time with Finn. It'd been months since my subconscious had sent me flashes of my memories, giving me mostly dreamless nights and allowing me to wrap my telepathy around Milo's mind while he slept.

Only Milo wasn't here. He'd continued working late since the incident with Theodore Whitlock, frightened he'd missed something and convinced some unknown horror lurked around the corner.

I didn't want to think about all the potential dangers of endless possible futures. Perhaps I lacked the constitution for it. What I wanted was to indulge in the simplicity of this school year, help my students, continue exploring my relationship with Milo, and, most of all, sleep peacefully wrapped inside a memory of a man I loved so much. A man whose memory no longer haunted me, one I'd slowly grieved and now found solace in our history.

I watched my past self long to grab Finn's hand as we strolled down the street, offer him a gentle squeeze, show a sign of affection, but instead, my younger self walked with his hands stuffed in his pockets, cursing about the rain and blaming the kitten for our wet misadventure.

Looking back on things, I supposed fate was real. Everything happened for a reason, right? Okay, maybe a stretch, but I would've never blinked twice at the sad faces of Charlie and Carlie if they hadn't reminded me so much of this day, so much of how I hoped to bring a smile to Finn's face. So, I failed to get the kitten then but ended up with two of the best later in life.

"*DORIAN!*"

I trembled, shaking loose from the strings of this memory and shrugging off the groggy fog of sleep.

"*Listen to me!*"

Each word hit like a hammer, cracking away the memory bit by bit until all that remained were shadows. Someone continued screaming my name on a loop, calling to me, begging me, but I couldn't understand…

A gurgle underwater flooded my eardrums.

My telepathy followed the shouting, followed the person calling to me as they reeled me further from my body and dragged my psychic energy through the night sky, then latched my magic to another person's mind. Another frequency. A familiar frequency.

My eyes snapped open, and I sprang forward off the bed, gasping on the phantom pain of water filling my lungs, drowning me. I dug my nails into the floorboards, almost unable to see the wood as murky waves filled my vision.

I struggled to steady my telepathy. It'd shot across the city, latching onto someone's pain, someone's suffering. My arms quaked, syncing to the frantic flailing of the set that resisted the currents. As I sank into their mind, I struggled to find my bearings from their pain, but also, in part, their inner core held this hollow vacancy.

"Jamie." I forced all my magic into the thread that yanked me awake, steered me to this moment, and warned me of the foreboding tragedy. "What's happening?"

Struggling to my feet, I reached for my phone, eyes lost in the darkness of the room and water it felt as if I had to wade through.

Jamie choked, finally surfacing the blanket of water that held him down. How did he end up there? Hands held Jamie by the collar of his shirt, tugging him above. My chest tightened, crushed by the pit in Jamie's frantic thoughts, but equally filled with relief by whoever helped him.

"Who would I be if I let you go so quickly?" The voice was unfamiliar but threatening, ominous, and twisted with a bizarre echo.

Jamie gasped, shoved back under.

NO!

I called Milo, reeling my telepathy back, attempting to see something, anything significant.

"Answer your phone, dammit." Come on, Milo. Please. I need—

My telepathy swelled, bursting all around me and painting the room in images of the rocky shoreline, the moonlit sky hitting a sign, and Jamie casting a small tidal wave of whirled water that didn't carry a hint of teleportation.

Why? Why wasn't he jumping through, vanishing? Instead, he fought against the man's grip, fled on foot, trudged through the water, and scrambled onto the slippery rocks.

"*Pay attention,* **you fucking** *idiot!*" My voice echoed, slamming me so hard it knocked the air out of my lungs.

No. This was Jamie's lungs. A residual effect of connecting to him, feeling him gasp as his attacker knocked him headfirst against the rocks, kicking his back until his chest cracked against rough ground.

I gritted my teeth as my telepathy smacked me with information. It was as chaotic and as broken as the images linking me to Jamie.

Peter Graham. It was a name I was familiar with. But where from? Entropy. Cellular absorption. Everything about the hauntingly eerie magic unraveled in my mind. Dangerous and deadly. Intel flickered by like a strobe light, giving me fractured pieces that I barely comprehended. Finally, everything settled on a clear image of the moonlit sign: Juneway Beach.

What was I going to do? I swallowed the lump in my throat. It tasted like blood and bile.

"Dorian. Dorian, are you there?" Milo's voice called out from my phone, doing what he did best: he pulled me back when my branch threatened to knock me into an infinite storm. "What's going on? You're freaking me out."

"Milo." I retrieved my phone. "Jamie Novak's at Juneway Beach. He's being attacked by someone named Peter Graham. I'm not sure how or why this is happening, but—"

"I'm on it."

"Wait. This guy, he's got a branch called—"

"I know it," Milo said. "I know him."

Enchanter Evergreen's image threatened to tear my telepathy away from Jamie Novak, who continued resisting futilely against Peter Graham. Milo rushed out of his office, abandoning a stack of paperwork and case files he sorted through tirelessly in search of leads to small threads he might've missed connecting to bigger warlock factions linked to Theodore Whitlock. Every part of Milo refused to believe an action so brazen as attempting to fight through the MDC only to turn tail the second an obstacle appeared that didn't carry an ulterior motive. He studied every connection to Theodore Whitlock in and outside of the jail, wondering what he'd missed.

Now he knew. Milo flew out the window, calculating every possibility of fighting against Peter Graham again. Again? Recollections surfaced in his thoughts as anxiety threatened to put him in a chokehold. The same chokehold Peter Graham had landed when Milo fought him without casting, the only sure way to defeat a foe so mighty. Everything Milo believed about Peter Graham was wrong. He was never supposed to land on this path, any path that made him a threat to others in the future. The Inevitable Future had carefully calculated everything. Yet now, he doubted his magic, magic he couldn't rely on for what came next.

"Wanted to drag this out, remind you of my reach," Peter said, pulling my telepathy back to the rocky beach shore, malice and venom in every word that left his lips, so cruel each syllable sent a shiver down my spine.

"It's…it's not supposed to…" Jamie coughed and gurgled.

"Gotta be quick, though." Peter smacked his own head a few times. "A friend of mine is being very naughty, pulling on strings he shouldn't be. Talking. Talking. Sending warnings to his betters. I'll need to show him a much longer lesson than you, Jamie."

I couldn't make sense of Peter's rantings, his nonsense. Whether because I was so closely linked to Jamie Novak or my telepathy had gone through a literal shredder of psychic energy, I couldn't glean the maddening thoughts bottled in Peter's head.

"This wasn't supposed to be my grand return." Peter sulked. "I wanted a feast; I wanted to revel in the mayhem as I shattered sanity. But perhaps a slaughter is unnecessary. Maybe only one has to die."

What the fuck is he talking about?

Peter kicked Jamie, rolling him onto his back and staring down at the frightened boy. His remorseless expression sent Jamie's thoughts deep into the abyss of trauma he carried everywhere with him.

"You think one is enough?" Peter cocked his head like he was searching for an answer, a response, but not from Jamie. "Honestly, I'm glad it's you, kiddo. This should've been your end all along."

"I don't want… I don't… I…" Blood and grime covered Jamie's face. His eyes widened when Peter reached out to grab him. Skin ripped, bones crunched, and tears streamed across Jamie's horrified face as Peter squeezed his grip. "*I don't want to die.*"

Peter whipped his hand in a swift, fluid motion and snapped Jamie's neck.

Every cell in my body vibrated. My insides were scraped out, gutted, and hollowed. I clung to the throbbing ache in my bones, the burning in my muscles, the agony that carried the last sensation I'd ever feel from Jamie Novak.

My telepathy exploded, whipping across the city chaotically until it found Milo, who flew closer and closer to save a life.

"*There's no point,*" I thought, linking to Milo as I collapsed to the floor and sobbed. "*He's dead.*"

Chapter Twenty-Seven

The days that followed Jamie Novak's death carried a suffocating routine of well-meaning expressions of grief. Guilds conveyed their sympathies to the mourning Novak family, a very public message meant to show the city itself shared in the sorrow. But Chicago didn't cry. Too many people were fighting their own battles, enduring their own struggles, surviving their own lives to grieve alongside the elite family that'd lost the heir few knew and even fewer liked.

Many bubbling thoughts, too many, carried doubts surrounding the situation, memories of the boy who housed a devil, the one people said was as cruel as a demon before becoming possessed by one. It made going anywhere and everywhere unbearable. When Finn died, hardly anyone knew the young enchanter, and those who did had excruciatingly kind thoughts surrounding the incident. *Incident.* Such a tactful way to say murder. But the news cycle ran with Jamie's death, fueling everyone's unwanted opinions.

Gemini's well-staged grief came with a grating exhaustion. Headmaster Dower had the best intentions, from the thoughtfully composed email to staff, her careful announcement to students, and her perfectly laid out agenda for what came next. She'd prepared for every conceivable step or reaction to grief.

A moment of silence on day one. The auxiliary gym was closed. She'd given staff a message to share with students, a list of questions to expect, possible responses to offer, resources and avenues for us to delegate this to someone more suited. Counselors were at the ready, with specialists contacted for those in more urgent need.

Even the substitute Headmaster Dower obtained for Mrs. Whitehurst's classes was top-notch. In all my years of teaching alongside Chanelle, I'd never seen her take a single sick day—hell, she even passed up half her personal leave time—yet she took three days, completely dropping off the radar, then returned Thursday ready to jump into the next fluid motion of the headmaster's stages of grief, where Chanelle helped prepare for the upcoming Gemini Academy vigil.

A moment of remembrance for Jamie Novak, a chance to share in the joys the students had, a timed ceremony not meant to impede learning but placed before the impending funeral services.

Impending. It sloshed around my head like a looming threat. It was, too. I hated funerals. I hated the sorrow in other's minds. I hated the other emotions more: frustration, annoyance, boredom, placating, tact, wishful musings, and a thousand other things in between.

Everything surrounding Jamie's death—his murder—had this step-by-step agenda meant to usher us through to the next checkpoint, hit our low, and move forward without missing a beat.

The organization for this week was meticulous. But I'd coped with grief… No. I'd survived alongside grief, existed in its waves for years on end, dragged to the depths of nearly drowning and rising to the surface through false hope only to be consumed in endless tidal waves of sorrow.

Grief didn't carry a timestamp. The best intentions couldn't simply sweep our staff and students hit the hardest by this loss.

Maybe I had bad coping mechanisms and handled loss poorly compared to those around me, but I couldn't focus on the next stage, the plan. That was what death did to me; it threw out all the plans I had, it—

"Mr. Frost." Gael's soft voice in a silent classroom pulled me from my thoughts.

He stood at my desk, fidgety, and clearly had to repeat himself a few times before pulling me out of the haze I walked through this week.

"Yes?"

"Can I get a pass to the library?" he asked sheepishly as he ran a hand through his shaggy hair.

Gael hadn't styled his spiky hairdo once since the attack on the party; his black roots even started growing, and given the season, I expected him to keep his autumn blend of colors perfectly on point. Seemed everyone had lost their focus.

This close to Thanksgiving break, I anticipated a loss of interest in learning. Honestly, over the years, I'd grown accustomed to lackluster performances around the holidays, so I took it upon myself to move toward recap mini-lessons and make-up work. But with everything that'd happened, I didn't even have the energy for that much.

Jamie's death was devastating, brutal, and held nearly everyone's attention, but several others were attacked at the party, injured, and carried the scars of that trauma everywhere they went on campus.

Unable to put together a real lesson this week, I'd allowed my students to do what they wanted. Train, study, goof off, sit with their thoughts—truly anything.

So, when Gael asked for a pass to the library, I obliged. Hell, I'd already given Layla and Melanie a pass to some math class for SAT prep. Not that either made it. I heard their wandering minds as they roamed the halls of Gemini.

I scribbled a sloppy pass in case Gael got a little lost on the way to the library, and admin wanted to know where his teacher had permitted him to go. "Do I need to add anyone else to this pass?"

Gael blinked a few times, shaking off his own haze of thoughts—something a lot of students had done since the party. Gael was affected especially hard, based on what I'd gleaned from him, from others, from reports, and from Milo's mind after he'd analyzed all the responding guild accounts.

Most of all, I could see it in Gael's somber blue aura, which had washed away the bright orange cheer of his personality. His thoughts were mostly in Spanish, so I struggled to comprehend more than half of the words and phrases, but I felt the similar chords of guilt he carried; they were reminiscent of those I held for Finn for far too long. What did Gael have to be guilty over?

"Just me." He faked a weak smile that hid his sharklike teeth.

I stared at his black eye, the deep bruising running along his face, similar to the abrasions along Tara's neck. They weren't the only ones injured at the party, but they put up the most fight. Or tried before…

At the end, even those injured considered themselves fortunate after the news of Jamie's murder was announced.

Part of me expected Gael to drag Kenzo to the library. Well, I expected Kenzo to drag him there. Kenzo didn't, though. He didn't do much of anything at school. He didn't train. He didn't study. He didn't strategize for the future. He simply sulked quietly. Even the thunderous words of his thoughts stirred softly like the patter of trickling raindrops.

Kenzo stared at the pages of a book, his expression calm and reserved, nothing like the Kenzo I'd grown to like since last year. No death stare at onlookers, no practiced scowl, no defaulted glare at the ready. "*What's the point?*"

So faint, so sad, it reminded me of Tara. Oh, Tara. She'd once again returned to isolating herself in the furthest corner of the classroom, avoiding everyone, including her friend Gael, who didn't cause mischief or burst into random fits of laughter. Even he sat quietly, contemplating while sharing a conversation with King Clucks in his thoughts. What I assumed to be a conversation, even if I only heard Gael's side.

There was guilt swimming at the edges of Tara's ocean, unlike the natural guilt she carried with her every single day. No, this new thread of blame came from the party. The tragedy Tara believed she'd caused.

Peter Graham said her brother's name, attacked a party she attended, and killed Jamie for interfering. It was difficult discerning more from her mind without delving into the powerful undertow of her thoughts that'd surely drown me. Still, Tara had convinced herself this was because of her. But it wasn't.

I'd connected enough dots eavesdropping on Milo to know that much. He hadn't stopped working since Jamie's murder. He analyzed all his notes, all his potential futures, all his contacts' information, and nothing indicated a connection, good or bad, between Theodore Whitlock and Peter Graham. Whatever drove Peter to that party, whatever malicious motives he harbored, Tara's presence was a mere coincidence.

Milo. Christ, how I wanted to talk with him. I wanted to lean on his shoulder, grieve, mourn, but we'd been down this road before, and Milo only knew me as the type of man who boxed up his grief and pushed away anyone who offered comfort. He did what he believed I wanted in this moment, which was to offer space while doing what he did best when grieving—he buried himself in work. He searched for answers. He fought for the best future even if his heart broke across the city, convinced he'd lost sight of the best futures for all.

With the classroom so silent, it didn't take much for my telepathy to reach out to Milo's mind, a soothing comfort after the way it'd found Jamie as I slumbered. I reeled back my branch, quelling my magic despite the psychic pain of breaking away from Milo right as his image materialized before my eyes.

I didn't understand why my magic sought Jamie out. I cared about the kid, wanted to help him, wanted to fix the damage the chimera had done, but I'd never truly linked my branch to his thoughts, his inner core. It was a haunting realization that my magic had developed so much since my own near-death experience and now might seek out those I cared about to any degree during their worst moments and give me a glimpse into horrors I couldn't prevent.

I swallowed the dread consuming me, knowing that I needed to sit down and do a real, proper evaluation of my growing branch magic. Updating a license, testing magical limitations, evolutions, improvements, or deteriorations was a lot like going to the doctor when you knew your body was broken. They were going to ask why I kept moving forward for so long with the check engine light flashing on repeat before finally figuring out what the hell was wrong. I hated surprises, but sometimes, ignorance was bliss, and as a mind reader, I rarely got to avoid the truth of things.

My phone buzzed.

Milo: How are you holding up?

A text. Which he immediately followed up with a gif because of course he fucking did. Some guy biting his lip while anxiously awaiting a response. I chuckled. Okay. That was a little funny.

Milo: Was wondering if you could help me out with something.

I stopped typing, watching the dance of three floating bubbles.

Milo: It's not like urgent but also sort of semi-important. You know?

Me: Anything.

Milo: Awesome.
Now, when you say anything...
Do you mean anything *anything* because I'd love to 🔨 some 🍑
Or we could just 🍭 🍆 😏

I stuffed my phone into my pocket, resisting the smile that came from each buzzing text of Milo deflecting his grief, his stress, with horny humor.

Desperate for a reprieve, I sped walked down the empty hallway toward the staff parking lot where I planned to hide for my entire planning period. The distance would alleviate the headache of emotions that ranged in far too many directions to handle, and perhaps a few cigarettes would decrease the massive amount of stress stacking atop my shoulders with each passing minute of the day.

As I reached the front doors, a spritz of water hit my arms. I paused, rubbing a hand along my dry shirt sleeves.

"Fuck," I mumbled.

The sensation of raindrops continued splashing against my skin. A light rain that carried the heavy weight of actual tears from someone's deep sorrow. I turned, staring down the halls in every direction, but found no one nearby.

I should've pushed through the door and let the sun outside dry away the emotional sadness that clung to my telepathy, yet this gnawing guilt ate away at me. Somewhere in this building, a student struggled with Jamie Novak's death so deeply that the emotions stretched across the academy and latched to my mind. This wasn't one of my students. No, I'd become familiar with their emotional frequencies, the most subtle echo of their thoughts, even when wordless, such as now.

"Fuck." I cracked my neck and turned on my heel in search of this broken kid, knowing full well I had absolutely nothing to offer in regard to lessening the sadness that spread throughout the building. Still, I couldn't help but want to help. Help. Help. Help. It was a word I heard from Jamie's cries as that warlock snuffed out his life.

Help. It was something I often failed to do.

Help. It was something I deluded myself into thinking I could offer.

Help. It was a word that began to lose all meaning in my mind.

As I reached the third-year student hallway, I found an aura of somber blue so deep and dark it resembled the blackness one might find at the bottom of an ocean. This mind radiated sadness, guilt, regret, rage, defeat, misery, and so many other emotions in tandem, I was shocked they'd managed to get out of bed and make it all the way to Gemini—even if all they did was hide from their classes in a part of the academy rarely used in the afternoons since third-year students spent most of their school days at internships.

Following the aura's trail, I opened the stairwell door and found Vik sitting crisscrossed at the bottom step with three shadow cats dancing in circles before collapsing into puddles of goop.

"I still can't get it." They wiggled their fingers like a puppeteer yanking on the strings of their magic, which reformed the shadow cat shape of three silhouettes.

Their magic was powerful, versatile, and capable of mimicking any and every magic conceivable, yet they sat in their sadness, believing their branch incapable of the simplest of tasks.

Bright yellow cut through the somber blue, casting sunlight in the stairwell that nearly made me wince from the sharp light.

"You're getting better at it," Katherine said, scooting closer to Vik.

From my vantage point, hidden at the top of the railing, I could barely see my student who was currently skipping her statistics class to sit in silence with Vik. Not that Katherine's attendance mattered this close to the holiday or given the fact she had a perfect score in the class.

"No, I'm really not getting better." Vik smashed one of their three shadow cats into black smoke between their hands while redirecting the two remaining cats. "I never tried hard enough during class. Never bothered when outside of school. Now, I can't work with him, so Jamie's branch is lost to the world. Not that some second-rate trash like me deserves to—"

"Stop that," Katherine said, an edge in her voice as her thoughts turned sour. She often believed in the best for everyone around her, so when Vik berated themself, it turned the edges of Katherine's joyful aura to a glint of crimson red.

"I just… I don't know…" Vik shrugged. "I thought it'd be a nice way to remember him."

"I did a hybrid spell with Jamie." Katherine retrieved her grimoire, flipping through the pages to the spell I'd encouraged her to work on as a way to subtly help Jamie.

Help. Jamie. There it was again, my delusional selfishness.

"Won't work." Vik managed to swirl the two shadow cats together into a black whirlpool. "I've copied Harrison's elixirs before. If his potion craft enchantments are anything like your spell craft, then all my branch can do is copy your ability to create spells, not the actual spell you created on a particular page."

I understood. Vik's mimicry would copy a blank page where they could, in turn, write down a spell of their own. But a spell that embodied Jamie's arcane magic would be among the most complex and sophisticated phrasing on parchment.

"Oh." Katherine released a bitter exhale, doing her best to push away the sadness that threatened to creep inside her.

It wasn't the same sadness carried by her classmates. Katherine didn't feel the loss of Jamie. I didn't believe she begrudged him, but there was no emotional pain to his death in her mind. No, the sadness Katherine carried came from how his death, his murder, rippled through the hearts of everyone around her that she so deeply cared for. She felt awful for what happened to Jamie, the act itself, but it pained her more to see those left so broken in different ways, heartache eating away at their joy, and she couldn't think of a single spell to fix all the sadness.

Katherine merely wanted to find ways to cut through that grief, pack it away for others, and move forward. It was a very Milo-esque philosophy. Admirable, if not mostly vexing.

There was one thought that sat in Katherine's throat like a bitter pill too big to swallow and too rude to speak. She'd dwelled on her ranking this year, having only moved up one slot from eighth to seventh, and upon seeing Jamie this semester, it dawned on her that she only managed to move up because Jamie's ranking had plummeted at the start of the new school year.

Vik's black whirlpool splattered onto the floor, and they released a heavy sigh and then waved their hands until the magic dissipated. I wished their sadness would've disappeared as easily, but it clung to their mind.

"You know, I might have another idea." Katherine slammed her grimoire, startling Vik, which sent a shudder through my body as my telepathy latched to their emotional uncertainty.

"W-was…was that necessary?" Vik's voice didn't carry nearly as loud through the stairwell as Katherine's action, which continued to echo.

“You want something to remember Jamie with, his magic, right?” Katherine asked, knowing her gesture pulled all of Vik’s focus from their thoughts and onto her question.

“Yeah, but…” Vik bit their lip, unable to form words for what they wanted. Even their thoughts lacked tangibility in what they hoped to express.

“I have an idea. Complicated idea. Complex idea? It’s an idea. A big one. Either really, really good, or plain awful.” Katherine smiled. Not the beaming expression that filled her entire face with joy but a soft smile meant to invite others to find a bit of happiness. “I need to talk to Caleb about it. He knows this stuff better than me, but I think we’ve got the right magics. Well, maybe. Depends. It’s something my dad and aunts did for my grandma way back when.”

Katherine strummed her fingers against the spine of her grimoire while her thoughts spun in a hundred different directions, weaving down the aisles of her mind, stitching together half-concocted plans and plotting to make everyone around her a little happier. I struggled to make sense of what she’d conceived since her aura burned bright, and her surface thoughts were almost as swift and methodic as Caleb’s.

I slinked back, slipping quietly through the door and leaving the two of them in the stairwell to sit with their feelings, realizing I had nothing to offer them. I couldn’t help them because I couldn’t help anyone. Not right now. Not until I dealt with my own grief and guilt.

Milo insisted on meeting me at the academy. Apparently, he couldn't be swayed to come back to my place since he had a late night of work. A late night of avoidance, but I'd take what I could get, and honestly, helping him in any small way was a wonderful distraction.

I leaned against the hood of my car, taking in the brisk air as I smoked a cigarette. Work had left me emotionally exhausted, enduring the barrage of thoughts in all their many forms. And truthfully, empty school days left me more drained than fast-paced classes. Doing nothing was sometimes the most tiring fucking thing in the world.

All I wanted was to go home and crash on the couch, but I waited for Milo alone in the empty parking lot.

"***Where the fuck is he?***' Kenzo's aggravation lit a spark that brushed away the chill outside.

Taking a deep inhale, I finished my smoke and wandered toward the front of the academy, where Kenzo sat with a book in his hands but none of the words in his thoughts. Nothing he did worked to focus his mind, retain the information, and escape the failure that loomed over him like a shadow.

"Waiting on your ride?"

Kenzo huffed. "Gael's in a study group. Which should've ended ten fucking minutes ago."

"Surprised you're not in there with him."

"Why would I?" he asked curtly, requiring and wanting no response. "I don't need to study. You've seen my grades."

"Pretty sure they're up there because of all the studying, training, hard work."

"Whatever." Kenzo tucked his book in his bag.

So much for having a moment. Geez, I wished Milo would show up already.

Past the shadow of failure weighing down on Kenzo's shoulders, luminescent orange cut through the skyline. Gael's joy had blossomed despite all the somber emotion he carried this week.

Curiously, instinctively, I reached out with telepathy, navigating the barren hallways of Gemini and reaching the library where others had just left, but Gael stood with shock and awe at the surprise visit from his idol, his hero, his inspiration: Enchanter Evergreen.

"What're you doing here, Mr. Enchanter Evergreen, sir?" Gael gulped, wishing he could go back and rewind this moment, undo his fumbling question, while also scrambling to fix his hair that he couldn't believe looked so bad.

Despite having met Enchanter Evergreen at several events and lucking out by landing in a class where his teacher dated The Inevitable Future, Gael had never once had a one-on-one conversation with Milo. There were a million things he wanted to say, to ask, but in the moment, his brain completely froze.

"*Why would Enchanter Evergreen want to talk to me?*"

A valid question and one I wanted an answer to as well. It seemed Milo's assistance involved keeping Kenzo occupied while he spoke with Gael. But why?

"*A head's up would've been nice.*" I linked to Milo's mind, which he masterfully ignored, not so much as revealing a micro expression to my intrusive comment.

"I know what happened has been weighing on you," Milo said with a gentle smile, the kind he donned when showing care over confidence.

"Yeah, it was…" Gael averted his eyes and paused.

"Peter Graham is a scary man, warlock, and I imagine it's brought up a lot of old wounds."

"Yeah, my folks said pretty much the same thing."

"You know what happened wasn't because of you, right?"

"I guess." Gael shrugged. "It's not really…I don't know. It's hard to say why he was there, and it's incredibly narcissistic to assume he showed up because of me. Doubt he even remembers me."

Peter did remember him, though. That much I gleaned from Milo's surface thoughts as he had set Peter on a potential path that'd keep him as far from interacting with the Martinez family ever again, along with never gaining access to his branch after all the damage he'd caused with the entropy magic. All this on top of instilling a degree of fear for authority that'd keep Peter compliant with the law. The thought weighed on Milo, wondering if he'd inaccurately predicted Peter's future if he'd steered him toward a breaking point, a cruel outlook where he'd take any measures for violence.

"What's got me down is that I froze," Gael said. "I didn't do anything to help. I needed to be saved. What's the point of training to be a professional enchanter if I choke the second trouble shows up? I basically did the same thing during the warlock incursion."

He didn't!

"That's not true," Milo said. "You played a vital role in support, making sure everyone stayed safe."

"Yeah, support. Not very good, and I couldn't even manage that much this time."

Milo studied Gael, thinking back to the events where their paths first crossed. For Milo, looking back on memories was more difficult than it was for me. His thoughts fluttered in and out of visions long since faded, discerning the potentials he'd skirted and the realities he'd cemented. How he made sense of what could've happened versus what actually happened was a miracle of his mind.

"Do you know why I arrived when I did that day your family was attacked?"

"Because you had a vision. Because you're Enchanter Evergreen, and saving people is what you do."

"Okay, but that's not why I arrived when I did. I was late, later than intended." Milo craned his neck, attempting to meet Gael's eyes as he kept his head turned away shamefully. "I had a vision of a very dangerous fight on my hands. I was terrified. I froze. Just a few minutes, but that fear felt all-consuming. And I was already an enchanter at that point. So, if pros are allowed to falter, to hesitate, shouldn't you be allowed, too?"

"But you did the right thing. I can't go back and…" Gael dwelled on Jamie's death.

"Fear and failure are not the same thing." Milo patted Gael's shoulder, a hand pressed against one of the larger spikes with his fingers carefully avoiding the smaller spikes that lined the one sprouting outward. "The world is filled with so much cruelty and needless chaos. Sometimes, staring directly into that chaos can be petrifying."

"Thank you." Gael looked Milo in the eyes. "Guessing you had a vision that brought you here. Despair or…I don't know. Something bad because of me. Sorry you had to come out here and—"

"I did. I have lots of visions. Currently having one now." Milo laughed. "But do you know what triggers my visions? My branch?"

"Yeah, there's a lot of factors." Gael's mind swirled in thoughts so swiftly and cumbersomely I could've mistaken him for Caleb, given all the data he had on the great Enchanter Evergreen.

"There are a lot of factors. One of them is how people's feelings are directed toward me."

What? I quirked a brow.

"If someone's frightened of me, I might get a vision of potential future nightmares they'll face or secrets they want to stay hidden, lots of random possibilities. If they express anger in my direction, sometimes I glimpse arguments, violence, battles, sporting events—usually with their team losing."

Gael listened intently, in awe, because Milo had never divulged this to anyone, and Gael would know since he'd watched, read, and listened to every single recorded interview Enchanter Evergreen had done.

"The best emotion, the reaction that I strive to bring out in others, is belief," Milo explained. "It's weird wanting people to put me on a pedestal, but that shows me futures where I can potentially do the most good, help the most people. It's the hope of others, their gift to me, that makes The Inevitable Future possible."

Emotions did carry such tremendous weight in this world. I only saw snippets of auras in the atmosphere, but they seemed to merge with nature itself, sparking chemistry and magic and so much more we had barely gleaned.

"The day I rescued you, the awe in your eyes, the gratitude in your smile, it gave me the very first snippet to a vision that helped make me the number one enchanter in Chicago."

"Wait, you mean the Night of the Fiend Massacre?" Gael asked, wide-eyed.

"It took some real investigation after that, months to fully unravel the vision and organize the guilds properly when the time came, but it might've never happened if I hadn't crossed paths with you that day, if you hadn't believed in me more than anyone else ever had."

"*Enchanter Evergreen es increíble.*" Gael smiled, truly smiled, for the first time since before the party where I worried he'd forever lost that spark of joy in his heart.

"I hope you'll remember to believe in yourself, Gael." Milo smiled back, almost as big and bright as Gael's sharklike teeth. "But if you ever falter, know that I believe in you."

I drifted from their conversation, content to let Milo handle what he saw as righting a future that'd strayed off course where he believed Gael was meant for.

"Gael's gonna be a minute." I plopped onto the bench beside Kenzo.

"Is he looking at those damn comic books again?"

I lit a cigarette, avoiding offering Kenzo an answer. Besides, half the time, I couldn't tell if he was being rhetorical or not. He rarely sought input, even when vocalizing a question.

"You know"—I forced out a deep exhale, letting the smoke waft with icy breath as I contemplated how to approach a much-needed discussion—"you're probably the most ambitious student I've ever had. And I've had some kids with big egos."

"Is that an insult?" Kenzo tsked, an act to remind me nothing I said could faze him, which was probably true. But he did more damage to himself with the words he slung inward than anyone else could ever hurl at him.

"You were scared when Peter Graham arrived, scared in a way I don't think you've ever been. Not since I've known you, and I've seen you faced against frightening odds." While Milo consoled Gael, rehashing the events of their first encounter, I took it upon myself to hopefully offer a bit of guidance to Kenzo.

"I wasn't scared." Kenzo ground his teeth.

He was. He replayed the events on a loop in his mind, freezing his thoughts, his memory, to the singular moment when he allowed his fear to let him flee.

"Do you know why I teach students about failure?" I asked, rhetorical as fuck, and savoring the tiny joy I got from Kenzo's internalized profanities over the question. "I do it because I need you all to understand it's okay to stumble, to falter, to fall flat on your face. I want these experiences to occur in a safe space because there's nothing safe about the casting industry. That said, you've held yourself with grace and skill in situations you should never have had to face at your age."

"I was ready for anything when he showed up and attacked." Kenzo stared at the concrete. "I just don't understand why I was so relieved when Tara pushed me out of the fight. I've never… I don't know who I am if I can't protect others, if I can't beat anyone. Everywhere I turn, there's someone with better magic than me, better skills, better belief in themselves, and I'm starting to think I'm not what the world needs."

"Your disruption, hell, the hex branch in general, is classified as a support magic. I've worked with a lot of students at Gemini. I've also read a lot of studies, researched enchanters across the nation, and I'm not sure I've ever seen someone with a disruption magic take on a team leader role, a combative licensing type, but here you are proving your magic would be what you made of it. You didn't let statistics determine who or what you saw for yourself, so don't let a few moments of hesitation wash away all the certainty you've got going."

My pep talk probably needed work, but bits of the apprehension in thc shadow looming ovcr Kcnzo crumblcd.

"It's okay to lose faith in yourself from time to time. It's all right to contemplate where you fit in the world. But it's important to listen to those whispers of belief in yourself, even when they're so soft and wispy you can't tell if they're there. They are. Take it from a telepath. It's okay to doubt, too, but it's important not to let those nagging thoughts consume you."

"Yeah, guess you're right."

"Obviously, since we both know you're not." I cracked the tiniest of smiles, which only aggravated Kenzo more. "I believe in you, and I'm okay believing in you even if you need to pause and contemplate."

"*Thanks...*" Static perfectly coiled Kenzo's hairline, creating a crown of sorts that buffered and blocked his surface thoughts.

"Impressive." I took an inhale from my cigarette.

Kenzo scoffed. "***Go have a Hallmark bullshit moment somewhere else, Frost.***"

I choked on a puff of smoke from laughing so hard, which Kenzo took as a personal slight to his proficiency. He stormed off into the parking lot to train since Gael was taking **for-fucking-ever**, as Kenzo, in his renewed sense of self, would put it.

"*You could've told me your favor involved helping one of my students.*" I linked to Milo's mind, stealing him from his chat with Gael, who had a thousand questions that he'd managed to narrow down to a healthy hundred.

"*Two students,*" Milo thought, managing to answer Gael's questions. "*Besides, if I told you, it would've altered the potential. You're really bad at rehearsed meaningful conversations.*"

"*That's not true.*" I huffed. "*I'm pretty bad at all forms of meaningful conversation.*"

Milo grinned. "*And I'm sorry I've been distant.*"

"*I get it. You need to work, need to solve...this.*"

"*It's not an excuse. I never saw this, not even an inkling.*" Milo acted out some fight against some warlock Gael mentioned from a decade ago, almost appearing joyfully lost in the moment. "*I'm here if you need me, Dorian. I just need to be there for others, too.*"

"*I understand, and honestly, I'm fine.*"

"*The four-letter word of doom. Does this mean you're gonna avoid me for the next six months?*"

"*Dick.*"

"*Save the dirty talk! I gotta get back to work after this.*"

"*I'm glad you're helping everyone. And I am fine. F I N E. But I want to make sure you're also okay, that you're not burning yourself out.*"

"And that's because The Inevitable Future always comes out on top," Milo said, answering Gael's question and responding to me without actually responding. "*I'm okay, Dorian. Thank you for your concern. It paints a pretty future.*"

"I love you, Milo," I whispered, sending all those emotions his way, every fiber I could muster through this sadness because I wanted him to only see futures that revealed my love, my hope, my happiness for him and everything he brought me.

"*I love you, too.*"

Chapter Twenty-Eight

I arrived at Jamie's funeral, my mind edgy and uncomfortable. Mourning fluttered throughout those in attendance, mixed with a multitude of thoughts for the hundreds who arrived, from guild members to classmates to staff to the dearest and nearest of the Novak family. Some were filled with regrets for what they said, what they didn't say, what they never could say to Jamie. Some were preoccupied with the pretense of grief. Some were aggravated by the chill in the air that no amount of bright sunlight above could penetrate.

All in all, emotions were strewn about in every damn direction with this massive group.

Quelling my telepathy wasn't an option, not with so many around and my mind in such a state of shame. Had I worked harder, done more, realized Jamie's pain sooner—none of this might've happened. I focused on those I cared for, minds like my students, Milo, Chanelle, and tried to let them ground me during this ordeal.

"*I'm fine,*" Chanelle thought.

I frowned. She believed I'd invaded her head to offer comfort, kindness, but it was selfishness on my part.

Chanelle stood with her husband, Kyle. Her thoughts would've been easy to latch onto, to offer relief for us both, but she didn't want that. Right now, she remained strong and composed, diligent in being her best self for the other students, the ones she hadn't failed. Her mind stirred to thoughts, to her past, to her mistakes she'd rather not share, so I buried the images before they cemented in my mind. I couldn't offer her solace, not with my own regrets, so I left her alone, content that Chanelle would reach out when she needed it. And I'd be there to talk, to listen, to focus on her pain and not make it about mine.

Speaking of someone who knew how to offer comfort when sinking in sorrow, Milo stood near his acolytes at the front of those gathered. First and foremost, he came to offer support, even if his mind rooted through visions, those he believed he'd missed and those yet to occur. I let him focus on guild work, let him fixate on offering the best potential outcomes in spite of believing he'd faltered too much. Keeping a careful eye on Milo, I watched him study his acolytes' changing futures, the shift of their colorful threads of destiny. Still intermingled from what Milo could tell, yet Lena's drifted, the indigo shade darkening, withering, and reaching for new pathways.

Milo didn't want that, didn't believe Lena's best future lay on her own, so he worked to subtly steer things, hoping to help her work through the grief in the same way he'd always wanted to help me. Only when Finn died, I pushed Milo away. I hoped Lena didn't turn into me, putting her life on pause and spiraling into isolation.

Lena appeared stoic on the surface, both in expression and her highest thoughts. Sorrow drifted around her, but she didn't sink into the depths. She didn't show her sadness, not the faintest trace on her face, and her thoughts prioritized what a Novak was meant to do. Even her parents remained pillars of support for those around them, refusing to crumble in their sorrow, sorrow Lena didn't believe they held for Jamie's loss, so she remained completely composed. A true pillar of support even in her grief.

But deep in her inner core, she thrashed chaotically, raging with a brewing storm strong enough to level a mountainside. Or worse, level a city. I couldn't hear anything past the muffled screams; if I reached out and touched her inner core, it'd shatter my mind. Still, the belief was there. It was in Milo's mind as he studied Lena. He feared her futures were pulling away from the paths he desired, the potential he believed would make Lena happiest alongside Ellie and Hayden. Love. Friendship. Passion. Support. Each thought glimmered as Milo analyzed visions, stringing together what he hoped wouldn't make the situation worse. Most of all, he sought the missing Peter Graham, who evaded all the guilds and sent a nagging reminder that no matter how much Milo prepared for everything, there were things he couldn't predict or prevent.

Everyone here infuriated Lena, pushing her thoughts further away from the sadness threatening to consume her and higher toward the peak of fury which fueled her magics. A storm of rage below, flames of wrathful heat above, it seemed only anger lay in Lena's future.

It was difficult to hone in on her thoughts, a struggle Milo must've also experienced. Lena was casting even here at the funeral. With so much of the semester spent listening to Kenzo's mind as he navigated ways to pinpoint Lena's branch at play, I found it easy to spot the subtle shimmer of bubbles before they popped. They were scattered throughout the cemetery, stretching further than my mind could follow. What was she doing?

The opening eulogy pulled Lena's attention, pulled my attention as her emotions settled. It was a lovely speech, filled with meaningless quotes to poetry Jamie never knew, achievements he'd never made, and completely swept aside the actual bravery he had, both when possessed and when facing the foul warlock who killed him. Lena didn't care for the rewritten narrative but understood that pretense dictated something more appropriate to survive the history books no one except future generations of Novaks would read. She wondered how many of their feats were lies made palatable for social graces.

Lena wasn't the only one. Tara listened to the speech, eyed those captive and proper during the eulogy, and was reminded of similar fabrications at Theodore's funeral. But everything about his death was a lie, including his death. That haunting truth ate away at Tara almost as much as Jamie's actual death did.

Tara shook, her face turned red, and the sorrow in her mind swirled so rapidly I thought she might pass out from her grief.

"HA!" She slapped a hand over her mouth, stifling a fit of giggles that bubbled.

Everyone turned, momentarily pausing during the eulogy. Lena scowled, quite ready to throw literal daggers at the Whitlock, who couldn't control herself. Ellie rested a hand on Lena's shoulder, steering her attention back to the continuing speech. Hayden shifted his stance, blocking Lena's view so she'd ignore the outburst.

Gael stood beside Tara, grimacing, while King Clucks raised his wings, hiding his face. This was possibly the only time I'd seen those two embarrassed, but neither seemed to know what to do while Tara convulsed, struggling to contain the giggle fit that consumed her.

“Let’s go,” Gael said in a loud hush, which was accurate given he had never learned to whisper in class, even when he believed no one would hear his vulgar asides practically belted across the classroom.

With Tara in tow, Gael led her through the row of people more annoyed than offended, though they feigned offense on Jamie’s behalf quite convincingly in their judgmental expressions despite some finding the eulogy more tedious than somber.

I followed their trial through the cemetery, making my way toward a mausoleum where Tara sat while Gael stood close by, offering support.

“What’s going on?”

“Totally sorry, Mr. Frosty. I made a killer coffin cock joke and realized it probably wasn’t the best timing, but Tara got swept up—because, like I said, it was a killer joke.”

“Ba-bawk!”

“Right, not killer. Hello, phrasing. My bad. I’m awful. The worst. Should just throw me in that grave, too.” Gael scrunched his face, thinking on a loop. “*Don’t think it, don’t think it, don’t think it.*”

Whatever horrid joke he didn’t want me to catch, I considered myself grateful he had the decency to take my telepathy into account.

Tara burst into her giggle fit again. “He’s lying. He’s not the ass here. I am.”

Gael averted his gaze. It seemed the only lies he held shame for getting caught in were ones that made Tara look bad. Here he was, willing to take the blame for the outburst when if I looked a little deeper into his thoughts, I saw the heavy burden of guilt he held for Jamie Novak's death. A death that wouldn't have happened if Gael hadn't thrown the party. A death that wouldn't have happened if he hadn't invited Jamie. A death that wouldn't have happened if he'd been nicer to Jamie after everything he'd endured. Each thought weighed on Gael's heart, making it difficult for him to navigate his typical prankster personality, now content with merely faking it for the sake of others.

Oh, Gael. How I wished to alleviate the heavy burden of misplaced guilt.

"You had no control over what happened." I stepped closer to Gael. "It's easy to look back on a situation and see all the right things we could've, should've, and would've done. It doesn't change what happened. Sometimes, the world is just simply awful."

"I'm fine." He smiled. "*Dammit, Clucks, I think he might be reading our thoughts. Quick, distract his brain from reading our brains!*"

"BAWK!" King Clucks belted out the most obnoxious noise before following it up with a crow that was not only startling but forced me to quell my telepathy from the onslaught of pissed-off people attending Jamie Novak's funeral.

"*Good job. That should keep him outta our heads and none the wiser.*"

And with that, I furrowed my brow and painfully silenced my telepathy.

The rooster's noisy eruption sent Tara spiraling into a laughing outburst, clutching her stomach and doing her best to stifle the furious fit of giggles that painfully clawed at her insides, searching for an escape. "I'm awful, I know, but watching everyone mourn…mourn. Mourn. God-fucking-dammit… Ha…mourn."

She said the word, fully grasping the meaning, yet in this second, it felt foreign to her.

"It's just hilarious and terrible, but everyone over there—most of them—they hated Jamie." Tara almost sank into the cruel memories she shared with Jamie Novak.

Not the cruelties of his actions last semester when possessed by a devil. No, Tara had a trove of past encounters with Jamie, from galas where he teased her to gatherings where he bullied and berated her. There was so much venom between the two. Quaint dinners meant only for the best of the best, where he reminded her that she shouldn't be on the guest list. Private school where he spread rumors. She kept trying to lock away all their sour encounters and ignore their tainted history because he'd endured so much—he died protecting her. She saw herself as a monster for simply not feeling bad, for not grieving and crying and being consumed by sorrow over his death. Most of all, she hated the tiny relief that hit, meaning she'd never have to process her awkward feelings of resentment that'd twisted into a desire for friendship or, at the very least, forgiveness.

She didn't have to process those feelings because he was dead, and that was what she told herself repeatedly. If only she knew that didn't offer an escape to unprocessed emotions, to regrets, to grief.

"Did you see Layla and Amani?" Tara asked, completely rhetorical and meaning to distract herself from the peaks and valleys of fluctuating feelings that threw her mind back and forth. "They look like they're about to burst into tears, but before today, they were telling everyone Jamie's a cuck. Basically, since the semester started."

"A what?" I quirked a brow.

"Oh, you do not wanna know, Mr. Frosty." Gael had an ominous expression, but crude delight brimmed behind his seriousness as he turned his head to Tara. "Surprised you know the term."

"I don't care for sex, but that doesn't mean I don't understand it or everything associated with it." Tara frowned. "In great part because of you."

"You're welcome." Gael gave a thumbs-up while his rooster mimicked the action by raising a wing.

"And I don't know, maybe they are sad. Maybe everyone here is actually really mourning, guilty…" That word clung to her throat like sludge threatening to suffocate her. "But watching everyone tear up and… It just seems so fucking fake."

I didn't know what to say, how to redirect the sad rage boiling the ocean in Tara's mind, the anger she hurled at herself, self-doubt meant to bury her beneath the currents of sorrow she'd become so accustomed to drifting through day in and out.

"Everyone handles their grief differently," I said, searching for something better to say, something that'd help Tara, but coming up short like I did far too often when shaping young minds.

"Not sure this is grief." Tara sulked, finally past her giggle fit. "I mean, who laughs at a funeral? A monster."

Hayden waltzed over, a smile on his face and glitter trailing his steps. "Personally, I'm a fan of your method."

I glowered, having no energy or patience for Hayden's jovial presence. His aura radiated cheer at an almost infectious rate.

"Totally," Gael said. "King Clucks and I have a wickedly morbid sense of humor. I mean, the coffin cock joke wasn't a lie. I just hadn't said it…yct. But it's good. Rcal good. Or bad bccausc, like, inapprops."

"I don't have anything inappropriate I want to say." Tara's face fell into its standard somber default meant to wall up all her emotions and carry on quietly like she did far too often. "I just have this strange relief. It comes and goes, and that's why I'm laughing, I think. I don't even know."

"To the things left unsaid." Hayden pantomimed a raised glass, one he wished he had. "I get that. When my best friend died, I had a moment of relief…just for a second, just for one fleeting moment."

Tara stared with wide eyes.

"We'd both applied to Crimson Guild—it's back in Jackson—and I knew he was gonna get the gig. We waited that summer for the news. Well, he waited for the yes, and I held onto the dread of getting that rejection to join the half dozen other rejection letters I'd already gotten from smaller guilds who had fewer applicants. If they said no, surely Crimson would too. Especially when they had…" Hayden paused, noticing his thicker country twang coming out the more he thought about life back home. "Guess we weren't really friends at that point. Competition getting the best of me made me a real dick, but an accident offered me an opportunity. I was awful for seeing it that way—even if just for a moment. It hurt having so much left unsaid, so much I wanted to go back and change."

I absorbed what Hayden said, the words that continued spilling from his lips unfiltered, undiluted, and completely raw. Honest. Making no amends or peace or pain, merely sharing his small truth the best he could. It captivated Tara. Captivated me.

In all the years I spent dwelling inside the minds of others, catching thoughts I wanted to glean and many more I hoped to avoid, I'd never seen such honesty. Hayden didn't twist the truth, he didn't misremember events to suit his mind's needs, and he didn't omit facts to shine a better light. He simply shared this vulnerability without hesitation in a way I never knew possible. Even Milo skirted his pain, and he handled tragedy better than any person I'd met.

This wasn't Hayden's most vulnerable moment, though. There were so many others on display, at the surface of his peaceful mind, ready for observation like I'd walked into an art exhibit. All the grief, the rage, the sorrow, the muddled mess of nonsense was contained like portraits on the wall.

How'd I miss so much depth to someone who held himself so vapidly?

"What'd you do?" Tara asked, stealing my attention from Hayden's thoughts, which I honestly found myself too unwilling to see even if he offered them to the world.

"A foolproof method." Hayden smiled. "It's not the best—there's gotta be better ways—but it helps."

"Yeah?"

Hayden looked up at the clouds, lost in the happiness they offered, the simple joy of floating along carefree, following their own schedule. He liked the idea of simply floating through life carefree and helping at his own schedule, unencumbered by expectations or pretense or destiny.

Destiny. Such a powerful word. Such conviction, so much connotation held in the thought, yet I couldn't linger on it with Tara and Gael pulling me from his thoughts with their own, which was better than the many others nearby.

"Let's head on up." Hayden nodded to the sky. "This isn't exactly the place for my super-secret infallible absolutely guaranteed way of handling grief foolproof method."

"You just said it wasn't the best," Tara said, flabbergasted by Hayden's enthusiasm and speed as he leapt into the sky.

"We can't just fly in the middle of a funeral." Tara crossed her arms, contemplating all the proper ways a Whitlock was meant to grieve publicly.

"Last one up is a rotten egg!" Gael shouted, letting King Clucks lead with his telekinesis. "*I'll be damned if Jamie gave us a perfect technique and then went and fucking died before I could say thank you, only for us to pass on a foolproof method of saying goodbye!*"

"Cl-cl-cluck!" His rooster sat squarely between Gael's shoulders, flapping his wings and draping Gael in a wave of telekinesis meant to ensure safety for the both of them as his human partner levitated high in the sky, trailing behind Hayden Russo.

"You ready?" I extended a hand to Tara, half willing to join on her behalf and moderately curious how someone as juvenile as Hayden handled his emotions in such a cathartic manner.

Tara floated ahead, soaring through levitation alone. Her root magic was so profoundly finessed that it pulled her to the sky ahead of Gael like she belonged in the heavens above.

I reached Gael, ready to move ahead but unwilling to abandon his slow rise as he fearfully reached heights he and his partner had never once considered. It was one thing to levitate a few feet, a full story above the ground, but to ascend so high that the ground became a greenish-brown blob. That terrified Gael.

That terror reached out and grabbed ahold of me; I willingly accepted it, hoping it eased the anxiety in Gael's mind, a sensation he wasn't used to.

"Ba-bawk!" King Clucks extended his delicate telekinetic grip, cradling me in the same wave that secured Gael.

Gael smirked, hiding his own concerns and happy he wasn't the only one a tiny bit kind of sort of frightened.

I floated with them until we reached Tara and Hayden.

"What's this masterful plan?" I asked, studying Hayden's shifting thoughts as he absorbed the rays of the sun, sprinkling glitter in a slow descent so it'd mix with the incoming rain from the clouds he envied.

Insufferable.

We hovered so high above the crowd at the funeral, I couldn't even hear Milo's mind.

"So, what we're gonna do is scream to the void," Hayden explained, fully intent on us actually shouting our feelings like we were five goddamn years old.

"Hell yeah!" Gael raised a fist. "When do we go?"

"Now," Hayden said, taking a deep inhale and shouting with all the force he could muster.

Without an ounce of hesitation, Gael joined him. The two of them went back and forth in the most annoying pattern of belting out their feelings. The pair flailed about, screaming at the top of their lungs and actually releasing the frustration weighing down their thoughts.

"I can't do that." Tara fidgeted, antsy, and as uncomfortable as me. Not at the heights we'd flown—neither of us worried about the massive plummet that'd end horribly, and it had nothing to do with King Clucks' mother hen hold over us but more to do with the broken pieces of our minds.

"Yes, you can," Hayden said. "It's easy to just let it out. Hard to start, but once you roar, everything comes together."

"It totally works," Gael said, followed by a commanding "bawk" from his rooster.

Tara spun around, drifting slightly further away. "I can't. It's just not me."

"You can," Gael said, scrambling forward in the sky, ignoring the faster beat of his heart as he tried to reach his friend, who already wove her telekinesis around King Clucks' casting.

"I can't." Tara eyed me. "You think this is silly, right? Screaming for no reason? It's just…no."

There was a reason, though. She had a mountain of reasons to test Hayden's silly foolproof method. I had a few myself.

Each one ate at me as Hayden and Gael stared, thoughts encouraging me to express what they shouted with such ease.

Clearing my throat, I yelled, slightly yelp-ish and without the same carefree dignity Hayden and Gael roared with. Pausing, I tried again, this time thinking about everything in my life I'd lost.

Finn, who'd died before I shared my honest feelings with him.

Milo, who endured over a decade of grief I had wedged between us.

Jamie, who I'd never know because I failed before I truly began.

And soon, the small stack became a mountain similar to Tara's, and I screamed without regret, releasing all the anger, sorrow, grief, and every other unsaid emotion in the sky too far for anyone else to hear.

I continued shouting, every moment, every regret, and it all brought me back to the most recent. Jamie Novak.

"AH!" Tara screamed, then quickly paused.

Gael's eyes held a motivating touch Tara had become so accustomed to; she didn't need to know the words to understand the meaning. Not only with Gael, but the squint of his familiar carried more meaning than an entire well-rehearsed speech I could've offered.

Without hesitation, without reservations, without a second of forethought, Tara screamed at the top of her lungs, releasing every ounce of grief she held onto. Grief for Jamie. Grief for her life. Grief for her brother. For her father. For the mother she barely remembered. For the life she never asked to inherit. For the magics she hadn't mastered. For the world she couldn't control. For the feelings she couldn't handle. For the loss she wanted to escape. For all the uncertainty she had in herself.

Tara screamed for everything in her life, finally raising her voice to the level of pain she carried deep in her chest, so much so it threatened to cave in and crush her heart most days. She screamed until the pain stopped. Only it didn't. The pain would never end, merely be subsided.

In awe, I watched the air ripple, the sky itself tear asunder until reality cracked at the release of her grief, her exhale of death, her mourning.

"I think you just exhibited another branch," I said, already regretting my words as Tara sulked.

"Fuck," she muttered.

"Is that an augmentation or alteration branch?" Hayden tilted his head, studying the rips in the sky, the literal slashes of sorrow that ate away at everything in its path before fading back into a peaceful blue.

"It looks like a Banshee's Wail," I said, having studied so many magics over the years and recognizing every single one that dealt with sorrow and sadness. "It's a psychic branch that feeds on pain."

Tara's gaze clung to the sky, the piece of it she tore apart with yet another magic she didn't understand. "Banshee's Wail?"

"It focuses on the vibrations carried through emotion, strong emotions, foreboding and mourning and…" I swallowed hard, trying to determine how much I had to offer on actual insight versus the lore behind the magic. If that was her new branch. She could possess something entirely different, but most sonic-based magics didn't rip through the fabric of the world. That type of energy, that type of expression, was purely psychic. I literally felt my grief sucked into the hole Tara tore into the sky.

"A Banshee's Wail." Gael rolled his neck, and I just knew he was gonna say something vulgar. "I mean, it's a cool magic and all, but all these branches and none compare to the massive cock I've got!"

Tara snickered, slapping a hand over her face once King Clucks pecked Gael.

"I didn't call you fat! I said massive. It's a compliment. You've got girth, buddy!" Gael cringed, bracing for the pecks. "The ladies like girth! Ow. Ow! OW!"

We hovered for a bit until Clucks finished his punishment. Then we descended to the ground as the funeral reached its end. Hayden joined Ellie, who'd been abandoned by Lena, desperate to escape the crowd of condolences from people she didn't even like. I almost confused the slight shimmer of microscopic bubbles during our descent for glitter cast by Hayden. Lena was still casting her branch far and wide, but it didn't disrupt our levitation or telekinesis. Though disrupting other magics remained the main function when casting her branch, she'd conjured tens of thousands for another reason. I tilted my head curiously. There were so many ways Lena could repurpose her arcane branch, and the way she left her thoughts exposed, raw, and raging, I realized she was sending her magic fluttering everywhere in search of the warlock who killed her brother.

I wished Tara's scream had pulled away a bit of Lena's sorrow, but hers clung too tightly to the anger that continued brewing into a thunderstorm I could see on the horizon of her aura.

"*I've got my eye on her, Dorian.*" Milo stood alone in the cemetery, far from the crowd making their way to the wake.

I walked toward him, closing our distance but not our minds. His was lost in visions, regrets, and determination. "She's going to need a lot of time to heal."

"She needs closure. I can't offer Lena much, but I can offer her that."

"So, you're chasing Peter Graham?"

"Someone has to, and I've stopped him once before."

"He's strong. Scary level type of magic."

"True." Milo stared through me, past me, and at the looping fates only he could truly track. "I'm less concerned about his magic, his strength, and more worried about how calculating he's gotten. The level of sophistication it takes to avoid my branch… It's discerning."

"You think he's the shadow?" The one Milo thought had vanished.

"Possibly."

"Could've learned something from Theodore, maybe got lessons in"—I shrugged—"evil patience."

"Peter Graham didn't have any interactions with Theodore Whitlock while at the MDC. Trust me, I checked. Peter didn't have many interactions, nothing involving comradery, that's for sure."

"I don't have any answers, but I wish you'd let someone else track him," I said. "He's a dangerous warlock."

"Warlock, yeah." Milo's expression turned quizzical, replaying my words, and then he buried his thoughts in visions; his eyes met mine, almost like he wanted to search my future above all else, but then his surface thoughts twisted back to Lena. "Dangerous or not, he made a grave error attacking Lena."

"Seriously?" I blinked. "Puns?"

"Oh, shit." The realization of his phrasing hit him, hit him like sunshine cutting through a blanket of ice, and melted away the stoic expression until a smile filled his face. "Unintended but amazing. Don't tell anyone, though. My PR team hates dark humor. They'd make me hold a press conference to apologize."

"I know you feel responsible because this involves one of your acolytes, but—"

"That's just it, I don't. I feel awful. I feel like I failed. But I don't feel responsible. That said, my connection to Lena allows me deeper insight into her future than others. When Peter Graham killed Jamie, he unintentionally wove his fate to Lena's. The two are entangled, and despite all he's done to hide his presence, I can glimpse the murky residue."

Whatever Milo had planned, whatever futures he weighed, he didn't want me interfering. He didn't want me knowing, carefully wearing his visions on the surface of his mind to hold back his thoughts.

"I can respect you have to do this, that you want to do this yourself, that it doesn't involve me. I'm even capable of holding back my magic, getting better every day, so when I say I'll respect your boundaries and let you do this, know that I mean it."

"That's a first." Milo teased.

"Ass." I glared, fighting off the smile Milo always gave me, even when joking. "The point is, where I was going with this before you felt the need to speak, was that I want you to know I'm here. Here for you in any way you need me, here for you when the dust settles."

He brushed the hair off my face, leaning in and kissing me. It wasn't filled with passion or lust, but comfort and love and caring meant to remind me while his magic kept his mind distant, his heart always stayed close by.

Milo pulled back, pressing his forehead to mine so our thoughts, our emotions, our very beings would meld from the contact. "Kind of morbid, kissing in a graveyard, I know."

I smirked. "Depends on who you're kissing."

"Bet your gothic heart is just beating with delight."

"When you're around, always."

Chapter Twenty-Nine

Doppler

I'd dwelled deep in the pits of darkness since the chimera killed Jamie Novak. My involvement, no matter how small and futile, was met with torment. The punishment would've been worth it if I'd actually managed to do something. All I did was falter too long to make any real difference.

"Oh, you made a difference." The chimera slinked through his shadows, circling me like the vulture he was, craving to pick at the remains of my hollow body. "Reaching out to Dorian the way you did—that was a very bad move."

The fact he hadn't slain me, hadn't crushed my being to dust yet meant Dorian didn't fully grasp my garbled message. He was still missing too many pieces of the puzzle because I'd kept them well hidden for so long.

"Because of you, Enchanter Evergreen is on my path, likely struggling to piece it all together, and it's only a matter of time until he realizes Peter Graham is much harder to read than once before. Then he'll connect the dots, learn a devil's at play, and do what The goddamn Inevitable Future always does, which is inter-fucking-fere."

Rage swelled, bubbles of tar boiled over and burst nearby, and I prepared myself for another grueling round of torment. But the anger subsided, and the chimera shifted his demeanor as the shadows took on a cooling effect, cradling my body almost like the perfect bedtime pillow.

"Obviously, I have to take Dorian's body now." The chimera knelt beside me, his expression painfully forced into a smile. "No more games, no more waiting. We could claim his body and both live the lives we want."

I laughed, wheezing as blood and tar soaked my chin. The amount of torture the chimera unleashed because of my actions, and yet he wanted to work with me.

"I'm offering you an opportunity, a chance to live, really live, puppet." His smile twisted into this bizarre sincerity like the nickname held affection or charm, yet he possessed neither. "No strings on you, right?"

"You're only asking because the devil's too weak to take Dorian." I slowed my laugh to a haunting chuckle meant to scare and mock the foolish demon. "Your plan failed, Dorian's mind didn't break, and now you're wondering, do you have time to kill all those kids? Will the guilds be staking them out? Discreetly, of course. How long before Milo realizes exactly who you are? What will you do without all your branches? After all, the thousands before didn't help. Enchanter fucking Evergreen thwarted you all the same. Will Dorian have his emotional walls at the ready if you did manage to skirt around threats and pick off one or two more students? Has the bastard learned some healthy coping mechanisms?"

"I see your telepathy is doing wonders."

"Don't need to be a mind reader to gauge what you're thinking." I resisted the shackles seeped in tar and the shadows of muck keeping me pinned on my back. "You're more transparent than you let on, demon."

"You will help me take Dorian's mind—"

"You think my finite magic can overpower the full extent of Dorian's branch? He'd shatter my very being if instinct took hold."

That was why I avoided him, that was why I had a plan to break his mind—chisel away at it layer by layer. That was why I went to such excruciating lengths to get the life I deserved with the two men I loved most: Finn and Milo.

Hell, I was surprised Dorian hadn't been destroying those he perceived as threats since I'd abandoned him. After all, it was the work of manifestations that kept Dorian's branch in check, preventing him from unintentional outbursts.

"You will help me." The chimera dug his fingers into my chest; they wriggled deeper, searching my hollow insides for sensations of pain to cast and agony to release, but the delay served as a humble reminder that I wasn't real. None of this was real.

I spit in his face, savoring his look of disgust as he wiped splattered blood and tar from his cheek. Whatever he intended, I wouldn't offer him the satisfaction of my fear, my willingness to barter or beg. "Do your fucking worst."

"If you resist me, I'll have no choice but to leave the city, wait patiently. After all, what's a few more decades in the grand scheme of things? But that magic you ran away with… I'll shred it to pieces and send Dorian a message in the form of your demise. Let his paranoid mind stew and suffer, waiting and wondering which corner I'll emerge from."

"You think I'm afraid to die?"

"You're petrified of it, puppet. Same as me. We both know the only thing awaiting us is oblivion. That's what happens to the souls of those who die in worlds they never belonged in."

Demons didn't belong in this world; they had their own realms to wander, but hubris and avarice compelled them to break through the walls of reality and worm their way into our dimension, desperate and hungry for the magic of witches.

But I did belong to this world, right? I was a manifestation, sure, but I was real. Everything I felt was real. Still, I did fear the universe didn't see me as anything other than a magical anomaly from some overpowered witch.

"Send me to oblivion. I don't care."

"So be it, but that'll mean I'll only have Finn to keep me company."

I quivered, and for a second, just a second, the feeling of my heart breaking hit, and the chimera used that false feeling to pluck the still-beating organ from my chest, willing it into existence the way only telepaths could do inside the mind of others.

"I will kill you," I said through gritted teeth.

The words echoed from every shadowed corner of his mind. Every dark crevice carried my twisting voice as I shouted again and again: I will kill you. Only, it wasn't my voice. Not any longer. And it didn't echo from within; it rattled and reverberated from outside the devil's mind from the street of the neighborhood block the chimera currently walked down.

We rose to the peak of his surface thoughts, taking in the scene of the setting sun as Lena Novak flew directly at us.

"You hear me, Peter?" She punched Peter's jaw so hard it cracked and broke. The recoil bloodied and bruised her knuckles as bubbles burst alongside the act of telekinesis. "I'm gonna fucking kill you."

It didn't take long for the entropy branch to steal nearby magic to mend the injury, something the chimera had to hold back his own demonic energy from doing. It'd reveal his status as a devil, and he couldn't allow such a revelation to appear on Enchanter Evergreen's radar, not when he'd worked so hard to copy my tactics and skirt Milo's mind with added immunity demons held for branch magics.

"I know your branch, know what it can do, and how to exploit it." Lena waved her hands, conjuring thousands of bubbles. They popped with an airy release; they burst with watery goop; they curdled inward; they expanded tenfold their size; each bubble held its own specific reaction when swarming Peter Graham.

```
Name: Lena Novak
Branch: Arcane (Bubble Burst)
```

The chimera pulled from my memories, which had melded and melted within the pits of tar and rot of his very being, stealing information I had on Lena Novak's magic. But the countless barrage made it difficult to focus and made it impossible for Peter's branch to absorb the shock of so many unique actions. Lena wielded her magic in ways I hadn't observed, in ways Dorian hadn't seen. Was she mixing and altering her frequency during casting blows?

"Like a demon, your branch wavers against the arcane, requiring time and understanding to drain the complexities in our branch." Lena swept in close, punching Peter, the chimera, and me again and again, hitting with telekinesis the cellular absorption couldn't keep up with. "Your branch isn't infallible, and just like a demon—I'll end you here and now!"

Lena's surface thoughts revealed the research she'd done on Peter Graham, from his encounter with Milo so many years ago to his battle against her brother, Jamie, and Lena carried that understanding high in her mind alongside a plan to eviscerate the warlock who dared.

"Enough!" The chimera channeled telekinesis, pushing Lena away but gaining only a few seconds of peace before the bubble burst magic continued chasing him. "How the hell did you even find me?"

The chimera rooted through the goopy slosh of his shadows, searching for slipups, wondering where he'd wandered that allowed someone to spot the most wanted man in Chicago. Suddenly, a flurry of bubbles exploded—blinding his vision, our sight outside his mind.

"My branch has endless possibilities, so searching the city might've taken every ounce of magic to scour your location, but I found you." Lena swooped in close, hitting the chimera with telekinetic strikes to further knock him off balance.

The tar in his mind boiled, enraged and incapable of gathering his thoughts. If he wanted, he could latch his telepathy to Lena, read her thoughts, and form a sight from her perspective. But he was arrogant, piecing together how such a simplistic branch caught him when he'd done so well to avoid the branch he feared most of all—Enchanter Evergreen's clairvoyance.

"I can manipulate my bubbles with over a hundred individualized commands." Lena's barrage of blows was unyielding. "Smother magic, absorb it, shield against, heal, distort, disrupt, merge, amplify, summon elements, transport—my arcane branch will be your death!"

This wasn't some arrogant boasting or a mistake in revealing her capabilities to offer a counter plan, but a powerful message meant to rattle the warlock Peter Graham, who believed his branch infallible. It worked, too, stunning the chimera as he attempted to think. He scrambled through the encyclopedic knowledge he held on branches, unable to think of one suitable to stop this arcane magic, furious he'd lost so many to begin with when he nearly died at the hands of Enchanter Evergreen, and now he found himself faltering against an acolyte of all fucking things. The insult.

Bubbles burst from every direction, even within, dropping his body to its knees. Tattered lungs seeped in black tar struggled to mend the damage that'd have surely killed Peter Graham if he weren't housing a demon, if he hadn't transcended to the state of a true devil.

"*His healing is holding out.*" Lena clenched her jaw. "*Good. Means I don't have to hold back anymore!*"

Hold back? Christ. This was her trying *not* to kill the warlock?

Lena slammed her hands together. The loud clap triggered a thousand more to follow. Bubbles popped against Peter's skin, scalding hot, searing cold, stabbing needles, sticky acid, and so many other sensations it made it impossible for the chimera to calculate the correct measures with his new entropy branch. Even his demonic energy couldn't develop an immunity against the arcane branch, quite possibly the most versatile arcane magic I'd ever seen in action as it bombarded him with extravagant damage.

Bubbles burrowed into the pores of Peter's skin. They traveled through blood vessels, exploding little landmines across his circulatory system. Cellular absorption continued stalling, struggling to gauge the frequency of Lena's fluctuating casting, making Peter's branch virtually useless to the chimera. Each burst shook the shadows that contained me here in the inner core. Tar swished through the host body, compensating for what should've been irreparable injuries.

"*Fucking arcane witch.*" The chimera seethed with rage, so lost in his distress that he didn't notice my released grip.

My legs were still bound in darkness, but I had a range of motion in my body, in my magic.

"You think you can stop me," the chimera shouted, his voice echoing with Peter's.

"I'm just getting started." Lena panted, her face coated in sweat as she channeled her magic. Despite the fury in her bones, the rage pumping through her blood, and the hate fanning her emotions, she'd pushed her casting to the brink of her limits.

If it were just Peter Graham, she'd have killed him a few dozen blows back, but the chimera could bide his time, conserve, and restore what had broken. The only true way Lena could remove the threat of the chimera was through banishment, but she leaned too heavily on her branch casting, and if she kept this up, she'd have nothing left to remove the devil who finally devoured the final round of bubbles in his body.

Reaching out with telepathy, I wanted to warn her, prepare her, help her end this fucking monstrosity.

"*Brilliant idea, puppet.*" The chimera turned his gaze back to me, clutching his fingers into a fist until shadows sprang forward and bound me once again. "*I've been playing defense when I should be targeting her weakest area—her mind.*"

The chimera quelled his body's natural branch like flipping a switch. It didn't come without a price. The sudden halt of one magic replaced entirely by a new one he'd wedged into a host body it didn't belong to caused his organs to heat and burn. Unlike when he possessed Jamie Novak for months, he didn't take care of Peter's body or heed his casting flow to slow the rot of his demonic presence inside the mortal coil.

"*Killing Jamie Novak brought such joy.*" The chimera reached out to Lena with telepathy, clawing at the walls of her mind with words meant to evoke misery. Not words. Images!

Jamie's gasping body, the resistance he put up, the struggle for escape, and the quick snap of his neck all rang through Lena's thoughts. He plastered the images, the memories, onto her surface thoughts, rattling the young acolyte.

"No!" Lena trembled, failing to shake away the thoughts with a poorly cast wave of bubbles meant to disrupt the connection. "*How the hell is he doing this? What is this?*"

"*I've got quite a few branches, though, not as many as when I wore your baby brother's face.*" The chimera cackled, thoughts turning the gears of Lena's mind as he helped connect dots to his truth, a truth he'd hoped to hide but now knew would offer him release from this battle. "*My only regret in killing Jamie Novak was that I couldn't savor his agony.*"

In a flash, he lunged ahead and jabbed Lena in the stomach with an open hand, fingers elongated and sharp due to the transformation of an augmentation branch the chimera still had access to.

"What're you?" Lena struggled, unable to back away as the chimera's clawed fingers curled into hooks meant to shred her insides to pieces.

"You know that answer." He sent an onslaught of Jamie's memories—no, his memories—which he'd saved and savored. They revealed atrocities to the torture and torment he caused while possessing the young witch. "*I'm the devil that took your brother's hopes, tore them asunder, and smothered them.*"

"Bastard." Lena squeezed his wrist, casting a pulse of banishment, but her body was too weak. The groggy side effects of banishment made her grip falter and her shoulders slump.

The chimera dug his hands deeper into her gut, laughing off the frantic frenzy of bubbles she summoned, each meant to simply assault him, so absorbing their damage proved easier than when she sent flurries with endless commands. "I'm going to take my time with your death, Lena. I'll pluck out your insides one by one, relishing every squirming scream, every agonizing second. Maybe my farewell gift to Chicago will be eradicating the Novak line before I go. How sweet a goodbye that would be."

"I'll kill you." Lena stifled a shout, still resisting, still fighting, still completely out of her league.

Her anger clung to me, empowering my own and giving me the strength to tear myself loose from the bonds of darkness.

"Lock!"

The chimera's body froze; every muscle, every joint, every drop of blood stopped.

"Lock, lock, lock!" Ellie Reed flew behind us, waving her key. "I can see your branches, see the threads of each one, and they'll do you no good here!"

```
Name: Ellie Reed
Branch: Ward (Skeleton Key)
```

Glitter formed in front of the chimera, scattering and carrying a telekinetic pulse in each shimmering speck. It burst wide, forcing his hand loose from Lena's stomach. His hooked claws were mere bloody fingers thanks to Ellie's warding branch.

The acolyte swooped past us, snatching her coven mate, and flew several yards away, where she immediately went to work locking Lena's injuries. Not only on the surface. Ellie carefully locked the most microscopic internal injuries. Her thoughts surged with anxiety as she counted up the damage, but it didn't derail her as she sealed tiny, fatal wounds with surgical precision. It motivated her to work faster, more precisely. She wouldn't let the woman she loved to loathe die on her so easily.

"Wha…" Lena gurgled. "What're you doing here?"

"You think we'd let you do this on your own?"

Lena tried to speak, her thoughts surging with a thousand warnings, but her throat constricted when she attempted to talk.

"You best believe I'm going to yell at you once we're outta here, Lena." Ellie smiled through her sadness, hoping her joy would wash away the terror-stricken expression consuming Lena.

"Get out of here, Finesse!" Hayden Russo appeared in the blink of an eye, then vanished just as abruptly.

"I can't move Lena. Not yet."

"Fine." Hayden reappeared on our right, punching Peter's jaw so hard it cracked. Not only the bones but the tar beneath holding this tattered body together started to crumble. The glimmer of glitter left the chimera's vision in a starry daze.

```
Name: Hayden Russo
Branch: Cosmic (Teleportation)
Branch: Cosmic (Glitter)
```

His telekinetic strike hit harder with the chimera's magics and demonic energy locked down by Acolyte Reed.

"How'd you find me?" Lena struggled to move, held down by Ellie, who tended to the injuries.

"You're not the only one who can scout with your branch." A wall of glitter obscured Hayden's body, flickering in and out every time he teleported. "And we'd never let you face this warlock alone, Mercury Rising!"

"You don't…you don't…" Lena coughed, choking and dripping blood down her chin. "*He's not a warlock.*"

"You think you can stop me!" The chimera lunged through thick swarms of floating glitter, silhouettes of Hayden Russo, which served as mere decoys as he continued rapidly teleporting, hitting his opponent from different angles and weak points each time.

"Don't drag this out," Ellie shouted. "He's got more than one branch."

Hayden flickered in front of the chimera, then clocked him in the back of the head having teleported behind us before his image fully faded amidst the glitter formed in front of us.

"He's not the only one born multi-branched." Hayden continued his taunting blows. "Besides, didn't you lock down his casting?"

"Yeah, but his threads, they're strange." Ellie studied Peter Graham's body, able to somehow see the branches the chimera had forced into his host body, but her warding sight didn't extend to demonic energy. She could tell there was something eerie in the air, but she'd need her sensory root to identify it, something none of these acolytes bothered accessing during the heat of battle.

It'd be their undoing.

"It'll be their deaths." The chimera leapt away from the glitter swirling around him, taking a free breath in the open street. "You have no idea who you're messing with, witch!"

Hayden flickered side-to-side, slowly approaching the chimera like a ghost as glitter shimmered all around us, revealing he'd laced the entire area with his magic from gravel at our feet, the air around us, to the cars and buildings nearby.

"No, you have no idea who you're facing, warlock." Hayden's voice came from every direction. "I'm The Infinite Light!"

It was a name carrying weight that left the chimera petrified. His magics were still bound until his demonic energy ate away at the shackles Ellie had placed throughout his body, but when he stared at Hayden Russo, he saw why the witch chose his name. The light pierced the darkness of his mind and revealed Hayden's infinite casting. A witch without limitations could surely banish a devil single-handedly.

Had Milo chosen this acolyte specifically for this reason? Was he aware of the looming threat that I'd kept alive in this world? Even without casting limits, Hayden couldn't eradicate the chimera unless he knew which magic to use. He'd need his roots, not his branches.

I had to tell him, warn him, see whatever future Milo weaved through his acolytes played out accordingly.

Chapter Thirty

Doppler

Glitter whirled everywhere like an inferno of bright lights, carrying Hayden in between the specks as he teleported again and again. Each tick of his rapidly beating heart carried him round and round, delivering countless blows to immobilize the chimera.

Hayden struck faster, harder, appearing everywhere at once. He punched the chimera in the face to knock him off balance, hit him with a flurry of strikes across his ribcage from either side, then kicked his calf to drop him. This continued in an almost methodical pattern of chaos. It was difficult to glean what Hayden's strategy was, if he had one at all. Hayden's mind lay fully displayed, revealing the surface of a serene lake that embodied his inner core, but with his cosmic branches at work, light reflected on the gentle ripples and obscured his thoughts.

With the chimera engaged in combat, his alertness dulled, I reached out with my telepathy to create a link to Hayden. His thoughts came in waves, but piecing together the intel he held proved challenging. Nothing from Milo appeared, and perhaps I overreached, assuming Enchanter Evergreen's involvement. Still, Hayden needed to know he faced a devil, needed to know how to end this here and now, once and for all.

Creating a connection to Hayden put a strain on my magic, nearly severing the thin thread I'd tossed into the ether. Hayden's cosmic branches caused interference with the psychic plane of existence where magic like telepathy reigned. He was truly something spectacular.

The chimera fumed, taking forced breaths to hasten the effects of feeding upon the glitter in the air, but he should've prioritized his demonic energy to continue gnawing away Acolyte Reed's intricate locks within Peter's body. "The warding is crumbling. Now, you're dead."

Hayden didn't acknowledge the comment; he merely flickered in close to the chimera's face, vanished, and sucker-punched him before kicking him from behind and dropping the devil to his knees once again.

The chimera swung his fists, flailing and missing his target by a fraction of a second each time as he scrambled to regain his senses, searching for the specific frequency of Hayden's casting so he could use demonic energy to nullify the effects the shimmering lights had on his vision.

Hayden's blows weren't only lethal. They provoked the chimera, mocking the devil, and pissed him off in a way I never could.

"I know how your entropy branch works." Hayden clocked the

chimera across the face, unfazed by the crackle in his bones completely reformed as mist seeped out of Peter's pores, stealing the magic in the air and healing him at a cellular level. "I get how it strengthens and heals you, but it also slows you down. We both know you can't keep absorbing magic without immobilizing yourself."

That was true of Peter, yes, but the demonic energy continuously ate away the casting before those side effects sank in. Still, the harder the chimera pushed himself while in this host body, the more it broke apart under the weight of possession.

"I don't need to keep casting. Just gotta drain your magic, then I'll eviscerate you and those little witches over there."

"I don't run out of magic." Hayden whirled by, swinging his arm across the chimera's throat and slamming him with a clothesline strike before shifting behind him and knocking him forward, then finally appeared low to the ground and kicked the chimera's right knee out of its socket.

I ground my teeth, synced to the brutal pain shooting through this body, and covered my ears from the piercing screech the chimera let out.

"Tell me again how you're gonna eviscerate me." Hayden scowled. "I wanna see that arrogance at its peak before I break every goddamn bone in your body."

Flashes of Lena's tears, Ellie's frown, and Jamie's body all flickered between the lights of Hayden's mind. Each somber moment made the calm of his lake fade, and soon, his anger hit like a tidal wave—intense and tremendous but vanishing quickly once it laid waste to the shore. Then his emotions settled, and the bright sunshine of his aura returned. I winced, covering my face to block the light I'd connected to. I didn't know if it was really that painfully cheerful or if the darkness of the chimera's inner core had dulled my vision, making it difficult to adjust.

Hayden bolted ahead, his heart surging almost as quickly as his body flickered. The chimera braced for the next assault, knowing he couldn't do anything until the warding faded. He needed a few more minutes. Hayden dragged this out, believing he had all the time in the world, and I had to tell him the importance of shifting tactics.

"He's not who you think!" I shouted at the top of my lungs, cutting through the light, unconcerned if the chimera heard. If Hayden accessed his banishment, it wouldn't matter.

My telepathy rippled along the surface of Hayden's serene lake, and the acolyte paused. Finally!

"I need you to listen," I said, looping my magic around his mind. "It's not his branches you need to—"

Every muscle in my body strained. The darkness around me exploded, sloshing everywhere and knocking me from one end of the inner core to the next.

Fuck. I gasped, fighting against the tar. It was so chaotic.

The chimera roared. His body buckled, and the ground beneath him cracked apart.

I struggled to see, to see past the shadows, but this wasn't the chimera's doing. This wasn't him stomping out my protest. Standing before us was Milo with telekinesis circulating throughout his entire body and funneled into a fist that he'd used to knock Peter Graham headfirst into the ground.

"It's time for you to get Acolyte Novak out of here." Milo cut his gaze toward the confused Hayden before locking his eyes back onto his target: the warlock.

"I can help," Hayden said.

"You will help by getting Acolyte Novak out of here."

"Ellie's got it under control," Hayden said, ready to protest with a thousand reasons he needed to help.

"Acolyte Reed's patch job can only do so much." Milo had a sternness in his voice. "Don't risk Lena's life so you can show off, Acolyte Russo!"

That struck a chord in Hayden's mind, and his magic settled. He gritted his teeth, heart pinching once he'd stopped casting, and suddenly I realized the erratic method behind his teleportation. It was linked to his heartbeat.

Hayden nodded apologetically. "On it."

As the three acolytes took flight, Milo's expression softened, almost to his default smile. The pride and hope he held for them radiated around him, and the beautiful familiarity of his mind helped empower me to rip loose from the tar mess and reach out to warn him of the true threat he faced.

Milo had defeated both Peter Graham and the chimera, but now he'd face them as one truly wrathful devil.

I reached out, shoving aside every ounce of demonic energy from the inner core, and sent my telepathy toward him, conjuring a link I'd avoided since attempting this foolish endeavor of creating a happily ever after that him, Finn, and I could share. This entire time, I'd skirted around Milo's mind, dodging his visions, and now I'd have to reveal everything I could to save his life.

"It's a real shame, taking this win from Mercury Rising, Finesse, and The Infinite Light. They would've solidified their position as elite enchanters if I'd let them banish a devil."

What? He knows.

Milo rolled up his sleeves, channeling magic to read potential futures. "But the fact is, you and I have unfinished business, and selfishly, I wanna be the one to end you. Correctly, this time."

Milo smirked. He knew it all. Well, not all. Not even close, but he'd pieced enough together and did what he always did: ensured the best possible future prevailed.

"You gotta tell me how you survived. That's been gnawing at me."

He played coy, but he was recalibrating outcomes based on sending his acolytes away. This had nothing to do with wanting to end the devil himself. Milo was right about Lena's injuries, but they were far from fatal. He'd merely painted that possibility for Hayden's imagination. Sure, the acolyte possessed a rare trait, infinite draw, but nothing was truly infinite. The boy's body would tire first, and Hayden's heart would never handle the levels of banishment necessary to eradicate a devil. Milo's body had barely endured it when channeling a hundred witches to kill the devil.

The chimera searched the streets, unraveling telepathy to pinpoint all the nearby minds in the neighborhood. They were plentiful and unaware of the danger outside; none were affiliated with guilds, meaning Milo didn't have a band of enchanters lurking around the corners of the city like the last time he'd faced off against the devil.

"Come to face me alone. The folly of mortals." The chimera shook his head and tsked. "Do you not recall what it took the last time you struck me down?"

"The hubris of devils." Milo hovered above the street, gravel crackling underfoot from the intense pressure of telekinesis. "The last time we encountered each other, you had thousands of branches at your disposal. Not that you could harness them all. My guess is you still can't. Not in an imperfect host."

And Milo didn't plan on allowing the chimera the opportunity again. He'd do everything he could to end what he believed he'd failed to do before, but he hadn't. It was my interference.

"*And you'll never know what a perfect host feels like!*" The thought soared above his surface, above his visions, above his plans, and reached out to rattle the chimera. Milo spent so much time with Dorian, he knew the second a telepath's magic touched his mind; thus, he felt the chimera and me rummaging around.

The threat provoked fear. It festered in the darkness, tense and recoiling, so much so that I tore away from the bits of muck that held me. Nothing I did truly disconnected me from the chimera's mind, from the darkness that'd attached itself to my being to the phantom sensations of Peter's body casting magic as his organs liquefied.

Smog filled the air, polluting the neighborhood with entropy casting meant to feed on the nearby magic. Not only Milo's but all the casual casting in the area. Soon, the chimera would be at full strength, in the body of a warlock that proved one of the most formidable opponents for Enchanter Evergreen.

"He can win this. He wouldn't be here if he couldn't," Finn said. He didn't whisper. He made his voice loud, evoking a shiver from the devil who'd died at the hands of Enchanter Evergreen once before.

Milo bolted ahead, taking that fraction of a second where the chimera turned inward, offended and distracted. The pulse of telekinesis hit so hard it caved in my chest.

I dropped to my knees, gasping and taking wispy breaths as the breaks along my hollow body cracked, simulating the harrowing destruction. The chimera's pain became mine as our essence entwined.

But the chimera healed, absorbing the last bits of Hayden's shimmering glitter through the entropy smog and repairing his broken bones.

"We have to help." Finn's voice pulled me away from the battle outside, where Milo clashed with the devil all on his own.

"I could reach out to Dorian while the chimera's distracted, have him send for guild members." I panicked, wincing from every blow that struck the chimera. This horrid sensation of being linked to the devil was awful. "If I warn Dorian now, I can ensure Milo doesn't face these odds alone."

"But he's not alone." Finn's cheeks twitched, quickly revealing then hiding the same pain he endured.

Being bound to the chimera meant sharing in his successes and failures. If he died, so would we.

"And if we die, we can take him with us." Finn channeled magic, drawing the tar toward him. Slimy, clawed hands reached from the shadows, ready to pluck out Finn's glowing eyes as he studied the histories of this body, of this entire neighborhood.

Casting without permission made him a beacon in the darkness, but it also escalated the rot in the host body. Outside, the battle raged, but the chimera's roar echoed, and his gaze turned inward to stop Finn's disruption. Only that led to a sluggish reaction of his body, offering Milo an opportunity, which he took by slamming the chimera onto the pavement.

I gasped, nearly buckling over, and left astonished by how Finn handled the brutal pain dealt onto the chimera that ricocheted through this broken host body and shattered our forms.

Once I gathered my bearings, I grabbed Finn by his collar, ready to drag him from the grasp of the clawed hands that had come to silence his branch casting, but he shoved me back and then hit every approaching piece of tar with banishment.

I stared, awestruck by the cleansed part of Peter's empty mind. "How'd you…"

"My casting's never been revoked, merely my will." Finn sent another wave of banishment to the encroaching tar come to reclaim the darkness. "That's the chimera's greatest strength, convincing the army of witch souls he held captive that nothing they did mattered. Nothing *we* did. If I'd believed in myself then, if I had the willpower I do now, I could've gathered every lost soul dwelling inside the chimera and destroyed him from within."

Searing tar lunged toward Finn like a net, ready to splatter and devour his futile resistance.

"No!" I banished the demonic energy until only wisps fluttered around Finn.

They were quickly banished by Milo's furious casting outside, tearing the chimera's insides apart every second.

As Milo struck outside and we cast from within, the rot set in and further decayed the chimera's host, leaving him more and more vulnerable with each passing second. His blood flow clotted, his organs boiled, and his casting receptors shriveled. Soon, the chimera would die.

"He could do this on his own," Finn said. "Milo's never walked into a mission without a plan for victory."

"But we should help him." I took the words right out of Finn's mouth, knowing he'd sooner embrace death than gamble on Milo's safety.

"We always were an awesome trio." Finn smiled, the kind that lit up his entire face in the darkness as he banished away creeping shadows. "The three meant to be, right?"

I choked on my response. Those were beautiful words, yet they belonged to Dorian, not me. Never me.

"Let's end this fucking devil once and for all." I grabbed Finn's hand, synchronizing our casting to strengthen the waves of banishment we cast.

Each time we struck, the sludge inside Peter Graham's body crumbled. Each time we struck, the harrowing darkness quaked. Each time we struck, our casting timed closer to Milo's outside this possessed body.

Shadows swept across the room, tightening to one small area and draping over the silhouette of a man crawling away from the banishment lingering all around this mind's inner core.

"You don't do this to me." His voice echoed, conjuring a storm of magic to stir as all but one branch faded. Peter's branch remained intact, draining the banishment outside where he resisted Milo's telekinesis and attempted to force himself off the ground much like he did inside the core of Peter's mind.

Finn squared my shoulders and locked his eyes onto me, his retrocognition in play and reading my entire history like I had a life worth living.

"What're you doing?"

"Sorry. It's a habit." Finn then pressed his hands to his heart. "Every soul tied to the devil will shatter before he crumbles. I need you to banish me."

"W-what?" I quivered, though I wanted to believe that terrified sensation came from syncing to the chimera's shaky body. "I can't do that."

"You knew this was the end result." Finn smiled.

"There's always a way," I said in unison with the scratchy voice of the chimera as he crawled toward us.

I turned away from Finn, ashamed that my thoughts, my desires, were as foul as the monster that held him captive for too long.

"It's okay to falter, to struggle, to make the wrong choices,"

Finn said. "But I'm asking for your help. I'm begging you not to make Milo cast the final surge of banishment. Don't let him feel my death. I wouldn't want him to live with that."

There were a thousand things I wanted to say, so much to apologize for, to beg, to plead, to offer the best farewell a better man could give. But instead, I brushed away tears that'd somehow begun to stream down my face, and I placed a hand on Finn's chest where the steady beat of his heart and the soft skin of his hands led my casting.

Without hesitation, I banished Finn. He shattered to nothingness almost instantaneously and fell away from the world, finally released from the devil, and given the peace I should've granted him months ago.

I trembled, hunching inward to console myself because I only had me. I was alone, forever alone.

"Guess it's just you and me now." I cast my gaze down at the chimera.

Not entirely alone. Not yet.

"If you banish me…if I die…you'll—"

"Die too?" I shrugged. "Sort of figured."

"You'll cease to be. There's nothing waiting for you, for me…but—"

"There's nothing waiting for me here either." I knelt next to the chimera.

"I can bring Finn back." The chimera panted, desperation in his eyes, which likely matched the hesitation and hope in mine.

In all the months of torment, torture, interrogation, and investigation, I had never seen the chimera appear so frightened.

"I just need the right branches, and I can give him to you again. The right way, the way you wanted to spend your life with him. Can give you Evergreen, too. I know some charming demons that'd love to sway his opinion for his—"

"Puppet?" I chuckled because he still believed he could pull my strings. "You wanna make the men I love into puppets for this puppet?"

"A term of endearment." The chimera smiled, feigning friendship he never comprehended.

"Your terrible nickname makes me realize I never learned your actual name." I scoffed. "Never learned a damn thing about you that you didn't want me to know, taunt me, goad me, manipulate me."

"My name is L—"

I cast banishment, shattering the entire lower half of his jaw. Droplets of tar scrambled from the vacant pits of Peter's mind, attempting to heal the broken consciousness of the chimera as he flailed and choked from his gaping wound. I banished the stray demonic energy moving toward us, cleansing this body of every piece of the chimera.

"I'd rather never learn your name. All I know will soon be carried back to Dorian, and it's best he's not burdened with any more knowledge of your existence than what there already is."

I dug my hand deep into the chimera's chest, watching the human form he favored shift and transform into his true demon self. Not that it held up with the waves of banishment I cast from within, accompanied by Milo's casting against an immobilized host body.

"Let the world forget you, devil."

Every part of the chimera had fallen away except for the tiniest of pieces attached to the fibers of my magic. It wasn't enough to do harm. Truthfully, I could continue, contain it, keep it a wisp of energy incapable of forming true sentience again.

That was my mistake before, my belief I could outwit a demon and gain insight on how to free Finn.

No. My true mistake was simply believing my own ego, feeding it, fueling it.

I let out an exhausting exhale and found my hollow insides syncing to Peter's body. The dead body releasing its final breath. But it wasn't entirely gone. I drifted forward to glimpse through the eyes of the fallen warlock.

Milo stood, tired but nowhere near the level of fatigue like the last time he'd banished the devil.

"Sorry it took me so long to figure out the right thing to do," I said through this body's voice.

Milo stared down at me, perplexed and already trying to glean potential futures. "Peter?"

Leave it to him to believe there might be potential in this riddled bag of meat.

"No, I'm not Peter. I'm…" I was unable to answer because I couldn't tell him who I was. I didn't rightfully know the answer myself. Suppose I never would now. "Just know it should make sense soon enough."

I smiled at him, knowing all I'd hidden from Dorian would be unveiled once I took my leave. How I wished I could've seen Milo smile one more time. Not the one he wore to battle, not the one he displayed for the public, interviews, and case meetings, but his true smile. The expression he reserved purely for Finn and Dorian. How I would've loved to see him smile at me that same way.

My vision of the outside world faltered as I sank back into the depths of Peter's corpse. This body would crumble soon. I pressed my hands to my chest, imitating the illusion of a heartbeat I so longed for in this world. Channeling what remained of my magic, I banished myself and the speck of the chimera that'd clung to my being in a futile and desperate plea for life.

"May we rot together in nothingness till the end of time."

The chimera and I deserved no less than to be lost to the universe and forgotten.

Chapter Thirty-One

I sat under the starlit night, smoking a cigarette while Finn and Milo bickered over constellations.

"That's Orion." Finn pointed. "Which you'd know if you even remotely paid attention in Guides to Channeling."

Milo tsked. "Pointless class. All she does is focus on cosmic channeling, anyway. I don't have a cosmic branch, so what's it really matter if I know the stars or not?"

"Cosmic branches burn brightest when drawing magic from the stars, but all witches can access it." Finn gestured, practically ready to read off his essay on the topic. Christ, he loved his essays. "Just like all witches can channel from nature, from the astral plane, from—"

"Again, all things you'd know if you actually paid attention in class," my younger self interjected, then blew smoke in his direction. A taunting act because at sixteen, I still hadn't sorted out how I felt for either of them aside from how happy they made me, which at the time, I found incredibly frustrating.

"I do pay attention; I just don't see why I need to know where my channeling comes from. It doesn't stop me from maintaining the highest root proficiency."

Ugh, Milo had that smug smile, not the one where he had mastered being cocky and sincere all at once, which people fucking loved. That expression would take him a few more years. But he couldn't help but be a braggart, given his second-year ranking shot up much higher than Finn's or mine.

"It is important," Finn said with his lecturing face because while he always dreamt of being an enchanter, his heart was happiest teaching others, helping them improve, and guiding them.

That might've influenced my choice to go into education. Not at the time, though. I wasn't sure it ever really dawned on me until now. I do think I gleaned the purpose of my subconscious throwing this particular memory at me, though.

I always dreamed about my past, reliving joys and regrets in equal measure. After gaining closure on Finn's loss, I finally stopped looking at memories of him through that lens of regret, so it helped me realize that maybe my mind was reminding me of certain moments for different reasons. Teaching. I'd slacked off lately, letting my students grieve, prepare for the holiday, and sink into a bit of my own sadness. But when the break ended, I needed to be ready to offer my students normalcy, even if the semester was coming to an end soon and another, longer winter break was a month away. Christ, this year was flying by.

"What do you think, Dorian?" Milo asked, perfect blue puppy-dog eyes at the ready to guilt me into siding with him, which worked if I remembered correctly.

"Stop fussing," I said, only it wasn't me who said it. Not the me in this memory, in this dream, but another version, who was almost as young, wrapped in his gothic ensemble. He plopped onto the end of a hospital bed where Finn lay.

What? I'd never visited Finn in the hospital. That never happened. Yet, in the corner of my eye, this new memory unraveled. Was I having some strange dream alteration? The last time my dreams went off script to my memories, it was the part of Finn deep in my subconscious warning me about the void vision.

"If you don't behave, you won't heal properly, and then you really will be in this bed forever."

Finn huffed. "Feels like I've been in this room for months."

"It's been two days. Dramatic much." The me in the hospital room frowned, fighting a smile, the same way I always did when with Finn or Milo.

My head cocked, making it impossible to see the hospital bed, to see the Finn and Dorian of that memory…moment…whatever it was. Instead, my eyes remained on Milo and Finn, shooting them a very dower and judgy expression. It seemed I couldn't deviate from the script of my dream.

"You'll tell me what I want, demon." Tar splattered between Milo and Finn as a new scene was unveiled before me.

I stood a few feet from myself, the younger version, as he walked in circles around a man shackled and on his knees. Only this wasn't me. I'd never done this, never lived this. Everything about this image was wrong and foreign.

"You're gonna have to do so much better than that, puppet."

I ground my teeth in disdain for the man's words.

No, not a man. The foulness in his gaze, the rot oozing from his hacked open flesh, and the wisps fluttering around to illuminate the dank dungeon—this was a devil. My chest tightened. I only ever knew one devil. The chimera. What the fuck was going on?

Tar erupted everywhere, erasing my dream and dropping me in pure, isolating darkness.

"Such a reversal of fortunes." The chimera's voice echoed in the dark. His hand reached out, delicately running his fingers along the person bound in shadows. "Would you like to know what I've got planned for Dorian?"

His fingers turned into talons; the first cut was shallow, but it dug deep into my core. Suddenly, every moment of torture he reveled in against me carried the weight of a new memory.

Slash. This wasn't me. Cut. It was me. Hack. A manifestation. What? Ripping through my hollow insides, I found every single thing the sentient extension of my magic withheld for nearly a year.

A year?

Severing the connection to my mind, my magic, my ability to summon new manifestations. Stealing Finn away. Saving the chimera. Skirting Milo's vision.

So much unraveled around my mind, flying by in a blur before I could fully comprehend a single image, yet each memory clung to me like I'd lived this second life.

I saw every moment of Finn's time confined by the chimera, memories my manifestation had hidden in a ploy to offer the man I loved a spark of life, a new life, a second chance in this world. I saw every argument with the chimera, the torment my manifestation dealt out on the demon, and what he endured once the demon bound him. I saw every person my manifestation hid inside, the memories of their daily lives, the lies he painted in their minds, the deceptions he weaved to obtain his goals, the manipulation meant to control Theodore Whitlock, and everything else that led up to the events of unleashing the chimera back into the world where he slaughtered Jamie Novak.

The searing agony of every memory pushed me deeper into the depths of my mind, buried under revelations.

And when I finally took a breath, escaped my slumbering mind, my bedroom vanished before my eyes as a hundred thousand visions paraded my sight at once. Every single potential future Milo spent years learning to control, cultivating and mastering, hit me simultaneously in a sea of carnage.

Everything looped round and round in my mind, stunning me and making it impossible to see anything other than these futures. Death. Romance. Mundane days. Smiles. Tears. Blood. Pain. Lust. Love. Confession. Concealment. Happiness. Nothing. Nothing. Everything! I couldn't discern one image, one word, one potential from the next. It all muddled together in a splotchy abstract.

Lips pressed to mine, beautiful and distracting and pulling me from a hundred thousand futures that sought to consume my mind until the end of all times. Every timeline, every potential vision held what felt like an entirely different world of events. But it vanished, and all that remained was Milo's kiss, standing in the rain.

The day our magics synced so perfectly, I glimpsed a void vision that put me on the path of saving my student, all my students, and brought me closer to Milo after so many years lost in grief. Had I really seen everything in Milo's mind during that kiss? Had my manifestation really managed to contain all those future images without shattering? I couldn't breathe while lost in the loop of Milo's futures hitting my magic, yet that piece of me, that dark and broken piece, plotted and conspired and wrought so much destruction.

I lay on the floor of my bedroom, absorbing the reality of what I had caused. A manifestation was nothing more than an extension of myself. This one clearly held all my narcissism and self-loathing—a lethal combination—but he was still me.

"What did I do?" I buried my face into my arms and sobbed.

Chapter Thirty-Two

I sank into the memories of my manifestation, doing my best over the course of Thanksgiving break to make sense of this madness, these vile actions, and the unadulterated hatred he held for me. Though I didn't believe in fate, not the same way Milo and Finn always did, I considered it quite fortunate this horrible truth hit me during time away from work.

There was no way I could face my students knowing the malcontent my manifestation held. I couldn't face Chanelle knowing what he—what I'd—allowed to happen to Jamie. I certainly couldn't face Milo.

Oh, Milo.

In years past, I preferred quiet, isolated holiday breaks. A reprieve from the world and all the expectations of human interaction. But this year, I'd been hopeful, even secretly eager, to spend my first Thanksgiving with Milo since he and Finn dragged me to some food bank to make the holiday meaningful. They wanted the good PR that came with it, naturally, but their intentions were genuine.

However, in the aftermath of Peter Graham's death, Enchanter Evergreen used this time to cement his image in the public and dissuade concern about the recent upheaval. He kept the details of the devil far from the press, from his thoughts, from me. But I'd seen more than him and had the horrors etched into my skull, scarring my mind. Milo wanted everyone to have a peaceful holiday, and I told him I wanted to be alone. In truth, I didn't want to have a much-needed conversation. I didn't know how to broach the topic or disclose what I'd done by extension.

For the days that passed, all I did was sit and dwell and make sense of the splotchy memories. They were thrown at me with such force that they landed in my bumbling brain, rearranged, fragmented, and in pure disarray. So, I sat in the quiet stillness of my home, deep in my own mind, ignoring those nearby and sorting out the chronicles of chaos I'd unleashed.

Charlie chirped, rubbing his head against my thigh and plopping onto my lap. This wasn't his way of asking for affection. Nope. This was merely his way of reminding me he was here, the way he'd always do when I was glum. Even Carlie joined her brother, nestling close to my hip and not once complaining about her late meals or lack of snacks.

They truly were too kind to me. I wasn't worthy of them, of anyone, or anything.

The holiday break had ended, and I hadn't sorted through half the nonsense my manifestation had caused. It left my mind in shambles. I wished I could blame the break for that. Often, a few days off made returning to the monotony of work an excruciating ordeal, shaking away the jetlag of freedom and rolling back into endless routines.

My routines didn't come easily, though. Milo continued working hard, picking up the slack of his acolytes who needed to recover. I didn't push him when he reached out with rainchecks. In fact, I invited the opportunity to avoid him and forgo the impending conversation where I'd have to explain everything I'd caused. Inadvertently or not, the manifestation came from my mind, my magic, my will. He was vile. Cruel. Selfish. Obsessive. Everything I pretended to have control over, pretended to have outgrown, pretended to strive for improvement. He was proof that I was still awful.

"Mr. Frost." Caleb strolled close to me as we approached my classroom. "Is it, um, well, would it be, um, okay if, um, I skipped—not *skipped* skipped—but like missed homeroom this morning for like a study session in the library where they're holding a library study session."

Looking at Caleb, every vision Milo had of him collided with my telepathy flashing by so quickly. The void vision rose to the top, the single most life-changing vision I'd held onto the day my magic synced perfectly with Milo, yet the others were there now, too. They'd always been there, it seemed.

I squinted, gleaning Caleb's frantic little mind because the words felt like a lie, but I was honestly grateful for the distraction of my own thoughts, of the past visions.

"A library study session during school hours?" My expression shifted into a scowl, forcing Caleb's hive of a mind to send the truth fluttering to his surface thoughts. "One they didn't send an email about?"

"Well, it's sort of an informal thing, so they didn't wanna clog emails up." He grimaced, then swallowed hard, burying the truth from escaping his lips but not his thoughts.

"*Gotcha.*"

Caleb clamped up, his shoulders raised, his eyes widened, and his mind revealed everything in apologetic bursts.

He planned on skipping morning homeroom in favor of some project Vik and Tia organized. Something involving a group casting. Caleb was instrumental in research components because of course he was, given his vast knowledge of branch magics.

He wasn't the only one. A group of students were selected.

Katherine, Layla, and Melanie among them—though Caleb only saw relevancy in Katherine's attendance given her branch magic. Each favored ditching instead of asking me for permission, something Caleb couldn't rightfully do. His polite anxiety made it impossible to "ask for forgiveness, not permission," as Katherine had encouraged.

"What are you all doing in the library?"

"Studying. Important project stuff." Caleb shivered as a cold sweat of deceit grabbed ahold of him. "It's a good cause, I swear. I'd never miss class intentionally, but this is really helpful. And we're probably not doing anything new in class anyway. I mean, before break, you were totally lax—so the opposite of your style, but understandable given everything that's happened. Which is awful, and I don't mean to make light of it or why class structure shifted."

Caleb avoided mentioning Jamie's death, even in his thoughts, as he referenced around the topic. "But you didn't even send an email before school today, which is weird because usually, before the end of a holiday or, like, even a three-day weekend, you send an email on what we should definitely be ready for when we return. But again, it completely makes sense. I just figured today would be a good day to miss since we wouldn't cover anything, and then we'd also learn something. Not that you aren't teaching. The reviews before break were fantastic and insightful, probably the best reviews I've ever had the chance to review—"

"Stop talking."

"Yes, sir." Caleb nodded profusely, like it'd somehow clear his mind, yet all it did was add to the growing headache his swirling thoughts caused.

"You're really gonna have to work on that whole oversharing thing if you want to have a successful interview as an industry professional one day."

"Of course. It's at the top of my list because I understand the importance of a solid social presence to help alleviate and support a community is—" Caleb tightened his lips to stop talking as he realized he was once again on the verge of oversharing.

"Let's go." I unlocked my classroom door, allowing a few students inside. I blocked Caleb from entering.

He fidgeted while I turned to those in class. Looking at the students who'd arrived, I saw everything Milo's magic had glimpsed of their potential futures. The mundane, the momentous, the mortifying. It all rumbled in my mind, threatening to crumble the very fabric of my being. I pushed all the visions aside, buried deep in the darkness of my subconscious, and fixated on their thoughts which helped alleviate the whirl of potential futures.

"I have to run to the library real quickly. Take this time to review"—I glared at Caleb, who averted his gaze—"or finish any missing work. Until I return, you're in charge, Gael."

"Hell yeah!" Gael jumped out of his seat, levitating until he stood on top of his desk.

Fuck. How was having Gael finally using his levitation root more exhausting than when he actively avoided it?

"This is a *dick*tatorship, and you will all obey the authority of my cock."

"Cl-cl-CLUCK!"

"Not you, Gael." I waved a hand, knocking him back into his seat with a thud, then turned my attention to Gael Martinez, who had a bubbly smile. "You're in charge. Please make sure everyone stays in the classroom and doesn't goof off—much."

"On it." Gael saluted me, then walked to the front of the classroom with a bit of swagger, already planning a brain game that mostly involved him drawing things on the whiteboard.

"Let's go." I dragged Caleb with me to the library, where I intended to learn the full extent of this project, for which so many felt the need to skip class.

Once we entered the library, Caleb's stomach twisted in knots, threatening to make me queasy with his anxious unease. Katherine eyed him from a few tables she'd sequestered from the rest of the library while setting up concoctions for a handful of other students. Caleb scrunched his face, trying to think of how to explain where it all went wrong.

"Go ahead and join them," I said, offering him a chance to tell Katherine why I'd joined despite the fact they sought to do this under the noses of their teachers. Whatever this was.

Truthfully, it couldn't be that terrible since they were in the academy library, but the secrecy, even Caleb's mind refusing to reveal exactly what they planned, made me too curious.

Amani handed the librarian a fake pass for her and Layla before making her way to the back, where Tia gestured for everyone to take their places.

```
Name: Amani Williams
Branch: Psychic (Glamour)
Ranking: 6
```

I walked over to the reference desk and eyed Ms. Abounader as she typed away on her computer, not so much as double-checking the glamour on the scraps of paper Amani handed her.

"You realize those passes are fake."

"Honey, I've been doing this for twenty-seven years, of course I know. Though, gotta say, Amani's glamours are a lot better than her dad's." She didn't look away from her computer, already searching class records on the students and concocting a list of books based on their interests—the limited amount she had—that she could casually influence them into giving a try. "Get outta my head, Dorian."

I cleared my throat, a bit flustered. Ms. Abounader was one of the few remaining staff members from when I attended the academy, and she treated me more like a student than an educator most days.

"That's because you've still got a lotta learning to do."

I frowned. For a busybody old biddy with a simple augmentation branch that allowed her to extend her limbs to those hard-to-reach places, she had a way of always knowing what people were thinking.

"You don't have to be psychic to know stuff."

Ms. Abounader vexed and annoyed me in equal measure.

"They're working." She gestured to the students. "They're not goofing off. They're not being disruptive. Honestly, there's a few I see in here quite often looking for a new book, and it's nice to see them dragging a couple friends in, too."

"You don't even know what they're doing in here," I said, having gleaned that much from her thoughts.

"Go ask 'em." She shooed me away. "No one's keeping you here."

Reluctantly, I took Ms. Abounader's advice and went to investigate.

"What exactly are you all doing?"

Vik hesitantly stepped forward, the role of leadership very much not what they wanted. It was essentially Katherine's idea, yet she'd insisted Vik came up with everything when presenting it to the others in the group. Their branch didn't even play a role, so Vik intended to pass the role of group leader off to someone else since Katherine wouldn't accept it.

```
Name: Vik Smythe
Branch: Arcane (Copycat)
Ranking: 158
```

They figured Layla or Amani would be the best leaders to coordinate this project. After all, they both enjoyed being the center of attention and were good at bossing people around. Instead, the pair pretty much bullied Vik into getting off their ass and making it happen.

I tilted my head, realizing Layla and Amani didn't do that precisely, but it certainly felt that way to Vik. The way folks reimagined their memories sometimes… It almost made me laugh.

"We're creating a living memory," Vik said.

I quirked a brow. Apparently, quite aggressively, with my stern, stone-like face that never faltered from peering through the souls of unfortunate bystanders. Seriously? That was what Vik thought from a single expression? Geez.

"It's a combination of several different magics." Vik kicked their foot into the floor, wishing they'd have copied a tunneling magic so they could burrow deep into the ground and disappear. "It's a high-tier enchantment spell. A few enchantment spells. Katherine knows more."

Katherine widened her eyes, waiting for Vik to continue before realizing they'd passed the mic to her. "Basically, it's a mix of spell craft, invocation, potion craft, glamouring, and a warding totem. We thought we'd need some psychic energy too, but Caleb's research says it'll work without any."

"What are you making?"

"A living memory." Katherine gestured to Vik. "Weren't you listening to them?"

"Of what, though?"

"Jamie," Katherine said, the only one in this group capable of flatly saying his name without becoming consumed by emotion. She really was the most level-headed of her peers, of most adults, too. "When he and I created a hybrid spell, it infused a living signature of his magic and presence. With this combination spell, we'll be able to create a snow globe effect on memories people hold of him."

Tia signed, leaving Harrison to interpret since she'd ditched her interpreter for this library adventure. And honestly, I supposed it was better than how she usually ditched her interpreter to take a vape break with whoever she could drag alongside her.

```
Name: Tatiana Owens
Branch: Enchantment (Invocation)
Ranking: 162
```

"My magic will create a command over the parchment from Katherine's grimoire and transfer that energy into the totems Layla bought."

"They're incredibly rare," Caleb chimed in. "I found a few knockoff versions online that would've probably done the trick, but this set definitely makes all the difference."

"It was nothing." Layla shrugged off the praise, wanting to bury everything about this as deep in her mind as possible, but I caught the regret, the guilt, the laborious work involved in procuring these totems from her grandmother's collection where they sat gathering dust like cheap trinkets hoarded and lorded at parties only a handful were worthy in attending.

In exchange, Layla agreed to spend winter break in The Hamptons, something she despised. It wouldn't be a simple vacation with her grandmother but a difficult testament of resisting persuasion, manipulation, and obligation for Layla. One where Layla's grandmother would encourage her to once again consider guild work in New York, Seattle, San Diego, or a dozen other handpicked cities where her grandmother held connections. It was important, after all, that the Smythe family balance their reach nationwide, and Layla's older brothers already cemented their place in Chicago.

I didn't have much sway in families that laid out futures for their children, but I could mull it over when helping Layla choose her internship next year. If I worked hard enough, I might find her a guild with an incredibly persuasive enchanter. Then it'd just be about making sure Layla rocked her internship. It wouldn't be the first time I nudged a student toward their interests over their family obligations, and it helped so much more when a top-notch enchanter encouraged that student to join their guild after graduation.

"Christ," Layla snarled, the roar in her thoughts pushing away my telepathy. "Are you seriously going to give a whole history lesson on the fucking totems?"

Caleb gulped. "I'm done."

"*Thank fucking god.*" Amani rolled her eyes at Layla, and the pair smirked.

"Once Tia's command is placed, the spells settle together in a nice combination, and then we'll be able to activate the final component of enchantment symmetry with a simple potion."

"Nothing simple about this." Harrison pulled out a few vials filled with a deep purple liquid. "It took all Thanksgiving break to get it right. Well, mostly because my uncle kept mixing his holiday hammered beer brew into my cauldron, but it's still a complex potion."

```
Name: Harrison Heywood
Branch: Enchantment (Potion Craft)
Ranking: 25
```

"Wait." I cocked my head. "How long have you all been putting this idea together?"

They all stared quietly, their thoughts revealing the time and dedication. Research, late nights, cross-analyzing spells, syncing all their casting frequencies, countless trials and errors, and so much more than any of them had learned from classes. Each one of them went above and beyond to put this together.

"What happens when the potion hits a totem?" I asked.

"Thanks to my glamours and Katherine's spell housing Jamie's magic, it allows the person holding a totem to relive a memory."

"I would've preferred a psychic magic like retrocognition," Caleb interjected, ready to offer an entire lecture behind retrocognition and how the magic allowed one to view the past, but I already knew that branch deeply, personally. He didn't share once Amani and Layla glared. "It's a really rare magic. Only five people in the state are even registered with the branch."

Which wasn't to say there weren't more, another tidbit Caleb wanted to drop because only licensed witches had to offer their branches for public records. Unlicensed branches remained confidential government records.

"This is a lovely idea you've all come together to create," I said. "Why not share this with me or your homeroom teacher?"

"Mrs. Whitehurst has enough going on," Amani said, then waved a hand at me dismissively. "And you're always hanging on her skirt every day. We didn't want you giving it away."

"Yeah," Vik said, fighting the nervous squeak in their voice. "We made one for Mrs. Whitehurst, too. As a surprise. But it's mostly for Jamie's family. You know?"

"I do." I nodded, truly impressed by the innovation and collaboration of these students.

Work was a beautiful distraction, so much so I was deeply saddened when the fast-paced classes came to an end and I had to go home. Each lecture, each activity, each question from a student kept my mind too busy and active to fixate on all the reasons I was a horrible person who'd ruined lives with my branch, with my manifestation.

Milo: Sorry I've been MIA.

I went to respond but lingered, watching the three dancing dots. He had more to say, and I didn't know where to begin.

Milo: Care if I swing by tonight?
Got cases and such but I miss your face. 😘

I grinned, skin buzzing at the simplest message. My spirits lifted, then sank back into insecurities, doubt, and the fact that once I told Milo the truth, the full extent of my part… I swallowed hard.

Me: I'd love to see you.

Fuck. Love. That made it sound like an easy-going, screw-your-brains-out kind of night when it wouldn't be. Not with the revelation I'd had.

I tossed my phone, ignoring the buzz, and whatever happy response followed. Hopefully, that'd settle any eager anticipation that tugged at my heartstrings where Milo's mind called out to me, excited to come over.

The hours passed, and I organized my thoughts, trying to find the best way to begin this conversation, yet when the knock at my door hit, my mind went blank. It didn't help that Milo barged right inside, using the playful rhythmic knock as a cutesy formality.

"Feels like you're a million miles away when I'm buried in work." He strolled over, a swagger in his walk, and plopped onto the couch beside me. "We have a lot to discuss."

"I should go first."

"Guessing you glimpsed the devil's resurrection or survival or a hundred other things I've been attempting to make sense of."

"No. Yes." I froze. Milo avoided me, too, not wanting me to learn the chimera had returned, had nefarious plans, and sought to blot out the perfect futures Enchanter Evergreen strived to make a reality. "I'm the reason the devil never died."

Milo's face fell, pensive and concerned, thoughts swirling into a thousand paranoid half-accurate assumptions that I'd lied about letting go of Finn, that it somehow unraveled all of this, how I must not love him if I kept something like this a secret.

"I do love you. And didn't mean to withhold any of this." I cleared my throat, fighting the crack of my gruff voice, turning pitchy as my eyes teared up. "It was my manifestation."

"You made a manifestation? I thought—"

"I couldn't?" I nodded. "So did I. Turns out that was because the last one I'd conjured hacked the strings connecting us and sort of did his own thing."

"What does that mean?"

I explained it all, everything that I knew, that I'd made sense of. Even with everything hurled back into my mind from the day the manifestation walked away from me to the night he perished, I still struggled to organize the memories mixed with hateful thoughts, torturous encounters, trauma, venom, visions, hopes, fears, desperations, and so much more.

I told Milo everything. How my manifestation stole away the wisp connected to Finn's being, containing the chimera, skirting Milo's visions, attempting to control Theodore Whitlock, failing, falling prey to the demon he couldn't ever control, the party, Jamie's death, the attack on his acolytes, and the final act where Finn convinced him, convinced me, to finally do the right thing and put an end to the devil who sought a perfect host.

Milo sat quietly, patiently listening, even simmering his thoughts that held a hundred questions I couldn't rightfully answer.

"You keep saying *you* did this."

"I did. It was my magic, my personality—and damn if that manifestation didn't hate how much we were the same."

"You always said your manifestations are extensions of yourself."

Most manifestations I created over the years were empty reflections of myself with no thought or will, merely a second sight of my being. But some of the stronger ones carried more quirks, more individuality. I'd never thought much of it, never suspected one could transform into something as terrible as this.

"But this manifestation was made of raw emotion mixed into magic."

"They are mostly reflections…were." Not that I'd ever make a manifestation again after all this. "The problem is it's my raw emotion, my magic, because they're me."

"They're pieces of you; they aren't you. You're more than your impulsive desire and self-loathing, which, from everything you've said, it sounds like this manifestation was a powerful combination of those two elements."

Milo scooted closer, unable to handle the distance between us, and truthfully, I wanted to collapse into his embrace and let the world fall away as he consoled me. But I didn't deserve it. I didn't deserve him.

"My magic killed a kid."

"No. A demon killed a kid. Your magic—not you, but your magic—made an error. Failed. Fucked up royally, but that's not on you." Milo placed a hand on my shoulder, squeezing it until the grip pulled me away from my thoughts. "You didn't see anything he did because he broke away, meaning he was a thought run wild on his own. You can't blame yourself for that."

"Someone has to."

"God knows you are the best when it comes to laying blame at your feet, but I need you to realize this wasn't you." Milo rubbed his hand up and down my arm. "I thought about killing Theodore Whitlock after what he did to you. I thought about killing Peter Graham all those years ago, snapping his neck, and watching the potential dangers he posed fade away. Does that make me a murderer for having the thought?"

I didn't respond because it wasn't the same. No, we weren't our thoughts; I learned that long ago after every mind surrounding my teenage brain bombarded my telepathy with a billion hypotheticals. But not everyone had to worry about their faintest fantasies or impulsive ideas springing to life and causing carnage like I did. They didn't have to worry about some manifestation they'd breathed life into then tearing loose and destroying the lives of everyone around them.

"Am I responsible for the lives they took?"

"What?" I choked on the word, my sight glossy from tears welling in my eyes, but Milo had the most sincere expression, no humor, no anger, no doubt as he asked.

"Am I responsible for the deaths Theodore continues to cause? Am I responsible for Jamie Novak's death?"

"No." My throat burned, and tears rolled down my face. "Never. You can't stop everything. Can't predict everything."

"But I did know the dangers Theodore, Peter, and a hundred others held and still hold. I know full well the potential harm they can cause. Not these deaths, but the potential remains. I chose to keep my conscience unburdened by bloodshed. Does that make me guilty? Culpable? Responsible? My magic saw a solution and showed me a possibility to snuff them out. Am I bad for not taking it?"

I fell forward into Milo's chest, burying my face and sobbing.

"You're not responsible, Dorian." He stroked my hair. "You're not to blame. You're not every bad result of your magic. This is a lesson I've seen you teach kids a thousand times over."

He meant in his visions. He had so many involving me. In the classroom. At home. With him. Alone. The happiest future for the two of us, something so bright and beautiful I still couldn't glimpse it amongst all the other visions flooding my mind simultaneously, but it existed. It could exist.

"I need you to realize this wasn't you." Milo squeezed me tighter as I trembled in his arms. "I need you to stop blaming yourself. I need you."

The words hit hard, harder than every burden I blamed myself for, harder than every desire to isolate myself, every desire to run away because I wrought Hell upon those around me.

"I love you, Dorian."

Milo held me all night, ignoring his phone and reminders of late-night cases, and sat with me as I struggled to get past what I—what my manifestation—had done.

Chapter Thirty-Three

"Are you sure you're up for a day at the academy?" Milo asked, his mind pulling me to his office from all the way across town. "Because they'd understand. It's not a requirement and—"

"I'm fine." Lena glowered, biting back something snippier, no doubt. In the month since losing her brother, attempting to stop Peter Graham, and nearly dying at the hands of a devil, she found the most grueling part of it was how her coven mates coddled her during the recovery.

Milo could see it on her face every day, and occasionally, I could hear it in her thoughts even though my mind usually clung close to Milo's alone.

Ellie hadn't given Lena nearly as much shit, Hayden actually showed up on time, and Enchanter Evergreen didn't hand out stacks of pointless paperwork for his acolytes to fill out on his behalf. Lena grew tired of all these acts of consideration, wanting the world to go back to something familiar. I related, which was possibly why her mind called out.

"Alrighty, then." Milo smirked. "You lot head on over to Gemini."

"You're not going?" Ellie asked.

"I've got a meeting." Milo waggled his eyebrows. "A super major awesome meeting with some Global Guild reps."

As his acolytes took their leave, Milo sat back in his chair and propped his legs onto his desk. "*I know you need space, time to decompress, working through the motions, and I hope it's going well.*"

Milo gave me the time to recover, to get my head screwed on right. No pressure, no rush, just a chance to focus on the end of the semester before winter break.

I did just that, working with students and preparing for midterms along with the second-year Spring Showcase just around the corner where I'd need my entire homeroom coven ready to impress every possible enchanter so they landed solid internships during their third year when I wouldn't be their instructor any longer.

I went into the semester with such grand plans, goals, hopes... And I failed to achieve any of them. In fact, the only lesson I successfully taught and lived through was how to cope with failure.

"*And yeah, you're probably not listening, doing your whole distancing thing while sorting through all the memories, the visions, the emotions.*" Milo smiled. "*But I'm secretly hoping you're eavesdropping. Hoping you can feel my love.*"

My heart hitched, and I went to link our thoughts to tell him I did. I did eavesdrop while taking the space I needed, I did feel his love, I did love him. But a wave of frustration wafted through the halls, hitting my telepathy.

I followed that thread of rage, finding an anxious Kenzo standing at the front doors of Gemini Academy. His heart hammered so hard against his chest, he thought he might pass out. The scowl on his face did wonders to deceive his peers while his insides twisted in knots over not being good enough. That this gesture meant nothing. That he needed a real declaration.

All in all, the self-doubt was Kenzo's alone, and Gael eagerly held his boyfriend's hand for the first time in public as they walked into school the day before winter break. Gael had styled his hair a bright red while somehow convincing Kenzo to add green streaks to his own. They had matching holiday hair, and Kenzo loathed the idea almost as much as Gael loved it.

I stared as they approached the classroom, Gael's sharklike teeth beaming as Kenzo frowned.

"What?" Static popped along Kenzo's brow, not hiding his thoughts but coursing across his pale skin while he continued training the full extent of his branch. "I'm holding my boyfriend's hand. There's no academy policy against that. If you got something to say, just fucking say it."

"Kenzo, chill." Gael chuckled.

I shrugged. "Nothing to say."

"Keep it that way." He dragged Gael into homeroom but paused once the eyes of everyone else fell on him. "Not. One. Word."

"Looks like love is in the air." Gael rocked his head side-to-side, humming some hit song while King Clucks mimicked the motion. Gael's faux hawk swished almost as much as the rooster's red comb jiggled.

Kenzo walked past, only releasing Gael Martinez's hand once they'd reached their seats, but Gael Rios-Vega's song continued, and his thoughts twisted into something minxy I figured he'd soon regret.

"It's beautiful to see my buddy happy with his beast." Gael winked at Gael, whose unyielding smile twisted into a grimace as his face flushed.

"Stop talking." Kenzo's face burned bright with annoyance, yet he'd found a way to be honest about his feelings leagues ahead of me. For a kid who wanted to isolate himself from the world while striving to be the best enchanter living in it, he couldn't fathom pushing Gael aside, even if it meant he had to deal with the other people in Gael's life—like Gael and King Clucks.

"What?" Gael grinned, mischievous as ever. "I'm just happy you're happy."

"No puedo decirte nada." Gael placed a spiky hand over his eyes.

"Yet you tell me everything." Gael smirked at Kenzo. "Everything. First comes hand holding, followed by sweet kisses, enchanting dates, lovely chats, and then it's all like sit on my face and—"

SLAM.

"***Motherfucker.***"

Static pulsed, lunging across the room and hitting Gael's stomach. He spun around, floating sideways until the motion met a bit of telekinesis from the other Gael, who sought to quiet his friend before his chatty personality embarrassed his boyfriend.

"I'm gonna be sick." Gael twirled, his cheeks puffing. "King Clucks, help me."

"Ba-ba-bawk." His familiar hopped off the desk and scampered over to Tara's seat, clearly content Gael's safety was not at risk.

Everyone in the class giggled as Gael fought to catch his seat while spinning round and round. Their surface thoughts were filled mostly with amusement for Gael's plight, completely overlooking the gesture Kenzo had made, already forgetting it like yesterday's news. All except Caleb.

"*It's nice to see Kenny happy. Genuinely happy.*" Memories of Caleb and his former best friend flashed in his mind, a lost childhood friend he couldn't relinquish.

I gripped Gael with a telekinetic hold, waiting for the hex to fade and pretty impressed by the level of improvement Kenzo had made with his casting. His disruption had gone from merely quelling active magics to amplifying them, proving his branch had extensive reach. All the same, I tossed Gael into his chair that he held onto for dear life while glaring at Kenzo.

"As entertaining as this is, we need to get to the auxiliary gym." I instructed everyone to gather their things so we could leave.

Chanelle's class met us halfway, irritation festering at the surface of her thoughts. I embraced it because there was no wave of grief burrowed beneath. She hadn't healed. No one really does when death strikes, but it got easier. Or so I'd seen from thousands of different minds over the course of my own dragged-out sorrow.

"You wouldn't believe the hell I've been through." Gael sulked, dragging his feet as he reached Tiffany. "Betrayal from every corner."

"Poor baby." She interlocked her arm with his as their familiars walked side-by-side. Quite a pair, King Clucks the rooster, and Duchess the beaver.

It appeared they'd gotten much closer this semester. Something told me Gael would only become more insufferable with a girlfriend who understood his minxy mind.

"*Not to be that person*"—Chanelle strutted close to me like it'd increase the volume of her thoughts—"*but what the actual hell are you doing?*"

"*It's a nice day for a little training before winter break.*"

"*You're full of shit.*"

I'd ruined Mrs. Whitehurst's Winter Wonderland World of Trivial…I honestly couldn't recall the full name. It was long and absurd and had too many rules that led to lots of children screaming in equal parts entertainment and frustration. Ugh. Personally, I rather enjoyed ruining her game day. She sent the kids off to all their classes high on sugar and demanding fun from every other class before vacation, so ruining her plans served as an added bonus to being a thoughtful assistant in today's agenda.

We arrived at the auxiliary gym, where Vik and Tia waited. While others had helped, these two orchestrated everything into place, so I was glad they stood here basking in the credit. Even though Tia had already conspired ways to sneak out for a vape break and Vik's face turned so ghostly white, they looked a moment from passing out with everyone's eyes on them.

"Here, I figured you just took an early vacation." Chanelle side-eyed her two students. "I'm still marking you both tardy."

Acolyte Novak and Reed entered the auxiliary gym.

"Where's Hayden?" Ellie eyed everyone from mine and Chanelle's homeroom covens. "I don't get it. We left at the same time. He even took off ahead of us. How's he not here?"

"He just texted." Lena shared her phone. "Look at this bullshit story about helping a little old lady cross the street."

Ellie huffed. "He needs better lies."

"Enchanter Evergreen should honestly fire him." Lena fought a smirk, not for the comment but for the tiniest sign of things moving back to normal.

My telepathy soared, searching for the serene light, which was easy to spot, and I found Hayden was, in fact, not lying. He really had gotten distracted when stopping to help someone get across a busy street. That guy was perplexing, to say the least.

"Why are they even here?" Kenzo asked, grumbling tone almost half as powerful as his irritated thoughts. "Didn't you cancel the midterm rematch?"

"I did—"

"Which is fortunate for you, squirt," Lena interjected.

"Squirt? What are you ninety?" Kenzo folded his arms at the same time as Lena, each studying the other with scrutiny. "Heard you went and got yourself impaled like some amateur."

Lena took bold steps toward us, but Kenzo noticed the weakened fluctuation in her constant casting as she recovered. "Were you hoping for an easy win?"

"Not a chance. I want you at your best when I wipe the floor with your smug face."

"Bring it on, kid. I'd love to slap you around a second time." Lena sneered. "And this time, I won't hold back when kicking your scrawny ass."

"Can't wait to show you how wrong you are." Kenzo scowled. "Anytime and anyplace."

Gael and Ellie grimaced at each other, half expecting a fight to break out between Kenzo and Lena this very second. It wouldn't. The two shared a sordid respect for one another. And honestly, I believed Kenzo would help guide Lena away from her grief while she helped him navigate his rage into success during combat, something I never rightfully fully grasped.

Changing my midterm so drastically wasn't ideal, but most of my students anticipated it. Not for the recent events. No, they braced for the pop quiz I gave them last week instead of a combative rematch because, apparently, it was still a very "Frosty" thing to do, changing lessons at the last possible second. The fact was I didn't want more fighting, combat, bloodshed—at least not until after the break. We'd return and focus on everything they needed to learn and prepare for next semester before moving into their third-year internships. I'd ensure it.

But first, we all still needed time.

I cleared my throat loudly to steer Kenzo and Lena away from their glaring contest, which would likely last forever, so we could focus on a little of that well-meaning time for mending.

Vik and Tia stared at the still chatty room.

"That was your cue," I said, clearing my throat again. "They're not gonna shut up until you start talking."

And even then, it took some serious effort to quiet a room full of teens.

Vik eyed Tia, who scrunched her face and signed. I wasn't sure what she signed, but her expression very much said, "I can't lead the discussion."

"We've been working on a project, um, all of us," Vik stammered a bit. "Well, not all of us, all of us. A group consisting of…"

Damn. They rambled through their well-rehearsed speech and threw in a bunch of added side comments they hadn't prepared to say. Everyone was pretty considerate. I backstepped from the group and approached Katherine, who watched Vik with awe, presenting the gift to everyone.

"You did a wonderful thing."

"Huh?" Katherine adjusted her glasses, attempting to hide her thoughts and failing terribly at it. I wouldn't tell her, though, since Katherine rarely failed. "I just made a couple enchantment spells. I hardly played a role in this massive collection of combo magic."

"I know this has been a tough semester, feeling like your ranking is stilted."

"Nope. Still top ten, so I've got nothing to complain about."

"The academy ranking system doesn't evaluate all the hard efforts of students." Something Katherine grasped more than others since she worked closely with her boyfriend, Caleb, who struggled to push his ranking higher. "But I see your efforts. Your determination. Your support. From making weighted blocks for Caleb and Tara to transcribing complex spell algorithms for Gael and Jamius, all the way to being an outlet of conversation for Jennifer and Carter."

I eyed those two, pausing as sometimes, when I focused on the pair, my thoughts flashed back to the singular moment that bonded them together. The day I nearly died. Those two had bounced around their feelings and friendship for a year now since they worked together to save my life. Skimming the surface of their minds, it didn't seem either knew whether these feelings were friendship or blossoming into something else. In any event, Katherine did what she did best—supported those around her.

"I also see your thoughts dancing in Spanish." I nodded as she finally found a trick to hide her words in a language I'd yet to learn. "You're teaching yourself. Another way to show support, offering Gael something to teach you when you're reviewing materials with him. I see that. I see the arguments you skirt when Kenzo annoys you. I see the study sessions you host for classes you're already breezing through because you want to make sure Yaritza, Layla, and Melanie's rankings aren't affected by a failing grade."

Katherine clutched her grimoire tightly, so tightly it distracted her from the joy of validation she felt selfish for basking in.

She shouldn't feel selfish for being acknowledged; she should be angry for how long I'd overlooked her. Even after telling myself this semester that I'd focus on all my students. Even after I noted the struggle Katherine internalized. Unfortunately, I let the struggles of other students pull my focus because when glimpsing at Katherine's mind, she always managed to pull herself out of the self-doubt, the frustration, the overwhelming emotions and persevere.

"I see everything you do, Katherine. You're an admirable person."

Those who always kept it together, never buckled under the weight of pressure, and constantly offered support to everyone around them were easy to overlook. They kept their composure; they acted as pillars of support—strong and sturdy, unyielding in their determination. They never appeared like they needed help. They didn't. They would survive without praise. I'd forgotten that sometimes, just because someone wasn't broken or struggling didn't mean they didn't require that emotional support, that kindness was too often reserved for those who needed it to stay strong.

"I'm sorry I don't acknowledge that more, don't express how grateful and fortunate I am to have such a talented and independent student in my homeroom coven."

Even though supporting everyone around her didn't pay off and grant Katherine guaranteed success, she carved out time every day to ensure a better tomorrow for those she cared about. I'd have to work on that next semester. Katherine wanted to see herself as a star. Katherine needed to feel supported in this program, too.

"Thank you, Mr. Frost." Katherine fixated on Vik's continued speech, so proud of them for making it this far without a panic attack like in the practices Katherine ran through with them.

I leaned in on Lena's mind since this gift was for her, her family, Chanelle, and a few others who might want to carry a piece of Jamie with them.

Lena's expression shifted, soft and surprised—forceful because she was in no way surprised. At the surface of her mind, Milo's spoilers rang through. Of course he told her. Anything involving her brother, his memory, the smallest possible trigger, he wanted her to go in prepared. She came here placating the forethought of others, quietly overjoyed for the sentiment put into this gift, and graciously accepted the totem along with the vial that would enact memories she carried of Jamie, recreating an illusion of their time together.

"Thank you so much." Chanelle hugged Vik and Tia, then eyed me. "*Thanks for not ruining the surprise.*"

"*It was the least I could do. I've sort of been a shitty friend.*"

"*Not at all.*" She grinned. "*Considering the low bar I keep you at, you're looking pretty top-notch.*"

I glared.

We let the students stay in the gym after the presentation while Lena and Ellie took their leave. Everyone relaxed, trained, or bounced off the walls—some quite literally—and then we sent them off to their next classes.

As the day wrapped up, I reached out to Milo's mind, missing him, missing us, missing the feeling of comfort his presence brought.

He soared through the sky, leaving a meeting and making his way to a case where he'd follow up with an interview he'd prepped for in his thoughts.

"*I appreciate the time and distance.*" I linked to his mind. "*Thank you for respecting my need, my addiction to distance, but I wish you wouldn't.*"

"*Huh?*"

"*I don't want time to decompress, to process. I mean, I do. It's important, but also, I don't want to be that guy who boxes everything away and shuts out the world.*" It was that exact type of behavior that led to the manifestation blossoming, finding a way to cut his strings and knowing me so well that he understood I'd never search the depths of my subconscious for the absence. "I don't want you to give me time."

"*So, you want me to pester you? Bug ya?*" Milo's smile filled the skyline he flew through. "*I can annoy you with lots of love. I'm good at it.*"

I sighed. "*I just need you to remind me that I'm not the worst person on the planet.*"

Milo scoffed. "*You barely make the top ten.*"

"Milo," I whined, not even sure that audible gravelly groan traveled through my telepathic connection, but I waited.

"*If you want me to stop by, I will. If you want me to overstay my welcome, I will. If you want me to refuse your commands on space, I will.*"

"*Well, I mean, a little space every now and then would—*"

"*Absolutely not.*"

I huffed. "*Thank you.*"

"*Just glad you want me in your life.*"

"*Always.*" I strengthened the connection, wanting to feel the warmth of his chest, his soft skin, his firm muscles. "*I need you in my life. Always.*"

Chapter Thirty-Four

Once I got home, I figured I'd have a few minutes to get ready for Milo's arrival, but a gust of wind hit the second I opened my front door, and I moved aside as he hovered in front of my doorstep, allowing him the space to properly parade inside.

"Didn't you have a meeting?"

"Oh, with the Global Guild?" Milo stepped in close. "Sometimes it's best to leave them waiting. Makes 'em want you more."

I turned away, face flushed and incapable of hiding the smile caused. "Since when do you want to join the Global Guild?"

He'd basically dodged them, their invitations, their requests, their summons, their uppity fucking everything since he was brought into the Global Rankings, making a name for himself on the international level, yet content remaining here in Chicago, far from their elite guild.

"I'm not really interested in the Global Guild buuuuut..." He dragged the word out with a grin that almost made me think he planned on making an ass joke. "Their influence here could paint a brighter future for everyone."

"The Global Guild isn't stationary." They moved where and when and how they saw fit. They didn't simply linger in a city for a time, not the way Milo's thoughts suggested. The Global Guild relocated regularly, completing missions only the best of the best could achieve. Even a devil at the doorstep of Chicago didn't entertain their fancy, not enough to garner aid from the most elite witches in the world. Not that Milo ever wanted their help or the implications it held.

With the Global Guild came strings, vulnerability, and the idea a city, state, or province couldn't defend itself. All the same, his mind weaved between blurry visions of what they might offer. Not blank visions. Blurry. Muddled. Just out of frame from my sight.

That's weird. It's like I can finally almost see Milo's magic in action.

"What're you planning?"

"It's sorta complicated, lots of random variables." Milo waved a hand like that somehow blew away the thoughts stirring around his spiky blond hair. "It's far off in the future, maybe. Nothing's certain."

"You and the future." I sighed. "You know, my manifestation knew a lot about your future or futures."

Milo stood silently, absorbing the distance in my phrasing. My manifestation. Not me. Because he wasn't me. Not really, not fully, not even a little bit. I hoped.

"He thought you hired Hayden as some potential to banish the devil." I shrugged. "But now I see you didn't plan that."

"And now you're wondering why I hired him. Of the nearly two thousand applicants, why Hayden Never-On-Time-For-His-Life Russo?"

I'd never asked. It didn't really strike me as something to look ahead at, but this was Milo. He never made a choice without thinking years into the future about the outcomes.

"I don't wanna talk about it. None of it." I brushed past him and headed toward the kitchen for a little liquid courage. "I didn't call you over to discuss visions, futures, your job."

"You brought it up."

"There's so much about your visions I can't make sense of." I poured a drink. "They're wrapped in my head, suffocating, weighty, and impossible to navigate."

"Not impossible, but certainly a challenge."

"I can see it all, well, all that you had the day our magics merged." I swallowed a scorching sip of vodka and sucked my teeth until the burning faded. "Everything that could happen, would happen, should happen, and…" I downed the rest of the heavy-handed shot I'd poured myself.

"And everything that'll never happen because the right fates didn't line up properly."

He meant the futures still involving Finn. Three young men stepping to the forefront of Cerberus Guild. Three powerful enchanters entangled in romance and heroism. Three meant to be the greatest protectors of Chicago. That was a future my manifestation believed he could force back into reality, wedge into the world despite Finn's death, despite me walking away from guild life, despite Enchanter Evergreen changing a million events between what could've been and what had happened.

It was astounding how Milo held onto every vision, saw every potential—even those that never held a flickering chance.

"So, you call me over here to help you sort through the rubble in your head?" Milo grinned, eager to dive into my mind and organize the visions that'd made a home in my head. I supposed it was his version of getting a sock drawer.

"No. I'm not ready for that." I pressed a hand to Milo's chest, fixating on the steady beat that never held anxiety when with me, the heart that beat with passion and love and kindness and courage and everything else beautiful in this world. "I called you because I don't wanna slip into comfortable patterns."

He quirked a brow.

"I freak out, drown in guilt, I struggle to go through the motions, I avoid you, dodge you, use you for sex, and push you away until the all-consuming grief finally stops. Only it never stops. Not for me. Not the way I resist feeling. But that pain subsides when you're here, really here, with me. I love having you in my life. I worry I'm not good enough. I worry I fuck up everything. I worry one day you'll realize the wrong partner died."

"Dorian—"

"Let me finish." My voice cracked, either from booze in my throat or the nerves of raw vulnerability. Personally, I hoped it was the liquor. "Despite all the daily guilt, the constant anxiety, the regrets I could bury myself in, I don't want to. I don't want to slip into the comfortable habits of taking ten years or more to navigate emotions I'll never master. I don't want to push you away ever."

"You already gave me permission to be insufferably unavoidable." Milo grabbed my hand, pulling it close to his face and delicately kissing my knuckles.

"I know in my head you have a point about the manifestation. He wasn't me. He was a piece. A bad piece. But I'll probably hang onto the blame until the day I die. It's just who I am." I caressed his face, running my fingers along his sharp jawline. "Still, I want to be who I am with you in my life, trying to see the world through the same happy lens you do."

"So, what do you wanna do right now?"

"Right now, I wanna bury my regrets while…" I grazed my knuckles along the tight fabric of his pants, brushing his crotch.

"While I bury my cock inside you?" Milo tilted his head, minxy grin and excitement in his bright blue eyes. "And here I thought you were trying not to fall back into avoidant tactics."

"This isn't me slipping into old habits. I'm not avoiding my emotions by being with you. I'd never do that to you, to us." I grabbed his belt, unfastening it. "I don't wanna use your body to dodge my feelings."

"And what do you want?"

"I wanna embrace how I feel, and right now, I wanna feel my boyfriend, feel your love, your passion, your satisfaction." I unzipped his pants. "The kind of things that remind me why I keep trying."

Milo kissed me, rough and fast. My lips barely kept up with his. I loved the taste of Milo. His hands had found their way onto my hips, pinning me against the countertop. I yanked his belt off and slid my hand down his slacks between his briefs. As his tongue led our mouths in a messy make-out, I grabbed his cock, jerking his bulge until it stiffened in my grip. Milo released my hips to adjust his pants and pull them down to free his fully erect dick.

"Damn." I kissed Milo's neck, breathy and teasing him with each exhale as I continued stroking. "That was fast."

"Gonna have to catch up." Milo pressed his full body against me, running his hands over me, tugging at my pants, gripping my thighs, kissing my shoulder, nibbling, and biting. I couldn't keep up with all the sensations, the desires, the full allure of his arousal.

Gentle telekinesis weaved between the roughness of his assertive hands, stroking my cock, wrapping around my ass, massaging my lower back, and a thousand other touches meant to ready me here and now.

Milo spun me around and pulled my pants down to my knees.

My breathing hitched when he stuck a finger inside me, wet and lubed, having already worked his magic to grab the bottle from my nightstand on the other side of the house.

"We could take this to the bedroom." I leaned so my back pressed against his chest, my ear close to his lips because I wanted to feel his words hit my skin.

"I want you here," he whispered, sliding a hand up my back one column at a time, and instructed me to bend forward.

With a firm hold, he kept my face and chest pressed to the cool countertop as he drove his cock inside me. My feet arched, stretching and bracing my stance on the high counter until his rough thrusts made my legs quake and my toes curl.

Suddenly, I relied purely on his magic to hold me. He hovered, clearly based on the angle of driving his dick down into me like a jackhammer pounding away so fast the empty glass shook, clinking when it reached the metallic edges of the sink.

I moaned, hand extending to catch it, but I missed, swept into the painful pleasure of Milo's increasing strokes. All I could do was brace against the counter. Every time he thrust, he went a bit deeper, fully plunging his cock all the way inside me, and mine began to throb.

With one hand pressed between my shoulder blades and the other holding my hip, Milo kept me pinned in place as he piledrived into me. Each second left me lost in delirium, in the excitement of Milo and the grunts that escaped both our lips, mixing with the slap of his skin hitting mine.

The clock on the stove ticked by, albeit completely inaccurate in its display of three in the morning, but I watched the minutes pass. Each one added to my throbbing cock bouncing against the kitchen drawer, sticky with precum.

Milo's relentless lust made me pant, the satisfaction he had asserting himself, fucking me as I whimpered in ecstasy. A true blissful euphoria. I never wanted it to end.

The pressure holding me against the countertop eased as Milo slid his hand down my back and slapped my ass. I yelped, startled and enthralled. He firmly squeezed the cheek while his other hand kept a grip on my hip. With me fully in his grasp, he pumped into me faster, unrelenting. Every breath he released carried a feral grunt, soothing me, calling me, enticing me more.

Unable to contain myself, I arched my back and leaned up. With my upper body freed, I stretched an arm over my head and yanked his hair. I pulled him closer, though I couldn't angle myself properly; I wanted his lips, to taste the sex on his tongue, to feel the sweetness of his love, to breathe in every exhale of passion he held.

"Milo," I whined, barely able to contain my climax.

His lips met mine, silencing me; his hand reached around and found my cock.

"Wait." I groaned, biting his bottom lip as he rhythmically pounded into me while stroking my cock until I couldn't stop myself.

My entire body warmed, vibrated, and all the tension in my muscles, in my mind, in my magic, exploded as I came.

Milo didn't stop. Kissing me. Thrusting. Controlling the ebb and flow of our bodies in the air as we spun around, shifting positions until I rode on top of him. He floated up to the ceiling, pinning me between his body and the rough surface of the wall. He grabbed my wrists, holding my arms in place as he teased me with his lips just out of reach. I bit the air between us, tasting his sweat and lust but wanting it all.

I wrapped my legs around his hips, guiding and instructing the pace, urging him to speed up. He was close. I could feel him twitch on the cusp of finishing.

His heightened thrusts were all-consuming. I gasped as he railed me harder and faster until finally cumming inside me. Milo bucked, still thrusting so he could pump every drop into me. I pressed my forehead to his, basking in his satisfied exhales as he panted, relishing in the pleasure of his release.

The exhaustion of his pure satiated delight showed as the full weight of my body fell into his, held up only by wobbly levitation.

I channeled some telekinesis to steady our slow descent to the kitchen floor, where I collapsed on top of a sweaty Milo.

"I need a fucking cigarette," I muttered.

Chapter Thirty-Five

I spent the rest of the evening restless. Yeah, struggling to get up and walk, but buzzed from the afterglow of sex. Milo, on the other hand, was teeming with energy by the time we moved into the bedroom and then passed out the second his head hit the pillow. His ability to shut out the whole world without overthinking a single thing before going to sleep was mesmerizing.

With him asleep, my mind wandering all over the place, and the kickoff to winter break, I figured it was as good a time as any to continue sorting through the visions, the memories, the chaos swirling around my inner core. No distractions or deadlines, just me and the daunting task of fixing my overloaded brain.

Laying back, I sank into the mattress until my consciousness fell deeper into the pits of my mind. A terrible mess that left the elegant rooms of my inner core trashed. Normally, here in my head, I could spot the thoughts of others trickling by, whispers and shouts alike, text on display, or images flickering about, but since regaining the lost knowledge, my fucking manifestation decided to drop on my lap in one sitting, everything in here became a jumbled trash heap.

Milo's visions flashed brightly from every direction like the most irritating gifs forming a movie reel where every frame was out of order or connected to a thousand different films. Mainly because they were. The words hurled from the lips of the chimera and manifestation were etched in the empty air of my mind, scarring my brain. Letters formed in deep scarlets or blackish blues, carrying the emotional wavelengths of their deep-seated disdain for one another. Toxic rage and venomous hatred threatened to bleed into my every thought if I didn't contain these awful memories. I wouldn't be controlled by these feelings. I wouldn't let them dictate my future or rewrite my past.

Taking a deep breath, I pulled the darkness of my subconscious high into my inner core and replaced the marble flooring I typically conjured. Not that I could see much of the floor with Milo's flashing visions playing everywhere.

If I didn't remove what had already seeped into my subconscious, I'd have to endure reliving the manifestation's short-lived life in my dreams. That wasn't about to fucking happen.

Milo rolled over in his sleep, and a soothing touch stirred in the darkness of my mind as he snuggled me and pulled me into a bearhug—his personal favorite while he slept. The warmth of his body pressed to mine made for a beautiful distraction as I extracted broken memories from my subconscious and sent them into a box I'd conjured.

Not a very big box and not too different from the filing sort Milo made in his inner core when sorting visions. I should make a thousand boxes for every single memory. But I didn't want to sort these memories or visions right now. I simply wanted them out of the way. Normally, boxing away things was a terrible way to repress traumas. They'd eventually explode, bleeding out in the worst ways at the worst moments, yet it was the only solution to the fog and guilt in my mind.

"You could ask for help." Milo's breath tickled my ear, stealing me from my mind and back to the bed where we lay. "I'm always here to help."

"I'm fine." I rubbed his arm, wrapped under my stomach and holding me in place.

"Just let me in." Milo kissed my neck. "Please."

It was as tempting an offer as it was mortifying, letting Milo into my head so he could help organize this mess, but then he'd see exactly how terrible everything had gotten. Not that he'd judge…probably.

Still, with everything in disarray, I couldn't invite him even if I wanted to. There was barely enough room in my chaotic mind for surface thoughts at this point. Hence, another big reason I needed to deal with this mess that my manifestation left. Sort of his big "fuck you, Dorian" before going off to die.

"Don't you trust me?" Milo whispered, making it hard to focus on my tasks in this semi-awake, half-dazed state.

"Implicitly."

"Then let me in." He kissed my neck again, gently and with just a touch of psychic energy meant to connect our minds, reaching out with a hand for me to grab, lips for me to meet.

"I can't. It's too crowded."

"I have a workaround." His skin vibrated, tingling against my body as he channeled magic. His other hand rubbed against my bare chest, cool to the touch and almost enough to make me open my eyes, but before I could, Milo stood inside my fractured, fucked-up head.

"How in the hell?" I quirked a brow.

"Remember that really fun enchantment I bought?" Milo grinned, thoughts stirring to the one and only time he'd used this particular type of enchantment which involved diving into my mind while he screwed me. Quite the surreal experience and not one I intended on repeating anytime soon.

"We're not doing that again."

"Doing what?" His coy expression did little to hide his minxy eyes.

"My head's too messy—as you can see—for any type of romance while traipsing about in here."

"Oh, so I should probably save the other enchantments I bought for special birthday requests?" He walked across the black flooring of my inner core, eyeing the flickering visions and studying the carved words of another's mind. "Thankfully, these enchantments are multi-purposed. You really need another psychic's help. And we both know you're not gonna see a professional."

I scoffed. "As if anyone could unravel my mind better than me."

"Why didn't you just ask me for help tonight?"

"You were tired."

"Please, I'm always tired." He thrust his hips. "And wired. I should've been in here sooner, given the major strobe light effect you've got going."

"I messed all this up, subliminally, sure. But I clearly wanted a manifestation to absorb and contain all the things my telepathy grabbed, held onto, saw, and made the day-to-day unbearable."

Quite the statement, considering most of what my mind dealt with each day felt like swimming against a current.

"You don't need to be self-conscious. Not around me."

"I'm not. I just sort of wanted to fix it up some before asking you."

"Look, we can do this little dance. You say you don't want help, don't wanna burden me, wanna learn to master your branch independently—which you will like you always have—but I already know you're gonna waste your whole vacation trying to sort out the rumblings in your head. And because of my branch—damn, clairvoyants. Yeah, yeah—I know you're not gonna make much headway, then right before school starts back up, you'll ask. Which, of course, I'll gladly offer my assistance." Milo jested. "Why don't we skip ahead so I can enjoy a little holiday time with you uninterrupted?"

I could see his thoughts teeming with events and festivities he planned on dragging me to.

I sighed. "Let's get started."

"Awesome." Milo waved a hand, rearranging his visions, stacking the flashing motions on top of one another in a way I couldn't. Whenever I tried, they repelled each other and ricocheted all over like the ultimate 'unknown error' popup.

"How'd you do that?"

"I know how to handle visions. Though, I'm actually digging the strobe light, dirty nightclub vibe you've got. Wasn't my jam at first, but it's growing on me." Milo wiggled his hips as he worked. "Uhn tiss uhn tiss uhn tiss."

And now he was dancing, organizing, and creating the most annoying melody in my head.

"Do you need to do that?"

"You love it." He moved his arms, calling me over but still arranging visions. "Come on. You need a little music in here."

"I'm gonna deal with memories while you sort visions."

"You're welcome." He uhn tissed to the rhythmic beat he'd awakened in my mind while he worked.

"Are you seriously going to dance the entire time you're in here?"

Milo continued to shimmy and shake, each step adding a flare of light to the black flooring, and then he stacked another set of visions together. "Music helps clear my head. And since we're renovating yours, figured it wouldn't hurt."

"And here I thought you just used music to skirt my telepathy."

"Added bonus." Milo puckered his lips. "Mwah."

The more he sorted visions, the more his mind sank into mine. His bright aura illuminated the darkness in my head. Each shake of his hips, snap of his fingers, and tap of his foot splattered paint in every direction. Sky blues where the visions had once crowded. Sunshine yellows over the black flooring. Bright oranges along the walls. Soon, my inner core was covered in pastel paints.

While Milo worked to place the visions I'd gleaned into one stacked corner of my mind, I sorted through memories of my manifestation, studying the illusions he had of Finn's time in the hospital bed, glossed over the tampered minds of those he afflicted with our magic, and endured the horrors of his time spent in the pits of the chimera's demonic energy. It was a difficult balancing act. I couldn't very well chuck this knowledge out of my head. Memories didn't work like that. But I wanted to prevent them from fully cementing into my subconscious, into my daily thoughts.

There were so many memories, so I took them one by one and boxed them away somewhere they wouldn't fester and rot my own thoughts. I found myself drawn to one bleak moment of my manifestation crawling through the black sludge of the chimera's mind, dragging himself out and toward Finn. Not the Finn he'd trapped in lies by tampering with his memories, but the Finn who'd suffered so long at the hands of the devil and found himself fully aware again. Because of me. Because of my goddamn manifestation.

"Where is he right now?" My manifestation asked in the memory.

I stared through his eyes as he surveyed the shadows, yet his gaze was drawn to the small light of hope Finn offered.

"Working. He often works," Finn said gently, instructive and calm. "If you're quiet, careful, you can hear him." Finn glanced up. "Right now, he's sending a message."

The frustration ripped at the edges of this memory as he tried and failed to glean what Finn meant, what he saw through the darkness.

"Here." Finn brushed the back of his hand against my manifestation's cheek.

I pressed a hand to my own cheek, sinking into the sweet sensation. A touch I'd almost forgotten.

It all swiftly melted away as Finn's magic stirred in the mind of my manifestation. He seared a memory of his own magic.

Every image flew by so quickly.

Theodore's sadistic smile. A wisp of energy. The carnage of Theodore's near escape. The delight in his eyes as he surrendered. The chimera slinking into Peter's mind as guards banished fiends and others escaped. Peter's possession. True possession. Blood. Tar. Magic. The city of Chicago flew by in a haze as the chimera searched for something. He stabbed his hand. Blood. So much blood. Then, letters etched onto parchment while he whispered words in Latin. The letter burned in blue flames of primal casting, and the ashes fluttered in the air with purpose, thoughts of Theodore as the sprinkled note vanished in the sky.

I froze each instantaneous flash and divided them, hoping to make sense of the seconds that carried hours' worth of knowledge.

Milo waltzed over, staring at the looped images I organized. "What's that?"

"A living memory." It worked the same way the students had banded together to create ones of Jamie Novak, only Finn's branch didn't require all the extra steps. "Finn showed this to my manifestation."

"What's the chimera doing?"

I shrugged. "Sending some note off. Nothing really came of it."

"To who?"

"No idea."

"It involves Theodore Whitlock, though?"

"Yeah," I said with a lump of guilt in my throat.

My manifestation was foolish enough to try and control the most dangerous warlock I'd ever encountered and ended up allowing him to conspire with the deadliest demon I'd ever met.

"Looks like the chimera was doing Theodore a favor." Milo studied each image, analyzing them intently. "My guess, something big enough, bold enough to convince the warlock to stay in lockup, so as to not interfere with the chimera's agenda. Must've been one hell of a favor, too."

"I thought Theodore stayed because he knew he couldn't escape."

"True. But everything about Theodore is reckless abandonment and diving headfirst into carnage. Calculating, yes. Patient, only at the advice of others." Milo drifted into his mind, flickering from my thoughts momentarily as he searched through visions. The enchantment held the tether between us.

"What is it?"

Milo's eyes flitted, rolling back as he searched through visions. "After the chimera and manifestation died, the futures blurred by demonic energy and skirted by psychic magic became clearer. I can see where the meddling occurred, but I can't tell which paths they affected. It's like a domino, and I don't know for certain which one they knocked over or which trail to track. I can hear the clink, feel the rattle of change, but can't quite see what's coming."

"And you think what the chimera did here caused something?"

"Maybe, maybe not." Milo grinned. "Another problem for another day. Dwelling never solves much other than feeding the beast of depression."

I squinted at him. "That felt like a personal attack."

"Never." He pursed his lips.

"You're insufferable."

"I know. Luckily, you're ad*dick*ted to me and all my insufferably uncharming ways." Milo giggled at his own terrible joke. "See what I did there?"

I huffed. "Can we work without the commentary?"

Milo's sleeping body pulled me into a tighter embrace, hugging me with intense love. The soothing touch comforted me as we worked in here, with him returning to the opposite side of my inner core to stack visions while I sorted the memories my manifestation had dropped back into my head. It was lovely to feel Milo, to work with him, to prepare for whatever came next.

I had no idea what ripple effects my manifestation had inadvertently brought about, whether Theodore Whitlock would prove a challenge, whether some unknown threat lurked, whether he'd shifted the happiest ever after that ever aftered. But I did know I wouldn't let it deter me. I'd master the magics I'd shrugged off for too long. I'd stay close to Milo, to the light and joy he offered. I'd train my students to be ready for any threat the future might bring. Most of all, I'd right the wrongs my magic caused.

Chapter Thirty-Six

Doppler

A secret part of me hoped my sacrifice would be rewarded by a burial in the deepest depths of Dorian's subconscious. When I banished the final fragments of the chimera's demonic energy, I felt the collision of all I knew swept back into Dorian's mind. All except me, it seemed.

Retribution for my betrayal, perhaps. Or, as I'd always suspected, Dorian was merely too weak to harness the full extent of his branch, and thus, I was lost to the ether of infinite space.

This must've been death. Oblivion, most likely. Complete and utter darkness. Alone with only my thoughts. It almost made me long for the days I'd sat in the depths of Dorian's mind, granted brief reprieves to search the minds of others, given fleeting images of Milo and Finn as they hung in Dorian's thoughts day in and day out. Now, I had only my own thoughts. Unfortunately, I was a shallow, hollow, broken piece of magic that had few stirring thoughts to keep me company in this eternal solitude.

"Geez, you're even more emo than Dorian, Dorian." Finn's giggle echoed in the chambers of black, creating a kaleidoscope of colors that sparkled and shimmered, revealing the twinkling lights of the cosmos.

No longer did I dwell in overcast shadows, but instead floated in what could only be described as the galaxy. Empty and infinite, beautiful and haunting.

"Did you hear my thoughts?" I turned, searching for Finn in this grand starlit space, finding nothing but more lights.

"I think you're thinking out loud." Finn snickered, drawing my eyes yet finding him nowhere. "It's hard to say. I've never experienced something like this before. And I've experienced a lot through the memories of my magic. It's like your words, your thoughts, sparkle in the distance, and I can hear them. Strange since I'm using my eyes. It's freaky cool."

This wasn't some unique branch at play. Otherwise, Finn would've identified it. His retrocognition made him a living text of history, the literal past incarnate.

"Whoa—now that's a major selling point to my branch. Wish you'd have helped me pitch it that way when I was actually alive." His hands found my shoulders, gently squeezing them as he'd squeezed Dorian's a thousand times before.

I spun around, finally facing Finn, who'd manifested from the stars themselves, bright and fiery and beautiful, warm and happy. "What's happening?"

"No clue. Assuming this is the afterlife or some type of afterlife." Finn shrugged. "There could be infinite numbers. Then again, this could simply be some fleeting sensation of our last drops of magic before the bleak nothingness of death swoops in."

"That's very morose."

"That's always been your philosophy, right?"

"Yes, no—" I scrunched my face, feeling the tension in my muscles for the first time in my life without pulling the sensation from another's body wrapped in some illusion. Ironic to finally feel now that I'd died.

Finn always believed in the infinite possibilities of life after death, the continuation of the consciousness, the flow of energy unbound, traveling the universe until the end of time, and then a little longer for one more trip around.

"You make it sound poetic." Finn smiled, boyish and sweet, somehow having more comprehension of this realm than myself, which seemed standard since he was often lightyears ahead of Dorian in all things. "You're a little hard on yourself, Dorian."

"I'm not…" I hesitated. I wasn't Dorian. I would never be Dorian. But I didn't know who I was.

"You're who you wanna be." Finn grabbed my hand. "So, who do you wanna be?"

"I'm not sure."

"Funny. I'm not sure either."

"What do you mean?"

"I'm Finn. But I'm not the Finn who died. I'm the piece who lived on inside a demon, a devil. Horrors and Hell and so many other experiences I couldn't forget if I wanted to."

"You don't want to?" I asked, contending with the lump in my throat as I nervously awaited his response.

It was peculiar, taking some solace in the fleeting sensations that struck me while basking in the presence of Finn.

"It's awful. It's not an experience I'd wish upon anyone, ever." Finn interlocked his fingers with mine. "But it made me who I am. Shaped me. As much as I wish it hadn't, I feel stronger overcoming it."

"Yeah, you're Finn, all right. Only Finn would look Hell in the eyes and celebrate that at least we could have smores thanks to the fire."

"I said that one time." Finn laughed, his thoughts stirring to memories of high school before we made it into the academy, times when Dorian said the entrance exam would be pure Hell, and Finn proceeded to jest.

It seemed my telepathy was intact.

"When I said my goodbyes to Dorian and Milo after they banished the chimera, the devil, I believed wholeheartedly that if and when I made it here—the other side, oo la la—that I'd want to find my other half. Find the Finn that I was so I could truly remember myself."

"Then I stopped you. Narcissistically stole you and failed to—"

"It was a bizarre experience, to say the least. We definitely have a lot to talk about, like manipulating a person's own magic to make them forget the bad memories because you believe you know best."

I pulled my hand away, but Finn strengthened his grip, refusing to release me.

"It's a conversation we'll have a long time to discuss. An eternity, perhaps." Finn released his hand. "If you'll have me."

My face fell, stunned. "Of course. But why? Why would you want to spend any time with me?"

"Because you're like me. Honestly, after remembering everything and dwelling inside the chimera again, I realized I was grateful for the reflection. The time to consider my options. I wouldn't want to burden Finn with my haunting memories. I can feel him, you know? That other piece. It's not quite magnetic, but there's breadcrumbs I could follow." Finn shook his head at the idea. "Let him wait peacefully for Dorian and Milo to rejoin him one day."

"You don't want to be whole again?"

"I'm still Finn, still me, even if I'm not that Finn."

"And I'm still Dorian even if I'm not *that* Dorian."

"You're pretty clever. Almost as smart as the *actual* Dorian."

"Bah." I waved a dismissive hand. "My intellect supersedes his in every…" I grimaced when Finn stifled a snicker. "And you were joking, poking fun because my ego is an easy target."

"Pretty much." Finn batted his eyes, his long lashes catching the starry light.

The twinkle sparkled and moved, casting a luminescent shadow, and our eyes followed that shooting star that landed far in the depths, tucked between a hundred others.

"Wait," a high-pitched squeaky voice cried out. "You're moving too fast."

Standing in the distance, a small blond boy panted. He kept his hands pressed to his knees, bracing himself even though he only stood in the shadows of space and could simply hover like us. This world truly was unlike anything I'd ever experienced.

"And who are you?" Finn asked.

The boy's eyes widened, surprised by our presence, wearing the fright on his face and in his surface thoughts. "How'd you get here?"

"We were just trying to figure that out." Finn slowly floated toward the lost and confused child.

The memories were warped, broken, and missing. Looking in his mind was like looking at this starry galaxy. Only the space in his head was more like an empty abyss, missing most of the lights to memories.

"That's your memory over there." Finn pointed to the shooting star the child chased.

"How'd you know that?" the boy asked.

"It's my magic; it allows me to see the past, and I can see yours is scattered all over the place."

"You can see me? My memories? I've been looking for them everywhere, but I got lost…they got lost…I don't know what to do." He frowned. "But I have to find them. I know it'll get better when I do."

Despite so much missing, the fear of darkness boomed in his mind, making this galaxy backdrop where we found ourselves the most frightening of places, where only the light held safety for him, yet the light fled, not wishing to return the pieces of his life it held.

"We can help you." Finn smiled.

"I don't know. My sister said to never talk to strangers."

"Your sister sounds very smart."

"No, she's really not." The boy pouted, folding his arms. "But I still don't know you."

"I'm Finn, and this is Dorian. We're a little lost too. Maybe your sister can help us find our way, and we can help you both catch those missing memories."

"She's not here." The boy backed away, nervous, like he was a second from hiding behind the shadows of outer space.

"You're all alone?" I asked, voice breaking that someone so small would be abandoned in the same afterlife Finn and I had found ourselves thrown into.

"I'm always alone." His eyes welled up. "That's all I really remember."

"You remember more than that," I said, wanting to help this child.

I wanted to help because Finn thought it was the right thing; I could feel his emotions, and I knew the boy wanted help but was too scared to ask. For once, maybe I could do the right thing without hesitating, without stumbling, without failing those around me.

I searched his mind, reaching for the faintest glimmers of thoughts, pulling them from the depths of his broken inner core. The casting didn't come with the fatigue it did when alive. There was a peacefulness to guiding these hidden memories, stitching the fractured history, but I couldn't sort them. There were too many missing.

This kid was right about his memories fleeing. So much was gone. The map of his memories was like the remnants of a cookie dough sheet after all the perfect cutouts had been plucked, and what remained were hollowed-out edges, barely enough to string together one solid cookie. Or, in this case, memory.

"That's because you're looking at them in all the wrong ways." Finn pressed a hand on my shoulder, guiding my telepathy with the reassurance of his retrocognition.

"Are you syncing your magic to mine?" My heart pattered quickly, experiencing something that'd once only been reserved for Dorian when he kissed Milo. A special bond that I craved, a connection unlike any other out there. True love and trust in mind, body, soul, and magic. That was the real reason I hid all the visions that struck Dorian's mind simultaneously, leaving him only with a single void vision. I envied the connection, the love he had.

"I can see his past, sort what's there so it all lines up, but you'll have to light the fuse so they'll connect to his thoughts."

Not many dots to connect, not until this child retrieved his missing memories, but I snapped my fingers and sparked the ones he had, the pieces he couldn't quite recall because they'd fallen apart.

As his blue eyes lit up, so did his mind. "How'd you do that?"

"A little touch of magic." Finn smiled. "We could probably use our branches to help piece together the other missing pieces as you find them, Jamie."

"Jamie," he said his name, clutching a hand to his chest and sitting with the familiarity of his past, revealing who he was, the parts he had at least. "I'm Jamie Novak."

"Yes, you are." I knelt in front of him. "If you want help, I'd gladly offer it."

"Really?" He quirked a brow. "You don't even know me."

"I know if I was missing pieces of myself, I'd want help finding them."

Finn chuckled, amused by the irony and making no effort to hide that fact.

"Okay. But you need to keep up." Jamie pointed a commanding finger.

"Of course," Finn said, happily nodding at the young Jamie who held no memory of the horrors he'd endured in his short life, no recollection of the pieces missing, or the fact that maybe he'd be happier if they stayed lost.

This joyful side of Jamie could know real peace wherever we were, and I hoped… I didn't know what I hoped for, but I worried unraveling the truth might make his eternity here somber.

"Can't know until we get there." Finn nudged me, pulling me from my thoughts.

In the seconds I spent lost in my head, Jamie had already made a move to chase the tiny star holding a piece of his past.

"It might be best for him if he doesn't remember everything," I said, unable to look Finn in the eyes.

"Best for who?" he asked. "Best for you? Best intentions by you?"

"What I did…" I stood and didn't respond. His questions summed up the entirety of my argument, my reasoning, my fatal flaw. "I just wanted you to be happy, to be ready, before learning all the horrors you'd experienced."

"And maybe that's what this place is for." Finn gestured to the bounty of stars surrounding us. "Maybe it's the universe's way of helping those who need a little extra time, those who need to sort through what's missing."

"We're not missing anything."

"How would we know if we were?" Finn smiled. "Besides, I don't think it's all missing memories. Other things can be missing, lost, need work, time, and a million other factors simple fellas like us just aren't ready to fully comprehend."

"You're assuming this place holds some grand design."

"That's the beauty of belief."

"I promise to do better, to do my best to help."

"No withholding memories unless he chooses that." Finn eyed Jamie, who continued wandering ahead. "Let's help him learn his history, unravel his truth, and if it's ever too much, we can offer him the choice of what he does and doesn't wanna fixate on. After all, we've got the perfect magics to help the kid out."

I scoffed. "You probably think this is fate or something."

"And you probably don't believe in such things."

We lingered together, his lips close enough to kiss. A kiss I wasn't ready or worthy of yet. There was so much love and lust I had for Finn, for this fragment of Finn, but I wanted to earn our first kiss, to be worthy of his touch, his compassion, his love, his forgiveness, his company and perfection and kindness.

Finn grinned. "My head is gonna be really hard to carry around with you inflating it so much."

"How are you doing that?"

He shrugged. "How's Jamie know those specks of stars are his memories and know the other ones aren't? Some of us just get it."

"And some of us don't." I rolled my eyes.

"Now you're getting it. Thankfully, we can help you as much as you profess wanting to help us." Finn grabbed my hand, interlocking his fingers, and we turned to follow after Jamie on a search for his history.

Who would've thought that I, a manifestation of Dorian, a piece of sentient magic, would spend my days alongside Finn and this joyful version of Jamie.

"A fragment of Finn," he clarified. "And you're less of a manifestation at this point and more of a doppler."

"A doppler?"

"Yeah." Finn used his free hand to gesture like he was unveiling a grand stage play ahead. "Fragment Finn and Doppler Dorian on their wacky adventures with Joyful Jamie. I like the ring to it."

"So do I."

"Will you two hurry up!" Jamie shouted. There was an annoyance in his tone, irritated by our conversation, yet a subtle fear he'd be left to search for his missing memories by himself again.

He wouldn't have to worry about being left all alone ever again. I'd see to it.

"We're coming!" I shouted back, hastening my steps.

Finn smirked. “There’s a joke there.”

“Ugh. Between you and Milo—insufferable.”

Finn broke out into laughter, sending joy cascading across the galaxy surrounding us, brightening the edges ever so.

I didn’t know what this place was, an afterlife, a waiting room, a figment from the last specks of our magic floating in the ether of space, but I planned to cherish every second I had. I couldn’t right the wrongs I’d done while desperately searching for a life that was never mine, but I could do everything in my power here to help guide Jamie, to work toward earning back Finn’s trust.

To finally live my own life.

“Minus the living part.” Finn shoulder bumped me.

“That whole knowing what I’m thinking is gonna get tiring real soon.”

“You get used to it.” His smile illuminated the farthest reaches of this infinite galaxy, and I finally began to see what Finn and Jamie saw when they looked out at the stars.

THE END

...until next semester.

Acknowledgments

Thank you so much to everyone who has continued joining in Dorian's journey throughout the Branches of Past and Future series. Creating a POV for one of Dorian's manifestations has been something I've been tinkering with since book one. Fun fact: I actually had a quirky conversation of banter and frustration between Dorian and a manifestation during book one but removed it from my early drafts. Ultimately, I realized that wasn't the right place to introduce the idea of self-awareness among the manifestations. I really hope you enjoyed meeting the Doppler, the villainous arc he presented, his questionable actions, and the perspective he offered on different facets of this wonderful world that Dorian doesn't always glimpse while working in the classroom with students.

It means so much that you took the time to read this story. If you have the chance, it'd mean the world if you left an honest rating and/or review. They help increase reader visibility and it's my hope that others will take a chance on Dorian's story. Since releasing *Three Meant To Be*, *Two Who Live On*, and now *One Has To Die*, I'm sure some are curious where things are going after this. I can't wait to share the next installment of this series and hope you'll return to join us in the second year spring semester.

Author's Bio

MN Bennet is a high school teacher, writer, and reader. He lives in the Midwest, still adjusting to the cold after being born and raised in the South.

He enjoys writing paranormal and fantasy stories with huge worlds (sometimes too big), loveable romances (with so much angst and banter), and Happily Ever Afters (once he's dragged his characters through some emotional turmoil).

When he's not balancing classes, writing, or reading, he can be found binge watching anime or replaying Dragon Age II for the millionth time.

Author website: https://www.mnbennet.com

Amazon page:
https://www.amazon.com/stores/MN-Bennet/author/B0BLJJK5NF

Goodreads page
https://www.goodreads.com/author/show/23017668.M_N_Bennet

Printed in the USA
CPSIA information can be obtained
at www.ICGtesting.com
CBHW031920090924
14022CB00006B/108

9 798990 149311